T0359679
AT THE FOOT OF THE CHERRY TREE
ALLI PARKER
HarperCollinsPublishers

HarperCollins*Publishers*
Australia • Brazil • Canada • France • Germany • Holland • India
Italy • Japan • Mexico • New Zealand • Poland • Spain • Sweden
Switzerland • United Kingdom • United States of America

HarperCollins acknowledges the Traditional Custodians
of the lands upon which we live and work, and pays respect
to Elders past and present.

First published on Gadigal Country in Australia in 2023
This edition published in 2024
by HarperCollins*Publishers* Australia Pty Limited
ABN 36 009 913 517
harpercollins.com.au

A catalogue record for this book is available from the National Library of Australia

ISBN 978 1 4607 6353 7 (paperback)
ISBN 978 1 4607 1592 5 (ebook)
ISBN 978 1 4607 4830 5 (audiobook)

Cover design by Louisa Maggio, HarperCollins Design Studio
Cover images by shutterstock.com and istockphoto.com
Author photograph by Leah Jing McIntosh
Typeset in Baskerville MT by Kirby Jones
Printed and bound in Australia by McPherson's Printing Group

This book is for:
Nobuko & Don,
Cherry & Gordon,
or, as I call you,
Grandma & Grandpa

PROLOGUE

August 1945

Death was in her hair.

Screams echoed in her ears, every blink brought a flash of fire and wrath, and death was in her hair. Dust and dirt clung to every strand, the once glossy black buried beneath a mask of darkened grey. Her eyebrows, her eyelashes, smudges against her vision, were sprinkled with fine powder she couldn't remove, painful grit and grime. Behind her was a trail of footprints and ash, leading back to a living nightmare. Her feet were bare, long since numb, a limping rhythm with every step she took. The world was empty, the world knew nothing, and she had seen it all.

The verdant sakura trees shivered as she passed beneath their boughs, a death angel on a dirt road. She lifted a shaking hand to brush her fingers through the leaves, to touch something real, to remind herself she existed. The leaves reached for her blackened hands, deep green stroking against dirt and ash and blood. The rough branches pressed into her skin, sensitive and tight, promising she was here in this moment. She was alive.

Bile rose in her throat and she doubled over, face throbbing as black sludge spilled onto the road. She gasped for air, convulsing, trying to breathe, to purge. The shaking started then, a quivering that wouldn't ease, tears snaking around cheekbones and mud and filth. She steadied herself, wiping her eyes, smearing the muck that covered her entire body. Thunder rumbled in the distance and, for the first time since she began her death march, she looked back.

In the valley far below, hidden beneath a blanket of deep grey clouds against an otherwise perfect summer sky, was a city screaming as it died. Her breath caught in her throat as she watched her home burn, heard the shuddering echo of buildings surrendering to the fall. There was only one place she could go and only one way to get there. She turned away and took one slow, painful step. The cuts on the soles of her feet split open as she limped forward, fresh blood spotting the path, ash snowing from her hair.

Hiroshima was gone.

She was not.

And so she walked.

CHAPTER ONE

GORDON: Melbourne, July 1945

It was war. Gordon Parker was armed, prowling through the undergrowth, scanning for his target. The wind rustled overhead, dancing across the back of his neck. Any moment now, he would find what he was hunting and attack.

A voice broke through his concentration.

'Have you got them yet?'

Gordon glared at his sister, gesturing for her to be quiet. June rolled her eyes and sat on the grass, opening a book, no longer interested in her brother. Somewhere above him, a kookaburra chortled, the gum trees sending leaves to the grass below.

There was a giggle.

Gordon stepped forward, feet soft. The sound came from the blackberry bushes. He couldn't see through the foliage but his target had finally revealed itself.

Gordon raised his weapon, readying for battle.

A roar, and the bush split apart as Gordon's prey launched at him. There was no time to react, his weapon – a tree branch posing as a gun – skittering aside as he was tackled by four of his younger siblings.

There were nine Parkers in all: Venn and Harry, plus their seven kids. June was the eldest, thirteen months older than Gordon, something she took great delight in. After Gordon was Donald, a year and a half younger, currently tugging at Gordon's right arm, trying to pull him to the ground. Jeanette was the fourth, sharp and observant, watching the fight in front of her and waiting for her moment. Then came his brother, Robin, thirteen years old, quiet, with cheeky eyes, too busy laughing to make use of the ambush, and a few years younger was Jennifer, raining gentle but considered blows on Gordon's stomach. It had seemed like the family was complete, until Jim arrived three years earlier, a surprise wartime baby.

If you needed anything, the door to the Parker farmhouse on Greenwood Avenue was always open. A sympathetic ear, your socks darned, a new jacket; nothing was too much trouble. Gordon often hid his favourite things under his mattress because, if they were easily in reach, Venn would gift them to someone who needed them more.

They didn't have much, but they had one another. That was more than most, with families divided across the world as the war against Japan stretched on.

As did the war under the gum trees.

It wasn't hard to fend off Donald, Robin and Jennifer. Gordon played it up, dodging imaginary bullets and closer hand-to-hand combat. Then Jeanette got involved. She sprinted and leapt at his chest, Gordon catching her at stomach height. They all collapsed to the ground, battle cries fading into the air.

'It's an ambush!' Gordon cried.

'It's good practice for when you go to fight!' Robin wrapped himself around Gordon's left leg, Gordon twitching it to kick his brother off.

'That's still a while away.'

'Why?' Robin held Gordon tightly, riding every kick. 'You're eighteen now.'

'Dad has to give permission. It's the same for anyone under twenty-one. You need permission from your parents.'

'I don't see why Dad won't let you go.' Donald dived onto Gordon, he and Jennifer taking an arm each. 'He was a Highlander when he was sixteen.'

'Yes, well, you all know how that conversation went.' Gordon had tried to convince his father to let him sign up a couple of years ago, at the same age Harry had fought in the Great War. The argument that followed had been heard in the main square in Ringwood, and Gordon hadn't been the one to get his way.

'It's probably just as well. If you can't beat us, you'll hardly beat the Japanese.' Donald's face contorted as he wrestled Gordon's arm.

'You're just lucky this isn't a real gun, otherwise you and any Japanese fighting out here would be long dead.' Gordon lifted his arm, picking up Jennifer, who shrieked. 'I might not be able to beat you alone, but with reinforcements ...'

The children stilled as they turned to June, sprawled in a patch of winter sunshine.

Her gaze never left her book. 'Can't.' She turned the page. 'Impossibly busy.'

'You'd let your favourite brother die for a book?'

'A very good book,' June replied.

'You're not her favourite brother, anyway!' Robin giggled as Gordon's spare hand darted around, poking him.

'I am!' Gordon and Donald said together, identical smiles on their faces.

June slammed her book shut. She stood, brushing the grass off her Land Army outfit, the bottle-green woollen jumper softened with wear. If June had been a boy, she would've enlisted the previous year when she turned eighteen, but volunteering with the Land Girls had been the perfect, if only, alternative for her. Working on the land, physical labour, getting her hands dirty: that was all June needed.

Her boots crunched on dried leaves as she stalked forward. No-one moved, waiting.

She pounced on Gordon.

'Wait, what?' Gordon tried to fend her off as she tickled him. Gleeful, the others joined in, Gordon powerless against several sets of tickling hands. With a roar, he burst to his feet, scooping Jennifer into his arms. 'I've taken a hostage! Shall we negotiate the terms of surrender?'

'Never!' June cried, and they surged forward, chasing Gordon as he ran laps around the gums, holding Jennifer as she shrieked with laughter. He clutched her close as Donald turned to trap them and Gordon retreated against the gum tree, a calm smile on his face, planning his way out.

'Coo-ee!'

The cry bounced off the bush, echoing against trees that seemed to shudder at the sound. Everyone froze.

'Coooo-ee!'

Robin drew closer to Gordon. 'What's that?'

'It's the cry of the fiercest enemy known to mankind.'

Robin's eyes grew wide. 'The Japanese?'

'Close,' Gordon said, adjusting Jennifer on his hip. 'Mum.'

They headed to the house, Robin and Donald fighting with two branches they'd found on their way back, furiously parrying, thrusting and dodging as they went. Gordon piggybacked Jennifer, breaking into a trot to stretch his legs, both laughing. June and Jeanette walked together, Jeanette claiming she had read her sister's book. Between the two of them, they were recounting a sprawling epic across fifteen countries that didn't seem like the likely plot of *Death on the Nile*.

Ahead of them, the farmhouse loomed. A huge two-storey building, a third storey if you included the attic, a great hiding spot if you didn't mind the dust, spiders or possums. It overlooked sprawling paddocks and a tennis court that was overgrown and seldom used. In one paddock was the family cow, a surprise purchase by Harry, declaring it their new automatic lawnmower. Greenwood House was constant, welcoming chaos.

On the veranda was their mother, Venn Parker, her light hair immaculately curled, an apron around her waist and toddler Jim perched on her hip. She thrust Jim at Donald, who took him and dropped the stick, Robin crowding around to pull faces at his youngest brother.

Venn forced a smile at Gordon. 'Your father wants to see you.'

Concern flared in Gordon's chest. 'Is everything all right?'

Venn cleared her throat. 'He wants to talk to you about something.' She hesitated as she searched for the words, then smiled, genuinely this time. 'He'll explain it.'

Gordon leapt up the steps to the house. Venn touched his arm as he passed, stopping him. She squeezed his shoulder, then turned her attention to the other children.

Confused, Gordon's heart thudded as he walked through to the living room, where the rich smoky scent of Harry's tobacco grew stronger. The repressed emotion from his mother made Gordon nervous.

Harry turned as Gordon entered, left hand tucked into his navy jacket pocket and right hand clutching the end of his pipe. He exhaled, tendrils of smoke snaking past his shining blond moustache and drifting across icy blue eyes identical to Gordon's own.

'You look terribly serious.' Harry's polished British accent was a stark contrast to his children's Australian ones. 'Has your mother lost her temper so soon after lunch?'

Gordon bit back a grin. 'Not yet, but there's still time.'

Harry chuckled and set his pipe down on an ashtray. 'I wonder if you may indulge me in a drive.'

'Is it to the council?' Harry rarely asked his children to join him at work. The local council offices were always busy and full of people, and the Parker children had a habit of getting unintentionally underfoot. Although Harry had been mayor of Ringwood a few years earlier, he worked as a councillor these days, providing what he could for the community and developing the country town. Perhaps Harry wanted to introduce Gordon to more of his colleagues, get him a job at the council now he was eighteen. A small way to carry on the Parker legacy.

Harry shook his head. 'It's a little further.'

'Does it have to be today? I promised Robin we could catch some frogs by the creek.'

'Very important birthday celebrations, I understand.'

Gordon laughed. 'Mum said you wanted to talk about something.'

'I thought we could discuss it on our drive. But as you have a previous appointment, perhaps now is not the time.' Harry ran his fingers through his silvering hair and sighed. 'Shame though. It's a long drive to Albert Park alone.'

Gordon frowned. The only things in Albert Park were the lake and the enlistment office.

Gordon stared at his father, the implication dawning. Harry reached into the inside breast pocket of his jacket and pulled out an envelope. In sloping dark ink, the curled letters read 'The Enlistment Officers of the Australian Army'.

Jeanette appeared in the doorway. 'Are you going or what?'

Gordon swept her into his arms, carrying her to the front door, unable to believe what was happening. The whole family spilt outside. Gordon gave Robin a tight hug and shook Donald's hand, a solemn nod between them. Donald was now the eldest son at home. He wrapped June in a bear hug, feeling a pang of regret as the reality dawned that he was leaving to fight. He wasn't expecting the lump in his throat as he kissed Jim, who grabbed at his older brother. The lump grew larger as Gordon turned to his mother. She was already crying, and pulled him into a tight embrace.

'Don't do anything foolish.'

'When have you known me to ever do anything foolish?' Gordon asked, trying to keep things light. 'I'm a Parker. We don't do foolish.'

'You come home.' Venn's voice was barely a breath. 'I'll hunt you down if you don't.'

'Now there's a threat if I've ever heard one. I'll be fine.' Venn held him for a moment longer, then Gordon stepped away as Harry hit the horn. 'See you later!' He jogged to the car and slipped into the passenger seat.

Harry adjusted his gloves, a pensive silence settling between them.

Gordon shifted, curious. 'Dad?'

Harry turned to his son, face grave. 'War is a time full of difficult choices. Sometimes those choices will not make sense. If you believe you are right, you must stick to your principles. But if you are wrong?' He exhaled deeply. 'If you are wrong, you must take your medicine, no matter how bitter.'

Gordon nodded. The weight of expectation settled onto his shoulders. It was tempered with a rush of nervous energy, exhilarating and anxiety-inducing. He was being taken seriously on his own terms.

Harry put the car into gear and Gordon stuck his head out the window, waving back to everyone congregated on the front steps as they drove away. Robin and Donald chased the car, laughing and shouting, until they were blurs in the distance.

Overwhelmed, Gordon gathered himself and took a breath.

Harry glanced to his son. 'Changed your mind?'

Gordon drew strength from his father's permanent calm. If Harry had fought the Germans at sixteen, there was no reason he couldn't fight the Japanese at eighteen.

'How long to Albert Park?'

CHAPTER TWO

GORDON: Cowra, August 1945

The training camp at Cowra in New South Wales was the furthest Gordon had ever been from home. It was strange to have everything laid out for him, a schedule for every moment of his day, but the routine of Army life made the adjustment easier. Gordon enjoyed the structure of basic training. He didn't need to think about it; he just went where he was told and did what was asked of him.

Still, in the evenings, after the lights went out and as he lay on the uncomfortable straw mattress, Gordon's thoughts drifted home. Had Robin stayed quiet so Harry and Venn could listen to the news broadcast? Had Jennifer managed her homework without him to guide her? Perhaps Venn had talked the ear off the butcher, telling him her eldest son had gone to do his basic training? Maybe Harry shared a cigar with his fellow councillors as they discussed where Gordon would be deployed first?

Those thoughts disappeared when he rose before dawn for the morning run. Two weeks in and he was running most mornings, hauling kitbags and guns, and clambering through obstacle courses as though it was second nature. He'd take an icy shower before breakfast at the mess, ducking and weaving among boys who shouted across tables as they ate and laughed.

Today, Gordon was heading out to the trenches. The camp had

built a replica of those in Europe, cut into the ground and sandbagged. Gordon hadn't done trench warfare training before, and the deep gashes hacked into the earth filled him with dread.

'Not to worry, cobber.' A stocky, russet-haired older bloke clapped Gordon on the shoulder as they approached the entrance. 'I'm told the real ones are much worse. The mud on the bottom will eat your whole boot and then some.'

'Mud?' Gordon asked. 'Isn't it summer in Europe?'

'It is.' The man grabbed his rifle before heading to his allocated trench, Gordon following behind. 'But there's no drainage and the dirt stays wet from constant piss and blood.' The man laughed. 'We won't be heading to the trenches though. The Germans are done. Old Hitler's eaten lead and there's none of these in the Pacific where the Japanese are hiding in the trees to shoot you on sight. It's a much nicer thought, isn't it? You'll never see death coming.' He flicked his hair out of his face, eyes glinting with amusement, and held out his hand. 'I'm Ticker Gammage.'

'Gordon Parker.' He shook Ticker's hand. 'The Japanese hide in the trees?'

The other man tilted his head. 'You're a little green, aren't you? You just eighteen? Maybe younger?'

'Eighteen,' Gordon said, firm.

'Stick with me and you'll be right. Some of these blokes you can't trust as far as you can throw them.'

'Speak for yourself.' A voice cut across them. Leaning on the back wall of the trench were two soldiers, one lighting up a cigarette.

'Mate, you're the worst of the lot,' Ticker said. 'You know Gordon Parker?'

'Yeah, we go back. A good ten seconds.' The soldier shook Gordon's hand. 'I'm Toby West. Call me Westy.' Toby inclined his head to the other soldier, chestnut hair falling to one side. 'This is Ken Goldsworthy.'

'Pleasure,' Ken said, holding his rifle loosely by his side. He seemed bored.

'You done this one before?' Gordon asked.

'Yeah.' Toby exhaled smoke with every word. 'Been here four weeks. There's only so many times you can fake shoot the enemy. Nearly as exciting as delivering the milk around town every morning.'

'Think it's target practice today.' Ken stepped up on a small ledge to peer over the top. 'Doesn't look like there's any fellas on the other side.'

'You fired a gun before, Parker?' Ticker asked.

'Yes,' Gordon said, unsure whether one evening shooting rabbits with his father counted.

Ken nestled his rifle into his shoulder, aiming across the top of the trench. 'It's pretty simple. Just aim and …' He mimicked pulling the trigger. 'You got a dead man on the other end and you live to fight another day.'

'That simple.' Ticker snorted, derisive, as Ken swung his gun down to prop it against the back of the trench once again. There was a loud, echoing crack and Ticker crumpled.

'Jesus Christ,' Ticker gasped as he clutched his leg. Blood bloomed against khaki trousers, soaking into the thick material. Ken went white.

'You shot him?' Toby snatched the gun up and placed it out of reach. Gordon rushed to Ticker's side. The blood was coming from Ticker's shin and Gordon pressed his hands against it. Ticker groaned and threw his head back, breathing hard.

'It's just a graze. You'll be right. But one of you better go get help quick-smart.' Gordon gave Toby a pointed look – Ken was shaking where he sat – and Toby sprinted off to find someone from Medical.

The bleeding wasn't slowing. They had to stop it, something Gordon knew from the day Donald had sliced his arm open on the wire fence at home. Gordon whistled at Ken to snap him out of his shock. 'Ken, mate. Come here for a sec. Need your help.' He moved, obedient, and Gordon put Ken's hands on Ticker's leg.

'Press down hard.' Gordon took his cigarettes out of his breast pocket, tucking them into his shorts, before whipping off his shirt and wrapping it around the wound. He tied the sleeves tight and moved to Ticker's side.

'Lie back and try to relax.'

Ticker groaned. 'Yeah, righto, no worries.'

Ignoring stares from the growing knot of curious soldiers around them, Gordon pulled a handkerchief from his pocket and wiped down Ken's hands.

'I don't know how it went off.' Ken's voice was faint. 'It was an accident.'

'We know, mate.'

'I know I'm annoying,' Ticker said, sprawled on the bottom of the trench, 'but you can just tell me to shut up. You don't have to shoot me.'

Gordon laughed, but Ken could only grimace.

'He's still talking so he can't be feeling too bad,' Gordon said, Ken's hands as clean as they were going to get. Gordon wiped the grimy cloth over his own fingers but the blood was already drying.

He checked Ticker's leg, the bleeding finally slowing, as shouts came down the trenches to clear the way, Toby skidding in with two medical officers. They examined Ticker and lifted him onto a stretcher. One spoke with Ken, who followed them out, leaving the other two men alone.

Gordon rubbed his forehead, adrenaline ebbing, then doubled over and vomited.

'She'll be apples, Parker.' Toby's voice sounded distant, the soft ringing in Gordon's ears blocking it out. Someone thrust a canteen of water at him and he sipped it, swished the water around in his mouth, then spat it out onto the dirt.

'I take it that's your shirt wrapped around Gammage's leg?' A Commanding Officer Gordon didn't recognise peered into the trenches from the ground above. 'You'd best come with me, lad.'

The CO didn't speak until they were in his office. Gordon shifted nervously in his seat. Had he been implicated in the gunshot? Perhaps they wanted his version of events. There was nothing to lie about – it had been a genuine accident – but Gordon's stomach tensed at the thought of being in trouble so soon after joining the Army.

'You did some impressive quick thinking out there.' The CO had his surname stitched onto his shirt. Newell. 'The boys in Medical want you to train with them alongside your usual duties.'

It took Gordon a minute to realise what was being asked of him. 'They want to train me for Medical? Does that mean I won't be able to fight?'

'Not necessarily. Any soldier with extra medical skills is worth their weight in gold out there. You can be a stretcher bearer, for example. It's up to you, but once the war is over, the Army tends to look kindly on those who trained in the hospitals. Send you to medical school in … where are you from?'

'Melbourne.'

'Fantastic medical schools in Melbourne. You'll come home a decorated soldier and be a doctor soon after that. Have a think about it.'

Gordon didn't have to think long. The son of a mayor, a returned soldier, a doctor. It was a simple choice.

His days became busier, with fitness, weapons training and time spent in the Army hospital, but he relished it all. He was careful around the guns, reprimanding others who became too cavalier. Ticker's leg healed quickly, the wound not too deep, but Ken was sent to Sydney. Desk work instead of carrying a rifle with shaky hands. Toby was rarely far from Gordon's side, switching his training to match Gordon's as much as possible. They ran together in the mornings, each trying to be the fastest that day, Gordon usually winning with his swift long legs but Toby sneaking in a victory every so often, surprisingly quick for a nuggety milkman. The only time of day Gordon was without his best mate was the hospital shifts. Toby wasn't one for dealing with injuries.

Gordon enjoyed the medical training. Almost everything was theoretical, mock surgeries as tests, only occasionally treating soldiers who came into the hospitals with real injuries like scrapes or perhaps a dislocated finger. There was generally a simple solution to every malady that came through the hospital tent flaps, and Gordon excelled. Every day brought him closer to getting on the battlefield against the Japanese, a thought both exciting and terrifying.

After a few weeks in Cowra, Toby came looking for Gordon one lunchtime.

'You chockers this arvo?' Toby asked, a mischievous glint in his eye.

'Don't think so,' Gordon said, wolfing down potatoes. 'Think I'm orienteering with Mitchell.'

Toby snorted. 'So no. You don't have anything on. Good. I've got us a seat on a truck heading somewhere far more interesting than anything that dozy old codger'll teach you.'

'There's nothing around here for miles, so I know you're having me on.'

'Four words for you, Parker. Prisoner of War Camp.'

The facility loomed out of nowhere, pockets of buildings in rows, the area divided equally into four. It felt like their training ground: uniform buildings in groups, beige against the green hills. Gordon and Toby were the first to tumble from the truck, the excitement growing to a crescendo during the drive to the prison camp.

When they arrived, Wilson, a portly redheaded guard, gave them the tour, almost amused by the delight thrumming through the group of six soldiers.

'Over there are the Italians,' Wilson said, pointing to buildings at the far side of the complex. 'Next to them are the Formosans, Koreans and that. But I reckon you want a squiz at our main attraction.'

Wilson led them towards a different group of buildings as Gordon's anticipation grew.

'Can't wait to show 'em what their mates are gonna fight.' Toby's face shone with glee. 'They'll be devastated to be stuck here. Sayonara, dropkicks!' Beaming, Toby ran ahead with the others, leaving Gordon a few steps behind. The group followed the fence line, the area behind it an outside yard where a handful of Japanese were gathered in the centre.

'Is that all of them?' Toby asked. 'Thought there were heaps more.'

'Most have been sent down to Victoria,' Wilson said. 'These'll move out soon.'

Discomfort sat in Gordon's chest. The prisoners deserved to be there, keeping them away from the fighting, but there was something pathetic in the way they hung together, heads down, quiet and morose. How had these men killed so many Allied soldiers? They barely looked capable of an arm wrestle, let alone a war.

There was one Japanese man near the fence. The rest of the soldiers moved ahead, jostling to stare at the bigger group of prisoners, but Gordon lingered. The man had a red gash healing along the side of his neck, and his clothes were dusty. His gaunt face seemed to take in everything. Including Gordon.

They stood, separated by the wire fence, sizing each other up. The man's stare was disconcerting and Gordon squared his shoulders to make himself bigger. The Japanese man didn't move, a curious expression on his face. The Australian refused to blink, to look away, regardless of how the man's dark eyes seemed to open into an empty well, almost hypnotic.

Gordon's brow furrowed, trying to strike fear into the prisoner but, before he could stop himself, he blinked.

It was a simple gesture but Gordon had lost. The Japanese man took a step forward. Fear shot through Gordon and he wrenched himself away, trotting towards the rest of the Australians. He threw a casual glance back to the man, who watched him retreat.

The soldiers were flinging rocks into the yard, aiming at the prisoners. Toby drew his arm back and let fly, the rock smacking into the shoulder of an older Japanese man, leaving a dirty smear where it landed.

'Bullseye,' Toby said smugly, as he walked to the fence to examine the damage. With a shriek, the man leapt towards the Australians, shouting. A few Japanese followed him, hurling angry, venomous words. The soldiers reeled back in fright. Seeing the young men flinch, the Japanese sneered, satisfied by their enemies' embarrassment.

Gordon cleared his throat. They shouldn't underestimate these men.

Pride wounded, Toby turned to Wilson. 'Bet they weren't laughing when you took the machine gun to them, hey?'

Wilson let out a low whistle. 'I wasn't here the night of the breakout but it wasn't pretty, that's for sure.'

The soldiers edged closer to the guard, curious. The Cowra breakout the year before had been worldwide news. During the early hours of the morning, the Japanese had swarmed the guards and fences trying to escape the camp. The two guards who were on duty fired machine guns into the stampede of prisoners to stop them, both dying when the Japanese overpowered them in their frenzied rush. Around 1100 Japanese were part of the breakout and nearly 360 escaped, many sacrificing themselves so others could flee. It seemed pointless – all of them were captured within ten days and security was tightened around the complex. None of the men here seemed capable of such an attack. But perhaps that was part of the Japanese cunning they had all heard so much about.

'Come on, Parker.' Toby tossed Gordon a pebble, which he caught. 'You're always saying you're a good throw.'

Gordon examined the stone. It was smooth and rounded, with a decent weight that would carry far. Choosing a target was harder. None of the prisoners were misbehaving or rowdy. Barely any were paying attention to the Australian soldiers by the fence now, bored by their impromptu audience. Gordon's throat went dry. He wished one of them would do something to deserve a clip around the ears.

'Who's the biggest pain in the arse?' he asked Wilson.

'Mate, they all look the same to me.'

The soldiers cackled and, despite himself, Gordon glanced back to the Japanese man from earlier. The man was still watching, eyes narrowed.

'Go for the skinny bloke in the middle.' Toby pointed. 'Unless you need a bigger bloke as an easier target?'

'Speak for yourself.' It seemed a cheap victory to lob the stone at a group of caged men, but the ripple of laughter that tore through the soldiers emboldened him. It wasn't something he'd write home about, but it would keep him in good stead with his mates. He closed his fingers around the stone and drew his arm back, ready to throw.

In the distance, a horn blared. One sharp blast, then several small ones.

Everyone tensed. The Australians and the Japanese. All turning towards the sound. Relief flooded through Gordon, quickly doused by a wave of fear. The soldiers drew closer together, readying themselves for a fight. All Gordon had to defend himself was the perfect pebble he hadn't thrown, which was hardly a weapon. One Japanese could be overpowered but if all of them came at once …

The horn grew louder. Dust drifted high in the distance as a vehicle veered through the complex. Everyone was watching, waiting to see what it meant.

Around the side of a building, an Army truck skidded into view. It was loaded with guards and soldiers, some hanging off the side. One was holding an Australian flag out the window, the blue material rippling as the vehicle sped towards Gordon's group. As they came closer, it was obvious the men weren't leaping into combat.

They were cheering.

The truck braked hard, dirt flying around them.

'Emperor Hirohito's finally surrendered, boys!' the driver announced as he pressed the horn again in triumph. 'We've only gone and won the bloody war.'

A moment of silence. Then uproar.

The soldiers erupted into celebration, Gordon unable to believe it. Everyone was laughing; someone pulled out a cigar. The jubilation was all-encompassing in front of a forgotten audience of Japanese prisoners; the news rushed through the outdoor yard in harried whispers, those that understood English sharing it with the others, dread creeping in.

Toby was quiet. Gordon joined him as the others cheered on a soldier who was tearing up a flag of Imperial Japan.

'You right?' Gordon asked.

'Well, that's it, yeah?' Toby crossed his arms. 'We don't get to go out now. I'll never get to kill one of those bastards.'

The excitement drained out of Gordon. Toby was right. The war was over. Gordon wouldn't get to serve his country. He'd never get overseas. He'd never be able to protect the people he loved. His war service amounted to all of a month's worth of training, scrapping around in the dirt, with nothing to show for it.

A sour feeling spread through his stomach as Gordon watched the soldiers tying tattered strips of the Imperial flag around their foreheads, laughing.

Toby pulled out a cigarette, then offered the packet to Gordon.

'So,' Gordon said as he lit his smoke. 'What do we do now then?'

CHAPTER THREE

GORDON: Pacific Ocean, April 1946

Gordon could never be a sailor. Three weeks aboard the SS *Pachaug Victory*, a creaking, stench-filled US troop carrier, was more than enough time on a warship. He'd shipped out with hundreds of other Australian and New Zealand men in the last week of March, 1946, waved off from Sydney by a crowd of press and cameras.Once the initial excitement had worn off, there was nothing much for them to do except play cards, gamble and sleep on their way to Japan to start their service as soldiers in the British Commonwealth Occupation Force, or BCOF, as they all called it. BCOF were the Commonwealth representatives resettling Japan post-war: Australians, New Zealanders, Indians, and British soldiers in the southern regions, with the American contingent stationed in Tokyo, overseen by the Supreme Commander of the Allied Powers, General Douglas MacArthur. Toby had found the advertisement calling for soldiers to help keep the Japanese in check, given rumours of residual fighting in Japan after surrender. It had been a tantalising prospect for something to do. The Army, unsure what to do with their newly enlisted soldiers that no longer had a war to fight in, had sent them to Queensland to complete their jungle training. This training consisted of several months of running obstacle courses in the tropical heat. Gordon and Toby had signed up on the spot. It was the closest thing to a fight they'd get.

Gordon had finished his book in the first week on the ship and had taken to re-reading *Know Japan*, a comprehensive guide about what to expect when they arrived. For days, they'd been in open water, nothing but watercolour shades of blue stretching in all directions. Gordon's listlessness wasn't helped by the fact Toby was horrendously seasick, confined to his bed with a bucket.

Gordon flicked through *Know Japan* once again, sitting on his bunk as Toby groaned on the bed below. Even though he almost knew the booklet by heart, Gordon skimmed the first page, outlining the anti-fraternisation policy. It made little sense to him. Who would have anything to do with the Japanese? They were still the enemy. He wouldn't see many of them anyway. He was assigned to the medical unit at the Regimental Aid Post in Kure to treat the BCOF soldiers, after excelling in his medical training at camp. Part of him wanted to be out in the thick of things, ready to fight, but there was something he loved in patching up bodies and fixing injuries.

Toby retched and Gordon threw aside the booklet. 'Maybe you should get some fresh air, mate.'

'And watch the horizon bob up and down? No sir-ee,' Toby said, breathing hard. 'Mind you, what I wouldn't give for a cigarette.'

'Here.' From a nearby bunk, Billy Richardson set aside the book he was reading and moved towards them, fingers slipping into his breast pocket. He withdrew a rolled cigarette and offered it to Toby. Toby coughed as he took the cigarette, his other hand wrapped around the metal frame of the bunk, bracing himself. Billy smirked and offered a smoke to Gordon. On the cigarette paper was a picture of a geisha, a photo from the *Know Japan* booklet.

Gordon rolled the smoke in his fingers, then handed it back. 'Not supposed to smoke below deck.'

'Suit yourself. I'll leave it here. Save it for later.' Billy set the cigarette on the bed in front of Gordon and climbed back onto his bunk. He flicked his lighter open and lit a cigarette, exhaling smoke into the air and winked, as though daring Gordon to stop him. Gordon flashed a half-hearted smile back, then picked up the cigarette and slid it into his pocket. Billy was rarely seen without his gang of soldiers and, even though Gordon had stuck close to Toby, he wasn't keen to put anyone's nose out of joint.

Toby groaned as the room pitched upwards, and he slumped to the side.

'You're all right, mate.' Gordon steadied his friend and sat next to him on the bed, propping him up. 'You'll have your land legs back soon enough and—'

There was a clattering on the stairs and Slim Mackie burst into the room, breathless, clutching his slouch hat over his blond curls, face shining with wild delight.

'We're coming into Japan, boys.'

Soldiers jostled for space on the packed deck, eager for their first glimpse of the country that would be their home for the next two years. Gordon and Toby grabbed a spot on the side, any seasickness forgotten. A shout went up from the bow, rippling through the crowd as they glided past a capsized Japanese warship, ropes hanging in severed tendrils from the bridge, windows smashed and deck torn apart. Gordon leaned out to look, adrenaline pumping at the sight of the damage from the American firebombing the year before. As they moved through the harbour, they passed more of these gigantic ships, wrecked in the bay, completely useless, toppled by the might of the Allied Powers.

'Pretty happy them Yanks were on our side,' Toby said, laughing. A commotion broke out as they moved past a small fishing boat with a solitary Japanese fisherman on its decks. The soldiers leaned out to jeer at him, a cascade of raucous noise. The fisherman ignored them.

'You reckon they'd be pleased to see us,' Gordon said to laughter from those around him. His own chuckle died in his throat as Kure city came fully into view.

Along the docks were dark, twisted remnants of buildings. The streets were filled with rubble, but somehow, perfectly untouched structures sat among the debris, a hint of life before the war. There were people among the ruins, shadows moving in the dark. Buildings had collapsed in on themselves, scorch marks from old fires burnt black into walls. Kure was a crumbling city on its knees.

The soldiers cheered, intoxicated by the scars of war.

Gordon's stomach lurched.

'Yeah, Westy,' he said, 'I'm pretty happy the Americans were on our side.'

After they disembarked, the soldiers were shepherded onto trucks that transported them to their new home: the British Commonwealth Occupation Force base in Kure. The mood had simmered down as the trucks wound through dirt and rubble, roads of ruin stretching towards the barracks. BCOF had taken over the naval base in Kure: Aussies and Kiwis now living in the buildings that had once been Japanese, then held briefly by the Americans until they moved north to Tokyo. It was incredible that the base was still intact, that the wooden buildings had escaped constant bombing and nearby fire.

Kitbags on their shoulders, Gordon and Toby tried to work out where they were billeted on the base.

'What's that one?' Gordon asked as Toby studied the front of the building.

'Blowed if I can figure it out,' he replied.

Gordon wrinkled his nose. The smell of the city wasn't as strong in the barracks, but it wafted in on the breeze, making his eyes water. It was an acrid mix of mud, burning rubble and human waste.

A soldier stuck his head out of a nearby door. 'You blokes lost?'

'Couldn't give us a tip, mate?' Toby asked, handing the man his slip.

The man studied it then grabbed Gordon's. 'West, you're in here. Parker, you're two buildings over. You better be quick. Lunch is up in five minutes.'

Gordon sprinted to his dorm, darting around soldiers who were on their way to the mess. The room was smaller than he expected, just two beds, attached to the side of a bigger building. One bed was obviously taken; the empty one was in the back corner of the room. Gordon ran to it, throwing his pack on the mattress.

Something squeaked.

Gordon stopped. Curious. He turned to see more clearly down the side of his bed.

Curled in a ball on the floor was a Japanese girl. Her face was buried in her knees, trying to make herself small. Near her feet were a bucket and brush, cast aside as she tried to hide from him. A cleaner, a housegirl, trembling behind the empty bed.

Heart thumping, Gordon took half a step forward, but she shrank away, white socks slipping on the floor. Not wanting her to panic, he moved back.

'Sorry,' he said. 'Didn't mean to frighten you.'

The girl lifted her head a fraction, looking up at Gordon. He raised his hands, trying to signify he meant no harm.

'Gomen-nasai,' she said, shifting to bow to him, pressing her head to the floor. 'Sumimasen.'

He shifted. 'Ah – I don't know any Japanese.'

'Gomen-nasai.' She didn't seem to hear him. Or maybe she spoke no English. It didn't matter. The only Japanese Gordon could think of was the word Toby had said in Cowra.

'Sigh … sigh-oh-nah-rah?' He probably hadn't said it right but the girl frowned. Slowly, she unfurled and stood, strands of dark hair brushing against her cheekbones. Her deep brown eyes took him in, and Gordon straightened beneath her gaze.

'Sayonara?' she asked, the word bouncing in the space between them.

Gordon nodded, letting out a loose laugh. 'Yeah. Sigh-oh-nara.'

She smiled back, her whole face lighting up. Gordon relaxed, relieved she was no longer panicked, until she bowed low and darted out of the room.

'No, wait—' Gordon moved to follow her but she was gone.

The mess hall was nearly identical to every other mess Gordon had been in since he enlisted, a comfort in such a strange place. It was full of soldiers, food at one end of the room near the kitchen, and he grabbed a plate to fill. The vegetables seemed mostly familiar. There was also some mystery meat and a tray of white grains behind a card reading 'rice'. He'd only ever seen rice the one time he'd been to a Chinese restaurant with his family. He loaded his plate with potatoes and carrots and was reaching for an apple when Billy joined him, Military Police armband strapped around his bicep.

'Didn't peg you as Military Police,' Gordon said.

'I'm an upstanding member of Australian society.' Billy served himself some meat. 'What's surprising about that?'

Gordon chuckled as they moved away from the food, unable to stop staring as they passed a Japanese woman moving swiftly through the mess, eyes downcast. She was dressed like the girl in Gordon's room, a worker on base. As she went past, Billy spat on the floor by her feet. The woman quickened her step, muttering something in Japanese as she hurried out. The officer smirked, catching Gordon's eye. Gordon offered a weak smile back but said nothing. Neither did anyone else. It didn't seem as though anyone had noticed. The Japanese were the enemy, after all.

'Join us, Parker,' Billy said as he stopped by a table filled with his mates.

Gordon glanced to where Toby was sitting alone. He didn't want to rub the Military Police officer up the wrong way but didn't want to be best mates either. 'Maybe tomorrow. Promised Westy I'd eat with him today.'

Billy shrugged and sat, leaving Gordon to head to Toby, whose meal was half eaten.

'You took your time,' Toby said.

'Some of us have respect and don't rush everything all the time,' Gordon said, stomach growling as he sat. His first bite of lunch was delicious simply by being eaten on ground that wasn't moving beneath him.

Toby poked a vegetable on Gordon's plate, curious. 'What's that, then?'

'Potato,' he replied, eyebrow arched.

'It's daikon.' A soldier set his plate on the table. He seemed older than them, perhaps twenty-three, all chest and dimpled cheeks. He didn't wait for an invitation as he pulled out his chair with a screech. 'Japanese radish. But I wouldn't eat it if I were you. The Japanese veg is all grown in bombed-out soil. Probably poisoned.'

Gordon's meal was loaded with lethal vegetables. He wiped his mouth with a handkerchief. 'What are we meant to eat then?'

'Most of the rest will be fine. You boys have brought supplies with you. Plus, anything that grows above ground is all right.'

'You saying that so you get more food to yourself?' Toby asked.

The man laughed. 'Absolutely. I'm Andrew Williams. Andy.' He turned to Gordon. 'You're Gordon Parker? You're with me in Medical. And we're bunkmates, so I hope you don't snore.'

'G'day,' Gordon said, still unsure about the food. 'This is Toby West.' Toby nodded in greeting, then looked down at the last roast potato on his plate, forlorn.

'Eat the food,' Andy said. 'Life's too short to die hungry.' Andy speared a carrot with his fork and bit into it, as though trying to prove the food was all right.

'How long have you been here?' Gordon asked, eating again. 'I thought we were the first to ship out from Sydney.'

'You were. The rest of us came across from Morotai, in Indonesia. Weren't ready to head home after the war ended so we jumped on another ship and ended up in the land of the rising sun.'

'How's it been?' Toby asked. 'How's the fighting?'

'Any chance I can volunteer with other units so I can get out of Medical sometimes?' Gordon asked.

Andy frowned. 'I wouldn't go chasing war here, lads. Fighting these blokes isn't as much fun as you'd reckon.'

'Nah,' Toby said. 'They promised fighting.'

'If there's been any, I haven't heard about it,' Andy replied. 'No official fighting, anyway.'

This place was nothing like Gordon had expected. Ruined cities, strange girls, dangerous food and no Japanese to fight. On top of that, he'd eaten all of his lunch without realising and the only things left were his apple and the damaged daikon.

Toby was just as unimpressed. 'So, what is there to do around this place then?'

Shouts exploded from outside the mess. Across the room, Billy leapt from his table and raced for the door, soldiers at his heels. Gordon and Toby exchanged an excited look, then bounded after them.

A brawl. Gordon tried to make sense of it as he watched the soldiers fight. A group of Australians, Billy included, were scrapping with a handful of Japanese. As he watched, a Japanese boy skidded to a stop at Gordon's feet. He couldn't have been much older than twelve. He glared at the Australian then dived back into the fray, as Gordon's stomach dropped. They were all kids. All scrabbling against the soldiers, heading in the same direction. Trying to get to the bins. Looking for food.

One of the boys flattened Billy with a kick to his stomach; he went down with a shout. The Japanese bolted, outstripping the soldiers who half-heartedly chased them. Billy stood, face red. Nearly every soldier who had been in the mess was now looking at the Military Police officer curiously.

'Thieving animals, the lot of them,' Billy said. He shook himself off and strode away, followed by the rest of his group.

Toby snorted. 'Hell of a first day.' He clapped Gordon on the shoulder then headed back into the mess, the crowd dissipating as the hubbub died. About to follow, a noise from behind the bins made Gordon stop.

There was a Japanese girl rummaging through a box filled with rotting vegetables.

'Hey!' It was out of his mouth before he could stop it. The girl leapt back, trembling. Her dress was dirty and torn, her dark hair matted and knotted, her eyes wide and scared.

He was still holding his apple. He held it up and pointed to it. 'You want this?' He put it on the ground between them, then moved back to allow her to take it. She watched him, unsure. He took another step back. Like a flash, she darted forward and swiped the apple, sprinting off.

Gordon sighed. Why wasn't anyone looking after these kids? The girl seemed about Jennifer's age. The thought of his siblings being caught up in this kind of world made him shudder.

He turned to head back into the mess. Outside a building nearby was the girl from his dorm, her head tilted to the side, curious. Now he could see her properly, she didn't seem much younger than him. She was a kid who'd survived this war too. Neither of them moved, her eyes locked on to him. This time it was Gordon who moved first, ducking inside, exhausted already by how different Japan was from Australia.

CHAPTER FOUR

NOBUKO: Kure, April 1946

It was dark by the time Nobuko Sakuramoto finished her work. The shadows stretched around her as she hurried through the barracks, head bowed, trying not to make eye contact with any of the Australian soldiers. No-one looked her way. The men were usually too absorbed in their own adventures to notice any of the Japanese girls around the base. Some girls in town wanted to be noticed, so the soldiers looked to them instead. Before the Australians arrived, the naval base had been occupied by the US military, and a few of the Japanese housegirls had gone to Tokyo chasing an American soldier. For most of them, that was the only way they'd ever get out of Kure. Nobuko didn't want that. She wasn't working to find a man to marry and be someone's wife, far away from home. Her family needed money and she was the only one left who could work. She needed to provide for her father and uncle, to hold the broken pieces of her family together.

It wasn't her first choice to work in the barracks. She didn't like being close to the ex-enemy soldiers, the dangerous men who had fought against her country for so long. Jobs, though, were scarce, and when her friend Hana suggested Nobuko come and work at the base with her, Nobuko had little choice but to take it. The money was okay but the real benefit was that they were fed two meals a day on the base and still allocated rations from the government. When Nobuko started, there were barely any ex-enemy soldiers around. It was easy to avoid them and most of the men never saw the invisible Japanese girls. Nobuko found the work simple, slipping in and out of rooms to clean them, avoiding any interaction with the Australians as more arrived. She hid in cupboards or peeked out from around the side of buildings to watch the tall, pale men laughing and smoking. They felt too big for Japan: loud, disrespectful and dirty. She kept out of their way, resolving never to meet any of them.

All that had changed now.

The man – he seemed a little older than her, perhaps a year or two – had surprised her. Nobuko always cleaned the dormitories at lunchtime as it was easier to avoid any ex-enemy soldiers. Over the past few weeks, she had never come close to an Australian, although she did study the photographs by their beds, of women and families, beaming faces in sepia and black and white. She'd been lingering by a photograph of a smiling young woman holding a puppy, her bucket and brush forgotten, when there was a rush of footsteps outside. She scrambled away and tucked herself in the corner of the room, nowhere else to hide. The man galloped in and made a beeline for her. Her heart thumped, she was too afraid to look up. He threw his bag onto his bed and Nobuko couldn't help the terrified squeak that escaped her throat. He must have seen her. He would be advancing on her now, ready to murder her where she sat …

He didn't. He tried to speak to her, his blue-grey eyes widened in surprise. Nobuko, shocked, recognised his garbled Japanese, heavily accented and terribly pronounced. She was apologising; he was saying goodbye. She didn't need more of a reason to leave, so she took the chance to escape while she could.

She'd been rattled for the rest of the day. He hadn't seemed as imposing as the Japanese government had promised the ex-enemy soldiers were, although he towered over her. Even more curious was that she had later seen him offer food to a starving girl. The urchins weren't rare. In Kure, everyone was starving and desperate. Many people had lost their homes, their families, their minds. The base was the most abundant place for food in the city, a veritable paradise compared to the meagre ration allocations doled out, and children snuck onto the base to hunt for any scraps.

The way he looked at her lingered in her thoughts as she hurried towards the bus stop when she left for the day. The stories she had been told about the Western soldiers were that they were murderers and had no soul behind their eyes. So far, this Australian hadn't killed her when he had the chance and had been kind when he didn't need to be.

'Nobuko-chan!'

Hana and Michiko arrived at the bus stop together, both laughing as they caught up with her. Hana bounced on her toes, cheeks flushed with excitement. The three of them wore matching grey dresses and whatever shoes they could find. There wasn't a strict uniform they were required to wear on the base but school uniforms were the easiest clothes to find and still fit them all at sixteen years old. Nobuko didn't have much more in her cupboard at home – a pair of sandals, a worn skirt and another blouse was all she had.

'Have you seen all the new soldiers?' Hana asked. 'They're so tall! One of them hit his head on the doorframe and I had to stuff my dress into my mouth to stop laughing.'

'If he'd seen you, you would've been in trouble,' Nobuko replied. 'We must be careful around these ex-enemy soldiers. They're dangerous.'

'But if they're still dangerous, how are they *ex-enemy* soldiers?' Hana asked, tucking a curl behind her ear. 'They can't be both.'

'I don't trust them.' Nobuko glanced up to see if the bus was coming.

'Cautious cautious Nobuko-chan,' Hana said, laughing. 'You wouldn't speak to the Americans either. But maybe if you had, you could be in Tokyo with Mina-chan.'

'You spoke to the Americans and you never went to Tokyo.' Nobuko stepped aside to make way for a grandmother who was also waiting for the bus. A small crowd was gathering now that most of the Japanese had finished their work: cleaners, builders, laundry workers. All were women and girls, except for one man standing a polite distance away. The war had taken a lot from Japan, including the nation's sons.

'I wonder if more soldiers will come,' Michiko said as the bus approached and shuddered to a stop. The doors creaked open, the crowd allowing the oldest on first. Nobuko and Hana stepped around a pile of debris, Michiko close behind, as they clambered on board. The three of them squashed together on a seat meant for two, allowing space for others, but also because it was more reassuring to be closer to one another when they drove through the darker parts of town.

'I hope so,' Hana said. 'I think they're funny.'

'I don't know,' Michiko said, sighing. 'Mother says they are dangerous. She says that if you get too close to them, your babies will be kangaroos.'

'What?' Nobuko asked, incredulous. Michiko nodded, serious.

'Your mother is crazy!' Hana said, cackling with laughter. 'I don't want to have babies with a foreign soldier.'

'That's the thing,' Michiko said, tapping the window idly as she spoke. 'They cast a spell on you if you get too close, because it's the only way they can trick girls into having kangaroo babies.'

'Are you sure?' Nobuko asked, confused. 'I haven't seen kangaroo babies in anyone's photographs.'

'It's not something they celebrate,' Michiko replied. 'But have any of the photographs you've seen had babies in them?'

Nobuko couldn't remember seeing any babies in the photographs but she hadn't been looking for them either.

'You silly girls.' A voice came from behind them. They turned to see the grandma from the bus stop shaking her head as she gripped the back of their seat tightly. 'The Australians will not give you kangaroo babies. They will eat you.'

Startled, Nobuko glanced at Michiko, who was equally shocked.

'Grandma, are you sure?' Hana asked, but the confidence had fallen from her voice.

'My friend's daughter went to Tokyo with the Americans a few months ago. Now, she is gone. No-one has heard from her since she left Kure. But my friend had a dream that the Americans cut her up and ate her for dinner. These white soldiers are the same.' The woman coughed.

Nobuko slipped her hand into Hana's, her heart beating fast. It had always been dangerous working on the Army base but it wasn't until now that she realised just how deadly it might be. She tried to calm herself. All she had to do was stay invisible and stay away from any soldiers.

Hana surveyed the old woman, then leaned into Nobuko's ear.

'I don't believe her,' she whispered. 'I've been working at the base for the longest of us all and I've never heard of anything like that. They can be scary but I don't think they would eat us. Besides,' Hana poked at Nobuko, 'there's no point! We're too skinny from rations. Nobuko-chan would barely feed one man!'

'I'm not feeding any man!' Nobuko said, as her friends laughed. 'I won't let any soldier eat me.'

'That's the spirit, dear,' the old woman said from behind them. Her eyes fluttered closed as the rocking of the bus put her to sleep. The girls giggled and Hana shifted in her seat.

'You're brave now, Nobuko-chan?' she asked. 'If you're so brave, speak to one of them someday.'

'Someday,' Michiko said, smirking. 'A hundred years from now.'

'I could speak to one,' Nobuko said, bristling. 'I just don't want to.'

'Because you're too scared,' Hana said.

'I like to be safe.' Nobuko wriggled against Hana, forcing her to move away from Michiko.

'One day you'll have to be brave.' Hana shot Michiko a conspiring look. 'You can't spend your life being safe and expect to have any fun.'

'I haven't always been safe,' Nobuko said. This made Hana and Michiko smile more, causing Nobuko's frustration to rise. 'During the war—'

'We were all brave during the war.' Michiko tossed her ponytail. 'That doesn't count—'

There was a loud bang and the bus slammed to a halt. Nobuko jolted forward, hitting her shoulder on the seat in front. She curled herself smaller, heart beating fast. An explosion? It didn't sound like a bomb. Nor did it sound like gunshots. No-one on the bus made a sound, a strange collection of fearful faces waiting for the air-raid siren, the roar of fire, the disaster of war.

There was a commotion outside, people yelling for others to help, passersby pushing forward. A man was carried to the side of the road. Headlights briefly illuminated an angry head wound and blood pouring across his face. His mouth was slack, his eyes open in shock. He was already dead.

'Do you think he jumped in front of the car?' Michiko murmured.

Neither Nobuko nor Hana said anything. Suicide rates were high and, although it never became less shocking, it was common for their route home to be interrupted by traffic held up while a body was removed from the road or a bicycle was pulled out from beneath a bus. Never one this close though.

Nobuko's heart ached. There was so much sadness after the war, so much desperation. Everyone was struggling, trying to live in this grim shadow of the proud and vibrant world they once had inhabited. Japan was in ruins. It was difficult to comprehend how quickly things had changed and how they might never change back.

The rest of the bus ride was sombre. Nobuko was relieved when they drew close to her neighbourhood, pleased to have the time alone to walk to her house. The bus rattled to a stop and she stood up.

'See you tomorrow,' she said, bowing quickly to Hana and Michiko. She caught the old woman's eye behind them, and instinctively nodded and smiled to her too. The woman inclined her head.

'Good night, brave Nobuko-chan,' Hana said, a small smile in her voice.

'Very brave Nobuko-chan,' Michiko echoed.

Nobuko smiled as she scrambled for the door of the bus. 'The bravest.'

The streets were dark and almost silent as Nobuko walked up the small hill to her uncle's house. She darted along the path, past the houses of her neighbours as they sat down to dinner. Candlelight flickered from windows, briefly silhouetting an older couple at their table, a mother with her baby, three sisters kneeling on the floor, sewing clothes.

An owl hooted softly above her, hidden in the twisted branches of the trees. Looking up into the sky, she suddenly felt overwhelmed. She stopped by a blossoming sakura tree, the pink flowers exploding on dark branches and blanketing the grass at her feet. She placed her hand on the trunk, setting one of her feet on the roots of the tree, and closed her eyes. The soft rustle of the flowers moving with the breeze surrounded her, calming her. Nobuko pressed her hand more firmly to the trunk, her palm curving around the flecks in the wood. She drew her other hand up blindly and placed it there as well, breathing deeply to steady herself. As though her heart knew what she was trying to do, it sped up. Faltering, Nobuko tried to stay grounded but her memories came screaming back and, with a gasp, she opened her eyes.

She was in Kure. She was nearly home. She was under the sakura.

She was safe.

Most days, when she could feel her nerves rising, connecting with the sakura trees helped her refocus and forget. Today was not most days.

Still overwhelmed, Nobuko set off again, trying to steady her breath. She wasn't far from home now. Her father would not want to see her weakened state.

His coughing echoed onto the street before the small shack she lived in came into view. Nothing else mattered for now. It was about Father and what he needed this evening.

Nobuko stepped onto the makeshift path that led to the hastily built house. Most people wouldn't call it a house, built within the ruins of where her Uncle Kazuo and Aunt Masako had lived. Three houses next to one another had been bombed, Kazuo and Masako's in the middle. The opposite side of the street was untouched. The shack wasn't much but she was grateful they had a few rooms inside, mirroring the layout of the previous house.

'I'm home,' Nobuko called as she took off her shoes at the door.

'Welcome home,' Uncle Kazuo said from the other room. She moved towards the kitchen, bowing to her father as she passed him. Noboru Sakuramoto looked to her from where he knelt, cigarette between his wrinkled lips, shining black eyes glinting in the dim light. 'You're late.'

'I'm sorry.' Nobuko bowed in apology and began to prepare the table for dinner. 'The bus was delayed.'

'This is why you should not work for enemy soldiers.' Noboru eased himself off the floor, cigarette smouldering. He stepped forward, filling the frame of the door into the kitchen. 'It is too far and they are—'

'Good evening!' Aunty Suma, their neighbour from across the street, called out from the front door as she bustled in. A knot of anxiety in Nobuko's stomach eased. Suma was carrying bowls of food – she must've been keeping an eye out for Nobuko's arrival home. She wasn't related to them, but Suma had become such a fixture in their lives that Nobuko wasn't sure they would survive without her.

'It is not very fancy but it will nourish you,' Suma said as she laid the bowls on the table. Well-practised, she and Nobuko then added mismatched plates and chopsticks around the food. Suma pooled all their rations together – what she was allocated with her niece, Amari, and what the Sakuramoto household received. Nobuko was grateful that they all benefited from her ration allocation when she didn't need to use it. Even if she was hungry when she arrived home from work, she wouldn't eat. She'd serve her father and uncle, sit at the table and listen to them talk, clear their plates away and tidy afterwards. It wasn't until much later that, if there was any food left, she would take a mouthful of rice before bed. Nobuko tried to eat as early and as late as possible at the base so she didn't take food away from her family.

'Maybe Nobuko should steal food from the Americans,' Noboru said, kneeling at the low chabudai table. 'They surely have enough.'

'And what if Nobuko was caught?' Suma asked, almost disinterested. It was a regular topic of conversation from Noboru, that the Americans owed them something. Nobuko picked up the bowl of rice and split it into four portions, then scooped a section into her father's bowl.

'They're not Americans, Father,' Nobuko said, gently. 'They're Australians.'

'Australia dropped the bomb?' Kazuo asked as he eased himself to the floor. His hip had been injured by flying debris in a bombing raid the previous year and hadn't healed properly. Nobuko served him rice and Suma ladled out a watery soup. It didn't look as though it had much flavour, even with the small sprinkling of nori on top. The rations rarely included anything besides the true basics, but Nobuko knew Suma had a stash of extra ingredients under her house. The days were hard enough and gloomy thoughts were often made worse by an empty stomach.

'No, the Americans had the bomb,' Suma said as she passed a bowl to Kazuo.

He frowned. 'Not the Australians?'

'The Australians are allies of the United States and Britain,' Suma said. 'But they didn't drop the bomb.'

Noboru slammed his fist onto the table. 'Whoever they are, they aren't Japanese. Nobuko should not work for the enemy – she should work for Japan!'

'Nobuko-chan?' Suma asked, ignoring Noboru's outburst and offering Nobuko some soup.

She shook her head. 'I've eaten.'

The older woman fixed her with a gentle stare. Tonight, though, Nobuko genuinely wasn't hungry. Her appetite had all but disappeared after her day. Perhaps her father was right – it was too dangerous to be working on the base and coming home so late each evening.

As she considered trying to find another job in Kure, Amari came inside.

'Good evening!' She stepped nimbly through the house in socked feet, kneeling at the table next to Nobuko. 'Sorry for my lateness – I was studying when Aunty came over.'

Noboru, mouth full of rice, nodded at Amari and gestured she should eat. Disappointment flicked across the younger girl's face as she saw the paltry serve of rice left in the bowl for her, and Nobuko's stomach clenched. If they had to share the same amount of food with one more person, everyone would go hungry. It wouldn't be easy to find another job that provided money and food as the Army base did. She would simply have to be Brave Nobuko so that she could help everyone she loved.

'How are your studies?' Noboru asked, reaching for his bowl of soup.

'They're going well,' Amari said, shifting on her knees. 'I'm hoping to study at the university in Osaka soon.'

'I don't see how English will help you.' Noboru clicked his tongue as he ate. 'You are in Japan. What do you need English for?'

'There are lots of reasons to learn English,' Suma said.

Amari nodded. 'Yes! Especially now that the ex-enemy soldiers are here. I have a chance to learn about the language. I can help the Japanese who can't speak English and do my part to rebuild Japan.'

Noboru straightened as he sipped his soup. Nobuko hid her smile. She, Suma and Amari had discussed the best ways to talk about Amari's English studies to Noboru and decided that appealing to his patriotism was the most effective. Even though Noboru was only a neighbour to Amari, he held a lot of influence over her. Amari's father, Suma's brother, had been killed in the Pacific during the war, after the ship he was on was bombed and sank, leaving her in Suma's care. At fourteen, Amari was two years younger than Nobuko, but she was incredibly smart and had had an interest in England since an Englishman who had visited her school had given her a book. The book had sparked a curiosity about lands far across the seas, a curiosity only intensified by fighting Britain in war.

'Perhaps Osaka will be good for you,' Noboru said, as Kazuo pulled out a cigarette. It was almost time to clear the table. Dinner didn't last long when there was barely any food.

'I think Osaka is a new opportunity for Amari,' Suma said. 'And any language is useful, but English especially so. Perhaps our niece can become a Japanese spy.'

Kazuo laughed, the sound bouncing around the room. 'Nobuko will have to get Amari a job at the base. Together they can be the Kure spies when they talk to the soldiers.'

'I don't talk to the soldiers,' Nobuko said quickly. 'My English is no good, anyway.' She didn't want to get in trouble for something she hadn't even done. Her father, however, had a soft, faraway look on his face.

'Nobuko and Amari,' he mused, then laughed. 'Girl spies. The enemy soldiers would have no idea!'

Nobuko twisted her slim fingers together, saying nothing. Kazuo lit his cigarette and she reached for his bowl through the thin tobacco smoke. If her father's attention was on Amari going to Osaka, he might not shift into his usual nightly routine of complaining. No sooner had Nobuko thought this than Noboru began to cough. A small one at first, then a gravelled, hacking cough that made everyone stop, concerned. Nobuko hovered by the entrance to the kitchen, watching her father, heart beating furiously.

He had started coughing in the last year of the war. It hadn't seemed significant at the time, to the point where none of them were sure when it had actually started. No-one could remember him coughing before the firebombing in Kure but neither were they sure if he had started after the first night of bombings or the fifth. Initially they had thought he was sick but there didn't seem to be any other consistent symptoms. Some days his energy was low and he couldn't move much. Other days he was okay. He refused to see a doctor, refused to have himself checked out. That stubbornness meant it was impossible for him to find work as he wasn't reliable. He'd done a few jobs since the surrender but had been fired from all of them – once for passing out in the middle of a shift, once for not showing up three days in a row, and once because someone had complained about Noboru's coughing fits and was too afraid to work in close proximity to him.

Noboru couldn't work because of his lungs, Kazuo because of his hips, and so it was Nobuko who was responsible for her family's survival.

This time, her father's cough settled and he cleared his throat. His hard eyes flicked around the room and Nobuko tried to avert her gaze, to avoid the bubbling anger that followed an attack. One thing Noboru couldn't abide was other people's pity.

'None of our girls will be spies.' He grasped a cup of water, a few droplets spilling over the side. 'Not Amari. Not Nobuko. No-one.' He levelled his gaze at Nobuko, who shrank back. 'You will do your work and come home. You will not to talk to anyone. You will do nothing more than what you are told. Do you understand?'

Nobuko nodded. Noboru rubbed his chest before draining his cup, then sat back on the floor, slumped in exhaustion. Suma shot Nobuko an apologetic look and Nobuko gave a shrug before she moved into the kitchen. She heard her aunt go to her father's side, chattering to ease him out of his discomfort. Nobuko placed the dinner bowls by the washing bucket and took a breath. Things might be hard but someone still had to clean the dishes.

There was never total quiet, even once the household retired to bed, but that reassured Nobuko. She lay on her futon on the tatami mat, her uncle already snoring in a dark corner. Her father's breath whistled, reminding her that she wasn't alone. Outside, there were footsteps of those going to their night jobs, dogs barking and running along the road. In the distance was the rhythmic clacking of a train, accompanied by the occasional blast of a horn. A breeze rustled through the pear tree in the yard. There was always some noise, something to anchor herself to.

Unable to fall asleep, she brushed her fingers across the tatami beneath her, back and forth. Tomorrow, the sun would bring a new day. As it would the day after that. Those days would grow to weeks, to months, to years, and perhaps one day things would be different. Japan would be healed; Noboru would recover and be able to work again; life would be better and Nobuko would be happy.

Tomorrow, however, she had to return to work. As she drifted into sleep, she wondered: would she be Brave Nobuko or not?

CHAPTER FIVE

GORDON: Kure, April 1946

Gordon was used to silent nights, occasionally punctuated by the bleat of a sheep, a chortling kookaburra, perhaps a barking dog. Otherwise, the Australian darkness brought with it thick quietness and calm until sunrise.

The Japanese darkness did not.

He knew his first night away would be strange, but the bed was hard and uncomfortable, the wooden frame cloaking the pillows in a pine and oak scent. The dorm room wasn't quite dark, the thin curtains allowing a vague glow into the room, even in the dead of night. Outside was constant noise. Voices, footsteps, laughter filtered through the walls as men moved past, the squeal of a wild animal echoed in the distance, and every time Gordon got comfortable enough to drop into sleep, a train would roar past and blast its horn. The third time it happened, he grunted out loud, earning a drowsy reply from Andy.

'You'll get used to it, Parker. They do it deliberately every night to wake us up. Don't get in a strop about it – that's how they win.'

It was easier said than done. Counting sheep gave him no relief. Throwing off his blanket did nothing either. Lying on his stomach was not an option, especially as his feet hung off the end of the bed.

Eventually, in the early hours of the morning, Gordon settled, feeling sleep reaching out for him, about to drop into oblivion—

Andy started to snore.

Gordon sat up. Outside, the sky slowly brightened, dawn beckoning. He got out of bed, pulled on a shirt and grabbed his boots, then slipped out of the dorm into the pre-dawn morning.

He wandered the empty base, blinking away his bleariness. There was a fence along the perimeter of the barracks, threaded with greenery that grew wild from the other side. A section of it had collapsed, half consumed by the straggly scrub, but there were marks of a walking track into the bush. He checked there was no-one else around before he stepped into the undergrowth.

Here was a welcome quiet. He could be the only bloke in the world right now, listening to the gentle lap of the unseen ocean somewhere to his right and a bird to his left digging through leaves to find food for its nest. The darkness lifted as the sun rose and the heavy smell of the city was far less pungent. The trees were painted with lush pink petals, pops of cherry blossom flowers smattered across the patches of green canopy around him.

The sound of a bubbling creek grew louder. The track opened up to a small watering hole, widening to a beach five hundred yards away. Cherry blossom trees arched over the water, a curtain of pink with a blanket of confetti beneath. Gordon sat on the stony creek bank, breathing deeply, watching the flowers sway in the breeze, this small pocket of paradise. Even in the shade, the humidity was rising, the day promising to be warm. The water rushed over rocks and branches, pooling in a deep, wide well of clear water, before heading further down to meet the sea. Unable to resist temptation, Gordon removed his shoes and rolled up the bottom of his trousers, dipping his toes in and bracing himself for ice. The initial shock of cold melted into a feeling deliciously pleasant. He waded in the shallows, torn between not getting his trousers wet and wanting to jump in further. The water looked too beautiful to ignore.

Naked, he rushed into the creek, diving shallowly into the wide pool and resurfacing, shaking his hair out of his eyes, beaming. The water cleared his mind, concerns easing with every plunge beneath the surface, shoulders relaxing. Perhaps if he could sneak out in the mornings for a swim, the next two years might not be so tough.

It was easy to lose track of time as he floated in the water. The sun peeked through the leafy trees, growing higher in the morning sky. How long had he been here for? Without his watch, it was impossible to tell. It could be almost breakfast. He swam to the edge of the creek, standing and shaking himself off, heading towards his clothes.

Before he could reach them, humming filtered through the trees. With no time, Gordon snatched up his clothes and covered himself, heart thudding. The humming stopped, the person hidden by the undergrowth.

'Who's there?' he said. 'Show yourself.'

Silence, then a girl stepped into view. She blinked at the sight of him, then frowned.

'Ah, g'day.' Gordon's cheeks grew hot. The girl said nothing, her head tilted to the side. 'Just … had a quick dip. Probably shouldn't have. Didn't know people used this track too much.'

Her black hair was tied back, a few strands waving in the breeze. She ran her fingers over her loose grey dress, perhaps a size too big, but still didn't speak. It wasn't until he noticed the white socks on her feet that a jolt of recognition shot through him. Was this the girl from yesterday?

She took a breath, then spoke a stream of Japanese, the words musical, rhythmic and completely incomprehensible. He laughed. 'No Japanese,' he said. 'English?' The girl's eyes flicked back and forth in thought. Now it seemed foolish that Gordon hadn't learnt any of the language before he arrived; but then, he hadn't been expecting to be ambushed stark naked on his second day in the country.

'Namae?' she asked, cautiously.

'Name?' Gordon repeated, and the girl nodded. 'I know that one. Gordon.' He pointed at himself, careful not to drop the fabric covering his modesty. 'Gordon.'

'Go … Go …' She faltered over the pronunciation.

'Ah, what about Don? Don.'

'Don.' She pointed to him. 'Don-san.'

'Yeah, sure. Don-san,' Gordon repeated. 'And you? Your namma-yay?'

The girl bit back a giggle at Gordon's attempt at Japanese. He ran a hand through his wet hair, pleased she was laughing and not running away.

'Sakuramoto Nobuko,' she said, the Japanese words crashing over Gordon, a collection of syllables and breath.

'Whoa, steady on,' Gordon said. 'Sakura-whatsit?'

The girl paused, then darted past him. He shrank back, unsure what she was doing, but she headed to the cherry blossom trees. Reaching up, she tangled her fingers in the blooms.

'Sakura-moto,' she repeated. 'Sakuramoto No-bu-ko.'

'Ah, sakura. Like the cherry blossoms.'

'Yes. Cherry,' she said.

He laughed. 'You do know English! You were having me on this whole time, hey?'

She shook her head, drawing away from him, alarmed.

He backtracked. 'Little bit of English then.'

'Yes. Little English,' she said, gesturing with her hands, showing a tiny gap between her two forefingers.

'Me, zero Japanese. No Japanese.' He shook his head to show what he meant.

'Sayonara,' she said with a small smile.

Gordon laughed, remembering their last meeting. 'One Japanese word then. Dunno what it means. Sigh-oh-nara.'

'Sayonara. Goodo-byo.' Cherry waved at him. 'Sayonara!' she called out, demonstrating, and Gordon understood.

'Righto. Goodbye. I'll remember that.' An awkward silence fell, neither knowing what to say. He was almost completely dry now. What was the best way to get her to turn around so he could get dressed?

Cherry pointed to the water, saying something in Japanese.

He laughed, embarrassed. 'I went for a swim. Swim.' He pinched his nose and took a deep breath before miming putting his head under the water. 'It was good.' He flashed her a big smile and a thumbs-up. Cherry gave him a thumbs-up too, standing underneath the cherry blossom tree. The branches seemed to reach down to wrap her up, a breeze making the blossoms fall like a light snow.

She spoke more Japanese, a clear question in the words. Gordon, at a loss, shrugged with a small chuckle and Cherry laughed too.

'Okay. Sayonara!' She turned and headed towards the base.

Stunned, Gordon watched as she left.

'Sigh-oh-nara, Cherry,' he called out after her. If she heard him, she gave no sign, and, once she'd disappeared into the greenery, he quickly dressed, hoping he wasn't late returning to base.

Gordon's first patient in the medical unit wasn't what he'd imagined. In his mind, he had thought his work would be almost heroic. A young man would be carried in, perhaps a bullet wound to the shoulder. Gordon would work quickly, the man drifting in and out of consciousness as Gordon found the bullet. He would stitch the injury closed, give the man something for the pain and that would be it. A life saved; an injury healed. June had always teased him about his delusions and daydreams.

In reality, Gordon was frozen as he looked at the screaming man on the bed. There was no bullet wound. There was no heroic life-saving moment. Strangest of all, the man was Japanese.

His name was Hiroshi, according to Cliff, the barrel-chested stockman turned translator who had brought him in with the help of another bloke from Engineering. There wasn't time to say much more. Gordon pressed down hard on the deep gash in Hiroshi's thigh to try to stop the bleeding. It didn't help that the man wouldn't lie still, his face pale and waxy with blood loss. He fought against Cliff's firm grip, pinning Hiroshi to the bed so that Andy and Gordon could work. The other soldier from Engineering held Hiroshi's legs down, to save all of them from losing their front teeth. The injured man flailed against them, screaming in Japanese that Cliff elected not to translate. As Andy readied the equipment to stitch the wound closed, the Japanese man's anger ebbed and he stopped thrashing, his energy declining from blood loss.

The lull in the fight made things easier. Andy instructed Gordon to keep the wound closed by keeping his hands on either side of the cut. Gordon tried not to look too closely, sure he would see the layers of muscles and fat and bone if he did. The older man didn't seem fazed, his stubby fingers working deftly to stitch up the injury. His work was neat and clean, experience evident in every movement. Gordon braced against Hiroshi as Andy inserted the needle but the Japanese man lay still, unconscious. Gordon had never seen an injury like this before and was glad he didn't have to take the lead on treating it.

Gordon pinned fresh white bandages over the wound. Andy stepped up next to him drying his hands, surveying the work. He gave a small noise of approval then took Hiroshi's pulse.

'He'll live,' Andy said, and nodded his thanks to Cliff, who was sitting on a nearby bed. The translator tapped the side of his nose in response. The other soldier had disappeared outside as soon as Hiroshi had slipped into unconsciousness. He was probably the person retching on the other side of the window.

'How'd you go?' Andy asked Gordon. 'First one's a goodie, isn't it?'

'Yeah,' Gordon said, letting out an overwhelmed breath. 'But what are they doing, bringing him here? I thought we weren't supposed to fraternise.'

To Gordon's surprise, Andy laughed. 'Mate, if you're gonna be a stickler for the rules, Medical might not be the best place for you. That anti-frat rule is impossible. Any conversation with any Japanese is forbidden? We're in Japan. This place is filled with Japanese.' Andy sniffed. 'We treat anyone who comes in here. Doesn't matter what their name is or where they're from. They're hurt, we fix them. If you can't do that, we can get you out somewhere else quick-smart.' He raised his eyebrows; a challenge.

Gordon shifted. He hadn't meant that he didn't want to treat any patients who came in – everyone deserved medical care. He was just surprised his first patient was Japanese, given the *Know Japan* booklet had been so firm about not fraternising with them. BCOF seemed to think that the Australians wouldn't have much to do with the Japanese at all. He'd met Cherry by the creek, sure, but he hadn't expected to see any of them in the medical unit, using the services of the Occupation Force. The city had its own hospitals and clinics. Although, given the destruction of Kure in the bombings, it was obvious the base had the best facilities around.

Gordon glanced at Cliff, who winked.

'No, it's fine,' Gordon said. 'I'm fine to stay.'

'Good lad,' Andy said, clapping a hand on Gordon's shoulder. 'I promise you'll be bored when you realise most of our patients are blokes with VD, begging for relief. Venereal disease isn't fun. You be smart if you ever spend time with a girl in town, okay?' Andy picked up the scissors and needle, taking them to the sink.

Gordon wandered over to Cliff. 'What happened to him, anyway?' Gordon asked, jerking his head towards Hiroshi.

Cliff's hazel eyes flicked to the man in the bed, then he clicked his tongue. 'They fossick through the debris, trying to find stuff to rebuild their houses,' he said in his slow Australian drawl. 'We watch them every day, pulling out huge hunks of whatever they can grab to build a shanty or a shack. He slipped while he was digging and cut himself on glass still stuck in a broken window frame.'

Gordon winced. There wasn't a good way to get injured but that sounded particularly gruesome. 'What do you do out there?' he asked.

'I translate mostly,' Cliff said. 'Sometimes I pretend I don't know what the Japanese are saying. Funny how much you can learn when you eavesdrop. But I'm with Engineering. At the moment, they're putting in poles so we can rig some electricity through the city. Lotta people are living by candlelight or just daylight. All pretty dire, really.'

'And you actually learnt Japanese?' Gordon asked. 'I mean, before you came here?'

'Yeah.' Cliff shrugged. 'Me stepmum's grandma was Japanese. Married to a pearl diver off the north-west coast. She looked after me a lot as a kid and her English wasn't too crash-hot, so we just kind of spoke to each other in both languages. I guess you can call me bilingual. Came in pretty handy during wartime though – no-one expects a stockman to speak decent English, let alone any Japanese.'

Gordon was surprised any Australian would speak Japanese. He couldn't think of a situation where you would need to speak anything other than English in Australia.

'You interested in learning?' Cliff asked. 'They've got classes here on the weekends if you want to stop in. I run it with Bisho for an hour at 10 am over in the main building.'

'I'll think about it,' Gordon said. Even though he had wanted to speak Japanese to Cherry, it seemed unlikely 'sorry I'm naked, I went for a skinny dip' would be part of Cliff's language curriculum. Would he get another chance to speak with her? He could be hauled in for fraternisation, if they were caught.

'You'd be surprised at how a konnichiwa, a genki dess ka and an arigato come in handy.' Cliff stood, rolling his sleeves up.

'Harry gar-toe?' Gordon repeated, confused.

Cliff smirked. 'Yeah, arigato. Thank you. Some blokes say Harry's garters or just Harry's. An easier way to remember it. Anyway, I've been gone long enough, I should head out. I'll check on Hiroshi later this arvo. If you need someone to translate and I'm not back yet, Bisho's in the kitchen today.'

'Righto,' Gordon said, shaking Cliff's hand. 'Thanks for your help today, mate.'

'Doe e-tashi-mash-tay,' Cliff said, winking. 'No worries at all.'

Gordon stacked bandages in the cupboard, determined to finish the task he had started before Hiroshi and Cliff had arrived. Even the medical unit wasn't what he had imagined. It was a long, simple room with six mismatched beds and only two privacy screens. Andy said their supplies had been pulled from anywhere possible and that they had been promised two more beds a month ago. It seemed like deliveries were patchy, although the cargo hold of the SS *Pachaug* had brought Andy boxes of kit from Sydney. Their main task over the next few days was to make a list of everything and keep a sharp eye on their stock. Apparently, it wasn't unusual for supplies to go missing, regardless of how closely Andy monitored things. Now, though, Andy had found a cabinet with a lock and key that, incredibly, still worked. It had been salvaged from town, probably from a bank. To everyone's disappointment, there was nothing inside. Nestled in the back corner of the room, the furthest point away from the door, it would be filled with gauze, saline, painkillers, medication and anything else Andy could lock in it.

Gordon had finished counting the bandages, stacking them into piles of ten, when a wail ripped through the hallway. It wasn't the cry of a man. A soldier burst into the room carrying a screaming Japanese boy.

'Give him a look over, would you?' The soldier dumped the boy on the bed and left, no interest in sticking around.

'We better find Bisho,' Andy said, heading for the door. Gordon waved at him to stop and slowly approached the bed. The kid looked about ten years old, tears tracking through the dust on his face. He reminded Gordon of his younger brother Robin when he had skinned his knees hunting rabbits.

'G'day, fella,' Gordon said, coming to the edge of the bed. 'I'm Don. Don-san.' He ignored the arch of Andy's eyebrow at the Japanese version of Gordon's name. 'Who are you?'

The boy didn't respond, sobbing harder. Gordon reached out to touch the boy's feet and he scrambled up the bed.

'Seems to be moving okay,' Andy said. 'Don't think he's hurting.'

'Might be hungry.'

'Good shout. I'll see if I can get something from the kitchens. Maybe bring Bisho back.' Andy left the room. The boy settled, eyes on Gordon, who eased himself onto the end of the bed, still keeping his distance, then reached into his pocket and pulled out a coin. It was a penny Gordon didn't have much use for, and he flicked it up and down. The kid watched as Gordon caught it then tossed it up again.

'You want to have a look?' Gordon held out the coin. The kid reached for it and Gordon palmed it into his other hand, making it disappear. The boy's mouth dropped open and he grabbed Gordon's arm, turning it over, looking all over the bed, but there was no sign of the penny.

'Hang on,' Gordon said. 'What's this?' He reached forward and pulled at the air behind the boy's ear, the coin pinched between his fingers. The kid gasped.

'Nani?' he said, then checked his ear to see if there was anything else there. Gordon handed him the penny; the boy seemed stunned by the magic trick, any pain forgotten.

When Andy returned with a bowl of rice, he stopped in the doorway. Gordon was stocking the cupboard and the boy was sitting on a bed, hair spiky and slick from being washed. He leafed through an English comic book, studying each page with intent.

'I leave you for five minutes and you've taught him to read English?' Andy said.

'He likes the pictures,' Gordon replied. 'Found the book in a drawer. Hope you don't mind. But here. Hey, Charlie?'

The kid looked up, eyes bright. 'Hai, Don-san?'

Gordon pointed at Andy. 'Andy-san.'

Charlie waved. 'Andy-san. Konnichiwa!'

Andy, shocked, waved back. He handed the food to Charlie, who pounced on it. Andy joined Gordon by the cabinet. 'Charlie?'

'He wouldn't tell me his Japanese name, so I called him Charlie.'

'Charlie!' the boy called across the room, mouth filled with rice. Andy stifled a laugh and turned back to Gordon.

'Righto. He's Charlie and you're going to be in trouble if you're not careful.'

'Hey, you're the bloke who said everyone who comes in here gets treatment,' Gordon said. 'Just following orders, boss.'

Andy studied him. Gordon squared his shoulders and held the older man's gaze, resolute.

Eventually, Andy shook his head. 'What was wrong with him, then?'

'No idea.' Gordon reached for a pile of bandages. 'As soon as I started talking to him like my younger brother, he calmed down. Doesn't seem to have any injuries as far as I can tell.'

'Funny, isn't it, that when you treat them like people, you find out they're just like us?' Andy moved past Gordon to carry on with his work, just as Charlie collapsed into peals of laughter, the comic book pressed firmly to his chest.

That night, Gordon and Toby hit the town. Toby had spent most of his day investigating what there was to do in the evenings from some of the boys in Explosives. There were rumours of weapons buried in the hills around Kure, the Japanese keeping extra stockpiles outside of military and naval bases, should the country be invaded by the Allies. A unit of men was assigned to work with the Japanese to find all the hidden ammunition in the area, then dump it in the sea. Gordon had no idea how Toby had struck up conversation with Explosives, given he was in a unit clearing debris and roads for the trucks and engineers, but Gordon had stopped marvelling at his friend's ability to find out anything from anyone.

Together, they headed into Kure. They had clearance to go out one night a week but with a curfew, so they wanted to make the most of it. Toby had the entire night planned. All Gordon had to do was follow along.

The ruined streets were mostly empty, many Japanese darting out of their way in the darkening twilight, slipping into shadows and watching them pass. Gordon kept half an eye out for Cherry but he hadn't seen her since that morning. He couldn't figure her out and even though they'd barely had half a conversation, he couldn't help wondering about her. The first day they'd met, she'd been terrified, but the second day she'd been braver and caught him on the hop. It was a good reminder to stay on his toes. It could have been someone else who had come across him in the creek, someone who might not have looked on him so kindly. Or worse, nicked his uniform.

There were lanterns hanging at the bottom of the hill, pinpricks of light that led into the busy market. As they moved closer to the town centre, they passed more people, the Japanese looking at the two Australian soldiers curiously. Toby ignored them as Gordon avoided eye contact.

'Are we allowed in there?' Gordon asked as Toby headed for the market.

'Mate, we're allowed everywhere,' Toby said. 'Besides, I've been told we have to head through here to get to the piece de resistance on the other side.'

'I hope your Japanese is better than your French,' Gordon said, laughing.

'I hope you're ready for the night of your life,' Toby replied.

The market was crammed with people, vendors dodging customers, stalls stretching around pathways, canopies hanging between doors of actual shops. There seemed to be anything and everything for sale here – Japanese clothes, samurai swords, towels, cigarettes, knives, even a bicycle. There were restaurants that were permanent but it wasn't any food Gordon recognised, strange spices and frying onions in the air. One restaurant packed with Japanese sold something called ramen – huge bowls of soup and vegetables. A sign in English declared that it was 'made from strong American wheat!' Why you'd put wheat in any soup was a mystery but they moved past before Gordon could have a closer look.

At one stall was an ornate dagger with a curved hilt, a shining red ruby about the size of a shilling embedded in the handle. Gordon stopped mid-step, astonished. The lantern light flickered on the blade, the carvings around the ruby almost dancing.

'Parker,' Toby called out; a warning. Gordon looked away from the knife. Three older Japanese men, the shopkeepers of the stall, glared at him. One was chewing tobacco, and he drew it through his teeth, the wet noise slurping against the man's lips.

'No time for window shopping,' Toby said, by Gordon's side again. Toby gave the Japanese men a small mock salute and the soldiers left, Gordon resisting the urge to turn back. 'Been told there's a couple of rules. Rule number one. Don't stop anywhere that sells weapons. You'll find it in your gut before you can say g'day,' he said. 'Besides, we've got better places to head to.'

'Where are we actually going?' Gordon asked, head turning as they walked, trying to take everything in. There really was anything you could want here, although there was a distinct lack of fresh food. Toby stepped around a Japanese woman who was slumped on the ground, clothed in dirty rags, head bowed and hands up.

'We're exploring the heights of Kure's extensive entertainment district,' Toby said. Gordon paused near the beggar, wanting to help, but Toby caught his elbow and steered him on. 'You give a little to someone and you'll be mobbed,' he muttered under his breath. 'Rule number two. Show no weakness. If they reckon they can stop you, they'll take everything and the shirt on your back.'

Gordon had every intention of walking through the market without stopping, when a stall selling tins of food with English on the labels caught his eye. He stopped, confused, and picked one up. It was a can of sweetened condensed milk with the BCOF supplies stamp on the label.

'This is from our canteen,' Gordon said, as Toby wheeled back, annoyed his friend had paused again.

'Yeah, the boys said it goes for heaps. Sugar's rationed so anything with a bit of sweetness, the Japanese lose their heads for. You want to get this stuff from the canteen though. There's a 400 per cent mark-updown here.' Toby took the can from Gordon, tossing it up and down. 'You should swipe medical supplies. You'd make a fortune.'

'Andy's got it all under lock and key,' Gordon said. 'Probably because your mates in Explosives were flogging it here.'

Toby smirked and set the can down on the table as an old Japanese woman shuffled out from the shadows. Her grey hair was tied back, her face weathered and tanned. The hem of her dirty dress was frayed from regularly brushing against the ground. She grasped Gordon's hand.

'You buy? You buy?' Her hands were cold against Gordon's skin despite the balmy night.

Toby swore under his breath and then smiled. 'No thanks, just looking.' He put his hand on the woman's wrist but she ignored him, looking to Gordon with a smile. Behind her, a young woman appeared and spoke to her in Japanese. The older woman listened, confused, and the younger steered the older away from the two men.

'Arigato. Arigato,' the older woman said, beaming. Gordon looked at Toby, hoping that he hadn't just lost his entire week's wage for being nice. The younger woman returned, cheeks rosy.

'What is your names?'

'I'm Gordon – Don. And this is Toby.' He gestured to Toby, then paused. His mate was staring at the girl as though she were an apparition, an incredulous smile on his face. The way the girl turned her full attention to Toby made Gordon suspect the girl hadn't missed the Australian's interest either.

'I am Yoneko,' she said. Toby still hadn't spoken. Gordon elbowed him.

'I'm Toby,' he said, collecting himself.

'Hello Toby-san.' Yoneko smiled. 'Would you like some sweet milk?'

Gordon roared with laughter as they left the centre of the market.

'It was a good deal,' Toby said, cheeks pink, brandishing his tin of condensed milk. 'She did me a great price!'

'Never seen anything like it.' Gordon wiped tears from his eyes. 'No wonder they say not to fraternise with the Japanese – that was some magic she did on you just then.'

'I'm no Jap sympathiser,' Toby said, vehement.

Gordon's amusement eased. 'Calm down. I'm not accusing you of that.' The crowd thinned as they left the market. 'Where are we heading now then?'

'After extensive research, I've discovered there are exactly two places to go in Kure. One is this cinema.' Toby pointed to a nondescript concrete building in front of them, one of a small pocket of buildings that were still standing in this section of the city. 'And the other is this hotel.' He gestured to a traditional Japanese hotel, a blue flag with Japanese script hanging over the wooden door. There were lanterns hanging outside but there didn't seem to be much happening inside it.

'What's so special about this hotel?' Gordon asked.

Toby put the condensed milk in his pocket. 'Let's go inside, shall we?'

The hotel was packed with BCOF soldiers. It was rowdy, men laughing and shouting, a haze of cigarette smoke blanketing the air. With most groups of men was a Japanese woman, some serving beer, others sitting on men's laps. The hotel wasn't just a hotel. It was a brothel.

'Now, I sense your hesitation,' Toby said, leaning into Gordon as they were guided to a table by a young woman. 'But trust me – this'll be great fun.'

'Andy said there's heaps of VD out here,' Gordon said. 'I don't want to catch anything.'

'I told you, I've done my research. You think this is the only place like this in town? The girls here are clean. It's basically a BCOF-approved establishment.'

'Really?'

'Figuratively.' Toby winked. 'What do you think of her?' Toby pointed to a woman dressed in a traditional Japanese kimono, serving drinks.

'You take your pick,' Gordon said. 'I'll just have a beer and make sure I'm back for curfew.'

'Tonight's the night you're going to be Perfect Parker?' Toby asked as he waved the girl over. 'This whole experience is going to be wasted on you.'

'Can't believe you've already forgotten about Yoneko,' Gordon said, teasing.

'I haven't. Yoneko is special. But tonight, I'm just looking for a bit of fun.' Toby smiled at the girl and pointed at the beer glasses. 'Two?' he asked, gesturing to Gordon and himself, then handed over some money. The girl nodded and moved away.

It was a strange kind of brothel. One big room that smelt like wood and beer, loud with male laughter and applause, women kneeling in kimonos to deliver drinks. Or perhaps it was exactly like an Australian brothel, if you took away the bamboo matting on the floors and the traditional dress. Gordon had never been to one of those either.

'There are no Japanese men here?' Gordon asked.

Toby waved his hand airily. 'They wouldn't come near the place. Lucky for them. There's only two types of Japanese, after all.' He flashed a smile at a girl who walked past, ignoring him. 'Pretty girls and bastards.'

Gordon let out a snort of laughter. Perhaps he was being prudish. What was the risk if the place was clean? Toby nudged him as a pair of girls wandered by, smiling coyly, and Gordon's stomach lurched. As much as a night here with any girl he could afford might be fun, a Japanese brothel wasn't the place he'd pictured his first time with a woman.

'Final answer?' Toby asked.

Gordon shook his head. 'Not tonight. Perhaps another time.'

Toby rolled his eyes. 'You are definitely going to regret this—' The words faded as the door slid open and in walked Commanding Officer Kerr. His ginger hair stuck out from beneath his hat, his impressive moustache full and sculpted. Silence fell as Kerr took in the room, the soldiers unsure whether to salute or bolt. Gordon was grateful he wasn't closest to the door – he wouldn't be the first to get in trouble and could sneak out without being noticed.

Kerr, however, threw a curt nod to the room and strode to the back, heading through a doorway that was covered by a short curtain with a samurai painted onto it. The tension in the room ebbed and, slowly, the merriment resumed.

Toby clapped Gordon on the shoulder. 'See? The COs have given the place their stamp of approval.' He leaned back as the girl returned with their drinks, his eyes roaming over her. Gordon, amused, shook his head. Toby reached into his pocket and offered her some Australian pounds. She took the money and put her hand into his.

'All you need is a bit of cash if you change your mind, mate,' Toby said.

'I'm fine with beer,' Gordon replied.

His friend laughed. 'Your loss. I bet you won't even last a week before you're entertaining a beautiful Japanese girl.' He let himself be led away and Gordon chuckled. A brothel wasn't his number-one priority for his time in Japan but, given the amount of soldiers here – mostly Australians but also a few New Zealanders, if he heard their accents correctly – it seemed like a popular spot. He sipped at the beer and grimaced. Weak beer and prostitutes. This was definitely not his kind of place.

He was several beers deep by the time Toby re-emerged, pink-cheeked, from the back room. Once the girls had realised Gordon wasn't looking for the usual entertainment, they left him alone. He was drawn into conversations with soldiers around the room as they drank. The beer wasn't as bitter as he was used to but he'd had enough to feel merry.

Toby hummed as they headed back to base.

'What time are we supposed to be back?' Gordon asked, stumbling into Toby as they clambered along a quiet road.

'I thought you knew,' Toby said, shocked. 'Why don't you know? You're the rule follower, Parker. I expect you to know these things.'

Gordon couldn't stop his laughter, the alcohol bubbling through him making everything a joke.

Toby sighed. 'Well, I'm not waiting another minute.' He took off at a run, heading into the darkness.

'We weren't waiting for anything!' Gordon called after him but his mate didn't stop. He continued, aware of how the beer seemed to be entirely in his head, the world a little less straight. He focussed on putting one foot in front of the other. If he took enough steps, he'd end up where he was supposed to be.

Soon enough, in the distance, he saw Toby sitting on the ground, head between his knees, breathing hard.

'You didn't get far,' Gordon said, laughing. 'Come on, we gotta keep moving—'

It wasn't Toby. Billy looked up at him, eyes glassy and red, a split lip bleeding over his chin. The MP officer pressed himself up, staggering as he came to his feet.

'You're gonna miss curfew, Parker,' he said, his words slurring.

'So are you,' Gordon said. Billy let out a harsh laugh, then slumped to the side. Gordon caught him, slinging the other man's arm over his shoulder. The two of them limped along, Gordon distracted by the blood on Billy's neck. 'What happened to your face?'

'I hate these Nips,' Billy said, glaring into the night. 'They're so fucking friendly.' Gordon readjusted his grip. The knuckles on Billy's right hand were grazed and bleeding. 'Trying to make us piss off by pretending they don't hate us. But I see through their mind games, you know. I'm smart. I know what they're trying to do.' He tapped his forehead hard with his left hand, swaying into Gordon, who caught the extra weight. As Gordon righted himself, he noticed something on the side of the road.

A body. A Japanese man sprawled in the dirt, unconscious. The left side of his face was swollen and bloody, shoulder hanging at an odd angle, breathing rasped and slow. Even in the dark, it was clear the man would die in minutes. Billy's fingers twitched over Gordon's shoulder. Gordon straightened up, sober and alert now, unease churning in the pit of his stomach. Billy's right hand. The left side of the Japanese man's face.

Billy didn't seem to notice the body. 'They hated us during the war, didn't they? Rounded us up, chucked us in camps, murdered us. Weren't so friendly then.'

'War's over now, Bill,' Gordon said.

Billy snorted. 'Tell that to Mum. Tell her the war's over and my brother'll come back from the dead after they starved him to death while he slaved away on the Burma Railway.'

Gordon's whole body chilled. The Australian prisoners of war were famous. Those who had survived. He had heard whispers, read articles in the newspaper about men who had been forced to leave their friends' dead bodies in the jungle as the Japanese oversaw the construction of railway lines between Burma and Thailand. The photographs of emaciated men, Army shirts limp against starved bodies, faces gaunt and hollow, were burnt into his memory. For all the Japanese talk of honour and pride, the Japanese had barely treated any of their prisoners of war with respect, nor the people of any of the other countries in the Pacific they'd invaded during their quest to rule the East.

'What about you?' Billy's words stabbed the air. 'You gonna work in Medical and treat any Jap who comes in for help? You dunno who they are or what they've done. Better to just leave them. Let all the bastards die.'

The words bounced off the rubble as they walked away from the slumped figure, Gordon unsure what to do. If he went back to help, Billy would be on him like a shot, and Gordon couldn't fend off an alcohol-fuelled frenzy. It didn't feel like the right thing to leave the man behind to die but there wasn't any other choice.

They walked through the darkened streets. He tried to forget what he'd seen, tried to ignore the gnawing guilt in his stomach. Someone else would come by this way soon. Someone else would find the man. Someone else would save him.

Perhaps if he told himself the lie often enough, he would start to believe it.

CHAPTER SIX

NOBUKO: Kure, April 1946

She had been Brave Nobuko. Her encounter with the Australian soldier sat warmly against her chest as she scrubbed floors, collected laundry and straightened beds. Her courage embraced her in a gentle hug as she sat with Hana and Michiko over lunch, the other two talking about the strange underwear that the Australians had. Hana took great delight in examining every piece of clothing she could when she had a day working in the laundry, amused by the small things she found. One soldier had embroidery inside his shirt cuffs, two symbols Hana couldn't read but she suspected were the mark of a wife or lover.

'Maybe one day, my name will be stitched into a man's shirt,' Hana said dreamily. 'Except I will put my name over his heart so it can beat against it forever.'

'Forever or until he wears a hole in it,' Michiko said, giggling. 'You need to be careful with your daydreams, Hana-chan. You'll get into trouble if you always live in a fantasy world.'

Hana sat up, zeroing in on Nobuko. 'Nobuko-chan, you are too quiet. Where are you?'

Nobuko needed to be careful about what she said or half of Kure would know her story by sunset. 'I am here. Thinking about work. I don't like polishing shoes. It makes my knees hurt.'

'Shoes and laundry are so bad!' Michiko agreed. The three of them were tucked away in the small eating area for the Japanese staff, clutching half-filled bowls. They weren't near the main mess hall; the staff area was isolated from the soldiers. None of the Japanese liked to eat with the ex-enemy men. There had been a few instances of violence and harassment against the Japanese from the soldiers and it was better to keep away. The food was basic but more than the rations – there was always plenty of rice on the base as none of the white soldiers seemed to eat it. The brown soldiers did, groups of men who came from India to serve with the British Forces, but they ate in another building. The ex-enemy soldiers were from Australia and New Zealand and, apart from a few Australian Aboriginal and Māori men, the majority were white.

Hana leaned towards Nobuko, suspicious. 'You weren't on the bus this morning.'

'No, I came in early,' Nobuko replied. 'Michiko told me about a path behind the base with blooming sakura and I wanted to see the trees.'

'Oh, did you go?' Michiko asked. 'They're beautiful by the stream.'

'They are! I haven't seen them so big before.'

'You must be careful if you go swimming. There are eels sometimes.'

'I didn't go swimming,' Nobuko said, unable to hide her smile.

Hana caught it. 'Why are you smiling?'

Nobuko hesitated, torn between wanting to keep her secret and wanting to tell her friends. Their excitement was infectious. 'I saw a soldier by the stream. He was swimming.'

Michiko gasped and Hana laughed.

'I knew it!' Hana said. 'Did you hide in the bushes and watch him?'

'No,' Nobuko said, indignant.

Hana grinned. 'I would've.'

'I said hello.' Nobuko tossed her hair slightly, courage stoking her bravado.

Michiko's mouth fell open. 'In English?'

'No, no.' What had she said in English? It hadn't been much. 'He told me his name. I told him mine. He is Don-san and I am …' Nobuko paused, thinking. 'I am Cherry.'

Hana and Michiko stared at her, both speechless.

Then Hana spoke. 'No. You are Brave Nobuko. Very Brave Nobuko-chan.'

The rest of the day sped by. Nobuko's fingers were pink and dry from polishing so many pairs of boots but her knees didn't hurt as much as usual. Even though she had told Hana and Michiko about Don, it still felt like a secret that was just hers, a moment in time that proved she could be more than what people expected of her. It never felt as though people expected much. She was a young Japanese woman, simply expected to maintain a household, get married and start a family. Even that was difficult, given that most young Japanese men Nobuko knew from her childhood hadn't returned from war, thousands dead on battlefields. To have a little secret that made her feel big was worth every minute polishing dirty pairs of ex-enemy boots.

The sun eased lower in the sky as Nobuko waited for the bus with Hana and Michiko. Nobuko hadn't seen Don since that morning. She wasn't sure if he worked on the base all day or if he was one of the many soldiers who worked in the city, pulling Kure back to its feet, to some kind of new post-war life. The bus was crowded, the girls unable to sit together, and Nobuko stood in the aisle, clutching a seat to steady herself, watching the rubble of the city roll past. As the bus moved through Kure, more passengers got on and she was pushed further away from her friends, so that when her stop came, she waved to them through gaps in heads and elbows before she got off the bus.

Trudging home, Nobuko's mind drifted to the stream, remembering Don standing there, his easy smile and kind eyes.

He had seemed embarrassed he was naked, something Nobuko found strange. Most Japanese didn't have any problem with nudity, especially after the war when many people were half-clothed out of necessity. Onsen baths were a staple of village culture and, while bath houses were segregated by gender, Nobuko didn't blush at the sight of naked people.

'Nobuko-chan!' Amari was running up behind her, breathless. 'I was coming from the city and thought I saw you.'

'Good evening, Amari-chan,' Nobuko said, smiling. Amari was the perfect person to walk home with. 'How are your studies?'

'They're good. English is very difficult though. I am trying my best but it is quite different to Japanese.' Amari twisted the end of her ponytail around her finger. 'Did you ever learn any English?'

'A little.' They crossed the small bridge that led them to the sakura on the other side. 'They stopped teaching us at school during the war.'

'Ah, lots of schools did that.' Amari nodded. 'I'm lucky for my teacher – he snuck me exercises to practise with even though it was forbidden.'

'Will you teach me?' Nobuko asked. The younger girl blinked, surprised. 'Only a little. It might be useful to speak a bit of English with the soldiers.'

Amari frowned and Nobuko wondered if she'd been too forward. She hadn't meant to ask her friend anything but Brave Nobuko had burst out. She wanted to speak with Don again. She wanted another secret to keep.

'We will have to be careful,' Amari said finally. 'Your father won't be happy if he catches me teaching you English. Aunty Suma told me I need to speak less about my studies as it angers him too much. If you want me to teach you, we'll have to make sure he won't find out.'

Nobuko nodded, heart thumping. 'We can keep it from him. Only simple English. Easy.'

Amari glanced at the empty road ahead of them. 'Maybe I can teach you some now, before we get home.'

'Now?' Nobuko asked, faltering.

'You're working tomorrow, aren't you? Why not start now? I'm sure you'll remember things as I teach you. It will be revision, not learning new words. And if I start now, your father will never know.'

Nobuko hesitated. She hadn't considered what her father might do if he found out she was learning how to speak to the ex-enemy soldiers. Of course he would be angry. Of course she would be punished. Did she really need to learn how to speak English to ask soldiers for their laundry? Did she need to know their names?

'Konnichiwa in English is hello,' Amari said, her voice soft. 'You would remember this. Hello. You can use this anytime of the day, it doesn't matter. It can be casual but this is how to greet people in English. Hello.'

Hello did seem familiar. It tugged at Nobuko's memory.

'Hello,' she repeated, the l's hard against the roof of her mouth.

Amari smiled. 'You're good!'

Nobuko waved her embarrassment away. 'No.'

Amari laughed. 'You're so Japanese. Okay. So konnichiwa is hello. Sayonara is—'

'Goodo-byo,' Nobuko said.

'Yes. Goodbye. Now, o-genki desu ka is how are you?'

'How are you?'

'Again.'

'How are you?'

'Good.'

The English lesson continued as they walked up the road, the conversation fading as their houses loomed ahead. Nobuko's heart thundered as though she'd stolen something from the market, not learnt English words on her way home from work.

'Tomorrow I will wait at the bottom of the hill,' Amari promised. 'We may not be able to do this every night but perhaps we can go somewhere together and spend longer studying, away from …' Amari trailed off as she glanced towards Nobuko's house.

Nobuko nodded. 'Thank you, Amari-chan.' She squeezed Amari's hand. 'I should go.' She checked the coast was clear and leaned in to her friend. 'Thank you,' she whispered in English.

Amari beamed. 'You're welcome,' she answered quietly, also in English. They shared a small conspiratorial smile, then parted, Amari heading to Suma's house and Nobuko heading to Uncle Kazuo's.

As she fell asleep that night, Nobuko practised English in her mind. Her dreams were patchy and fluid, shifting from one place to another. None of them made sense, full of unfamiliar places and strangers. Until the one that was all too familiar.

Darkness. Flashes of amber and orange. Dust and stale air. She couldn't breathe. She couldn't move. Her fingers desperately scratching upwards, trying to free herself, trying to escape.

Nobuko woke. It was before sunrise. She crawled onto her knees, reached out her hands and pressed them to the tatami beneath her, her body bowed forward, her breath shaky. She tried to ground herself, to push herself harder into the floor, wanting to feel anchored, present, whole. Slowly, her breath came back to her. The tension in her body eased. She sat up and looked into the darkness, the faintest tinge of morning light sneaking in through the windows.

She stood up and got ready to head to base.

As she walked to the bus stop, she practised English under her breath. Walking the way she had come last night made things stronger in her mind – a certain word, a pronunciation she'd stumbled on. The more she tried to remember, the more other words came to the fore. She remembered numbers in English, her mind stumbling over one to ten, fighting to remember the English way to say 'four' and 'five', the f sound very different to her Japanese. At the bus stop she got stuck on the number that should follow eight, and for most of the ride she racked her brain trying to remember it, counting repeatedly from one to eight, trying to prise it from her memory. It wasn't until she arrived at base, opting to enter through the main gate, that it came free.

Nine.

Eight. Nine. Ten.

Nobuko picked up her bucket and brush, on dormitory cleaning duties. She gripped the handle as she crossed the base, heading to the rows of small buildings that housed the Australians. She remembered vividly which building Don was sleeping in and, suddenly nervous, veered away from it, opting to start somewhere else, to work up her courage to speak to him. Nobuko could become invisible or small in front of any other foreigner, but she had a feeling that if Don was to see her, he would try to talk to her again. She wasn't ready for that.

Or so she thought. Every scrub of her brush on the floor made her wonder if she should have gone to Don's room first, to see if he was there. To have an English conversation, to impress him a little. She pressed harder with the brush, bristles splaying to the sides, the rhythmic scrubbing becoming annoying, almost teasing her. *Not brave*, the brush seemed to chide her. *Not brave. Not brave. Not brave.*

She finished the room. Cleaning the floor, straightening the beds, even clearing the dust off the small windowsill; refusing to rush. There was a chance Don would not even be in his room now. For weeks, the timing of the cleaning rounds had been a blessing, a way to avoid any foreigners easily. Now, though, there was no reason that he would be anywhere near his room at this time of the day. She could be getting herself worked up over nothing.

She headed to Don's building next.

What would she do if she saw him? Would she even speak English with him? In reality, she could hardly say much – a few pleasantries were not a fluent conversation. Maybe he would laugh at her. Perhaps it was better if she said nothing at all. She could wait to speak with him. With more time, she would learn more from Amari and have a better conversation. Today it would be better if she said nothing.

Yet in her mind, a small voice spoke in English.

Hello. How are you? I am well. Thank you. Goodbye.

Hello. How are you? I am well. Thank you. Goodbye.

Hello. How are you? I am—

A dormitory door burst open and a jostle of soldiers spilled out. Nobuko stopped. They whistled and Don leapt outside, jogging to catch them. She hadn't expected a group.

The men headed away from Nobuko without noticing her. Don laughed at something, a shorter man pushing him away as they walked towards the gates. She had missed him.

Relief and disappointment thrummed through her as she headed to his dormitory, slipping her shoes off at the door and stepping inside with her socks on.

The room was empty. She took a breath as she collected her thoughts. It was better this way. She would have made a fool of herself if she'd tried to speak to him. Perhaps he wouldn't have remembered who she was. She was getting caught in a daydream that didn't even exist.

Sighing, Nobuko took her bucket to the back of the room to start scrubbing. It was near Don's bed, sure, but it was also easier to clean the floor from the back wall to the door. A small thrill ran through her as she noticed he had pinned up photographs by his bed. She left her bucket and padded over, curious.

Several faces grinned at her. There was one photograph with a mountain of people, two adults and a pile of children. Off to the left was Don, holding another boy upside down. They were both laughing, the younger boy blurred with movement. The older woman appeared to be exasperated, but the others were looking at the camera, unaware of the action happening on the side of the frame. They looked like Don's family but there were so many of them – maybe they were cousins and friends too.

A sneeze.

Nobuko, startled, stepped away from Don's bed. Perhaps it had come from outside; perhaps someone had been looking in the door. Either way, she needed to get back to work. Hurriedly, she fished the wet brush out of her bucket, shook off the excess, then pressed it to the cold floor near Don's bed.

Underneath it was a boy, wrapped in a blanket.

Nobuko squealed. Scrambling away, she leapt to her feet, then dived forward and pulled him out.

'What are you doing?' Nobuko snapped.

'Sleeping,' the boy replied.

'You can't sleep here! You must go home, you can't stay.'

The boy stepped away from her, grimacing. 'No.'

Nobuko shook her head, panicked. 'It is dangerous – they will punish you if they find you. Where do you live?'

'Here.' The boy crossed his arms, petulant. 'Don-san said I could sleep here!'

Nobuko stopped. 'Don-san knows you are here?'

'Yes. He gave me a lucky coin.'

She stared at the boy, who seemed to be waiting for a reprimand but was simultaneously defiant. One hand was thrust in his pocket, fist tight, the other hand clutched his blanket.

She softened. 'What's your name?'

'Hamada Mitsuhiro,' the boy replied. 'Everyone here calls me Charlie.'

She hesitated. 'I'm Nobuko. It's nice to meet you, Charlie,' she said, bowing.

He bowed lower, pressing his grubby hands together. 'Will you make me leave?' His voice was vulnerable, bravado gone. His dirty grey shirt was two sizes too big, his trousers had a hole in the knee. He looked at her with desperate eyes.

'If Don-san knows you're here, I won't make you go,' Nobuko said, gentle. 'But you must be careful. I don't clean here every day – if someone else finds you, you could be in trouble.'

Charlie nodded quickly. 'I will. Do you know Don-san, Nobuko-san?'

She paused. 'A little,' she said. 'Maybe one day we will be friends.'

'Can we be friends?' he asked.

His earnestness shifted something inside her. 'Yes. We can be friends.'

Charlie beamed and picked up her bucket. 'If anyone asks what I'm doing, I'll say I'm helping a friend clean the base.'

Nobuko laughed and dipped her brush in the bucket. 'We should make sure we clean then. Come on.'

No ex-enemy soldiers noticed Nobuko's new helper and none of the Japanese said anything about the appearance of Charlie. New faces appeared every day, old ones disappeared without a word. It was simply the way of this new world.

CHAPTER SEVEN

GORDON: Kure, August 1946

The late May weather merged into a humid June and July. In August, the Japanese sun was relentless, the open areas of the city providing little shade with few buildings still standing over head height. Gordon and Andy treated more and more cases of sunstroke as summer arrived in Kure.

While the soldiers couldn't hide their symptoms of exposure to the heat, they were much more embarrassed about their symptoms of venereal disease. Gordon spent the days with his hands in cold water, swapping out wet cloths to cool the dehydrated men while they slept, then the evenings dodging soldiers who wanted to be slipped medication and not go through official channels. The first few times, Gordon had tried to be discreet, signing out penicillin and handing it to his patient with a nod. Word soon got around and for weeks he could barely move without being approached by someone wanting treatment from him, to avoid coming to Medical. Eventually, he told people to come in the afternoons to collect, refusing to deal with anyone outside of the unit walls. Andy was amused but not surprised.

'Half the bloody Army's got it, at this rate,' he said. 'It's the worst-kept secret on base – everyone knows it. Who cares if someone sees you ducking into Medical?'

Some boys never seemed to learn, Gordon wryly noting repeat visitors who appeared every Monday or Tuesday after a weekend in town. Toby wasn't a regular but had been one of Gordon's first patients, ashamed that his information about the brothel being clean was incorrect. Instead, Toby had turned his focus to Yoneko, often coming back from the market with a new trinket or purchase, both pleased by her attention and frustrated he wasn't wooing her faster.

It seemed impossible that Japan had now been Gordon's home for three months. He'd fallen into an easy routine, a contained life on base. Even though he'd come wanting to fight, he was glad that he spent his days inside. The injuries that came in from those who were working in the city were intense – missing legs, arms slashed open, broken limbs – which was to say nothing about the men who died immediately from their injuries and never made it to the base at all.

Charlie had become Gordon's shadow, helping in the medical unit and fetching supplies to allow the Australians to focus solely on their patients. When the heatstroke cases rose, Charlie disappeared for two days, and Gordon worried he might have got himself into trouble. Instead, the boy returned with natural ice to keep their cloths and flannels cold. Gordon had no idea how Charlie had found it. Over the past few months, small things they needed had started to appear in the unit. Gordon and Andy started calling Charlie the most resourceful kid in Kure.

Gordon had asked his mum to send over some picture books and toys to give away to the kids in Japan. Venn had overdelivered, Gordon not surprised at the size of the box she'd sent over. Inside were books, knitted toys, clothes, magazines; anything she could rustle up from the locals and probably the house at Greenwood Avenue. He recognised a pair of gloves that had been his in the pile. Laughable to think about gloves when the weather was so hot. Charlie got first pick, the boy unable to believe the treasure inside. Gordon had expected him to go for the tennis balls, maybe even the Aussie Rules football – he was already thinking about teaching Charlie how to kick it. To his surprise, Charlie had picked out a book, *Blinky Bill*, about a koala in the Australian bush. He had sat down to flick through it and pored over it every day since.

Today, Charlie sat on the floor reading, fingers running underneath the English, mouthing out the words as he read the letters to himself. Usually, he sat on a bed, but today Medical was half filled with feverish soldiers, and other beds had been stripped to be made up again, so there was only one clean bed for patients. Gordon pulled out fresh sheets to make up the empty beds, the starchy material coarse against his fingers. He never saw who washed them; they just appeared in the cupboard every morning, the housegirls almost invisible. Gordon tried to imagine June or any of his sisters living in Japan, working as a housegirl in the barracks. He chuckled to himself – it was an impossible image. June would tower over the small Japanese girls, and if a soldier gave her his boots to polish, she would probably throw them straight back.

Quick footsteps outside made Gordon turn. A soldier he didn't know, a towering, mousy-haired man, shoved a Japanese girl through the door. She was crying, holding her left arm across her chest, shoulder popped out of place.

Gordon was immediately at her side. 'What happened?'

'Dunno. Found her like this.'

Gordon studied the man, who didn't flinch. Gordon turned to the girl but she backed away, clearly in intense pain.

'Mate, what'd you do to her?' But the soldier was gone. Gordon's mind whirled. Andy had left to get supplies from the Officers Quarters, and if he left to find a translator, the girl would probably make a run for it. Charlie watched from across the room, concerned.

'Charlie, mate, you know Cliff? Cliff-san?' Gordon asked. The boy nodded, abandoning his book as he leapt to his feet. 'Bring him here. Find Cliff-san and bring him here. For help.' He gesticulated as he spoke but wasn't sure if Charlie knew what he was talking about. The boy, though, dashed out of the room without a second's pause.

Gordon grabbed the screen to block off the clean bed in the back of the room. The girl sat on the floor, breathing hard. Satisfied the other soldiers couldn't see her, he turned to the girl and patted the bed, trying to tell her to sit on it.

The girl burst into tears. Alarmed, he moved towards her but an anguished wail ripped from her lips and he retreated.

'Don-san,' he said, pointing to himself. 'Namay Don-san.' He snatched up some bandages and showed them to her. 'I help. I help you.'

The girl didn't move, hiccoughing through her tears. Gordon tried to remember any Japanese he'd picked up but nothing more than the basics came to mind. Telling her goodbye was the last thing he wanted to do.

Relief coursed through Gordon as the door swung open and Charlie ran in.

'Help, Don-san,' Charlie said.

'Thanks, mate.' Gordon turned around. 'Cliff, I'm—'

Cherry stood in the doorway. 'Okay, Don-san?'

There was no time to find anyone else. Cherry could get the girl onside better than Cliff, given that Gordon had a few ideas how she'd ended up with a dislocated shoulder, all of them to do with the ill intentions of an Australian soldier and none of them the girl's fault.

'Arry-gato, Cherry. Okay. Where pain?' He gestured at the girl then pointed on himself. 'Shoulder? Arm? Leg?'

Cherry knelt down by the girl, speaking to her in rapid Japanese. The girl pointed at the bed, then threw furtive glances over Cherry's shoulder to Gordon. He kept his distance. Cherry turned to Gordon.

'Ami-chan, beddo?' she asked.

'She's Ami-chan?' Gordon said, then nodded. 'Yeah, on the bed. Beddo. Easier. Easy to fix.'

Cherry spoke to Ami, who took another look at Gordon, then stood. Leaning on Cherry, Ami moved slowly to the bed and slid onto it, breathing hard. The two girls spoke again, then Cherry came to Gordon.

'Pain,' Cherry said in English, reaching up to touch Gordon. She laid her warm palms against his shirt and gently touched the front and the back of his left shoulder. 'Also here.' She moved her hands down to Gordon's wrist, wrapping her fingers around it. 'He pull,' she whispered. Gordon cleared his throat, fighting rising anger. He needed a level head to focus on Ami.

'Thanks, Cherry. It okay for me to look?' Gordon gestured, moving towards Ami, who caught the movement. Tremulously, she nodded, and he approached her with raised hands, asking for permission to touch.

'Okay?' he asked.

'Okay,' Ami said, voice thick with tears.

Gordon touched her shoulder as gently as he could, but she still tensed under his hands. It was dislocated but not so badly that he couldn't slip it back in. He'd dealt with this kind of thing before – he'd dislocated his fingers playing footy, and Donald had fallen out of a tree and popped out his shoulder a few years earlier. It felt different when it wasn't family, and even more different on a girl.

'I need to move your arm,' he said, pulling his own arm back to demonstrate. 'Then slip it back into place.' Again, Gordon mimicked putting the shoulder back in, then shook out his body and smiled wide, overplaying it. 'Then you'll be okay.'

The girls nodded. He had no idea if they'd understood his English but his gestures seemed to work. Gordon took Ami's hand, careful not to move it unnecessarily, avoiding the finger marks around her wrist. He put his other hand on the back of her shoulder to give himself something to push against. Cherry stood close to Ami, the injured girl trying to compose herself.

'Okay.' Gordon swallowed, bracing himself and trying not to think about what might happen if he made things worse. He breathed in deeply and the two girls copied him. It helped take him out of his own head, a swift smile darting across his face.

'Ichi. Ni. San.' Gordon counted to three and then lifted Ami's arm up, ignoring her squeal of pain. The shoulder socket slipped back and Gordon left his hand on it as Ami's pain eased, her breath coming in short bursts but with no screaming. His breath was fast too but the adrenaline was waning, relief moving through him instead.

'Now, pain is okay?' Gordon asked. Cherry turned to Ami, who took a shaky breath.

'Okay,' Ami said.

Gordon beamed. 'Righto, excellent. You stay here.' He gestured they should stay before stepping out from behind the screen. Charlie was there waiting, a raft of medical supplies laid on the unmade bed next to him.

'Arry-gato, mate,' he said as he picked up a sling. 'You did good.'

He paused before he headed back behind the screen, hearing quiet Japanese. He leaned around the side and watched as Cherry squeezed Ami's hand, rubbing the girl's back as she spoke, soothing her. There was something gentle in this moment, Gordon enthralled by Cherry's care and grace.

Realising he was staring, Gordon moved forward. He held up the sling and demonstrated putting his arm in it. Ami nodded and he folded the material and put it around her arm. She looked at Cherry, who hesitated. Gordon kept working, pretending he hadn't seen. Despite Ami clearly wanting Cherry to communicate something, Cherry didn't speak until he was done.

'Don-san, thank you very much,' Cherry said in English, her voice faltering over the words. 'Ami-chan happy you help.' Her cheeks were pink and she refused to look at him.

Gordon chuckled. 'If Ami-chan ever needs more help, come to me,' he said. 'And, jeez, your English is very good, Cherry. You had me fooled.'

'No,' she said, shaking her head. 'No good yet.'

'Well, if you ever want someone to practise with, come by anytime.'

Her blush deepened. There was something about her humble embarrassment that was entirely endearing.

Ami giggled, which made him laugh.

'If you're giggling now, Ami-chan, you must be feeling better. Here.' He darted out to grab a cool cloth soaked in ice water and wrapped it around her wrist. 'You go home,' he said. 'You sleep.' He put his hands under his head like a pillow, closed his eyes and let out a soft snore, making the two girls laugh. 'You be okay soon.'

Ami eased herself off the bed, cupping her left arm and sling in her right. 'Arigato, Don-san.'

'No worries,' Gordon replied, at her side to help her if she needed it. He winked at Cherry, who hovered close by. 'Arry-gato, Cherry.'

'No wor-rees,' Cherry said, causing the girls to collapse into laughter. Gordon grinned. If he could make Cherry smile that much, he didn't mind being the butt of the joke.

A few weeks later, Gordon was writing letters home. Jennifer's and Jim's birthdays were coming up and Gordon knew he'd never hear the end of it if he didn't send something back for them. He'd bought some origami paper and paper dolls as gifts, knowing they'd be interesting for everyone back home and easy to post. Gordon was finishing up when Toby appeared in the dorm, breathing as though he'd been running but affecting a casual stance.

'What are you up to today, Parker?' Toby asked.

'I get the sense you're about to tell me,' Gordon replied, arching an eyebrow.

'Don't suppose you'd be interested in a road trip out of town?' Toby crossed his arms, leaning against the doorframe.

'I suspect I might be.' It would be foolish to question Toby's plan.

'Good man.' Toby clapped his hands. 'We leave in ten.'

'Any clues where we're headed?' Gordon asked, putting his letters under his pillow.

Toby smirked. 'You're gonna love it. It's gonna blow your mind.'

Gordon and Toby weren't the only ones on the road trip. A handful of blokes had come along for the ride, including Slim Mackie, a bloke you should never play in a game of poker (something Gordon had found out the hard way); and Henry Evans, captain of the unofficial BCOF Australian Rules football team. Driving the Jeep was a bearded redhead, Patrick McNeary, who had barely said two words since they'd piled into the truck.

They rolled out of the city, the rubbled streets giving way to green countryside. Every so often, children would spot the truck and run after it, laughing and waving at the soldiers as they chased them. Gordon threw out sticks of gum, the kids cheering as they pounced on the loot, shrinking into the distance as the truck drove away.

'Don't make too much noise about this, hey fellas?' Toby said. 'Paddy'll get in trouble if the COs find out he's smuggling us through.'

Gordon frowned at Toby. Surely he didn't mean they were heading to the one place every bloke wanted to explore. It wasn't forbidden but it wasn't smiled upon either. A rush of excitement ran through Gordon as Toby nodded, smug.

They were heading to the city that ended the war.

Hiroshima.

If you asked directly, no-one had visited the city, only ever stopping by the BCOF outpost, which wasn't near the epicentre of the blast. If you asked indirectly, it seemed nearly every soldier who had been in Japan for longer than a few weeks had made the trek out. Some came back with small souvenirs – fused glass or melted metal. Others refused to talk about it and changed the subject. Gordon knew he'd visit eventually, but he wasn't among the more macabre blokes in the barracks who got out there as soon as they could. Still, most of them agreed: without the bomb being dropped, Japan never would've surrendered. Standing in Hiroshima would be standing in the middle of history.

'Some blokes came down to the Atomic City last week,' Slim said. 'They reckon it's pretty much back to normal now.'

'Is that why you thought you'd pop along?' Toby asked, voice dry. 'To check out normal Hiroshima?'

Slim bit back a laugh and shrugged.

The truck slowed and Patrick pulled up the handbrake. 'Righto, boys,' he said, stepping out of the driver's side door.

'Let's check out the might of the American Air Force, hey?' Toby said, excited. He stepped off the truck, the rest of the blokes close behind.

Gordon walked around the side to properly view the city.

There was no city.

There was just … nothing. Piles of dirt, huge structural beams jutting out of the rubble, the occasional power pole marking where the side of the road was. Broken foundations that sat two inches above the ground traced where buildings and houses had once been, roof palings and sheeting slammed into the dirt beneath. The openness of the destruction felt wrong. It was different to the bombing at Kure, where patches of the city were still untouched. The carnage at Hiroshima was complete. Even a year later, the city was still devastated. Blackened trees poked up on the horizon, stripped of their leaves and growth, looking more like oversized twigs than the lush, abundant green in pockets of Kure. The air was sharp, the faint scent of an extinguished fire mixed with something almost metallic, washed out by the dense, stagnant smell of the river. The quiet was eerie. A soft whistle of wind as it moved through the destroyed city but no rustle of branches. No voices or traffic. A creak of a stack of rubble, shifting in the breeze. The sound of their footsteps on the dusty ground.

No-one spoke as they fanned out, away from one another, faces grim. Gordon's boots crunched as he stepped through the debris, testing each step he took to make sure it would take his weight. Glass shards tinkled to the ground as he walked, falling from broken window frames. In the distance were the mountains that surrounded the city, nestling Hiroshima in its seaside valley. There was a horizon that didn't make sense, uneven and lumpy; no buildings, just rubble. On the ground was a curled black-and-white photograph, half buried beneath a car tyre. A young mother and father, dressed in their best kimonos, the mother clutching a pudgy baby who stared at the camera, mouth slightly open. The sides of the photograph were singed but the faces were still visible. Clearing his throat, Gordon moved on. He stepped around shards of ceramic, crumbling rocks of concrete, and greyed, burnt sticks that looked suspiciously like human bone.

Discomfort growing, the idea of walking through a mass graveyard heavy on his mind, Gordon looked back to the truck. Patrick was leaning against the grille, smoking as he watched them. Slim was there with him, lighting his own cigarette. Henry was fossicking through the ruins and Toby had his back to Gordon, looking at the town hall that had been half blasted apart, the skeleton of a dome still visible on the top. It was one of the only moderately intact buildings for miles, the only others crumbling brick and concrete structures that protruded from the ground like collapsed sandcastles. Not wanting to stick around, Gordon worked his way back towards the truck, hoping the sudden sweat on his neck wasn't obvious.

His pace quickened as he moved over familiar ground, not nearly as careful as he had been before. He stepped onto a section of a wooden fence or wall and his right foot went straight through the palings, leg sinking into the rubble below. Panic caught in his throat. His knee was hidden, swallowed by the Hiroshima ruins, the splintered wood like sharpened teeth. Slim and Patrick shouted and rushed to him; Gordon focussed on not falling further. He put his hands on anything he could touch that wouldn't slide away or break beneath his fingers. There wasn't much strong enough to hold his weight – anything he pushed against crumbled into the darkness below.

'Must be a basement,' Patrick said as he and Slim arrived, both scanning the rubble for the safest way to get to Gordon.

'I came around that way,' Gordon said, pointing to his right. 'Guess I swung too far left on my way back out.'

Slim was on the ruins, carefully making his way over, Patrick close behind. 'Is your foot on anything or are you hanging?'

Gordon felt below him. The toes of his boot could touch something, perhaps a flooring beam, but his heel wasn't braced against anything. 'I don't reckon there's much but empty space under there,' he said. He tried not to dwell on the idea of anyone dead in the space below or the fact he may soon join them. His left leg was pinned under him, knee at an awkward angle.

'You right?' Patrick asked as Slim inched around to Gordon's other side.

'Yeah, mate, I'm just stuck in a pile of rubbish at a bomb site. I'm having a ripper day.'

'Ah, you wouldn't joke around if you were in serious strife,' Patrick said, winking at Slim. 'You'll be right, Parker.'

Gordon wriggled his toes. He could still move them, so there was no serious damage to his legs. More than anything, he was embarrassed he'd been the one to get into trouble while they were out here.

Slim shuffled close enough to grab Gordon's shoulder. Patrick eased towards Gordon, something cracking, causing him to adjust his approach. Beneath them, the ground groaned, like a weary tree heralding its intention moments before it snaps. They exchanged a look but said nothing.

'You got him?' Slim asked as Patrick manoeuvred himself into place, grabbing Gordon's other shoulder.

'Don't step on the wood,' Gordon said as Slim and Patrick braced themselves to lift him.

'Nah, you already tested it for us,' Slim said. 'Cheers for that.'

The levity ebbed as Toby skidded to a halt on the nearest patch of road. 'Need help?'

'I reckon we're already stretching the friendship with three of us up here,' Patrick said. 'Seen this stuff collapse with less blokes on top of it.'

Gordon ignored his thudding heart as a creaking groan rang out once again.

'Your other leg all right, Parker?' Slim said. 'You reckon you'll be able to put weight on it when we get you out?'

'I reckon you should just get me out and we'll worry about the rest of it later,' Gordon snapped.

'Righto,' Slim said, taking a breath. 'There's a chunk of concrete behind us. That's the safe spot – it's not going anywhere. We get you out, we go back, we stand on that. On the count of three, Paddy …'

Gordon braced his toe against whatever was underneath him, trying to get any leverage he could. Slim and Patrick gripped his shoulders, one of their arms under his armpit, the other holding the top of his shoulders.

'One. Two. Three.' They pulled. Gordon pushed his foot into the debris and the three of them lifted him up.

'Jeez, you weigh a bloody ton,' Slim said, straining.

Once his knee was out of the wood, there was enough of a gap for Gordon to pull himself out, the three of them scrambling backwards to safety. The concrete seemed to be a wall of a building that had stood there once. Slim's assessment of it was right. It barely shifted under the weight of them.

'You right, Don?' Patrick asked as Gordon examined his leg. Much to his relief, other than a tear in his trouser leg, there were no cuts or open wounds.

'Dramatic,' Slim said idly, all tension gone.

Gordon laughed, unable to believe it. 'Cheers, fellas,' he said, clapping them both on the back. 'Thought I was done for—'

A loud creak filled the air and there was a crack that whipped across their faces. The pile of rubble they had just stumbled away from was swallowed whole, like the land had opened its mouth and sucked in anything on top of it. Dust and dirt flew into the air, the three of them instinctively turning away to protect their faces, but the fine powder covered everything. Coughing, Gordon steadied as he stared at the place they'd all just been standing. All three of them could've been smothered under the ruins of Hiroshima.

'Let's go,' Gordon suggested. No-one needed any more convincing. They joined Toby and walked in single file back to the truck, Patrick leading. Henry was still coming over to meet them, the furthest away in his exploration of the debris. Gordon's foot caught something as they walked.

It was the wheel to a tricycle. The rest of the tricycle was trapped beneath stone, the nut and bolt loosened enough to free the wheel. It looked exactly like the wheel on the tricycle his brothers and sisters had ridden at home, the wheel Gordon had fixed just before he'd left so Jim could ride it.

Gordon swallowed, unable to tear his gaze from it, then kicked it out of his path and followed the others to the Jeep.

The truck rumbled as they headed off. Everyone was silent. Gordon stared blankly at the carnage rolling past them. His heart leapt as he spotted a group of school kids sitting among the rubble, a teacher holding up a page of Japanese lettering, still trying to teach the children.

'Why Hiroshima?' Gordon asked. 'Kure had a naval base. Tokyo, Osaka – sure, that makes sense. But here? There wasn't any Army presence. They were just people.'

'Japanese people,' Henry said. 'They were trying to kill us too. You remember that?'

'So we kill them all first?' Gordon frowned, trying to make sense of it.

'Who's to say the war wouldn't have ended if the Yanks hadn't done it?' Slim asked.

Gordon nodded mutely. Part of him agreed with Slim, but seeing the devastation that Hiroshima and Kure had suffered threw the whole thing into a different light. It was real. It had happened. The evidence of that was all around them.

'What'd you find?' he asked Henry, wanting to change the subject.

Henry sorted through his treasures. 'Some melted glass ... think this was a belt buckle or something.' He lay them on his knee, green and gold glass fused together in a strange pseudo-Venn diagram of colours, a faint imprint still visible on the glass. The belt buckle was a brown-black, round once but now warped and misshapen.

Gordon's stomach churned. He wished he hadn't come, wished Toby had told him where they were going in the first place. It felt perverse to be here, digging among the ruins, picking out a memento to brag about.

The truck stopped. They were still in the city, amid the destruction. Patrick got out of the truck and came around the back.

'West, there's a box under your seat there – hand it over, would you?' Toby felt around under his seat and pulled it out. It was filled with tins of food, supplies and a blanket down the bottom. Toby passed it to Slim, who handed it to Patrick. He walked away from the truck. Curious, Gordon got out to follow him, the rest of the blokes not far behind.

They were in the middle of town, the only sound the gentle hum of the river. There were no buildings, no people. Patrick didn't break stride, heading over to a taller pile of wood and bricks off the side of the road, clearly familiar with where he was going. He let out a low whistle.

From behind the heap of rubble, people stepped out. All young, around Gordon's age or younger. They moved together, some with misshapen limbs, many with burn scars on their arms, one girl leaning on a stick, her left leg missing. Survivors. A kid around four years old ran to Patrick, who handed him an apple from the box.

'Pikadon. Pikadon. Pikadon,' the boy said, running away from the soldiers, clutching his apple like a jewel.

'That's what they call the bomb,' Patrick said. 'Pikadon.'

A girl around sixteen stepped towards them, timid. Her clothes hung off her shoulders, ragged and torn, revealing angry scarring over her shoulder. It was a strange pattern, criss-crossed but curved and raised, tucking under her arm.

Patrick caught Gordon staring. 'Apparently she was wearing a striped kimono that morning.' He set the box on the ground and threw an icy look at Henry. 'But who gives a shit. They're just Japanese people, right?'

Henry sniffed, uninterested in Patrick's lecture. He drifted away, kicking aside stones and wood while he waited for them to finish.

Gordon reached into the box and pulled out the blanket, offering it to the girl with the scars. She took it and bowed her head in thanks. He mimicked the movement without realising and she smiled and bowed again. Toby and Slim hung back, neither sure what to do.

'Oi,' Gordon said. 'Want to give us a hand?'

It didn't take long to distribute the small stash of supplies Patrick had brought. Those living in the rubble clearly knew him, an established system between them. He had specific things for some people – tinned peaches for a boy whose right eye slumped downwards, the right corner of his mouth pointing to the ground. He yelped with delight when he saw them, snatching the tin. Patrick told Gordon, Toby and Slim he'd found the survivors by accident, spotting movement among the debris as he drove to the Hiro camp. Every time he made the trip from Kure, he'd bring a box of something. They were outcasts, other Japanese preferring not to look at them. Patrick wanted to help, even a little.

As they headed back to the truck, a boy ran up to Toby and touched his hand. The boy's own hand had no fingers, but as Toby turned to look at him, the boy beamed and waved. Toby stared at him, wordless and unmoving. Patrick cleared his throat and waved at the boy, prompting Toby to do the same, Gordon and Slim joining in. It didn't escape Gordon's notice that Toby rubbed at the hand the boy had touched once they were in the truck, wiping his hand on his trousers surreptitiously.

Gordon turned to Henry as they climbed in. 'Where'd you go then?' he asked.

'Figured I'd see what else I could find,' Henry said. 'And, I reckon this is the cherry on top.' He held up a small handleless cup, blue ceramic with a chip in the lip. It seemed bizarre that among all the damage a fragile piece of clay had somehow survived. 'Might send it home to Mum. She can chuck it up on the mantelpiece – be a good talking point when the Country Women's Association come around, don't you reckon?'

Something in Gordon snapped. He seized the cup from Henry, drew his arm back and threw it out of the truck. It hit the road and shattered into pieces. Henry lunged forward and Slim caught him, stopping him from pouncing on Gordon.

'You're asking for trouble, Parker—'

Gordon sat tall, filling the back of the cabin. 'Try me.'

Henry hesitated, then sat back. 'Gone all soft, mate,' he said, thin-lipped. 'Bet you celebrated the end of the war just as much as I did. Don't get narky just because you've seen what war actually is now. We wouldn't have won if it hadn't been for all this beautiful destruction. You wouldn't spit on Truman or Churchill or Chifley if they came to say g'day. Don't act like that out there isn't what we've all wanted for years.'

Toby laid a warning hand on Gordon's shoulder. Gordon shook it off but said nothing, looking out of the truck away from Henry. Of course the end of the war was what they'd wanted. He'd gone to the enlistment office on his birthday to play his part. But the destruction of Hiroshima felt wrong. It wasn't a few bullets embedded into walls as soldiers fought valiantly in the street. It was an annihilation. Indiscriminate mass murder. Gordon cleared his throat as he tried to shake the thought from his mind. The war needed to end, absolutely. But with Germany and the Italians toppled by the Allies, who was to say that Japan wouldn't have fallen soon enough without the American bombers? Without Hiroshima and Nagasaki?

They turned away from the city, heading back towards Kure and civilisation. The last thing Gordon saw before they drove out of the impact zone was a white flower, sneaking between bricks and debris, searching for the sun.

CHAPTER EIGHT

NOBUKO: Kure, September 1946

Nobuko hadn't been to a festival since before the war. Obon, Hinamatsuri – they'd all stopped during the war years. There had been a small Tanabata festival in Kure a few months earlier, a shadow of its previous celebrations, but Nobuko had stayed home to look after her father. The bigger Obon festival had been combined with an anniversary of the Pikadon in Hiroshima. Slowly, small things she recognised were creeping back into life after surrender.

Tonight one of the Shinto shrines was putting on a small local festival in town. Nobuko hadn't wanted to go but Hana and Michiko were adamant they all should. Drink some sake, make a wish, there were even rumours of fireworks. Nobuko had asked her father, expecting him to say no, but he had agreed. As they got ready to leave, Suma helped dress Nobuko in a yukata, a kimono made from lighter fabric, borrowed from a friend.

Suma finished tying the yukata and stepped back to view her handiwork. She was wearing a kimono of her own. Red and pink flowers on white fabric, golden lines across the material. Amari wore a green yukata with orange koi fish on it. Nobuko's was plain, white and red flowers on a navy backdrop. It had been such a long time since she'd worn traditional dress that even just feeling the folds of fabric envelop her body, the rope tight against her ribs, made her feel like an empress.

'It's a little small,' Suma said, frowning.

'It's perfect.' Nobuko brushed down the stiff material. 'A small yukata for a small festival.'

'I'll see if I can find you another one.' Suma adjusted Nobuko's collar, getting it to sit straight with a gap at the back of her neck.

'Thank you, Aunty.' Nobuko ran her fingers through her hair. It hung in curls to her shoulders, a wave around her face that tucked in at the ends.

'Your hair is so pretty.' Amari sighed. 'Mine is so straight.'

'How about mine?' Suma asked. She'd pinned hers back with a comb, a pearlescent sheen to the seashell on it.

'Where did you get that?' Amari asked, amazed.

'It was a gift,' Suma said. 'Sato gave it to me when I took her some food. She said it was for her daughter but …' She trailed off. They all knew why Sato's daughter wouldn't be getting the comb.

'It's beautiful,' Nobuko said as Amari nodded.

'Shall we go?' Suma said, standing. 'Nobuko-chan, are we going with your father and uncle?'

'No, they're going separately.' Nobuko moved to put on her wooden geta sandals. 'I'm meeting my friends there. We don't need to wait for my father.'

The crowd was bigger than she expected. As they approached the Shinto shrine, there were people dressed in their best clothes – kimono, yukata, Western dress. There were children everywhere, racing among the crowd, darting through people's legs as they chased one another. Nobuko scanned the crowd, looking for Hana and Michiko. Amari and Suma held hands as they walked, Amari's face pinched and nervous.

'Are you okay, Amari-chan?' Nobuko asked.

Amari nodded but didn't speak.

'We might not stay long,' Suma said, her voice light. 'I'm tired already and sometimes lots of people are overwhelming. When you find your friends, you don't need to worry about us.'

Nobuko eyed Suma, understanding passing between the two. Amari had been trapped in a bomb shelter after a raid, when a fallen tree blocked the entrance. Two other people in the shelter died and Amari had been claustrophobic in crowds since.

'I'll find my friends and see you tomorrow,' Nobuko said, smiling at Amari to lift her spirits but the other girl barely looked at her. 'If you see my father and uncle, make sure they don't drink too much sake.'

'I fear that may be impossible,' Suma replied, laughing. 'Have fun, Nobuko-chan. You deserve a good night.'

Nobuko dived into the crowd. She moved around a group of young Japanese boys who leered at her, passing a bottle of sake between them, seeming to fancy themselves as yakuza, Japanese gangsters.

'Hi, cute girl,' one of them called out as she hurried past. 'Why don't you stop awhile?'

The group's laughter faded into the noise of the festival as she drew closer to the shrine. At the entranceway was a towering grey Torii gate, and off to the side were Hana and Michiko.

'Nobuko-chan!' Michiko waved her over. They were in yukata too: Michiko's purple and yellow, Hana's blue and pink. 'Come, come, let's make a wish.'

They headed into the shrine grounds, bowing at the tall Torii gate. The air was heavy with music, bells and a shamisen ringing out around them as they walked, creating a festive air. There were stalls of food, clouds of smoke rising above the festival as vendors cooked sweet potatoes in coals and roasted nuts over open flames, and there was even a stall selling mochi, sweet rice cakes. Around them, the trees were filled with paper, people writing their wishes and tying them to the branches, the paper intensifying the shuddering of the changing autumn leaves when the breeze rustled through.

If Nobuko ignored the people limping or the children who clearly had no parents to watch them race around, it almost could've been a scene from before the war.

She took a deep breath, the air tinged with charcoal and sweetness. 'Let's make a wish,' she said, and the three of them rushed over to claim their paper and thread. She considered what to wish for but it was impossible to ask for so much. Instead, she wrote one word in kanji.

Peace.

The night was mild and filled with laughter. It was wonderful to do something fun after so long fighting for survival. Nobuko briefly glimpsed her father and uncle smoking and drinking on the grass around the shrine. The crowd grew as the night wore on and soon she became weary, fatigued by the intense socialising.

She was thinking about leaving when Hana touched Nobuko's arm. 'I see some strange-looking men,' Hana said, a note of soft amusement in her voice.

Nobuko braced herself. There were many victims of war, missing limbs or badly scarred. They were painful to see, her own memories of war enhancing their shared pain.

To her surprise, they weren't Japanese men at all.

In the middle of the crowd, having staked their own small patch of grass, were a group of Australian soldiers in uniform. Nobuko didn't recognise them all but her stomach flipped as she saw Don. At his side was Charlie.

'What are they doing here?' Michiko asked, surprised.

Hana shrugged. 'Anyone can come to the festival.'

'Are you sure they're welcome?' Michiko glanced at the crowd. The Japanese didn't seem to look at the Australians, but the locals were certainly hyperaware of their presence, hurrying past or avoiding watching them for too long. The soldiers were relaxed and jovial, Don clutching a bottle of beer. As though he could sense her, he looked to Nobuko. His eyes widened at the sight of her in her yukata, then he waved. Nobuko, Hana and Michiko waved back together, causing Don and the soldiers to laugh. The other soldiers waved as a troop, an almost choreographed dance, the girls falling into giggles.

'Let's talk to them,' Hana said.

'No,' Nobuko said, alarmed. 'My English isn't good enough.'

'Neither is mine but maybe we can practise.' Michiko tossed her hair. Nobuko was about to argue when Charlie appeared by her side.

'Hi Charlie-kun,' Nobuko said.

Charlie said nothing, then wrapped his arms around her waist in a hug. She started, not sure what was happening, then he pulled back.

'From Don-san,' Charlie explained, then darted back to the soldiers. Nobuko, stunned, glanced to Don, who was beaming at her.

'I don't think that one cares if your English is bad,' Hana said, dryly. 'We should speak—'

A shout ripped through the crowd. The group of young Japanese men who had called out to Nobuko earlier raced forward and dived onto the Australians, fuelled by sake and bravado. Pandemonium erupted. People scattered, a frenzied stampede for the exits.

Michiko grabbed Hana's and Nobuko's hands. 'Let's go.' They ran the opposite way to the masses, trying to escape the bottleneck by the main Torii gate. Nobuko looked back. Don ducked under one punch, then took another to the jaw. She gasped and Michiko dragged her away.

'We don't want to stay.'

They spilled onto the street, through a gate on the other side of the shrine, others moving with them. Whistles blasted as people ran towards the festival site.

'Police!' The cry whipped through the crowd, people moving faster to get out of the way of the oncoming officers. Nobuko's hand lost Michiko's; she was now alone in the storm. Heart thumping, she drew back towards a building, shrinking into the shadows and counting softly to herself, waiting for the frenzy to subside. The crowd was still in the shrine, riotous and loud, all scuffles and shouts.

Slowly, the noise settled. Nobuko leaned her head back against the cool wooden wall of the building behind her, breathing slow.

Eventually, she stood. She could go back to what was left of the festival, to try to find Michiko and Hana or even Suma and Amari if they hadn't already left. Instead, she turned away from the shrine and began her walk home in the darkened night.

It seemed impossible that they would ever go back to what life was like before the war. Even the small taste of normality tonight was tinged with reminders that life had been changed forever. The orphans trying to make the most of the evening, to scavenge what they could. The volatility towards the ex-enemy soldiers. Nobuko averted her eyes as she walked past a section of the city that had once been a music hall and was now burnt-out remains. It had been her Aunt Masako's favourite building.

Nobuko's breath caught in her throat. She didn't want to think about her aunt.

Instead, she focussed on the things she could see. The lantern outside the soba restaurant was still lit but the lights weren't on inside. A tabby cat stared at her as she walked past, looking up from a pile of rubbish where it had been foraging for mice. A man was doubled over by the sakura, breathing hard.

Nobuko frowned. As she drew closer, she realised the man wasn't Japanese. He was a foreigner and he seemed to be alone. He groaned and drew himself up, Nobuko catching a glimpse of his face.

'Don-san?' She stepped forward, cautious. Don blinked hard, as though he was struggling to focus. His lip was split and bleeding, hair tousled from the fight. His nose had been hit, a smudged line of crimson across his cheek where he'd tried to wipe the blood away. The top button of his shirt was ripped off, the olive-green material hanging open at his chest.

He stared at her, a small crease in his forehead. 'Cherry?'

Nobuko led him back to her house, his steps slow and laboured. She worried that he could have a head injury. She knew there was a risk that her father would be home by now, but she might be able to convince Suma to help. As they neared Suma's, silhouettes moved in the windows. Her heart sank. She would need to take him to her house, empty and dark, across the street.

Nobuko turned to Don. 'Please, wait.' He nodded, fixated on the ruins of a house they'd just walked past. Hoping he wouldn't get in trouble, Nobuko moved towards the shack, listening hard. She slid open the door.

'I'm home.' Her voice echoed in the darkness. There was no answer. She slipped off her wooden sandals and crept into the main room. It was empty. Satisfied, Nobuko put on shoes that were easier to walk in and headed back to Don.

He wasn't there. Panicked, Nobuko looked around. Had someone found him on the street? Had he wandered off? Perhaps someone had seen them together and attacked him.

'Cherry?' Don's voice came out of the darkness. He was hiding under a twisted maple tree, shielded from sight. 'Some of your neighbours came past.'

Nobuko reached for him. 'Please, come,' she said, leading him into the house. She didn't look at him as she moved towards the door, but she heard him stop. She turned.

Don's mouth was open, staring at the rubble they had tried to push to the back, the walls that stood at odd angles, built from anything they could find to create a home with a roof.

'Don-san, quick.' That made him move. She took off her shoes as she came in, Don stooping low as he followed her. He made to step inside but she stopped him.

'Please.' She pointed to his boots.

He was too big for the house. Don's presence seemed to fill the whole place. He ducked under doorways and awkwardly folded himself onto the floor while she lit a candle and put some water from the drinking bucket into a bowl to wash his face. Nobuko found a small towel and poured some water into a cup for him to drink.

'Okay,' she said as she came back to him. Don's eyes settled on her and her stomach lurched. He took the cup and drank it in one gulp, wincing as he pressed his lips to the ceramic. Nobuko hesitated, unsure if she should offer him more. They didn't have much water left for the week. Deciding to leave that for now, she knelt in front of him with the cloth and dipped it in the small bowl.

'You don't have to do that,' Don said. Nobuko paused, filtering the English words through her head to translate them. 'I can—' He reached for the towel and she understood him. She shook her head.

'Stop. I do.' His arm fell away and she shuffled forward, putting her hand on his chin and tilting his head towards the light. As gently as she could, she dabbed at the cut on his lip, cleaning up the blood. It had stopped bleeding but it was swollen, Don wincing as the cloth touched his mouth.

'Sorry,' Nobuko said.

'It's fine,' he assured her. 'I'm being a bit of a wimp.'

'Wimp?' she repeated, confused.

He smiled, the edges of the wound threatening to split. 'I'm being a coward,' he said. 'Not brave.'

'You brave. You fight.'

Don laughed, a hollow sound. 'Probably not the bravest thing to do. Would've been braver to walk away once we'd got them off us.'

Nobuko didn't say anything, squeezing out the small towel and wiping the blood off his cheeks. His eyes were fixed on her. She tried to avoid his gaze, aware of how close they were.

'You're good at this,' he said, voice soft. 'You should come work with me and Charlie in Medical.'

'Thank you but I clean.' Her heart was hammering. This seemed too intimate, too close.

'I'd like to have you there,' Don said. 'Maybe we can sort something out.'

His gaze pierced her, looking into her soul. Overwhelmed, she looked away and noticed blood on the back of his hand. She wiped it, hoping the light was too dim to show how red her cheeks were.

'Any more else?' Nobuko asked. Don's hand, clean and hot, was holding hers. Her eyes crashed into his again, her breath tight in her throat.

The door slid open.

Nobuko's heart dropped. She scrambled backwards, already preparing an excuse, bracing for Noboru's wrath.

It was Suma.

She stared at Nobuko and Don, shocked.

Don raised a hand and waved half-heartedly. 'G'day.'

Suma took in the scene, then turned to Nobuko and spoke urgently in Japanese. 'Your father and uncle are at my house. They wanted me to lay out the futons while they get ready to leave.'

Nobuko grabbed Don's boots and her shoes. She tugged on his elbow. 'Please, come.' She pulled him to his feet and led him towards the side door.

'Nobuko,' Suma said. Nobuko turned, surprised to see her so worried. 'Be careful.'

Nobuko ushered Don out, gesturing to keep quiet. She put her shoes on and peered out through the garden. Noboru and Kazuo hadn't left Suma's house yet.

She turned back to Don, who looked a little frightened. In spite of her own fear, she smiled. 'Please, we go now.'

The two of them moved down the road, Don stepping carefully in his grey socks, until Nobuko was convinced they were out of sight. She passed him his boots and he sat down to pull them on.

'Sorry,' Nobuko said as he dusted off his feet. 'Father not like ex-enemy.'

Don nodded, sympathetic. 'Can't think of many men who would like their daughter alone with a strange soldier.'

'Maybe if you had come before the war. Before the Pikadon. Father was different then.' She sighed and Don looked at her, the crease in his forehead appearing as he considered her words.

'Pikadon?' Don asked.

Nobuko paused, surprised. 'You know Pikadon?' She shook her head. 'Very bad day. Very …' Nobuko searched for the English word. 'Very scary.'

Even in the dim evening light, she could see Don's face pale.

'Cherry,' he said, voice grave. 'Were you at Hiroshima?'

All the energy dropped out of Nobuko's body. Don watched her, concern etched into his features.

Nobuko paused.

It wasn't an easy answer.

'Come.'

The streets were quiet as Nobuko led Don into the centre of town so he could return to the barracks. She was acutely aware of him following her as they walked. She lingered by a Torii gate, an entrance to another Shinto shrine. She wanted to pray, to ask permission for what she was about to do. Don cleared his throat and she gestured for him to continue behind her. Their footsteps echoed as they walked into the grounds, towards the shrine ahead of them. Nobuko moved to the small temizuya pavilion to cleanse her hands, the small fountain of water equipped with two hishaku ladles. She scooped up the water with the ladle, washing her left hand, then her right, and letting the last of the water trickle down over the handle. Don tried to copy her movements, clumsy and unsure, nearly running out of water as he finished.

Nobuko walked over to the saisenbako altar to pray. Don hung back, watching from a distance. The shrine had been mostly undamaged during the war, heavy beams of wood balanced against one another to make the pointed building. The inner area of the shrine was restricted to priests only, a wooden fence built around the edge to stop visitors from going too far in. There was a box to throw in coins for prayer, although tonight there were a few small piles of rice grains along the edge. Nobuko didn't have any coins but she had to hope the gods wouldn't mind. She grasped the thick red rope, pulling hard, to ring the golden bell. The clanging calmed her, the ritual familiar and steadying. Nobuko closed her eyes and bowed her head to pray. She clapped, waking up the gods to ask them for permission. The answer came quickly, an instinct in her mind. Nobuko bowed, grateful. She allowed herself a small smile as she gave another deep bow, knowing she was making the right decision.

She turned back to Don, who was looking at her with a sense of wonder. She imagined what he could see. A Japanese girl in a yukata, praying by a shrine, lit by the flickering lanterns.

She sat next to him and folded her hands in her lap. Her English wasn't good enough to tell him everything, but she would try.

She remembered it all. Every detail.

'Don-san,' Nobuko said. 'I tell you about Hiroshima.'

CHAPTER NINE

NOBUKO: Hiroshima, 6 August 1945

Nobuko was winding wool. Her fingers were deft as she pulled apart a navy knitted jumper, her well-practised movements tugging the stitches loose as she wound a new ball to be re-knitted into something else. It was her father's sweater, a small hole at the bottom prompting her to unpick the stitches and reuse the yarn. She missed him. Every so often, as another row came free, she'd get a scent of tobacco and grass, almost as though he was there with them. Nobuko and her parents, Noboru and Tsudo, had left Hiroshima to stay with her Aunt Masako and Uncle Kazuo in Kure, moving out of the big city to be closer to family as the Americans turned their focus to Japan. It had been an ill-timed decision, as they'd arrived shortly before the US Airforce began targeted firebombing on Kure, aiming for the naval base. After Masako died running for an air-raid shelter, caught in the path of several bombs dropped by B-29 planes, and the house they were living in was destroyed, Noboru decided it was too dangerous for them to stay. Kazuo refused to leave, so Noboru stayed with him and sent his wife and daughter back to where they had lived for the majority of the war until the men could join them.

Back to Hiroshima.

For Nobuko, after months away, it was comforting to be back in familiar places with her mother, Tsudo. The small three-roomed house with the patched crack in the kitchen wall hadn't changed but Nobuko had. She was older. Wiser. More mature.

They both had war work, doing what they could to help the government keep the country running. Tsudo spent her days at the docks, unloading food and weapons from ships that transported supplies along the coast, taking stock of shipments, and arranging deliveries to merchants and businesses in town. She worked almost exclusively with women who were waiting for their husbands to come home from war, though there was the occasional older man who had been deemed unfit to fight. Nobuko visited older members of the community to help them. Every day, she got dressed in her school uniform, then walked to different elders in town and helped them to cook, clean or tend to their garden, or just sat and listened to their stories. Some girls hated the idea of spending time with older people, but Nobuko didn't mind. Many of the people she helped were alone, their sons on the battlefields or serving Japan.

Every night, Nobuko and Tsudo would lie together on the same futon in the tatami room – their second futon had long since been given away to someone else who needed it – curled against each other as they slept. Sometimes when Nobuko woke in the night, she would move closer to her mother, wrapping around her to feel safe. Living in Kure had been hard, but they had managed. Nobuko's favourite thing to do was to walk through the bustling town with her mother and Aunt Masako, often pausing outside the music hall to listen to the upbeat music, Tsudo and Masako dancing together as Nobuko clapped. A reminder there was time for joy and delight, even in the midst of war. In Hiroshima, there was less worry, less tension in the air. People were cautious, but less afraid.

Today, Nobuko was ready earlier than usual, so she had packed the futon into their small wooden cupboard, opened the sliding door to let some fresh air and light in, and started winding the wool. The radio was playing, a constant source of noise, as Tsudo emerged from the small washroom.

'Nobuko,' Tsudo called. 'Are you visiting Matsui-san today?'

'Yes, she's my first visit this morning.' Nobuko frowned as the wool snagged. She separated it, careful not to damage the fibres as she pulled.

'Do we have any mochi left?' Tsudo asked.

'One,' Nobuko replied. 'But I was saving it for your birthday.'

Her mother entered the room, pinning back her dark hair. She wore a pair of Noboru's navy trousers to make her work easier at the docks, and she was wearing a white shirt with a soft grey jumper tied around her shoulders. Nobuko's heart leapt. She'd finished knitting the jumper last week. The wool had come from Matsui, who had pressed it upon Nobuko when she spotted it in the bottom of the cupboard.

'I can't do anything with it,' Matsui had said, pushing the balls of wool into Nobuko's arms, the old woman's hands gnarled and stiff. 'Make something useful.'

To see her mother wearing it made Nobuko proud.

'That's kind,' Tsudo said, placing the mochi on the table. 'But my birthday isn't for a few more days and I'm sure Matsui-san would appreciate the mochi more. Some thanks from us for her wool.' Tsudo was moving into the kitchen when a horn sounded. Both of them froze.

The air-raid siren. It rang out through the radio, reverberating on the streets. It had sounded a few times since they had returned to Hiroshima, but the planes had headed elsewhere. Kure, Osaka, Tokyo. The moments between the air-raid siren sounding and the announcement of where the planes were heading were the hardest. In Kure, they hadn't waited. They heard the first siren and left for a shelter, knowing they were a likely target. In Hiroshima, it was more uncertain. More confusing. More frightening.

'Pack the things we need.' Tsudo's low voice shook. 'Go now, Nobuko.'

She scrambled to her feet and opened the top drawer to a cupboard that sat behind the table. She grabbed a ring that her mother kept there, next to a photograph of Nobuko's grandparents. The ring was gold with an emerald nestled into the band, visible on Nobuko's grandmother's finger in the photo. She lay them in a piece of fabric then, as an afterthought, picked up the only photograph they had of the three of them – Nobuko, Noboru and Tsudo, taken a few years beforehand – wrapped it in the small cloth bundle, and tucked it into the waistband of her skirt.

She came into the kitchen as Tsudo finished packing what little food they had in their pantry. She was calmer. A voice crackled out of the radio between blasts of the alarm.

'It's an early warning,' her mother said. 'There are American aircrafts heading towards the south of Japan. They are letting all the cities know.'

Nobuko nodded, her fear easing only a little. The screeching sirens threw up memories of Kure: outrunning planes for the air-raid shelters, scurrying to safety and hoping they would survive this time.

'Such an awful noise.' Tsudo rubbed her temples and turned the radio down, kneeling at the table. 'I wish they would find something nicer.'

'If the alarm was too nice, people would stop to dance to it instead of getting to safety.' Nobuko picked up her wool and twisted it back through her fingers. 'It would be an even bigger disaster.'

'Perhaps you're right.' Tsudo glanced at a small clock on a wooden cupboard behind the table. 'I will wait a little before I go to work,' she said.

Relief flooded through Nobuko. It was always safer with her mother nearby.

'Let's eat something.' Tsudo unwrapped the food, laying what they had on the low chabudai table. Nobuko fetched two bowls from the cupboard and passed them to Tsudo. Rice and nori was their staple breakfast, a quick and easy meal in the mornings, and today was no exception.

After putting a small scoop of rice into each bowl, Tsudo shredded nori into flakes and sprinkled it over. 'Chopsticks?' she asked, then smiled. Nobuko had already laid out two sets of chopsticks for them both. One set was her father's pair. They hadn't had word from him in weeks, but that wasn't unusual. Noboru had told Nobuko when she had left Kure that no letters were better than a message that brought news of death and destruction.

Tsudo passed over a bowl, Nobuko touching her mother's calloused hands. The food hadn't been divided equally, Tsudo taking less. Her mother did more physical labour than her, so Nobuko reached across the table and swapped their bowls. Tsudo sighed, then gave a soft smile of thanks. They'd had arguments over how to split their rations enough times that they no longer needed to talk about it. It didn't make much difference: neither portion was enough.

It was no way to live. The relentlessness of infinite fear, worried every decision they made may take them into the path of danger, may lead to their final moments. Nobuko was exhausted by it.

'Does war ever end?' she asked abruptly, catching her mother's deep amber gaze. Tsudo chewed on her rice before she set the chopsticks down.

'Do you remember a time before war?' Tsudo asked. This battle with Britain and America had stretched on for years, creeping closer and closer to Japan, and now it was on their doorstep. Before that, Japan was at war with China. All Nobuko's memories seemed tinged by the shadow of fighting. Her earliest memory was of her father, celebrating a battle victory, dancing on the tatami as the radio broadcast Imperial Japan's success against their enemy.

'No,' Nobuko replied. 'Barely. There only ever seems to be war. Somewhere, even in peacetime.'

'Some say peace is merely the time between wars,' Tsudo said, her shoulders slumped forward.

Nobuko sat up. She didn't want her mother to be sad. 'One day, I will live in peace,' she said. 'No more fighting. No more rations. No more sirens. But all the wool we need.'

Her mother smiled. 'A worthy dream.'

The radio noise shifted. A burst of staccato beats. Both of them looked to it, Tsudo listening hard. Nobuko could barely hear it from across the room, but her mother visibly relaxed.

'It's a reconnaissance raid,' Tsudo said. 'Only a few planes. Not enough for an air raid.'

The tension oozed out of Nobuko's body. 'I hope there's never a raid here. If there's any damage to the city, I'll need to go out and clear the roads for the fire trucks to get through. I'm not strong enough to do that.'

'You are very strong, Nobuko,' Tsudo said, a reprimand in her voice. 'Your strength is not measured in muscle, you know.'

Warmth spread through Nobuko, but she found it difficult to take the compliment. 'I suppose we will have to go to work, after all,' she said.

'Luckily!' Tsudo said. 'I want to show off the top my wonderful daughter knitted for me.'

Nobuko blushed.

'You will have to be careful. Eto-san will be jealous and want one of her own,' her mother continued.

'I'll make her one,' Nobuko said. 'I'll need more wool, but I can make them for everyone.'

'Find the wool first,' Tsudo suggested. 'Don't make promises if you can't keep them.'

Nobuko nodded, thinking about where she may be able to get yarn. There wasn't a lot of spare clothing, but if moths had eaten away at old knits, Nobuko could pull them apart and create a continuous thread from lots of different pieces, remaking it into something new and functional.

'Let's eat!' Tsudo said, clapping her hands together.

'Let's eat!' Nobuko repeated, pressing her hands into a prayer before picking up her chopsticks and bowl, stirring the nori flakes into the rice.

'Tanaka-san might have some old wool garments I can take,' Nobuko said, unable to let go of this new idea. 'I'll ask him today. I think I remember a red scarf he had.'

'Don't be pushy.' Tsudo swallowed a mouthful of rice. 'Remember people don't have much to spare.'

'Of course,' Nobuko said. 'I won't be rude. I'll be polite—'

A flash of bright light swept through the house, followed by an ear-splitting explosion. The ground beneath them shook. An earthquake. Nobuko's eyes jammed shut as something threw her backwards and the world around her tumbled, the house falling down around them with a shudder.

In the darkness behind Nobuko's closed eyes was the silhouette of her mother sitting opposite her, in front of the window. The image throbbed and then faded. A trick of the light.

Silence.

There was something heavy on top of her, pinning her down. Opening her eyes, there was nothing but darkness. Then, a small shaft of low light. Nobuko couldn't move. Her chest was heaving but she couldn't hear her breath. There was a low ringing in her ears, growing louder and louder. Pain streaked through her back as whatever was above her forced her to stay hunched over. She whimpered, trying to get on her hands and knees, the bamboo lines of the tatami mat pressing hard into her legs. She needed to get out. As she moved, there was a tinkle of broken glass and crockery. The cupboard behind her. It had fallen with the impact of the earthquake. Was it an earthquake? An earthquake didn't bring with it blinding light.

'Mother?' Nobuko's voice was a croak, her mouth filled with dust and dirt. She coughed, the movement sparking pain in her shoulder and chest. 'Help! I'm stuck!'

Nobuko groaned as she pressed against the heavy wood above her, but she couldn't shift it. Panic rose, heart thudding. She was going to die here, smothered in the wreckage of her home.

'Mother!' Nobuko screamed, sobs tearing from her throat. She scrabbled through the debris, trying to find a grip on the ground.

There was a slick wetness beneath her, making it hard to move but, as she gasped for breath, she managed to get both her feet on the floor. She gritted her teeth and counted to three.

'Ichi. Ni. San.' Nobuko pushed hard, using all her strength to lift the cupboard above her. It barely moved, scraping back against the floor. She released her body, coming back to a foetal position, unable to stop sobbing. She was going to die. She would never see the sky again, never see her sakura blooms next spring. Death, who had been hunting her through all these years of war, had finally found her, here, at her home in Hiroshima.

No.

She was brave. She was strong. In mind and in muscle. Nobuko let out a breath, coughing as she then inhaled a lungful of dirt and dust, and repositioned herself on her feet and hands, crouched like a frog in the dark. Gritting her teeth, ignoring the screams in her back as the cupboard pressed against her, she steadied herself.

'Ichi. Ni. San.' She pushed with everything she had, grunting with the exertion. The weight above her shifted and she pressed harder, the cupboard eventually falling aside, a cloud of dust and ash flying around her.

She could see the sky. At least, it seemed like the sky. The roof was gone, a fetid breeze snaking through the air around her, revealing roiling darkness above. Thick smoke billowed over the city, black stormy greys, hiding any hint of the sun that had risen that morning. A red haze reached for her, a warning of danger that was already too close. The air reeked of charcoal and ash and mass burning, a bonfire that had spread wildly out of control.

Her house was around her knees. The walls were ripped apart like paper, foundation beams snapped like matchsticks. Where her home had once stood was nothing more than a pile of oversized twigs. Every building was a lump of rubble, as far as she could see through the haze of ash and dust.

'Mother,' Nobuko whispered, still barely able to hear her own voice. Panic jolted through her and she scrambled onto the rubble, feet clad only in socks, looking for any sign of Tsudo. 'Mother!' Nobuko shrieked, slipping as the wreckage shifted under her weight. A chunk of wood moved aside, revealing an arm buried beneath the surface. Wailing, Nobuko began to dig, ignoring glass that cut into her hands, ignoring splinters and pain and bruising. She pushed against a heavy wooden post, an electricity pole, now plunged into the middle of the tatami room. It didn't budge.

'It's okay, Mama,' Nobuko said, voice hoarse and soft. 'I'm here, I'm coming.' She scrabbled hard, unable to stop the sob of relief as the soft grey yarn of her mother's jumper, now blood-soaked and crimson, appeared beneath the debris. She cleared as much as she could, but when she pushed aside a plank of wood to reveal her mother's face, Nobuko froze.

Tsudo lay there, eyes open, skin pale, mouth agape. Dead.

Nobuko hiccoughed. Her mother couldn't be dead. She would blink, she would know what to do, she would protect them and get them out.

Except she didn't.

Shaking, Nobuko stared at her mother. Around her, the wind grew stronger, whipping through her tangled hair, the smell of acrid burning intensifying. She coughed and looked up, startled to see hungry orange flames in the distance. As much as she wanted to stay, to give her mother the respect in death she deserved, Nobuko couldn't if she wanted to survive. A tortured moan escaped from somewhere deep in her chest and she touched Tsudo's head.

'I'm sorry,' Nobuko whispered, saying a prayer for her mother's spirit, tears flowing freely and unnoticed. Anguished, she fought her instincts to stay, to curl against her mother's chest, to let death take them both. She wrenched herself away, the movement dislodging something beneath her and she slipped down as the debris tipped back over her mother's body, burying her once again.

Nobuko staggered from the house, disoriented. There was nothing she recognised. No roads, only ruin. The scraps of her home city cut into her feet, smears of blood marking her steps, no safe path and no shoes for her to wear. She stumbled forward as the air grew thicker with ash and smoke. Her foot stepped on something both hard and soft and she jumped back, horrified. It was a burnt body, blackened and ashen, arms and legs contorted at odd angles. She wanted to scream, but there was nothing left in her lungs to make a noise. She moved faster, desperate. The fire behind her grew bigger, greedier, eating anything in its path, blanketing the city in a frightening red sheen. The entire world was burning.

This was no earthquake.

Breathing hard, she pressed on, focussing on each agonising step. Someone called out for help, but when she found the source of the voice, the woman was already dead. Nobuko shrank in on herself. It was too much. It was far too much. She walked past people, some clothed, some naked, some injured and screaming. The river curled through the city, dirty and muck filled, ash and debris already flowing downstream.

'Please.' The voice was hoarse and barely a whisper. 'Water. Please.' Nobuko couldn't look. A hand grabbed her ankle, reddened fingers cinching painfully tight.

Terror flew through her. 'Stop, please! Let go!' The hand didn't yield, the person dragging themselves closer to her. Their clothes were rags, hair burnt off, a patch of spiky black. Their left eye was swollen shut, mouth red and bleeding.

'Water,' they asked again. Nobuko was sobbing, terrified. Then it began to rain. Fat raindrops fell from the sky, landing heavily on the ground. One or two at first, then several. With a sigh, the hand let go of her ankle and the person rolled onto their back, opening their reddened mouth to catch whatever rainwater they could. A raindrop fell onto their face.

The water was black.

A wave of fear threatened to engulf her whole body and Nobuko's feet propelled her forward. Around her, the injured were desperately trying to drink the black rain, throats parched, but she kept her head down, not wanting any of it. The rain was unavoidable; sharp raindrops flicked against her skin and clothes, a prickle of pain every time another found her as its target. Her once white shirt was long dirtied with ash and dust, but Nobuko paused when she noticed a small hole by her waist. The edges were black and uneven, as though moths had found it and eaten away at the fabric. Desperate to get out of the rain as it grew heavier, she stumbled towards the river, grateful the bridge still stretched over the water. She skidded down the river bank, ignoring the pain in her body, and staggered under the bridge to shelter, a safe haven for now.

She wasn't alone. Several others had gathered there, clinging to one another, some shocked and silent, some rocking themselves as they sobbed. Nobuko didn't recognise anyone – they were all covered in a layer of dirt and grime and blood. As was she. A troupe of death angels. She sank to her knees, light-headed. Her home city was gone. There was nothing standing, nothing but the landscape of hell. This couldn't be real. This was her fear running rampant, bringing the monsters out of the dark. She was trapped in a nightmare, a horrible dream, sparked by memories of the firebombing in Kure. She would wake soon.

Nobuko pinched her arm. A tight throb of pain shot over her elbow, but nothing changed. She slapped her arm, the connection stinging. She didn't wake up. Desperation growing, she hit any part of her body she could, her thighs, her chest, her face, welts of red barely visible through the powdered grime on her skin. The nightmare remained, the stench of smoke stronger now, spiked with the smell of burning bodies.

Something dug into her hip. In the waistband of her skirt were the flaky remnants of the photograph of her grandparents, the picture destroyed. The photograph of Noboru, Tsudo and Nobuko was crinkled but intact. The emerald ring, too, had survived.

Nobuko touched her mother's image, numb once again. Next to her, someone stood and moved to the river's edge, peering into the water. In the river, something floated downstream. As it drew closer, everyone beneath the bridge turned to look.

It was a body. Half burnt and mutilated. Then came another. And another. There was a mass of debris moving with the current, but it wasn't debris. The survivors watched the slow-moving tsunami of the dead, hundreds of people seeking relief in the river and dying before they found it. The procession of death wasn't only blackened and mangled corpses though. Some were unmarked but glassy eyed; others bloodied but cleansed by the Ōta River. The dead moved as one, embraced by the water, parading by the group of survivors, on their final path out of life.

Behind Nobuko, a scream. A man collapsed on the ground, his daughter trying to shake him awake. 'Father. Father!' The girl grabbed at him, the edges of his burnt kimono disintegrating in her fingers, but her father did not move.

Nobuko blinked. Her father. He would be worried. He was the only person she had left. There was no-one here for her in Hiroshima now.

Before she realised, Nobuko was on her feet. She pulled a wide plank of wood from a pile of nearby rubble and groaned as she set it on her back. The black rain was still falling. She staggered out from underneath the bridge, ignoring people who stared as she scrambled up to the road once again. The raindrops hit the plank of wood with a soft hiss, but didn't eat through to harm her. Her socks had long since disappeared and her feet were bloodied and dirty. She coughed and a soft cloud of ash shook itself from her hair, twisted tendrils of anguish that hung around her face as she walked.

It was death. Death was in her hair.

The dirt road was quiet, the silence almost painful after the noise of the ruined city. Her makeshift wooden umbrella had become too heavy for her and she'd left it by the side of the road moments ago – or was it hours? – no longer needing it once she was out of the black rain. The sun hurt her eyes, the world too bright after being caught in the darkened storm at Hiroshima, ravaged by fire and smoke. Nobuko saw nothing ahead of her, her footsteps slow and laboured, her breathing sharp and short. The sakura gleamed in the sunshine, the rustle of the leaves echoing the roar of the explosion, the screams of those dying where they sat a dull ringing in her ears.

Her feet throbbed, but the pain was numbed, a tension and tightness in her blackened limbs. She had to keep moving. If she stopped, she would fall, and she might never get back up. She blinked and the swirling flames and rubble appeared. She coughed and her mother smiled across the chabudai table, kneeling to start a breakfast they would never finish.

The road wound to the side, nestling against the mirrored curve of the river. She stepped off the main path, limping towards the rushing water and then sinking her toes into the current. Her body relaxed, the cool temperature briefly easing her pain. There was no rubble or dust or dirt in the pristine water, rushing over stones as it raced on its path towards the ocean, ever moving. The river teased out streams of crimson, dirt and grime, tendrils snaking in curls across the surface of the water.

Her reflection stared up at her. Unrecognisable. A cloak of powder and dust, grey and black caked in her eyebrows, her eyelashes, her hair. She tilted her head to the side and so did the demon in the water, neither sure what they were looking at. Nobuko reached a shaking hand out to the river, the demon mimicking her movements.

Her finger touched the water and she recoiled. She needed to keep moving, still miles from Kure. She needed to get to her father.

She walked. She came across people on the road who fell silent as she approached, staring. Some tried to speak as she limped through towns, but Nobuko didn't have the energy to stop. She didn't know what to say. How could she tell them what had happened at Hiroshima? A woman asked her about the black cloud in the sky at the bottom of the valley, how it hung heavily over the city. Where had it come from? Nobuko couldn't answer. She didn't know. A bicycle flew past, a man heading to the ruined city, but he was gone before she could warn him to stop. A boy took her hand and tried to pull her off the path, but Nobuko wrenched her hand from his grasp. He tried again, rougher this time, but she started screaming. He scrambled backwards, shocked and frightened, but left her alone.

Villagers shied away from Nobuko as she staggered along the road, one mother standing in front of her child. But Nobuko didn't stop. She didn't want them. She wanted her home. She wanted her father.

Nobuko's chest ached, her ribs were whining, bolts of pain shot through her body with every step. This was the only road to Kure; she simply had to keep on it.

Except now a horse and cart blocked the entire roadway. Nobuko stopped inches before she walked into it, barely seeing it. She placed her hand on the back of the wooden cart, filled with bales of hay, to steady herself, trying to work out the best way around it.

The driver of the cart emerged from around the side, patting the flank of the chestnut mare, placing its hoof back on the ground. The horse neighed and the woman slapped its back, talking to it.

'You're complaining over nothing. We're going to be late now you've stopped us.' The woman moved to climb onto the back of the cart when she noticed Nobuko, staring into nothingness. Immediately, she was at Nobuko's side.

'What happened?' The woman's soft brown gaze flicked over the girl. 'Where have you come from?'

'Hiroshima.' Nobuko's voice was hoarse and deep. She braced herself for the questions she couldn't answer, the words she couldn't speak. The woman hesitated. She was dusty too, but from manual labour instead of collapsed buildings. There were strands of straw in her black hair, she wore working clothes and her cheeks were reddened by the sun, a smattering of freckles over her nose.

'You walked all the way from Hiroshima?' the woman asked.

'I have to get home. To my father. In Kure.' Exhaustion was catching up with Nobuko now. She knew it. Her body would refuse to move, she would stumble to her knees and stay where she fell on the side of the road to Kure. She would never see her father again. Nobuko slumped as her energy failed, but the woman caught her.

'You can't walk. I'll take you. Here.' The woman helped her onto the back of the cart, nestling her among the hay. Nobuko relaxed. No need to keep fighting. 'My name is Suma.' Suma clicked her tongue in disapproval as she noticed Nobuko's damaged feet. 'You walked all this way with no shoes. We will go quickly. To your father.'

'His name is Sakuramoto Noboru,' Nobuko said.

The other woman stopped in shock. 'You are Sakuramoto-san's daughter?' She clicked her tongue and hurried to the front of the cart. 'Quickly, quickly, quickly.'

Nobuko stared at the sky, soft white clouds fluffy against the bright clear blue. The sakura leaves waved at Nobuko in the dappled sunlight as she lay exactly as Suma had placed her, unmoving against the bed of straw. People stared as the woman steered the cart quickly into Kure, catching sight of the smudge of a girl in the back of the cart. Suma chattered constantly, Nobuko hearing none of it.

She closed her eyes.

Somewhere, far away, was the voice of her uncle.

'Who are you?'

'Suma. Please. I must find Sakuramoto-san.'

'He is not here.'

'Where is he?'

'There was a bomb at Hiroshima. He went there to look for his wife and daughter, hours ago.'

'I have his daughter.'

'Nobuko? What?'

'She is here. She walked from Hiroshima until I found her halfway on the south road. He must've passed her on his way.'

'What of his wife?'

Darkness.

Sleep.

Silence.

Nobuko couldn't look at Don. She wiped away her tears, wishing her hands would stop shaking. She wasn't sure how much he had understood, how good her halting English had become over the past few months, but he seemed to have understood enough. Many words she hadn't known, but Don had nodded, offering her an answer, filling in her sentences. Some things she couldn't even begin to describe, and he had covered her hand with his, holding it tightly as she cried. There had been moments he cleared his throat, tears brimming too. His emotions helped her hold on to her own and continue her story.

She had never talked about what had happened that day. There wasn't anyone who would listen. Her father didn't want to talk about her mother. Once Noboru had returned two days later, convinced his wife and daughter were dead, his grief for Tsudo and guilt that he had sent his family to Hiroshima eroded any joy at finding Nobuko alive. Kazuo was still grieving for Masako. Suma had tended Nobuko's wounds and nursed her back to health, but they had never spoken about Hiroshima. There were no words.

Don listened. Don heard her. His hand grasped hers more tightly. 'Cherry …' But no more words came. He took a breath and fear chilled her. She had told him too much, shown too much.

The silver moonlight shone above them and Don leaned forward. He pulled her into his chest, holding her close. Nobuko stiffened, surprised. She'd never been so close to a stranger before, although surely Don was no longer a stranger. His warmth enveloped her and she relaxed, allowing him to hold her, feeling his heartbeat beneath his chest. He smelt like summer, like strength.

'Thank you for sharing that.' Don nodded at her, face grave. 'For telling me that.' He let out a heavy exhale and Nobuko's chest tightened. She had burdened him with her story. Now he was carrying that weight too.

Before she could think about it too much, she moved forward and kissed his cheek.

'Thank you. For listen.' Nobuko couldn't help her own smile, mirroring Don's own. He held her gaze, and Nobuko's stomach flipped over. Would he kiss her? Did she want him to?

Before Nobuko could think about this any more, Don looked away.

'No worries for listen,' Don said. 'No worries at all.'

Nobuko blinked back tears. Her shoulders weren't tensed, her body softer than usual. It was a small thing, to have someone to talk to. When the world itself was ever-changing and moving, it was something she could hold on to and brace herself against.

CHAPTER TEN

GORDON: Kure, December 1946

Gordon hadn't stopped thinking about that night at the shrine with Cherry, haunted by what she had gone through. The living graveyard of Hiroshima, the complete destruction of the city, was burnt into his mind. She had somehow survived that. Now she was living in a glorified shack, coming to work every day in the same clothes, still greeting him with a smile. The smile that illuminated his dreams.

There were other things from that night he couldn't stop thinking about. The way her hand had felt in his, how she fitted perfectly in his arms, the stiff fabric of her yukata against the worn fabric of his uniform. He hadn't had a girl back home; every girl in Ringwood knew his mum or sister, after all. Their meddling would've made courting anyone nearly impossible. He had friends who'd married before they'd been sent off to war, and there were boys who had gone into town during basic training to find a girl for the night, but Gordon had never understood all that.

Holding Cherry gave him a glimpse of what he had been missing.

It was impossible though. The anti-fraternisation rules were still in place, even though there were plenty of BCOF soldiers who took up with Japanese girls, some for the night, some for longer. A few of the men had wives back home, but they'd give a wink as they whisked their new girl away for an evening in town. A handful of blokes were careful, not wanting to get on the wrong side of the COs or the Military Police, but most of the soldiers didn't care. They got their time with a pretty Japanese lass, then could ignore her for a week, pleading that they needed to lie low and not get caught. Not amused that there seemed to be so much fraternisation when it had been expressly forbidden, the Military Police stepped up their game. They frequently raided the few restaurants in town that didn't care if the Westerners and the Japanese mixed as long as they paid for their meals. The MPs would punish the soldier by barring him from town for a week or so, and the girl would be hauled off for testing since they were prostitutes more often than not. Sometimes Gordon was dispatched to the MP's office to patch up some bloodied knuckles or check out a black eye. Billy Richardson took to the raids with relish and Gordon was glad they'd never become mates.

Still, Gordon daydreamed of afternoons with Cherry, fuelled by the brief moments they saw each other at the base. How much bigger would her smile be if he could take her out somewhere nice. In Melbourne, they could have lunches or afternoon teas. It would be far harder to do that in Japan but, as more of his friends became interested in Japanese girls, Gordon started to consider it. Cherry wasn't a prostitute, so that wouldn't be a problem. As long as they were smart, neither of them would get in trouble. Slowly, he figured out a plan.

Toby had been caught with Yoneko a few weeks earlier. They were walking back to her market stall after they'd been by the river, when they were stopped by some MPs. Yoneko had escaped, but Toby had been reprimanded for walking next to a Japanese girl in public. When he relayed this story, Gordon suggested that next time Yoneko walk either in front of Toby or just behind him. The suggestion had worked. Toby hadn't stood next to Yoneko as they walked and they'd never been caught again. This loophole raced around the barracks like wildfire.

With this in mind, Gordon summoned his courage to ask Cherry to go to the movies. He barely looked at her, terrified she would say no, speaking so fast she asked him to repeat himself.

Through the biggest smile he had seen from her yet, she said yes.

With the most difficult part done, he simply had to pick his moment. He didn't want to rush it, especially now the MPs were targeting fraternisation as their major crime. It seemed ridiculous. The anti-fraternisation rules were useless. On the boat over, it had seemed like it would be easy to avoid any Japanese. He was on an Australian Army base under the command of British generals. Why would he need to speak to the Japanese? Now he was settled, he realised there was constant need. Every day, he would treat a Japanese person for an injury, whether minor or major. When Gordon was in town, Charlie would appear and take him to someone who needed medical attention. The Kure hospitals were working at half capacity and many children in the city were orphaned and alone. Gordon wouldn't refuse to treat them because a piece of paper told him he couldn't. He didn't agree with Billy on much, but sometimes tearing the anti-fraternisation page out of *Know Japan* for cigarette paper, as Billy had done on the ship, seemed like a good idea.

The market was in a mid-afternoon lull as Gordon wandered through it, looking for gifts to send home. Slim had picked up a Japanese doll to send to his mother as Christmas wasn't far away and postage times were so slow. Realising he should do the same, Gordon headed into town on his day off to find something that would satisfy everyone rather than trying to choose and pack individual gifts.

He was examining a china tea set, intricate blue flowers painted onto every piece, when Charlie appeared at his side.

'Don-san, you come please.'

The boy led Gordon out of the market, the two of them hurrying through the streets. Charlie moved at a run, Gordon jogging behind him as they ducked and weaved around horses, bicycles, people and rubble. They turned into a section of the city that was still bombed out, a kind of shanty village where people were living until the ground could be levelled and cleared. String hung in diagonals between half walls or fallen trees, and power poles created washing lines. People stared as Charlie darted a familiar path through the shacks, Gordon stumbling to keep up.

Charlie stopped by a towering pile of concrete blocks, impossibly braced against one another but somehow sturdy. At the base sat an old Japanese woman who was clutching her hand, surrounded by children and adults, all chattering and trying to help her. When they saw Charlie and Gordon, they fell silent and moved aside to let the Australian through.

A splintered stake pierced the woman's left hand, trails of blood snaking down her wrist. She whispered in Japanese, rocking herself ever so slightly as she prayed.

Gordon knelt next to her. 'Ko-nichi-wa.' He pointed to himself. 'Don. Don-san. Namay?'

'She is Obaa-san,' Charlie said.

'Nice to meet you, Obaa-san. Can I … ?' Gordon reached for her hand and she let him take it. The wood had gone straight through and it was impossible to know how bad the injury would be once the stake was removed. He turned to Charlie. 'Is there any cloth? I want to tie this so it won't move.'

Charlie called out to the crowd in Japanese and several people disappeared. Gordon smiled at Obaa-san. 'I'll sort you out, don't you worry.'

She spoke back to him in Japanese and patted his hand. To Gordon's surprise, the small crowd broke into laughter. He looked to Charlie, eyebrows raised.

The boy giggled, shaking his head. 'She wish her daughter meet you. She say you are handsome.'

Gordon laughed. 'Well, that's very kind of her. But tell her I'm spoken for. I've already got a girl.'

Charlie translated for Obaa-san, who scoffed before lilting Japanese fell from her mouth.

Charlie went pink.

'What'd she say?' Gordon asked.

'She say you need a Japanese girl, not a white girl.'

Gordon chuckled. 'She is a Japanese girl. Not sure she's mine yet but maybe one day.'

Charlie paused. 'Maybe I not translate this for Obaa-san.'

Gordon understood. 'Tell her I think she's a lovely woman.'

There wasn't much more he could do than wrap the cloth around the stake and enlist her neighbours to take her to the closest hospital. She waved as she left, Gordon giving her a small salute.

He was left with a group of children, all staring at him.

'Charlie, you want to take these kids home?'

'This is home. They live with Obaa-san.'

Gordon took in the pile of rubble that had been stacked and fashioned into a cave among the debris. There was a makeshift kitchen in the front, and blankets and towels at the back that would become a bed at night. It was a sorry excuse for a home.

Not sure what to do, Gordon bundled up the excess cloth and tied it together, making a ball with it. He tossed it around in his hands absentmindedly. It was a move from Australian Rules football he did habitually when holding something vaguely football shaped, curling his right hand into a fist and gently using the thumb side to punch the ball into the air and catch it.

The children were fascinated.

Gordon went back the next day with the football Venn had sent and taught them how to kick the oval-shaped ball to one another and how to mark or catch it. He also hid a pile of canned food in the kitchen so that it would be ready for Obaa-san when she returned from the hospital. He made sure he left the improvised orphanage alone, cautious of any Military Police who were patrolling the area, determined not to get caught.

His desire not to get caught was the reason Gordon hadn't taken Cherry to the movies yet. She'd been through enough trouble in her life; he wouldn't be the cause of more. Gordon would send Charlie to give Cherry messages, the two becoming almost like brother and sister as they interacted more and more. Gordon felt a prickle of jealousy when the two of them chatted as they worked and, after speaking to Cliff, Gordon started attending Japanese classes on the base. The language made Gordon's head spin. The words were all in the wrong place, reading was impossible and he pronounced everything incorrectly. Then he'd hesitantly say something to Cherry in Japanese, and she'd beam at him, the biggest smile this side of the Pacific, and Gordon didn't care how hard it was. Her English was coming along too, although she spoke a half-English, half-Japanese style of speech most of the time, a kind of hybrid language. A lot of the girls did. The best moments were when Cherry threw in an Australian word out of nowhere. The first time she talked about a kangaroo nearly knocked him flat.

The weather was cooling down as winter approached. There were rumours of snow over the cold months, something that seemed strange to Gordon. In his experience, snow was something you drove a long way to, not something that arrived on your doorstep.

The Christmas celebrations weren't a big holiday for the Japanese. They had festivals throughout the year, although Gordon hadn't dared sneak out to another one. The impending holiday had given an air of merriment to the base, the boys hanging paper chains in the mess, and the dorm buildings had wreaths made of unfamiliar plants hanging on the outside doors. This break would be a prime opportunity to take Cherry out. Stolen conversations in ten-minute grabs were hardly enough. The Japanese didn't celebrate Christmas, and neither Cherry nor Charlie had heard of it before. It didn't seem that everything would close down in December, which is why Gordon was surprised when Toby came into the medical unit and told him the cinema was closing for a month.

'It's what?' Gordon asked, washing his hands as Toby leaned against the cupboard near the sink.

'I know, I don't get it either. The last screening is tonight and they're not reopening until the New Year.'

'But we get time off soon. What's the point in giving us time off if they shut down one of the only things we can do for fun around here?'

'There's going to be entertainment but strictly on base.' Toby handed Gordon a towel to dry his hands. 'Some singing and dancing performances from the boys in Engineering, apparently. Maybe you and Andy can sign up to be a double act.'

Gordon ignored the joke. 'If all the shows are on the base, I'm guessing that means none of the Japanese girls can come.'

'I reckon you're probably right.' Toby sniffed. 'Almost like they did that deliberately for our first real holiday here.'

Gordon's heart sank. It had been frustrating enough waiting to take Cherry out. He didn't want to wait until January for his next opportunity.

'Are you and Yonnie doing anything tonight?' Gordon asked.

Toby's eyes lit up. 'You thinking a double date?'

It wasn't a double date in the traditional sense. There wasn't a place they could take Cherry and Yoneko, share a table, talk and laugh together. The BCOF definition of a double date was Gordon and Toby heading into town, slipping through the market, Gordon chatting in simple English to the Japanese who recognised him and came over to say hello. Tonight of all nights, Gordon didn't want to draw any attention to himself. They made it to the other side of town, the door to the brothel shut but life pulsing within. Instead, Gordon and Toby headed for the cinema.

The cinema was an open hall with a projector, showing movies that no-one really understood – either the plot or how the films had ended up in Kure. When the cinema had first opened, there were no seats, but as it was the only legitimate form of entertainment in town outside of the hotels and izakaya drinking spots, it had acquired more furniture and moulded itself to the requests of the Western soldiers.

Gordon unlaced his boots to slide them off his feet. Toby was less bothered, kicking his off and leaving them in a heap at the back of the room. No shoes in the cinema was the one rule that hadn't changed with the BCOF presence in Kure. Many places Gordon went were run by Westerners in some capacity, so his shoes didn't need to come off. It wasn't often he went somewhere he was required to slip off his heavy Army boots, unless Charlie dragged him to someone's house or Gordon needed to go into a Japanese building. Setting his boots next to each other, Gordon headed in. Toby moved to go right but Gordon caught his arm.

'Let's sit here.' Gordon steered Toby to the left, a small aisle in the middle splitting the rows.

'Nah, but don't we want to be closer?'

'I think here's just fine in case there's any funny business.'

Toby grumbled but took a seat, Gordon settling next to him. There were already a handful of soldiers sitting on their own on the left, seats empty between them.

On the right were an equal amount of Japanese girls.

One row ahead of them on the right side of the aisle were Cherry and Yoneko, Toby's intended destination. Cherry glanced to Gordon, her face shining in the low light. Happiness shot through him. At least he had been able to give her this. They weren't sitting together, but that was a safer option, in case someone reported back to the MPs and, two days from now, Gordon found himself in trouble. The other girls there were a mix of housegirls from the base and street girls. Some of the soldiers brought the girls regularly, trying to curry favour with a night out and a date instead of paying.

Yoneko waved, standing so they could see her. Toby waved back, even more enthusiastically. Cherry pulled Yoneko back down and Gordon elbowed Toby in the ribs.

'Don't blow our cover.'

'Calm down, Parker.' Toby's gaze was fixed on the back of Yoneko's head. 'Everyone here's in the same boat.'

They wouldn't get another chance to do this, even with Gordon's date sitting miles away. Gordon settled back in his seat, his long legs stretching out in front of him, watching Cherry as she spoke with Yoneko, heads bowed. He didn't know how she did it, but she was always bubbling with happiness, even sitting here with a girl she barely knew. The two of them had met only hours earlier and had come together, the parallel of Gordon and Toby.

The lights dimmed and a hush fell over the audience. Cherry threw a final look back to Gordon as the lights faded, and he gave her a wink as she disappeared in the darkness.

The movie had barely started when a whistle screeched, the doors bursting open. The lights snapped on, revealing four Military Police officers. Instinctively leaping to his feet, Gordon's heart sank as Billy charged in, whistle in his mouth. None of the MPs took off their boots, the dust and dirt of the city falling from their shoes onto the tatami floors as they crashed into the room.

'That's enough of that,' Billy said, sneering.

'Enough of what?' Toby asked.

Billy shook his head. 'I could book you all, right here and now, for fraternisation.'

'How?' The word was out of Gordon's mouth before he could stop it. Behind Billy, Gordon could see Cherry and Yoneko, on their feet and far away from their seats, having retreated at the MPs arrival. Cherry clung to Yoneko, terrified. Gordon stood taller. 'I'm here with Westy. I haven't fraternised with any of the Japanese, unless you count the bloke I bought the ticket from, and I don't think it's against the rules to buy something. I haven't said a peep to any of those Japanese sheilas. None of us have.'

'He hasn't.' A voice piped up behind Gordon, another soldier. 'He's been with his mate the whole time.'

'Or are there new rules where you can't be within one yard of a Japanese now?' Toby asked.

No-one moved, waiting for Billy to make a decision.

Bolstered by Billy's silence, Gordon crossed his arms. 'Mate, do you mind if we get back to the film?'

Billy stepped up to Gordon, who refused to give ground. 'I'm watching you, Parker. I don't know which of these is your Nip girl but when I find out ...'

'Chuck a sock in it, Richardson,' Toby said. 'You're the only one who likes the sound of your voice.'

Billy scanned over the girls, as though trying to work out who was there with Gordon. Gordon refused to look at Cherry. Thwarted, Billy strode out, followed by his fellow officers, dusty boots thudding into the distance.

Gordon steadied himself and Toby clapped his hands, the nervous energy in the room thrumming. Some of the girls drifted over to their dates, seeking comfort and reassurance. Cherry and Yoneko stayed away, stealing glances at Gordon and Toby.

'Guess we should've picked that,' Toby said. 'Tonight's the last night, after all. Makes sense they'd have a sniff around.'

'Do you reckon they'll come back?' Gordon asked. Cherry and Yoneko were talking with some of the other girls. 'I don't reckon Billy's done for the night.'

'She'll be right.' Toby shrugged. 'You're being paranoid.'

Discomfort lodged in Gordon's chest.

'You stick around then.' He rummaged in his pocket for a scrap of paper. 'I'm not going to wait for Richardson to spring me.' He pulled a pen from Toby's pocket and gestured for him to turn around. Using Toby's back as a table, Gordon drew one of the only kanji symbols he knew – the character for river – onto it. Three vertical lines, the left with a small curve at the bottom. Gordon folded it up and tossed it towards Cherry and Yoneko as he walked back down the aisle. Toby hesitated, torn, then darted after him.

'You're so bloody cautious,' Toby said, pulling on his boots. 'It's like being best mates with Safety Sam.'

'Yeah, well, if everything was up to you, we'd probably have been sent back to Australia by now, so don't get all funny about me trying to keep us out of trouble.' Gordon laced his boots, determined not to look back at Cherry. He hoped she'd seen him drop the paper and understand that 'river' meant the spot by the creek where they'd met months ago. Toby struggled to get his boots on, Gordon waiting impatiently with him. The other soldiers shared Toby's view, it seemed, that now the MPs had done their sweep, it was safe to publicly couple with their date, arms slung over shoulders, whispering in ears. Cherry and Yoneko had taken their seats again, but Gordon couldn't see if his message was still on the floor.

Toby scowled as he stood. 'That could be us, mate.' He gestured towards a soldier who was laughing with his girl, and sighed as they left.

They stepped into the fresh winter air. Toby continued to grumble as they headed through the market, still bustling with nightlife. Gordon ignored Toby's complaints as they walked back to base, cutting through the yard to the back fence to get to the creek. The moon was bright, lighting their way as they picked through the undergrowth, found the small clearing and waited.

Twenty minutes later, Yoneko burst through the bushes, sprinting into Toby's arms, shrieking as he spun her around. Gordon stood as Cherry appeared, cheeks pink.

'You all right?' he asked. To his surprise, she wrapped her arms around him. Gordon swallowed as blood rushed through him with Cherry pressed against his body.

'They arrest all people,' Cherry said. 'Yoneko and I leave with some girls and then men come back. They catch all girls with soldiers, take all away. We just miss. Very close.'

'We're safe here.' Gordon cupped her face in his hands. 'No-one knows about this spot except us.' He pulled her into a hug, trying to quell the thud of his own heart. Over the top of her head, he shot a pointed look to Toby.

'We're fine, aren't we?' Toby said. 'We listened to you. Maybe it wasn't such a bad idea, after all.'

Gordon fought the urge to roll his eyes. 'You owe me, West.'

'You've got a pretty girl in your arms and half the night to spend with her.' Toby was wrapped around Yoneko. 'Don't waste it thinking about me.' He kissed Yoneko and they left the clearing, giggling as they went further into the scrub.

The night settled around them as Gordon and Cherry sat on the bank of the creek.

'Sorry the movie turned out so bad,' Gordon said, then summoned his courage. 'Gomen-na-sigh, Cherry. Should've probably guessed it. Er – wa-ru-ee dess. De-shi-ta. It was bad.'

Cherry bit back a smile and Gordon's face flushed.

'My Japanese is bad too, yeah. Er – ni-hon-go wa wa-ru-ee dess.' Gordon racked his brain as he tried to remember the Japanese word for 'too'. He couldn't. 'As well.'

Cherry shifted to look at him. 'Your Japanese good. Just more practice,' she said. 'You say – nihongo mo warui desu-ne.'

Gordon couldn't hide the laugh that tore out of his throat. The words fell off her tongue so beautifully. When Cherry spoke Japanese, it was like music. Sometimes Japanese sounded sharp, a tight rhythm to the language, but Cherry's voice was soft and lilting, and Gordon had no idea how she ever understood a word he said. His Japanese was ugly and ragged, badly pronounced in his Australian accent, and some of the sounds he could never get his tongue around.

'I don't even know where to start with that.' Gordon ran a hand through his hair. 'Japanese isn't easy to learn.'

'Japanese difficult for you? Muzukashii desu ka?'

'My word, is it ever.' Gordon turned a pebble over in his hands. 'You say everything back to front. I can't read any of the actual words. I can barely count to ten most days.'

Cherry laughed. 'Count to ten very easy. We practise.' She picked up his hand, her slender fingers dwarfed by his calloused ones. Gordon's breath caught but Cherry didn't seem to notice. She took the rock from his hands and set it down, then touched his left thumb, then his left forefinger.

'One, two. Ichi, ni.'

'I know them. Itchy knee. I get to three and then I forget them. Itchy knee, san …'

'Shi.' Cherry touched his ring finger. 'Go.' She touched his little finger for number five.

'She go.' Gordon's voice was soft. He was intensely aware of Cherry's touch, the warmth in her hands flaring against his own. Could she feel how his palms had started to sweat? 'Itchy knee, san, she go.'

'Hai. Yes.' Cherry moved to his right thumb and counted off the rest of his fingers. 'Roku. Shichi. Hachi. Kyuu. Jyuu.' She came back to his right thumb, her arm resting gently against his thigh. Gordon tried to focus.

'Rock. Hitchy. Hatchi. Queue. Jew.'

'Very good. From start?' Cherry's hands moved back to the beginning, one hand around Gordon's wrist, the other tapping against his fingers.

'Itchy knee. San … She go.' Gordon swallowed as Cherry shifted to his other hand. 'Rock. Er … '

'Shichi.'

'Yeah, righto. Hitchy. Hatchi. Queue. Jew.'

'Again?'

'Itchy knee.' Gordon wanted to kiss her. 'San. She go.' There wasn't any way Cherry couldn't feel how hot he was. 'Rock. Hitchy. Hatchi.' Her eyes sparkled in the moonlight, smile wide as she brushed her fingers over his. 'Queue. Jew.' He had to have slipped into a dream.

'Perfect!' Cherry said, beaming. Gordon clasped her hands tighter. 'Totemo jouzu desu. You are very skilled.'

'You're a good teacher,' he said. He stroked the back of her hand with his thumb. Cherry kept smiling. A wave of relief rushed through him and, before he could overthink it, Gordon leaned forward and kissed her.

She was still at first. Gordon's heart hammered and he pulled away, terrified he'd overstepped. Cherry looked shocked, unable to hide her surprise.

'Sorry,' Gordon said. 'I'm sorry, I—'

Then Cherry leaned forward and kissed him back.

CHAPTER ELEVEN

NOBUKO: Kure, December 1946

The memory of their first kiss kept Nobuko company as she waited for the bus, her breath small puffs of fog in the cool night. The memory of their second kiss wound itself around the wait to collect the cleaning supplies for the day. Their third and fourth kisses waited for Nobuko as she stepped into rooms to clean them, those remembered moments tantalising and sweet. Over the weeks since their trip to the cinema, Don often met her by the creek. One night, a night he called Christmas Eve, he met her with his bag. Nobuko was worried he was leaving, but he pulled out something wrapped in newspaper.

'It's not much, but I had to get you a Christmas pressie.'

She opened the package and her heart dropped. Inside was a blue woollen dress, plus a hand-knitted scarf and mittens, in beautiful red and navy.

'What is this?' Nobuko realised she'd spoken in Japanese. 'What is this?' she said again in English.

Don's eyes were downcast, almost as though he couldn't make eye contact. 'You're always wearing the same clothes and it's cold now. So I wrote to Mum and asked her to send one of June's old dresses. But I think this is from a shop in town. And Mum made the scarf and mittens for me, but I wanted to give them to you. They're Melbourne colours. Red and blue Demons.'

'Demons?' Cherry asked, frowning.

'It's a footy team. Sports. Australian Rules football. Not real demons.'

The English took a moment to translate. 'These come from Australia?'

He nodded. 'Yup. Ridgy-didge Mrs Parker special.'

She brought the scarf to her nose and inhaled. It smelt like wool, a deep note of sheep buried beneath soap, perhaps a touch of lavender. A small souvenir from Down Under, knitted by his mother. The dress was heavy and beautiful. It would keep her warm as winter chilled further.

'You tell Mum about me?'

Don hesitated. 'Not exactly. I said I've got some good Japanese friends who need some warm clothes and that it's expensive here. She sent some things for Charlie too.'

It was too much for Nobuko to accept the gifts, especially the scarf with such beautiful and neat stitching, so she pushed them back into Don's hands. 'I cannot have. Thank you. These are yours.'

He deftly wrapped the scarf around her neck. 'You can have. Harry-gato. I've got more than enough stuff to keep me warm over winter and I don't want you to catch a cold. Please take it. Kudda-sigh.'

Nobuko bit back a smile. Don's Japanese pronunciation needed a lot of work, but she loved that he tried. 'Okay. I keep them safe. I wear.'

'That'd make me real happy.'

Nobuko wasn't sure what number kiss they were up to now. She just hoped they never stopped.

For a few days after Christmas Eve, Nobuko was given holidays from her work on the base. She didn't want to take them but had no choice. Instead, she cooked and sewed with Suma and Amari, holding her secrets tightly to herself. She hadn't told anyone about Don, and Suma hadn't said anything after she'd caught them together the night of the festival. Nobuko had hidden the scarf and mittens in the back of a cupboard, determined to keep them safe. It was easier to smuggle them out of the house and only put them on once she was halfway to the bus stop. Noboru had barely even noticed the new woollen dress.

Nobuko tried to focus on her sewing as Amari talked about going to Osaka for her studies later in the year. As the others chatted, Nobuko unpicked stitches in a dress that had a hole in one side. The good material would be repurposed and the damaged material would become rags. It was mindless, repetitive work and Nobuko's thoughts drifted to her favourite subject. Don.

The fact that several months ago she had been terrified of working on the base and now she desperately wanted to be there wasn't lost on Nobuko. A simple connection had completely changed her everyday world. She thought about Don more and more, wondering if he was busy tending to a patient, or racing towards the mess hall for lunch. If she had been on the base, she would have chosen paths to take her close to Medical, just to catch a glimpse of him. Don had said that Andy didn't mind her coming in, that he considered her to be an honorary member of staff after Nobuko had helped with Ami's dislocated shoulder.

There was something captivating for Nobuko in watching Don when he worked; his head bowed over a patient, the way his forehead creased between his eyebrows. She never loitered anywhere for long, scared she would get in trouble, but no-one ever really noticed her. When Don wasn't around, she was another invisible Japanese girl. Most of the time, anyway. Sometimes the ex-enemy soldiers would shout out things to her as she walked off the base at twilight, the men already a little drunk. Nobuko didn't need to understand their words to recognise the intent. There were stories of other girls who had worked at the base, enough to make her cautious. Some girls who had welcomed the attention from Westerners had disappeared and no longer worked for the Army. Other girls refused to return to work after they'd been approached by a group of soldiers. It didn't seem to matter what country they were from, dangerous men lurked in every unit of BCOF.

'Nobuko, what are you thinking about?' Suma looked over from where she was drying bowls. 'You're scrunching up your face.'

'These stitches are tight,' Nobuko said, shaking out fingers that had locked around Suma's small unpicker. Nobuko had no idea where Suma had found it, especially considering it had English on the handle. The letters spelt *England*, somewhere Suma had never been. The small tool made tearing the thread much easier than using a knife or scissors.

'Nobuko, maybe you should come to Osaka with me,' Amari said. Nobuko looked up, surprised. 'You have a few days off work, don't you? Perhaps we could go on an adventure together.'

She didn't know what to say. Since Hiroshima, Nobuko hated the idea of travelling outside of Kure without her father. Regardless of how late she worked or how early she needed to leave the next morning, she always came home to her father at night. Even on the days he was sick or angry, he was her anchor point. If he was still there in the morning, so was she.

'I'm sorry, it's not a good time for me now,' she said, carefully choosing her words. 'Perhaps when you are set up at university, I will come to visit.'

'But I thought you could practise your English.' Amari said. Nobuko shot her a panicked look, but she didn't notice. 'There will be lots of people who speak it, maybe even Englishmen—'

'You are learning English, Nobuko-chan?' Suma asked, her voice sharp.

'A little,' Nobuko said, meekly. 'It was difficult on the base to have no English. Amari taught me for work.'

'What English do you know?' Suma's voice betrayed her suspicion and Nobuko exchanged a look with Amari, whose hands were on her mouth, apologetic.

'Laundaree, please,' Nobuko said, the English bouncing off her tongue. 'Boots, please. Thank you very much. Goodbye.'

Suma held Nobuko's gaze, unimpressed. 'Anything else?'

Nobuko gave a small smile. 'Ge-day matu.'

Nobuko did not go to Osaka. Suma decided it was better for Amari to go on her own. Nobuko stayed in Kure, counting the days until she was back on the base. It felt like an eternity, but the moment she stepped off the bus, it seemed like the time had passed in an instant. She didn't enter through the main gates, instead heading to the stream in case Don had had the same idea. Even if he hadn't, Nobuko wanted to take a deep breath in a place that felt like theirs, to soak up her daydreams before her work started.

As she stepped through the undergrowth, whistling filtered through the bare sakura branches. Had someone else found their spot? Nobuko braced herself to dart past the clearing. She clutched the end of her Demons scarf and peered through the trees.

It was Don. He was sitting on a rock, wrapped in a heavy coat against the cold, whistling as he focussed on something in his hands. Nobuko stepped out, unable to hide her smile.

'Good morning, Don-san!'

Don's head whipped around, lighting up with delight. He bounded over to her. 'Oh-hi-yo, Cherry-san. That scarf looks swell on you. Really great.' He wrapped her in his arms, his warm body enveloping hers. Nobuko breathed him in, warmth and spice and safety. Too soon, he pulled away. 'I had an inkling, you know. Just had a feeling you might come this way this morning.'

'I happy you are here, Don-san.'

'Me too. Wa-ta-shi mo. You sure are a sight for sore eyes.'

Nobuko wasn't sure what he meant, but his smile told her everything. He led her back to where he was sitting, a letter on the ground where he had dropped it.

'From home?' she asked.

Don had told her about his family. He had lots of brothers and sisters. June was saving up to buy a motorcycle and Don's father was considering running for mayor of Ringwood for the second time.

Nobuko was curious about Don's mother most of all, the woman that had raised children in the Australian bush and knitted scarves for Demons.

He picked up the letter. 'Yes, it's from home.'

'Will you read to me?'

'You don't want to hear this – there's nothing interesting in it.'

'From Mum?'

'Yeah.'

'That is interesting for me.'

Don looked at her, amused. 'You sure? You won't find it boring?' Nobuko shook her head. 'No worries. Let's see.'

The two of them huddled together in the frosty morning as he read the letter aloud. Nobuko didn't understand it all, especially when Don went off on tangents to explain things to her in lengthy chunks of English. She didn't mind. It wasn't the contents of the letter she was interested in. It was the way his eyes sparkled when something connected to his heart. The pride in his voice. The homesickness that slipped out among the delight. He missed his family. Nobuko often stopped by his bed to look at his photos, but now she knew their names. Don's words flowed over her, his voice a deep melody, rough around the edges. A voice she could listen to forever.

'We all miss you very much and can't wait to have you back among the gum trees. Love Mum, Dad and all of us.' Don folded the letter shut.

Nobuko touched his hands. 'What is gum trees?'

'They're big silver trees. Like sakura but taller. They have green leaves and you never want to put your tent under one. They drop their branches if you sneeze nearby. Koalas live in them.'

'Ko-a-las?'

'Koalas?' Don exhaled. 'How can I explain koalas? They're grey and fluffy. Big ears. Like mine.' Don touched his ears and Nobuko laughed.

'Maybe one day I write letter to Mum. Say konnichiwa from Japan?'

Don hesitated, then nodded. 'Sure. Yeah. If you write one, I'll send it with mine.'

She couldn't stop thinking about the letter. It seemed foolish that she'd offered, but it would be more embarrassing if she didn't give something to Don. Her English writing needed work and Amari still wasn't back from Osaka. In her mind, Nobuko composed version after version, unsure what to say but wanting to remain polite and respectful. Don didn't press her for it and Nobuko was glad, desperate for Amari to return before he sent anything home. After over a month, Nobuko had something she was happy with, written in Amari's notebook, Amari keeping it safe so Noboru would never find it.

Nobuko sent best wishes from Kure and hoped they had a good Christmas and New Year, even though both holidays would be a distant memory by the time the letter arrived in Ringwood. At the end, she wrote that she hoped to visit them in Australia one day, a sentiment she wrote more to be polite than truthful. She signed her name in her Japanese kanji, then wrote the English underneath – Cherry.

Before she could overthink it, she gave the letter to Don, who seemed surprised. He promised he'd include it in his next parcel to Australia and tucked it into his pocket.

Nobuko forgot about the letter. She focussed on her work, on spending time when she could with Don. One day, when the snow had thawed and the sun shone through a brittle spring morning, Nobuko was astonished to discover she'd been assigned to work in the medical unit as their main cleaner. She floated to the medical wing, barely aware of where she was going, until suddenly she was standing in front of a sheepish Don.

'Andy and I reckoned we could use a bit of extra help. If you don't want to, that's okay. I can get someone else.'

'I want to,' Nobuko said, heart soaring. 'I want to.'

Twice a week, Nobuko met Don early at the stream so they could sit and talk. He would return to the base first and she would walk back to the main gate of the compound to catch the bus. She spent her mornings in the medical unit cleaning, making beds or tidying, keeping out of the way if there were several patients there. Nobuko had been worried Andy would be annoyed by her friendship with Don, but Andy seemed to enjoy having her around. There were moments when she thought he might ask her something, terrified whether her English would be good enough to understand him, but he would just say she was doing a bonza job. Nobuko asked Don what it meant.

'Bonza? It means great. The best there is. Bit of Aussie slang for you.'

'Bon-za,' Nobuko repeated, the word odd on her tongue. Charlie parroted it and, clutching a toy aeroplane from the battered box in the corner that Don's mother had sent months ago, raced around the room repeating it over and over.

'Tell you what. Why don't we do some English lessons when things aren't too busy here? Maybe you could teach me some Japanese too.'

They did. As the days rolled by, Nobuko picked up more English, sneaking time with Don by the stream, often with Toby and Yoneko nearby. They were much more open about their relationship than Don and Nobuko were, Yoneko already dreaming about marrying the gaijin – the foreigner. She constantly talked about her dream life in Newcastle with Toby, married with children and money.

Yoneko wasn't the only girl dreaming of an Australian life. The longer the soldiers were in Japan, the more girls they became involved with and the more the Army seemed to be concerned about fraternisation. Nobuko overheard Don and Andy talking one afternoon, discussing how the BCOF officials had closed down the hotels in town, in a bid to stop disease from spreading. Some soldiers who came to the medical unit didn't seem to have anything wrong with them and Don went pink when Nobuko asked why they were there, sidestepping her question. His avoidance explained everything.

Her job on the base meant she had a steady income and was fed while she worked. Many other women didn't have that choice. Some, called suki-suki girls, sold their bodies to soldiers from the relative safety of the brothels. Others walked the streets to find a drunk BCOF soldier with some spare yen. There were stories of women snatched up by Western soldiers who decided that the lady in front of him was a suki-suki girl, whether that was true or not. A few yen tossed to them after they were finished made them a suki-suki girl regardless.

Some women had no other way but prostitution to make their money. Work on the base was highly sought after and Nobuko was thankful she had work that gave her safety and provided for her family without her needing to sell herself.

'That is very kind, thank you,' Don said.

'That is very kind, thank you,' Nobuko and Charlie chorused in English. She folded the sheets as Don sorted through the supplies cupboard, Charlie helping stack what they had left.

'No, I don't want any.' Don shook his head, exaggerated.

She copied him. 'No, I don't want any.'

Charlie giggled and Don caught Nobuko's eye.

'You look beautiful today.'

She couldn't hide her smile, smoothing out the creases in the sheets. Andy walked in, interrupting the moment.

'What's all this? Don Sensei's English lesson?'

'Something like that.' Don dusted off his hands. 'Don Sensei's running low on bandages and gauze. Reckon I should do a run to the hospital?'

'Wouldn't hurt.' Andy rubbed his chin. 'Might need to take a translator along with you.'

Don turned to Nobuko and took a steadying breath.

'Cherry, will you come to the hospital with me?' he said in his best Japanese yet.

Nobuko followed Gordon at a distance as they walked to the hospital, ready to catch every glance he threw her way. He took them on a longer, winding route and she was happy for it, pleased to spend the time with him, although he was yards ahead of her. They walked through the market, Don lingering by stalls before moving on, Nobuko copying him, picking up the trinket he'd been admiring moments before. The warmth of his hand transferred from the object into her palm, touching invisible fingerprints.

Their game was interrupted by a squeal. Yoneko burst through the crowd, racing to Nobuko, neatly dressed and face flushed.

'We did it! We did it!' she shrieked in Japanese.

'Did what?' Nobuko asked. Behind Yoneko, Toby was with Don, looking stunned.

'We got married!' Yoneko declared, spinning on the spot.

Nobuko stared at her friend. 'Where? How?'

'There's a shrine outside town. The priest marries soldiers to local girls for some yen. Toby looked so handsome!'

'It was a real Japanese ceremony?'

'Without the kimono and the expense but it was real. I'm Toby's wife now.' Yoneko sighed, her hands clasped over her chest. Nobuko smiled with her.

Scanning the crowd and seeing no Military Police, Nobuko picked her way to the Australian soldiers. 'This good news,' Nobuko said in English. Don nodded, punching Toby on the shoulder. 'Don-san, we buy wedding present?'

There was a paper stall at the edge of the market, filled with a limited supply of washi paper, silk threads, cord and parchment. Nobuko wanted the best quality to make a mizuhiki knot to bring Toby and Yoneko luck in their marriage. Don loitered nearby. There was a pre-tied musubi-kiri knot, the paper and silken threads twisted around themselves, the knot symbolising the fastening of marriage.

'Maybe this.' Nobuko showed it to him. 'This is marriage knot. Very special. Perfect gift for Japanese wedding.'

'Righto, if you say so. Let's give them that.' He put his hand into his pocket, the stall owner stepping forward. Before Nobuko could say anything, a sharp whistle pierced the air.

An MP officer strode over from a nearby truck, a second following close behind. Nobuko's stomach clenched. It was the man who had been at the cinema. She shrank back against the stall as the officers stopped in front of Don.

'Parker, were you talking to this woman?'

'Billy, this is Miss Sakuramoto.' Don gestured to Nobuko. She didn't move. 'She's a housegirl at the barracks and we're headed to the hospital to get some extra supplies.'

Billy looked around the paper stall. 'This doesn't look like the hospital. What do you think, Jones?'

Jones scoffed.

Don let out a chuckle. 'We got a bit waylaid. It's still official BCOF business—'

'I'm charging you under breach of the BCOF anti-fraternisation rules—'

'Mate—'

'I am not your mate.' Billy's words cut across Don, the surprise on Don's face sending dread through Nobuko. 'As a member of the Military Police, I am expected to keep Australian troops safe from nefarious influences.'

Don bristled. Nobuko repeated the sentence in her head, trying to unpick the meaning.

'What are you trying to say?' Don's voice was rough but wary.

Billy smirked and turned to Nobuko. 'I am arresting you under suspicion of prostitution.'

Billy's English was quick and sharp, but she knew what that word meant. Prostitute. 'No, please—'

'Wait on—' Don stepped forward and Jones grabbed him. Billy grasped Nobuko's wrists. She tried to pull away, but he gripped her more tightly.

'We'll take you for examination for any evidence of VD—'

Nobuko couldn't understand him now. She only knew the panic in her body and his rough hands on her wrists.

Don's voice broke through her terror. 'You're bloody joking. She's no prostitute. She works in the barracks, for Pete's sake—'

'What's she doing with you then?'

'Because I asked her.'

Billy dragged her forward, Nobuko pulling against his grip. Helplessness descended on her, a fear she hadn't felt since she had walked away from the ruins at Hiroshima.

Billy leaned into Don, Don still restrained by Jones.

'If I had sixpence for every bloke who swore their girl wasn't a prostitute, I'd be richer than the bloody King of England.' Billy grinned. 'Told you I'd get your girl one day, Parker.'

Billy pulled at Nobuko. The sharp tug on her shoulders sent a throb of pain through her back and she found her voice. 'No! Please! Don-san! No!' She was thrown into the back of a truck, sobbing as she scrambled for the window. Don shoved Jones aside and raced for her.

Billy stepped in front of him. 'Careful.' His voice was laced with smug warning. 'I swear you're starting to go slanty-eyed.'

Even from the small window in the truck, Nobuko could see Don was shaking with rage.

'Be sure to report to CO Kerr to discuss your fraternisation charge.' Billy and Jones stepped away from Don and climbed into the truck.

As soon as the doors shut, Don darted to the window. 'Don't worry, Cherry. I'll get you out. They're bastards, the lot of them.'

'Don-san, please—' Nobuko's voice was swallowed as the engine roared to life, the vibration making her unsteady. The truck lurched forward and she caught herself from falling. Don shouted, running alongside the truck as they drove, refusing to stop until the truck had outpaced him.

Nobuko stared after him, his distraught face etched in her memory, still able to see him even after he'd disappeared into dust, after they'd turned corner after corner, taking her away from Kure.

She didn't know where they were going, but it wasn't a short drive. She sat on one of the bench seats, the vehicle dark and dirty, every bump in the road jolting through her body.

Outside, the city around them dissolved into rubble. Nobuko's breath constricted in her throat. They were heading to Hiroshima. She turned away, her fear solidifying to numbness, staring into the middle distance. She didn't want to look out the window. She didn't want to remember.

The truck stopped. Nobuko was thrown forward, barely able to put her hands out to protect herself. She scrambled away from the entrance. Billy appeared, a cigarette on his lips. He clicked his fingers at her.

'Come on.'

Nobuko didn't move. Couldn't move. Billy climbed into the truck, grabbing her dress.

'I said, come on.' He pushed her out of the truck, dust flying as she landed on her knees. They were outside a Japanese police station. Billy wrapped his hand around Nobuko's upper arm and pulled her towards the building. She stopped resisting. There was no point.

Billy handed her over to the police officer, who eyed her with distaste, then she was thrown into a room with three other women. None of them spoke. One woman's dress was torn at the side, a ragged hole revealing her stomach and chest. She desperately tried to hold it closed. One woman lay curled on the floor, asleep. The third sat with her back against the wall, legs tucked up in front of her, hair knotted and one of her eyes swollen shut. Nobuko sat on the floor near her. She gave Nobuko a sympathetic smile, reached out and took Nobuko's hand. Nobuko wrapped her fingers around the woman's, grateful for even a little kindness.

One by one, the other women disappeared. Fetched by a policeman, taken away as the door closed with a thud. Outside, the day ended and night crept in. Nobuko was alone in the room, shaking. She had no idea how long she had been there for.

It was dark when the door opened once again.

They took her to a room. A cold medical bed was inside. They pushed her to it, instructed her to lie down. A male police officer stood at the head of the bed, a male doctor at the foot. They spoke but she could barely comprehend them, the words holding no meaning.

The policeman slapped her across the face.

'Open your legs,' he said. Nobuko shook her head. 'Open them.'

'I'm a housegirl,' she whispered. 'I work at BCOF in Kure. I am no prostitute.'

The policeman sniffed. 'Open your legs. We need to test if you're clean. If you don't, I will hold you down so we can do it, anyway. It's better if you co-operate.'

Nobuko closed her eyes.

And opened her legs.

CHAPTER TWELVE

GORDON: Kure, April 1947

'She's not in Kure.'

The words sat like lead in Gordon's chest. 'What? What do you mean?'

'They must've taken her somewhere else.'

Gordon stared at his CO, Harold Kerr, not comprehending. When the truck had disappeared, he'd sprinted back to base and demanded to speak with Kerr. Panicked, he tried to convince Kerr to help find Cherry, his CO promising to call the MPs to find out where she might've been sent.

Cherry wasn't in Kure.

'Why would they take her at all? She's a bloody housegirl, not some prostitute—'

'You know the rules on fraternisation, Parker.' Kerr's ginger moustache bounced as he spoke, his pale eyes sympathetic. 'You shouldn't have been with her in the first place.'

'We were on BCOF business,' Gordon said. 'We were going to the hospital to get supplies for Medical.'

'Then why did they take her?' Kerr asked. 'Where were you at the time?'

Gordon hesitated. 'We stopped at a shop. But it wasn't anything dodgy.'

Kerr sighed. 'I'd like to help you. I would. But this, coupled with the letter … my hands are tied, I'm afraid.'

'What letter?' Gordon asked.

'I have received a message from your mother.'

It took Gordon a second to comprehend what Kerr had said.

'She's concerned about your friendship with a Japanese girl. I assume it's this Cherry.'

'Wait on, my *mother* wrote to you?'

'Don't fret, I will reply and assure your mother there is nothing between you and this girl. You will be restricted to base for the next month—'

'Sir—'

'You are not to leave the confines of the grounds for any reason. The rules on fraternisation are strict. There's nothing else I can do.'

Gordon's head spun. Kerr was a CO. Surely he could do anything. It wasn't right that Cherry had been seized because Billy was a mongrel. It wasn't right that Kerr was refusing to help because Gordon's mother had written a letter to the Army.

Gordon seethed with anger. Squaring his shoulders, he spoke before he could change his mind. 'Perhaps I should report you for fraternisation then, sir.'

Kerr looked at him, incredulous. 'Come again, boy?'

There was an unmistakable warning in his superior's tone and Gordon faltered. He couldn't get the image of Cherry's frightened face pressed against the window of the truck out of his mind. It was enough. 'I imagine it was quite a blow when your favourite brothel closed down. They've shut down the brothels for all servicemen, haven't they? Or is there an exception for Commanding Officers?'

Kerr leaned forward. 'Are you sure you want to play it this way, son?'

Gordon held Kerr's gaze. He and Cherry hadn't done anything wrong. If he was the only person who would stand up for Cherry, so be it.

Kerr took a deep, controlled breath. 'Wait here. Don't you move an inch, Parker.'

He strode out of the room. The door shut behind him and Gordon exhaled, the tension leaching out of his body. He'd threatened his CO. There was a chance that Kerr had gone to fetch an MP officer, ready to throw Gordon onto the first boat back to Sydney. He refused to think about it. He'd done it for a good reason. Cherry didn't deserve to be treated badly just because she was friends with him. He'd done what was right. It was what his father had always taught him.

The door opened and Kerr returned. He didn't look at Gordon as he sat at his desk, rifling through paperwork. Gordon waited, resisting the urge to beg Kerr for information.

Eventually, Kerr looked up. 'They took her to the Hiroshima police.'

'Great,' Gordon said. 'So get her back.'

Kerr shook his head. 'This is above me now. There's nothing more I can do. The MPs have done nothing wrong. If they suspected her of prostitution, they have to send her for testing.'

'This is Richardson.' Gordon paced, fury building. 'He's trying to get to me, trying to piss me off.'

'Seems like it's working,' Kerr said, voice dry. Gordon glared at him, the CO raising a single eyebrow. 'If you want my advice, I'd take this opportunity to forget her. Take up with an Australian girl. There'll be nurses arriving soon from home. Pick one of them. Trust me. It'll be better for your kids.'

It was all Gordon could do to control his anger. Bursting from Kerr's office, he made for the creek, sitting under the budding cherry blossom tree, its dark branches jutting into the sky. He couldn't sit still, frustration coursing through him as he paced, furious that his mother had meddled where she had no right to. Even from the other side of the world. How had she even become so fixated on Cherry?

Gordon stopped walking.

It was his fault. He'd sent Cherry's letter home. He hadn't been sure about it, but the letter hadn't had anything incriminating inside. It had been a last-minute addition to his own letters, which only mentioned Cherry and Charlie in passing. Gordon hadn't told his family anything about him and Cherry. It wasn't any of their business and yet they'd become suspicious anyway. He should have known better. He should have known Venn would read it and get her nose out of joint. She got suspicious if Gordon even mentioned a girl in passing and he'd asked his mother to send supplies and winter clothes for Cherry. Even though it had been in the same sentence as Charlie, Cherry was a girl, a Japanese girl. Thinking about it now, it seemed obvious Venn would have misgivings about any Japanese girl Gordon mentioned. He'd just never imagined his mother would write a letter full of those misgivings to his CO.

Gordon groaned as he sank down among the roots of the tree, watching the path, waiting for Cherry to appear, to assure him she was all right. It was his fault she was in this mess.

She didn't show up.

Gordon couldn't focus on work the next day. He had barely slept, guilt tearing through him, stomach churning as he saw Cherry screaming at him from the back of the truck, Billy's smug grin as he stepped into the vehicle. Gordon had got confident, thought he'd found the right loophole to protect them both, but had put them in danger instead.

'What's up your nose?' Andy asked, exasperated, when Gordon glanced to the door once again. The footsteps continued past Medical and didn't stop.

Disappointed, Gordon sagged. 'They arrested Cherry yesterday.'

Andy said nothing. His silence spoke volumes.

The door squeaked open. Gordon turned, hopeful. 'Cherry?'

A different housegirl stood in the doorway, looking terrified. Gordon's heart sank.

'Sorry,' she said, and began to back out of the room.

'Wait.' Gordon stopped himself from grabbing her arm. 'Cherry. Cherry-san, the girl who usually cleans this room – where is she? Is she back yet?'

'Sorry,' the girl said again. 'No English.'

'Nobuko,' Gordon said, desperate. 'You know Nobuko?'

The girl shook her head and hurried away. Gordon rubbed his face, angry and frustrated all at once.

Gordon left the base as soon as he'd finished for the day, sneaking out through the creek to get into town. He wasn't sure who was on the gate and didn't want to risk being caught, considering he was supposed to be confined to the barracks. If Cherry had come to work and greeted him with her radiant smile, he would've served out his punishment impatiently but fully. She never arrived. Gordon hadn't seen Billy either and, while that was less strange, he couldn't shake the feeling that Billy had done something to Cherry to make a point.

He boarded a bus heading away from BCOF, ignoring the stares of Japanese passengers who couldn't tear their eyes away from the white man on their route. He'd paid too much for the fare, but when the driver had stood up to give the right change, Gordon had waved him away, cheeks burning. In the small mirror by the steering wheel, Gordon watched the driver slip the change into his pocket. The city rolled past and he scanned the horizon, trying to find something familiar, waiting for the shrine where the festival had been held. Once there, he retraced his steps, trying to recall which way he had gone to end up on Cherry's road, wading through blurry, concussed memories. He'd been walking for almost an hour when he recognised a sakura tree. Cherry had found him there the night of the festival, his lip split and bleeding.

Heart pounding, he followed the path up the hill, ignoring surprised looks from the locals. He wasn't welcome here, a stranger in khaki, an ex-enemy man. Pausing under the maple tree, his hiding place after the festival, he wondered if this was a good idea. Cherry's shack was so close though. He couldn't leave now. He had to know if she was all right.

Gordon stepped into the small garden of the shack. There was light inside, but the building was silent. Morose. Or maybe he was imagining it.

He knocked against the frame of the open door, the wood stinging his knuckles.

'Excuse me?' he called out, his voice breaking through the night. 'Sumi-masen?'

There was movement inside and, after a moment, a man came to the door. He had to be Cherry's father. They had the same shape to their chins, the same high cheekbones. He wore a navy kimono, the folds falling around his skinny body, shoulders slumped forward as he leaned against the door frame. His chest heaved with each breath, the effort of coming to the door clearly taxing. The man eyed Gordon, his anger obvious.

This no longer seemed like a good idea.

'Nobuko-san, is she here?' Gordon said in Japanese, his voice faltering.

'You,' the man replied, stepping towards Gordon. 'It is you.'

Gordon took a step back. Nobuko's father continued speaking Japanese, but Gordon's language skills were too poor to comprehend it. All he knew was that with every word, the man in front of him grew angrier.

'Nobuko,' Gordon said, racking his brain to find the words he needed. 'I am looking for Nobuko.'

In response, Cherry's father punched him in the face.

Gordon stumbled, pain erupting around his head, a metallic taste at the back of his mouth. He spat blood on the ground, trying to get clarity back. Another man ran out and pushed Gordon away. There was no sign of Cherry, not even a glimpse of her peeking out from around a door or a window.

'Is she okay?' Gordon asked in Japanese, his voice nasal and fluid. 'Nobuko-san. Is she okay?'

The two men disappeared inside, ignoring him. Defeated, Gordon left.

Cherry wasn't on the base the next day. Or the day after that. Another girl came to clean Medical, three girls on rotating shifts during the week. Gordon's anger simmered close to the surface, barely within his control. He snapped at Charlie, sending him into the city to see what he could find out, but the boy didn't reappear for two days. Gordon fought his own sense of guilt, no idea where Charlie had slept or where he had gone. The boy finally returned, but with no information. Refusing to give up, Gordon begged Yoneko to see what she could discover, sending her a message through Toby. He also tried to find Cherry's friends on the base, Hana or Michiko, but every time he spotted them, they would slip away before he got close. They were avoiding him. Not that he could blame them, but it made not knowing anything even harder.

Wrestling with an aching sense of hopelessness, Gordon did as he was told, staying on the base and not heading into town, determined not to give anyone a reason to ship him home before he found out where Cherry was. Toby, frustratingly happy in the wake of his marriage to Yoneko, reported that the shack near the maple tree was empty, with no sign of Cherry or her family. Yoneko promised to keep looking, but Gordon wasn't sure that he would ever see Cherry again.

Days turned into weeks. Gordon kept his head down, desperate for the day he could hunt for Cherry himself. He didn't have a plan, didn't know what he could do that others hadn't already tried, but he needed to do something. Letters arrived from his family but Gordon couldn't bring himself to read them, still furious his mother had gone over his head. He had a tentative hold on his temper as the end of his confinement to the base drew nearer.

Two days before he was allowed back into the outside world, Gordon, Toby and Slim were heading to the mess when they neared a group of MPs smoking by their trucks. Gordon's heart stopped when he saw Billy among them, laughing. He took a step forward, but Slim and Toby caught one arm each to stop him.

'Whoa, Nelly,' Slim said. 'Let's think this through before you go off accosting MPs.'

'He knows what happened to Cherry.' Gordon tried to shake them off, but both men kept their grip. 'He's the only one who knows.'

'She's a strong girl,' Toby said. 'Cherry'll be fine. Maybe she got a new job. Yonnie's still looking. She was waiting for someone who lives near the Hiroshima outpost to come by the market. We'll find her.'

'If you get up Richardson's nose, that's one way to be sure you never find out what happened to your girl,' Slim said. 'He'll make it easy for you to punch him so he can march you onto the next ship out of here.'

Gordon forced himself to settle.

'That's the way,' Toby said, letting go. At Gordon's stiff nod, Slim let go too. 'The best way to deal with the MPs is to ignore the bastards.'

They moved towards the mess, walking past Billy and his mates, who watched them as they passed. Gordon looked at the ground, oblivious to the forced conversation from Slim and Toby. They were trying to distract him, to keep Gordon's focus elsewhere. He could only hear a ringing in his ears, the thump of his heart in his chest, in his throat. He was determined not to look at Billy, not to give him the satisfaction of seeing how angry he was.

Billy's words cut through it all. 'Hey, Parker. Seen your girl lately?'

Gordon paused. Next to him, Toby and Slim tensed.

'Leave it,' Toby murmured.

'Thought you said she was a housegirl here.' Billy swaggered towards them. 'Don't reckon I've seen her in a while.'

Gordon stood still, body tight. He didn't trust himself to lift his foot. He couldn't be sure he wouldn't grab the front of Billy's shirt.

'Suppose I was right, then.' The officer sighed. 'Guess she was just another dirty prostitute.'

The word echoed, bouncing off nearby buildings, rebounding to repeat itself over and over in Gordon's ears. He tried to quell the fury in his stomach, to calm his heart as it tried to leap out of his throat, to still his hands that were ready to strangle Billy. Toby and Slim stood shoulder to shoulder with Gordon, all three men trying to keep their composure in the face of Billy's deliberate provocation.

Harry's words rang out in Gordon's mind, the advice his father had given before Gordon had left Melbourne.

'War is a time full of difficult choices. Sometimes those choices will not make sense. If you believe you are right, you must stick to your principles. But if you are wrong, you must take your medicine, no matter how bitter.'

Gordon drew himself up and rolled his shoulders back. A breath. He caught Billy's gaze, raised his right hand to his forehead and gave a small, casual salute.

'Hope you boys are having a good day,' Gordon said, the words tipping heavily from his mouth. 'You lot haven't got the easiest job on the base, after all.' He nodded and, with difficulty, forced himself to walk away. He didn't look back, hearing the scuffle of Toby's and Slim's footsteps as they hurried after him, confused silence from the MPs as the three soldiers retreated.

'I was about to clock him myself,' Toby said. 'I don't know how you didn't.'

'Wasn't what I wanted,' Gordon said, jaw tight, 'but it was the right thing to do. Wouldn't have helped anyone if I'd knocked Richardson's block off.'

'Yeah, but I bet it would've felt bloody good,' Slim said, and the tension eased as they stepped into the mess hall. Gordon composed himself, knowing that when he awoke in his dormitory tomorrow morning, he would have no regrets about not punching Billy. For the most part.

Gordon's restrictions were lifted, but he was cautious about breaking any more rules. He and Charlie went into town, asking questions of anyone at the market, anyone who might know something about Cherry, but Gordon's limited Japanese made things difficult; many Japanese were suspicious of why an ex-enemy soldier was looking for a particular young woman, even when Charlie tried to convince them otherwise. He resisted the urge to go back to Cherry's house, scared he would cause more trouble.

The weeks rolled on, surprisingly fast and agonisingly slow. His mind was never far from Cherry. Splashing each other as they swam in the creek. Darting through the market stalls, apart but together. The more he thought of her, the bigger his daydreams became. Cherry sunning herself beneath the creaking gum trees at Greenwood House, her and June laughing while Gordon and his brothers played cricket. Every night as he fell asleep, he'd think of her. Her sparkling, deep brown eyes, the way her entire face lit up when she smiled, the soft nod she gave when she was listening, translating his English to Japanese so she could understand him.

Not seeing her, not knowing where or how she was, was torturous.

Gordon stayed late most evenings in Medical, looking for an excuse to avoid spending time with Toby. Every night, Toby would head into town to find Yoneko, to spoil his wife before the sun rose the next morning. At first, Gordon had been pleased to join them, but seeing them together was painful. Their happiness was a constant reminder of what Gordon had lost.

It didn't help that when he went into town in the evenings, the number of soldiers who were wrapped up in Japanese girls was growing. Now the official brothels were closed down, many men found themselves in Japanese houses or even chasing girls in the street. Gordon struggled to keep his composure when he walked past soldiers with arms around girls, no fear of being caught by the MPs. There were too many men to arrest, too many women to seize. Gordon and Cherry had simply been at the wrong place at the wrong time.

It was easier to work late rather than be out on the streets. The quiet evenings in Medical gave him time to think, time to plan how he was going to track down Cherry.

He had to find her. He had to know she was all right.

CHAPTER THIRTEEN

NOBUKO: Kure, April 1947

They let her go. When it became obvious to the doctor that Nobuko bore no signs of venereal disease, he dismissed her and left. The police officer stood by the door, impatiently waiting for her to gather herself. With shaking hands, she smoothed down her skirt, then walked out of the room.

A police officer drove her back to Kure. Nobuko sat in the back seat, rubbing her arms to release the memory of the policeman's grip holding her down. She crossed her legs to hide the feeling of the doctor's hands on her thighs. She had moved, an instinct, and they had intervened. At least any bruises would be easy to hide.

The policeman dropped her at the bottom of the hill, the road up to the house stretching for miles in front of her. She walked quickly, already dreaming of scrubbing herself with icy cold water before she went to sleep. Perhaps the water would wash the touch of the doctor and policeman from her body.

As the maple tree appeared in front of her, Nobuko almost sank to her knees with relief. The house was dark, no sign of anyone awake. She would deal with her father in the morning, give an excuse about needing to work late or missing the last bus. Right now, all she wanted to do was lie down and sleep.

Moving quietly, she slid the door open and took off her shoes. She struck a match to light a small lantern, dimming it as the flame caught.

Noboru stepped into the light, arms crossed, mouth pressed tightly closed.

Nobuko faltered. 'Father, I'm sorry I'm so late. I—'

'I know where you have been.' The volume of his voice made Nobuko start.

'Father, please, you don't need to yell—'

'You were arrested! Suzuki saw you! What kind of girl gets picked up by the police?'

Nobuko struggled to hold back her tears. Suzuki was one of the biggest gossips in Kure. Noboru would have known she'd been arrested before the truck had arrived in Hiroshima. Her silence seemed to enrage her father further.

'A thief! A criminal! A prostitute! So which are you?'

'It was a mistake.'

'They didn't arrest you for no reason.'

Nobuko sank to her knees, head bowed, hot with shame.

'I was with a soldier. We—'

Noboru advanced on her. 'A prostitute. My daughter.' She shook her head, but her father ignored her. 'What would your mother think?'

Her breath caught. 'I'm sorry.'

He knelt beside her and held out his hand. 'The money.' Nobuko looked at him, confused. He clicked his tongue. 'The money from your extra work. Give it to me.'

'There is none.' She sat up. 'It was a mistake. I haven't been … I've only worked at the base.' She swallowed, trying to push the memory of the doctor away. 'They sent me home because I was clean. I am clean. I'm not selling myself to them.'

Noboru fixed her with a look and she held it. He sighed. 'So everyone will think you are a prostitute and we won't even get money from it.' He stood. 'This soldier. He works on the base? You see him often?'

She saw no point in lying. 'Yes.'

Noboru nodded. 'He will give us supplies and we will sell them at the market. You tell him.' He nudged her with his foot. 'Do you hear me?'

'He won't do it. I won't ask him.'

'He would do it if you asked him.'

Nobuko didn't answer. Her father was right. Don would help if she asked. But she wouldn't.

Noboru snarled, angered by her silence. He grabbed her shirt and pulled her to her feet. 'You will not go back to that base then. You will have nothing more to do with the ex-enemy soldiers. You are not to leave the house. Do you understand me?'

Nobuko nodded, her collar pulling tight against the back of her neck. Noboru dropped her and she slumped to the ground. He cleared his throat, a coughing fit threatening to burst from him, but he controlled it.

'Go to sleep. I don't want to look at you again until the morning.'

Ten minutes later, she curled into a ball on her futon, wishing for the darkness of sleep.

It would not come.

Noboru kept Nobuko at home the next day, instead sending Kazuo to pick up their rations. Suma tried to visit, but Noboru pushed his daughter into the back of the house and sent Suma away, maintaining that everything was all right.

Nobuko spent the day cleaning. She went over every inch of the kitchen, the small tatami room, the washtub outside, and scrubbed, dusted and wiped everything down. She cooked lunch, a bowl of rice with rare lotus root, then went back to sweeping and cleaning the floors. Noboru came in to inspect her handiwork and, most of the time, made her begin again. Her fingers went red from the water and work, but she continued to scrub, only stopping to cook and serve dinner. She barely spoke; she didn't look at her father or her uncle. They barely looked at her either.

Nobuko was sweeping around the back door after dinner when a familiar voice called out from the front of the house. Chills raced through her. Don. He had come for her. She started moving towards the door, when Kazuo appeared, blocking her path. Nobuko sat in the dirt and listened.

Don was clearly concerned for her, a thought that made her heart leap. The conversation didn't last long. A thud, a yelp, and her uncle sprinted through the house, shouting at Noboru to stop. Nobuko didn't move.

Noboru burst from the house, rage flaring, knuckles bloody. In one quick movement, he slapped her. Dazed, she pressed her forehead to the ground in a deep apology, cheek stinging.

'See what you have done?' Noboru roared. 'This man shows up looking for you. Everyone sees him here! All I have tried to do is give you a good life, a better life, and this is how you repay me? Running around with foreign men, arrested by police, giving yourself to anyone who calls your name? And to him? He is not a good man.'

Something inside Nobuko broke.

'You think this is a better life?' she asked, rising to her feet. 'Mother is dead. We have barely enough food. We are still fighting, even though the war is done. Japan is in ruins. We are treated like criminals in our own country. This is not a better life.' Noboru took half a step back as she met his eye. 'The Japan you know is gone. We are forever changed. All of us. If you think this life you have given me is better, you're a fool.'

'You think I'm a fool? These men will leave. They are not from here. What happens when they do? You think this man will take you to Australia with him? Why would he? You are nothing. You are no-one.' Disgust filled her father's face. 'No Japanese man will have you either now. You are a woman of the ex-enemy. No-one will touch you.'

'All the good Japanese men are dead.' Nobuko's words were sharp.

Noboru curled his lip. 'Get out.' The words were so soft, she almost didn't hear them. 'Get out!' he said, shouting.

She pushed past him, heading to where she hid Don's scarf and mittens. About to leave, she spotted the photograph of her parents and her, the precious photograph she had saved from Hiroshima, which sat on the family shrine. Her mother's mouth bore no smile but her eyes shone, urging Nobuko to have strength, to stay firm. It was enough. She left the photograph where it was displayed, clutching Don's gifts to her chest, and strode past Uncle Kazuo, who averted his gaze as she walked out.

Nobuko didn't look back. She glanced down the hill to see if Don was visible in the low light. There was no sign of him and she didn't have the energy to follow. She crossed the street and went to Suma's house.

There was a young woman a few years older than Nobuko sitting near the front door, smoking, her purple yukata tied loosely around her. She took one look at Nobuko and stood.

'I'll find Suma,' she said, and disappeared into the house.

After Amari had moved to Osaka, Suma had opened her house to young women who had no parents, or had nowhere to live. Some stayed a night or two, others weeks, the house filled with transient women, all with different stories and tragedies. Women who had lost their entire families in the firebombing at Tokyo and moved from city to city to find somewhere new to build their lives. Women who escaped men who beat them, who had been living in the wreckage of bombed-out houses, forced out of the only shelter they could find, sleeping on the side of the road until Suma found them and took them in. She knew what it was like to have nothing. She was one of the only divorced women in Kure, a fact she didn't hide. Her acceptance of it made her more scandalous in some people's eyes.

The women watched Nobuko from the corners of their eyes, conversation halting when she walked into the room. She heard their whispers. She was a prostitute, a comfort woman for the enemy soldiers, thinking too highly of herself to take a Japanese husband, seducing the gaijin instead.

Their judgement made things worse. Nobuko hid in a back room, too embarrassed to come out. Two days after her father had disowned her, Noboru and Kazuo left the house with their few belongings. She watched from the window, but neither man even glanced towards Suma's house. Part of her wanted to run after her father, throw herself at his feet, beg for his forgiveness. She forced herself to stay where she was. She wouldn't chase him.

The last remnants of her broken family disappeared down the hill, two retreating backs carrying their whole lives with them.

Nobuko stayed at the window long after they were gone.

Suma suggested she move into the empty shack, but Nobuko didn't want to live in a house of ghosts. She went in one night to collect some of her things, and to see what her father had left behind. The photograph was gone – taken or destroyed, Nobuko didn't know. The only thing that remained hidden, forgotten by Noboru, was the emerald ring, dug into a hole beneath the tatami. Nobuko sewed it into the lining of her skirt, intending never to go back to her uncle's house again. It held nothing but memories of the family she had tried to hold together, a family torn apart by war.

Nobuko didn't speak to anyone, even Suma, keeping to her futon in the corner of the tatami room, then staying in the garden to keep out of the way. The house was filled with women coming and going, but Nobuko wasn't part of the activity; she was an outcast, a war orphan, damaged. Noboru may have been angry, but he was right. People kept their distance from women who were involved with ex-enemy soldiers. Nobuko was grateful for it.

Every time she considered going back to her job on the base, she felt violently ill. She needed to figure out how to make money, but the idea of being surrounded by soldiers who might report her, might send her back to be examined once more, was terrifying. She could barely move from her futon most days, trying to focus on how to breathe or sleep. Weeks turned into months, but Nobuko had no energy for work. She took over the cooking and cleaning to contribute, keeping the house in order, miserable and exhausted every day.

Until the day she saw a fox.

It appeared while Nobuko was washing the crockery in the bucket outside. It snuck in through the shrubs on the perimeter of the garden and stopped when it saw Nobuko with her hands in the wash bucket. Instead of fleeing, it tilted its head to the side, as though studying her. She moved her head in the same way, mirroring the animal's movements, amused. It took a step towards her, then another, sniffing the air around her. Then it sat, white tail curling around its body, as though waiting. She stayed still. There was a message in this moment, something significant, Nobuko waiting for a sign from the gods to tell her what to do next. The fox stood, let out a loose, guttural bark, held her gaze, then loped back into the green, disappearing the way it had come.

It was time to be Brave Nobuko once more. If things were going to change, she needed to change them herself.

CHAPTER FOURTEEN

GORDON: Kure, November 1947

'Mate, you need to take a night off.' Andy was replacing the morphine drip of a sleeping soldier as Gordon took the old medicine away. 'You've stayed here so long, you've become boring, and no-one likes a boring man.'

'Speak for yourself.' Gordon looked to Charlie, who was counting syringes. 'Charlie likes me just fine. Don't you, Charlie?'

'Yes, Don-san. We mates.'

'My word we are.' Gordon threw a pointed look at Andy, who sighed.

'Righto, I'll stick my nose elsewhere. But sulking around here isn't going to bring Cherry back. She's gone, mate. You need to forget about her.'

Andy's logic made sense but, even though it had been six months since the arrest, Gordon refused to let it go. Yoneko was adamant Cherry's family had left town, taking her with them. No-one had seen Cherry for months. Still, Gordon wasn't satisfied. If she had been forced to leave Kure, surely she would've tried to get a message to him somehow, wouldn't she?

There was a clatter of footsteps at the door and Gordon turned. A boy of about ten was standing there, peering into the medical wing.

Gordon couldn't figure out why the kid seemed so strange. Then it hit him.

The boy was white.

'Hello there, young man,' Gordon said. 'What can we do for you?'

'They said there was a hospital here. I wanted to see. I'm Peter.'

Gordon threw a confused look to Andy, who seemed just as puzzled. The older man stepped forward. 'This isn't quite a hospital but it is the medical unit on base. I'm Andy, this is Gordon, and we look after anyone who needs help if they're injured or sick.'

'Just the Australians?' Peter asked.

'We help lots of people.' Gordon said. 'The base has a lot of Australian soldiers, yes. But there's also men from New Zealand, India, England who serve here. And sometimes the Japanese need help too.'

Peter scrunched up his nose. 'Why do you help the Japanese?'

Gordon knelt beside the boy. 'Because they need it. And that's the best reason to help someone.'

Peter scowled. Outside in the hall, there was the click of heels on the floor. 'Peter? Where did you go?'

Andy opened the door. 'Ma'am, he's in here.'

A harried woman stepped into the room, pearls adorning her ears and neck, lips a strange bright red. In her makeup she seemed almost alien to Gordon, who was so used to the Japanese women he saw every day.

'Thank you,' she said, breathless. 'He can't stay still, this boy. I'm Rose Evans.'

Andy offered his hand and introduced himself and Gordon. Gordon gave a small salute. 'Forgive me, we don't often see women on the base. What are you and Peter doing here?'

Rose smoothed the sides of her hair back. 'We just moved from South Australia. Not onto the base. We live closer to the camp near Hiroshima, actually. They built a town for the Australian families. It's called Nijimura. Means rainbow village, apparently, which is quite fanciful.' At the blank looks from Gordon and Andy, she explained. 'The Army brought over some of the men's families to live here with them. Bring a touch of normality. Remind them of home.'

It did spark something in Gordon's memory, but he hadn't paid much attention to the fact the Army had built a town for Australian families given that he had no wife or children to bring over himself. Something else tugged at his mind. 'Mrs Evans? Henry's wife?'

Rose nodded, her smile widening. 'You know Henry? That's lovely. From his letters it was obvious he was frightfully homesick, so here we are! Peter and I have only been here two weeks, but he wanted to show us the Kure base. I must say, this place is quite unusual, isn't it?'

Gordon cleared his throat. Even though he'd barely spoken to the man since their trip to Hiroshima, he had seen Henry in town in the evenings. His Japanese girl's name was Ana and, if the rumours were true, he paid for her to stay in a house just past the market, like a lot of the boys did to keep their girls out of the brothels. He doubted Rose knew anything about Ana.

'Well, thanks for your visit. Did you want to see anything else here, Peter?' Andy asked. The boy shook his head.

Rose nudged him. 'Say thank you to the kind men.'

'Thank you,' Peter said, the words singsonging through the unit.

After Rose and Peter had disappeared, Gordon shook his head. 'Henry better sort himself out or else he's gonna be in trouble if the MPs pick him and Ana up. And not only from the MPs.'

Andy held up a hand, weary. 'All right, all right. Enough about the MPs. If you're going to stick around here late again tonight, tell me now. I've got a girl to pick up.'

'Where are you going?' asked Gordon.

'Most of the COs have headed up to that Japanese hotel in the mountains to get a glimpse of General MacArthur,' Andy replied. 'When the cat's away, the mice'll have a party down the back of the dorms. A bunch of us are bringing our girls along.'

Gordon nodded, heart aching. He'd have loved to take Cherry to that. 'Righto. I'll stick around here. Enjoy your night.'

Andy stopped by the door. 'I reckon Toby's girl is right. Cherry's dad found out about what happened and they left town. She's safe somewhere, mate. I can feel it.'

'Maybe. Maybe not. I just gotta hope we'll hear something.'

Gordon worked alone for the next few minutes, making up fresh beds, wishing for some music to fill the empty room. The door to Medical swung open but Gordon barely glanced at it, tucking the sheets under the thin mattress, expecting it to be Charlie.

'Don-san?'

The hairs on the back of Gordon's neck stood up, heart in his throat. There, standing by the door in her navy woollen dress, was Cherry. She blinked as their eyes met, her hands twisting together.

'Cherry.' Gordon crossed the room and swept her up in his arms. She was smaller than he remembered, or had he become taller? Her hair brushed against his chin, catching on his smattering of whiskers.

She trembled and Gordon released her, worried he was hurting her, but she laughed, tears shining on her cheeks.

'I think maybe they send you to Australia.' Cherry wiped her face. 'Maybe Andy-san is here but not Don-san.'

'I'm here.' Gordon grabbed her hands. 'I'm always here. Me and Charlie. We've been waiting for you.'

At Charlie's name, the boy seemed to appear out of nowhere, hopping with excitement but not wanting to interrupt. Cherry smiled at him and he turned pink, giving her a deep bow. She bowed back and the two of them chattered in rapid Japanese that Gordon couldn't understand. What he could understand was the happiness that radiated from Cherry as Charlie spoke, her eyes flicking between them both.

'What's he saying?' Gordon asked.

'He says …' Cherry paused. 'He says you miss me very much.'

Tears welled in his eyes, his breath cut short. 'My word, I did.' He cleared his throat, his voice a gravelled murmur. 'I missed you like you wouldn't believe. I've been looking for you. I went to your house. I saw your father.'

Cherry's face darkened and Gordon's heart stilled. 'I have no father,' she said. 'No parents. My mother die in Pikadon. Now also my father gone.'

Gordon had a thousand questions, but right now none of them mattered. All that mattered was that Cherry was here, with him again.

He touched her face. His heart leapt as her eyes fluttered closed, the warmth of her cheek in his hand electric.

'You've got me. You've always got me.' The next words were out of Gordon's mouth before he could think about them. 'I love you.'

Cherry didn't move. Maybe she didn't know the English. He hesitated, not wanting to say the wrong words, but he knew them. He'd deliberately looked them up weeks ago, just in case. 'I love you,' he repeated in Japanese.

Still, she didn't smile. She glanced at Charlie, and Gordon understood.

'Charlie, mate, fetch us some chocolate – chokoreto – from my bunk. We need to celebrate Cherry's return.'

Charlie nodded and darted out, leaving the two of them alone.

'Maybe I shouldn't have said that,' Gordon said, certain she could hear his heartbeat as it thundered in his chest. 'Sorry.'

'It's okay,' Cherry said. 'But there is problem. Maybe you not love me because of problem.'

'I don't care.' He shook his head, adamant. 'Any problem we've got, we'll sort it out together.'

'You want children?' she asked. The question was so out of left field, it took Gordon a second to follow what she was saying.

'Yes. Someday.'

Her eyes clouded over. Walking to the nearest bed, she sat down, Gordon at her side. Now he had her back, he wouldn't rush her. He waited patiently for her to speak.

'Some Hiroshima girls have trouble with babies. Maybe bleeding. Baby die before born. Die after born.' Cherry twisted her fingers in her hands, not looking at him. 'Maybe me too. Have trouble. Maybe you don't love me then.'

Gordon's heart swelled. He cupped her chin and tilted her head back so she could see how genuine his words were.

'I love you. I don't care if you're Japanese or German, or you barrack for the Collingwood Football Club. I don't care if we have three babies, ten babies, or no babies. I love you, Nobuko Sakuramoto. You are the only thing I care about.'

Cherry smiled and Gordon's entire world stopped. He leaned forward and kissed her deeply, all his anxiety and fears melting away.

When they broke apart, it was as though Gordon could breathe properly for the first time since Billy had taken Cherry away. Head whirling, almost drunk, he took her hand again.

This time he got down on one knee.

'Nobuko-chan. Will you marry me?'

Gordon raced through the dormitory buildings, searching for Toby. He could barely contain his excitement. There was no sign of Toby or Yoneko at the raucous party, the soldiers taking advantage of the absent COs to smuggle Japanese girls onto the base. Before Gordon headed to the creek, he doubled back to check Toby's dorm, in case he was getting ready to head out for the night.

Gordon burst through the door but there was only one man inside. Matthews was lying on his bed reading a book.

'You know where Westy is?' Gordon asked.

'Probably halfway home by now.'

'What do you mean?'

'The bloke married a Japanese girl and then tried to get the Army to sign off on it.' Matthews inclined his head towards Toby's bed. It was empty, no sign that anyone had slept in it, no photographs taped to the wall above. Gordon's heart sank. 'I dunno what the bloke was thinking. There's the anti-fraternisation policy for a start. It's bullshit but it's there. And no Japanese is ever going to be allowed to set foot in Australia. What does he think the White Australia policy is for?'

'The White Australia policy?'

'Stops anyone who's not British coming into Australia. Well, anyone who's not white. The clue's in the name.'

'But war brides wouldn't count.' Dread crept through Gordon's body. 'I know blokes who met their wives in France in the Great War. They were allowed to move home with their husbands.'

'Yeah, but girls from France don't look all that different to us, do they?' Matthews said. 'Lots of soldiers bring home their war brides but I only know ones from England or America, maybe Canada. Dunno if you've noticed but we're definitely not in Canada.' Matthews stretched his neck from side to side. 'West obviously figured the chips would fall his way, but as soon as he mentioned his Japanese wife, the COs packed him up on the first boat back to Sydney. I don't blame them. You don't want to mix yellow and white. It's not pretty.'

Gordon stumbled from the dorm, panic whirling, breathing hard in the cool night air. In the distance, the not-so-secret party echoed through the buildings around him. He pressed his hands into his knees, almost as though he'd been punched in the stomach.

He had to be smart about this. Toby had always rushed into things without thinking about them and now he was on a ship in the middle of the Pacific. Gordon needed time to consider his options, to figure out the best way forward. They'd be married one day; he'd made his promise to Cherry. The wedding didn't need to be tomorrow.

At this thought, Gordon started laughing, delight and relief flooding through him. It seemed impossible that so much had happened so quickly.

Toby was gone. Cherry was back.

Now he needed to work out how to do this right.

CHAPTER FIFTEEN

NOBUKO: Kure, March 1948

The kimono was folded neatly in the cupboard, hidden beneath the blankets, a secret Nobuko had been hiding for weeks. One of the girls on the base, already married by the Shinto priest to an Australian soldier, had lent it to her. Through glowing praise from Don and Andy, Nobuko had been given her job back in the medical unit. With the money she was earning, she bought them both a small Christmas present to say thank you: a small daruma each, the red-and-gold painted round doll a symbol of good luck. Don had laughed with glee, convinced that the daruma looked like a demon. An echo of his Melbourne Demons. Don had given her a small silver wristwatch, a gift she treasured every day.

It had been difficult to return to the base. Nobuko avoided any soldiers she didn't know and refused to go near the Military Police offices. She had, however, discovered a small community of housegirls who had used the same priest as Yoneko to marry their soldiers and would help any girl who wanted to do the same. Don didn't want to rush it, wanting to make sure everything was right before they married. As the weeks rolled by, Nobuko found out what she could in whispered moments swapping buckets or collecting laundry.

One spring afternoon, a married housegirl called Keiko delivered sheets to Medical. Keiko turned up the corner of the material to reveal a kimono tucked among the cotton.

'For good luck,' the girl whispered to Nobuko, cheeks pink. 'Many housegirls have worn this kimono for their weddings. The love kimono. Please pass it on to someone else who needs it after you.'

Nobuko had taken it home to Suma's and hidden it in the cupboard. Today, though, she needed to wear it. After months of waiting, she and Don were finally getting married.

The kimono smelt like citrus and cigarettes and would take time to put on. Nobuko needed the house to be empty; she hadn't told anyone at Suma's about the proposal, cautious of the backlash. Nobuko was meeting Don at the shrine in a little over two hours. She didn't have much more time to spare.

Finally, the only other woman in the house called out that she was leaving. Nobuko wished her a good day, listening to the receding footsteps before she snuck to the window to check that she was alone.

She pulled the stiff material from the cupboard, shaking it out to air it. There was a slight texture to the fabric, extra embroidery to accentuate the patterns. It wasn't a traditional wedding kimono, but it was beautiful. She was just about to step out of her skirt when the front door slid open.

'Hello?'

Nobuko froze. It was Yoneko. Shoving the material aside, she straightened herself. 'Yoneko-san?' She moved to the front door, to keep her guest away from the kimono.

Yoneko bustled inside. 'Good. I hoped you were here. Has Don-san had a letter from Toby-san?'

Nobuko shook her head. Don had received no word from Toby since he'd left Japan months ago, even though Don had written several letters. Toby was all Yoneko wanted to talk about since he left, Nobuko already weary of the conversation they were about to have.

Instead of talking, her friend burst into tears. Startled, Nobuko came to her side. 'Letters from Australia take a long time. He can't send them through the base and the Japanese post is so slow.'

Yoneko lifted her gaze to meet Nobuko's, eyes filled with fear.

'I'm pregnant,' she whispered.

Nobuko took a step back. 'Are you sure?'

Yoneko nodded, miserable. 'I thought it was possible but I wanted to wait to be sure. I wrote to him last month to tell him, but he's not replying to any of my letters.'

Nobuko, mind whirling, gently touched Yoneko's knee. They were all skinny, the rations not enough to properly satisfy hunger, but she seemed all bone and no muscle.

Yoneko took a shuddering breath. 'What if it was all a lie?'

'No. Toby loves you. A month isn't that long from Australia.'

'What about my other letters?' Yoneko let out a strangled sob. 'He hasn't written once. What if he doesn't come back for me? What if he's forgotten about me?'

Yoneko's words gutted Nobuko. She was about to commit herself to Don, another ex-enemy soldier and Toby's best friend. Would the same thing happen to her? Was Don the same as Toby?

Yoneko snarled, trying to wrest back her emotions. 'Maybe everyone else is right. Maybe we cannot trust these Australians.'

For the next half hour, Yoneko swung between upset, angry and trying to convince herself she was being irrational. Nobuko tried to weather all the emotional shifts until she finally told Yoneko she really had to get to the market.

'But please, stay here as long as you need to.' Nobuko pulled a futon from the other room, resolutely ignoring the pile of kimono fabric in the corner and the knot in her stomach. 'Sleep. You will feel better when you wake.'

Yoneko fell asleep almost immediately. Nobuko gathered the kimono fabric and rushed out of the house. It wasn't until she was halfway down the hill, stopping underneath the budding pink sakura trees, that she stopped to think, kimono folded on the grass next to her.

What if these weddings were worthless to the Australians? As far as Nobuko knew, none of the women who had married soldiers had gone to Australia with them. Granted, most of the soldiers were still serving with BCOF, but were all of them really going to bring home Japanese wives?

That wasn't the question she needed to ask.

Was Don going to bring home a Japanese wife?

Above her, the sakura shivered in the breeze. She placed her hand on the trunk, breathing deeply into the ancient energy of the wood, asking for guidance.

Nobuko was so late. Her wristwatch ticked every second, every minute away, as she hurried to the shrine, no clue whether Don would still be there.

She stepped through the Torii gate, heading towards the altar.

When it came into view, she stopped.

Don sat on the steps, head bowed, dressed in his Army uniform, the khaki stiff and starched. Her heart leapt at the sight of him and she picked up the skirt of her kimono, rushing forward. Don looked up at the sound of her footsteps, a relieved smile stretching across his face.

Everything would be okay.

'You … you look … wow.' He was nervous too, his hands trembling as he reached for hers. 'I didn't think you were coming.'

'Sorry, Don-san. Sorry. Difficult to leave the house. But maybe it is still okay to marry?'

Don squeezed her hand. 'There's nothing I would rather do more.'

Nobuko gave a nervous giggle. 'Where is Charlie?'

'Keeping watch,' Don said. 'Lots of raids from the MPs have been happening around here lately – someone tipped them off to these weddings. I've told him to run in and tell us if he sees anything.'

Nobuko tensed. It was terrifying to think that this day could be ruined by MPs. If they were caught together again, Don would be sent home and Nobuko would be even more disgraced. Perhaps it would be better to cancel the wedding, to be safe.

Then Nobuko met Don's eyes. Within them was an infinite grey-blue galaxy of possibility, of safety, of love.

He patted her hand. 'I checked the patrols. They're on the other side of town today, so we should be right. I'm just being extra careful.'

Don stood up, gesturing that she move past him up the stairs.

All she needed in this moment was to be Brave Nobuko.

She straightened her kimono. 'Let's get married.'

It was a simple ceremony, a poor imitation of a traditional Japanese wedding. Nobuko barely took it in, intensely aware of Don beside her, trying to concentrate on the Shinto priest in front of them. They were in the middle of their san-san-kudo ceremony, drinking sake from three shallow cups in varying sizes, when a yell went up outside the gates, followed by a sharp whistle.

Don tensed. 'A patrol?'

Nobuko's heart leapt into her throat. 'They are here?'

'Looks like.'

'Faster,' she said to the priest, who nodded. The priest quickly moved through the end of the ceremony, asking Nobuko and Don to leave sprigs of evergreen at the altar.

Outside were more shouts and the sound of running. It was likely Charlie, trying to outrun the Australian police. If he was smart, he would lead them in the wrong direction.

Don was throwing glances towards the Torii gate, waiting for the moment Billy burst onto the grounds. He snatched up the scroll that declared them married and grasped Nobuko's hand to pull her up from where she knelt.

'Come on, Mrs Parker,' he said, a grin on his face regardless of the commotion. 'Let's get out of here.'

They bowed to the priest and then ran. Ducking out a side gate, Don pulled Nobuko along as she struggled to keep up with him in her wooden sandals. The whistles and shouting grew louder, the Australian accents punctuating the air as the officers converged on the main entrance to the shrine, missing them by moments.

Don and Nobuko snuck into a small hotel. After he had taken off his boots, careful to remain out of sight of the door, he placed money on the counter. The man running the establishment looked Nobuko up and down, eyebrows raised, and fear ran down her spine, but he handed over a room key and pointed up the stairs. Don led the way, heading into their room, pulling Nobuko inside. He peered out the window to look on to the street below, as she fought to get her breath back.

'Charlie – where is he?' Nobuko asked, hopeful Don could see him out the window.

'Not sure,' he said. 'But Charlie's more slippery than a bar of soap. He'll be fine, don't you worry.' He turned to look at her and smiled. She looked away, self-conscious under the intensity of his gaze. 'I think they're gone. The MPs. I don't reckon they'll find us here.'

His confidence was reassuring. Don undid the buttons around his throat, his shirt falling open as he moved across the room towards her. He looked slightly dazed.

'Mrs Parker,' Don said, sounding out the words on his tongue. 'My wife. Cherry Parker.' He kissed her, not seeming to notice her hesitation as she considered her English name. From Nobuko Sakuramoto to Cherry Parker. It felt strange, her Japanese identity gone. Or was it adapting? Melding into something new? Her past and future meeting. It felt strong, like Cherry Parker was her true name. Cherry Parker was the woman who married an Australian soldier, who stood up to her father, who wasn't afraid of the world. Nobuko Sakuramoto was a child, a girl whom people ignored and forgot about. Cherry Parker had her whole life ahead of her, a life that she could barely begin to imagine.

Right now, Cherry Parker was kissing her husband, touching his face, his back, his arms.

'You are beautiful,' Don said, taking a step back to look at her properly. He touched the sleeve of her kimono.

'Not my kimono,' Cherry said, voice gentle. 'Must be careful.'

'Maybe we should get you out of it,' Don said. 'Then we won't need to worry about damaging it.'

Cherry nodded, breathless, nerves threatening to overwhelm her.

He frowned. 'Wait on, how does this thing come off?'

Cherry giggled and they kissed, his lips soft on hers, then his mouth became hungrier, more urgent as he pressed himself against her. She trailed her hands down his chest, tracing around the buttons on his thin cotton shirt. Don stopped, his mouth almost on hers, breath quickening, a shudder of anticipation at her touch. Guided by instinct, ignoring her thudding, anxious heart, she moved her face aside, her breath brushing over his neck and collarbone as she undid the Army regulation buttons on his shirt, a soft tremor in her hands; Don hastened to undo his belt, both undressing him together. It wasn't until he stood in front of her naked that she caught her breath. He watched her, waiting for her to take the next step, his cheeks flaring pink. Her husband. The man she had risked her entire future for. She reached for her obi, the sash on her kimono, and undid it, Don helping to manoeuvre the folds of white fabric as they eased away from her body, her ribs unfurling to take a deep, full breath once more. She stepped out of the mound of material, deliberately avoiding his gaze as she arranged the kimono neatly to one side, steeling herself. She didn't know exactly what to do, but she turned back to him and it no longer mattered. She reached out to hold him as he pressed her body against his, skin to skin, chest to chest, and their mouths crashed together once more with renewed longing and desire.

The futon welcomed them, their clumsy movements, their whispered apologies in Japanese and soft questions in English. Their words melted into breaths, a universal body language between them. And as the day outside gave way to darkness, the two of them found themselves within each other, separate and whole in the same, shivering moment.

Don looked so peaceful in sleep. His breath was soft and deep, blond eyelashes flickering against his cheek. Cherry watched him, wrapped in a blanket. The smoky orange light from the streets outside drifted through gaps in the paper that covered the windows, painting the room a strange, warm colour in the night.

The day had been driven by instinct, by fear. All those moments had led her here. A husband in bed, his bare chest rising and falling, one arm open outwards, an invitation to nestle into him. She hovered her fingers over his skin, feeling his warmth without the contact. He was her family.

Grief exploded in her chest, a deep ache for her mother and father. Weddings were supposed to be a union of families, an entwining of two threads into one. If it had been a proper ceremony, Tsudo would have helped Cherry dress in her wedding kimono. Noboru would have escorted her into the shrine. Both their families would have been present for the celebrations.

The thought of Noboru among Don's family made her shudder. It wouldn't have been a beautiful union; her father would not have been able to hide his contempt for the Australians. It was impossible to imagine how Tsudo would have felt. Perhaps she would have calmed Noboru, to smooth over any disagreements. Perhaps she would have dazzled Venn and Harry, been charming and vivacious to their guests. Perhaps she would have refused to attend the ceremony, rejecting the idea of her daughter with an ex-enemy soldier.

These thoughts were vicious and sharp. Cherry pressed her face against the rough blanket to stifle her sobs as grief ripped through her. Her family was gone. There was nothing but an imagined world for them now, a daydream that would never materialise. Nothing real.

Except the man in the bed next to her. He was real. His flop of blond hair, eyes that mirrored dawn-blue skies, his rolling voice and quick smile. It seemed a foolish thing to be considering her decisions now, whether Don was the right choice. He was the only choice. She couldn't move to another city: she didn't have the means or money. There were hardly any Japanese men to marry, most having never returned from war.

But there was this man. This man who was loyal and sweet, who stood up to the police when they threatened her, who loved her so much he had married her. He wasn't the man she thought she would marry, but this wasn't the life she expected to live. Her world had been destroyed and the path she walked led her here to this moment, asking her to be vulnerable, asking her to trust. In Don. In herself.

She took a deep breath, the air shaky in her throat. She wiped the tears from her eyes and touched Don's face. He stirred in his sleep and reached for her, his slender, long fingers hooking around her hip.

'Cherry?'

'Here, Don-san.'

He sighed, a small sleepy smile on his lips. 'I love you.'

She lay in his arms and he pulled her into him, still mostly asleep. The tightness of his arms was a safe hollow for her to be protected in, to fully surrender to this moment.

The wind whistled through the trees outside, a scuttle of leaves scraping along the path. Sweeping aside old hurts and wounds, making way for things to come.

She burrowed into him, breathing in this new world. Her new home. Hers.

'I love you too.'

Now they were married, Cherry felt like she had even more to lose. She stayed living with Suma, becoming more involved with the other women in the house, not making friends but no longer keeping out of everyone's way. Yoneko, pregnancy now showing, had moved in too and was prone to fits of extreme sadness as the months passed without hearing from Toby. Cherry, on the other hand, was the happiest she'd ever been, finding strength and security in Don. He was always excited to see her when she was on the base, greeting her with a wave and a smile. Even though there was so much joy to be had, Cherry couldn't fully appreciate it. Things couldn't always be so easy, so light. Any day was the day it could all be taken away. Every time they went into town, there was a higher risk of being caught, a higher chance of Don being sent home for fraternisation and the two of them being forced apart. She consoled herself with the idea that, when Don's service in Japan finished in December, she would follow him on the first civilian ship leaving Kure.

Her fear grew with each passing day. Even seeing the Military Police trucks on the base would bring on a panic that threatened to overwhelm her, and she would retreat to a cupboard to claw her breath back. Soon even the thought of meeting Don in town or stepping off the base together was too much, Cherry adamant they stay in the medical unit until she went back to Suma's at night. Don seemed baffled by her behaviour, but after the first few times he tried to encourage her to go into town, he dropped it. Cherry hated letting him down, hated seeing him frustrated she wouldn't go out with him when many of their friends were regularly dating and some MPs had started to turn a blind eye to fraternisation. A handful of them had a Japanese girl of their own. Sometimes all Cherry wanted to do was put on a pretty dress and go into town with her husband but the moment she thought about getting ready, she was overcome with nausea and could barely move. All it took was one MP officer to destroy everything.

Instead, Don would come to Suma's when he wasn't working. It wasn't ideal either. Many of the women who lived there weren't comfortable in the presence of an ex-enemy soldier and Suma tried to keep out of Don's way when he was there. Still, he visited as often as he could.

One day, Don came around with a small bag of tools, Charlie at his side.

'Noticed when it rained that there was a leak in the eaves. Thought I might fix it up.'

Cherry made tea while Don got to work. Charlie appeared with some pieces of wood, which he and Don set about cutting to size to replace what was damaged.

'Oh good, Cherry. Give us a hand. Tell me if this is straight.' Don aligned the wood with the angle of the house, the right side dipping lower.

'Maybe a little more left,' she said. He tilted it right, increasing the angle. He threw a sly smile back to her. 'Left. Left!' The more Cherry insisted Don needed to move it left, in either Japanese or English, the more he shifted it the other way, the wood hanging at a right angle to the house. Charlie burst into laughter, Cherry unable to stop her giggles either.

Don studied how he was holding the plank. 'This isn't right. You should've told me to move it to the left.'

She laughed harder as he straightened the plank and hammered it into place. The air around them shimmered with joy, Charlie almost crying with delight.

'What is this?' Suma said in Japanese, standing behind them, arms filled with her basket. The three of them fell silent. Don glanced at Cherry, concerned.

'Don-san noticed the roof was leaking. He wanted to fix it.' Cherry spoke in Japanese, moving forward to help Suma. 'Can I carry something?'

'Charlie, there is more.' Suma tilted her head towards the road and Charlie swiftly escaped to grab the rest of Suma's things.

'Sorry, Suma-san. Don-san was trying to help.' Cherry took the basket of apples from Suma. Don stayed silent, as though waiting for his punishment.

Suma snorted. 'I am sure that is why he's here. He cannot come every day, Nobuko-chan.'

Cherry nodded. Suma looked the Australian up and down, then walked past him as she went inside. Cherry offered him a faltering smile. 'It is okay. She says thank you for fixing.'

Relief washed over him. 'No worries at all.' He'd barely turned back to the roof when Charlie came flying in.

'Don-san. MPs are coming.'

Cherry's heart jumped into her throat. Surely not. Surely they wouldn't be coming here.

No-one moved. Then Don looked around, face wild. 'I need somewhere to hide.'

There was no way out through the back of the small garden, and if Don tried to sneak out the front gate, the MPs would spot him. There were no bushes or shrubbery big enough to conceal him and the house had no cupboards. They would be caught again. Cherry would be seized and sent to the police once more.

She put the basket down, worried she would drop it, and tried to control her breathing. Dimly, she was aware of Charlie and Don trying to find somewhere for the soldier to hide. It was all she could do to focus on herself.

Someone patted her cheeks, gentle but firm. Suma.

'What is happening?' Suma asked in Japanese.

'The MPs are coming. They will be here soon. They will arrest us.'

Suma's mouth tightened. Don had stopped looking for a hiding place, resigned to his fate. Charlie looked terrified. Cherry knew she must look the same.

Suma strode past them and slid open a wooden panel that led underneath the house. There was a small cavity where she kept food that would last longer in cooler temperatures. 'Quickly.' She gestured to Don and he sprinted over, scrambling into the darkness on his stomach.

Charlie rushed over to help Suma reset the panel and scuffed the dirt to hide any footprints. Suma came to Cherry's side, picking up the basket. Her body language was casual but she fixed Cherry with a firm look.

'You must not make them suspicious. Don-san was never here. We are hiding nothing.'

Cherry nodded, trying to ease the tension in her body.

'Good,' Suma said. She picked up an apple from the basket. 'Ah, these are okay. I hoped there would be more at the market, but fruit sells so quickly, doesn't it?'

The change in Suma's behaviour was so fast, it took Cherry a moment to register it. It was then that they heard footsteps. Suma shot her a look and she steeled herself.

'So quickly,' Cherry agreed, amazed at how light her own voice sounded. 'Although any fruit is better than none.'

'Under the orders of the British Commonwealth Occupation Force, we are conducting a raid on this location.' Three MPs moved through the gate, Billy in the lead. Cherry's stomach curled at the sight of him.

'What is this?' Suma demanded in Japanese. Billy ignored her.

Cherry summoned her courage. 'A raid?' she asked in English. 'We are the only people here.'

Charlie joined the two women as Billy handed them a small slip of paper. It was a notice with the BCOF stamp at the top of the page, in tiny handwritten English that would be impossible for any of them to read. That was probably the point.

'There have been reports of Australian soldiers visiting Japanese members of the public on this road.' Billy's eyes shone with malice. 'We are simply taking precautions to keep everyone safe.'

The other two officers moved into the house. Suma chased after them when they didn't remove their shoes, shrieking at them to take them off.

Billy stayed with Cherry and Charlie, never shifting his gaze from her. She fought to keep her face impassive, almost bored, as the other officers searched. Her heart jolted as she noticed the small pile of tools Don had been using on the ground, just near Billy's foot. She shifted to keep them out of his eyeline, the man moving with her as she took a small step to her right.

'Have you seen Parker lately?' he asked, his tone airy. 'I heard he's taken up with another girl south of the market. Pretty little thing. For one of you, anyway.'

All Cherry's energy was being directed into nonchalance so she barely registered what the officer had even said until the moment had passed. Was he trying to make her suspicious of Don? Jealous, even? He seemed to sense his shot hadn't landed and he shoved Cherry aside to move into the house. Her heart was thumping so fast she was sure Billy could hear it, but she followed him, keeping her distance.

'What's taking so long?'

'She won't stop shouting at us, sir.'

Suma screeched as Billy stepped inside. She dived onto his feet, forcibly unlacing his boots.

'Fucking hell.' He tried to kick her off but she curled around his legs, untying the knots. He glared at his officers. 'Did you find Parker?'

'There's no-one here.'

'Let's go before she puts a curse on us or something.'

The soldiers filed out, Suma shooing them away. Cherry and Charlie stepped back to let them pass, Cherry refusing to look towards where Don was hidden. Billy hurried out of the gate, laces flapping as he walked, Suma screaming after them about respect until they were out of earshot.

She turned back and grinned at Cherry and Charlie, who were silent.

'Perhaps next time they won't bother.' Suma moved to the side of the house and pulled the panel open. Don wriggled out, covered in dirt and dust, spiderwebs caught in his hair. Cherry rushed to him, carefully brushing aside leaves. Suma was less gentle, roughly clapping the dust off his back.

When they'd done the best they could, Don gave Suma a small bow and spoke in Japanese. 'Thank you.'

Suma raised her eyebrow. 'When you've finished with the roof, there's a windowsill in the back room that needs replacing too.'

She took the basket of apples from Cherry and walked inside.

Don shot Cherry a quizzical look, not understanding Suma, but Cherry shook her head. 'Suma-san is happy you safe. Me too. That was much scary.'

'Sorry. I didn't realise they were raiding houses. We'll have to be more careful.' He laughed. 'Not that it'll matter much longer. I've only got a few months left here, anyway.'

The atmosphere between them chilled at this reminder. Cherry turned away from him. She didn't like to think about Don leaving. She wanted to ask about when she would come to Australia after him, but she didn't have the energy. Dealing with Billy had been hard enough. The travel arrangements for her trip to Melbourne could wait.

There was also a tiny part of her that didn't want to ask in case Don said she wouldn't be coming.

Without Suma's house as a regular refuge, it became harder for Cherry and Don to see each other outside of work. Occasionally Don would book them a hotel room, but neither of them liked that. There was a risk the manager of the hotel would report them to the MPs and it would be harder to deny prostitution if they were discovered in bed together. They were married, but the Australian government and Don's superiors didn't see it that way. The time they had together was flying by faster than either of them wanted, Don's discharge date approaching with unrelenting speed. Don tried to get his service extended but his CO, Officer Kerr, had told him there was no chance of Don staying longer. He'd been punished for fraternisation and he was still considered to be too friendly with the Japanese he dealt with in an 'official' capacity to stay.

Pushing aside her worries about being left in Kure until she could join her husband in Australia, Cherry set about creating the perfect goodbye present. She collected wool from anywhere she could, pulling anything knitted apart, winding the wool into several balls. When she arrived home from work, she'd knit a few rows, creating a jumper in mismatched yarn for Don to have with him in Australia. As she worked, she murmured under her breath, knitting her words into every stitch.

'I love you. Be safe. Don't forget me.'

Cherry was working on the jumper on her day off when Charlie appeared at the door, instructing her to follow him. He led her to two bicycles he'd scrounged.

They rode to the sea, where Hana and Michiko were waiting on a jetty near a small fishing boat.

'What are we doing?' Cherry asked as she and Charlie joined them.

Hana shrugged. 'I don't know. I got a note to meet here.'

'Me too,' Michiko said. 'It wasn't either of you?'

Hana and Cherry shook their heads. Charlie let out a low whistle and an old fisherman emerged from the boat, eyes crinkled and kind. 'Please, come on board.'

Perplexed, none of the girls moved. Charlie gave Cherry a small thumbs-up, taking her bicycle. This was something of Don's making. Emboldened, Cherry stepped onto the boat, Hana and Michiko following.

'Are you coming too, Charlie-kun?' Cherry asked.

Charlie shook his head as the fisherman threw the rope off and started the engine, the boat spluttering to life with a blast of petrol fumes. The fisherman guided them away from the city and towards the smaller islands off the coast, dread settling in the pit of Cherry's stomach. Perhaps it had been foolish to get on this boat. Perhaps it wasn't Don's idea, after all.

The roar of a speedboat and cheering behind them made Cherry turn. A small dinghy shot across the water, in the prow a handful of Australian soldiers. Don, Andy and Slim. They shouted to the girls, waving and whooping, skidding past to overtake them. Excited now, the girls squealed, and the fisherman put more pace into the engine.

The boats pulled up on a small secluded island, Cherry first to clamber onto the sand. Don was sprinting to her, arms wide, grin broad. She tensed. It was risky to show this much affection in public. Then it hit her: there was no-one on the island. There were no MPs, no COs, no-one to arrest any of them.

They were safe.

Don swept her into his arms, holding her tightly, burying his face in her neck. His breath caressed her skin, an electric current down her back. Cherry couldn't breathe, not from the strength of Don's grip but from the way her stomach flipped at his touch.

'No-one can get us here,' he whispered. 'It's only us.'

'Only us,' she repeated, then kissed him on the cheek. He kissed her properly, his hands in her hair, her hands around his waist.

'Slim found the boat and fixed the engine. I figured we could get away for the day,' he murmured. 'And bring some of our friends too, you know. Just so you didn't think Mr Yoshimoto was kidnapping you.'

Cherry didn't know what to say, overwhelmed. She could only smile. He winked, brimming with delight.

'Cherry-san!' Michiko's voice rang out across the sand and she gestured for Cherry to come to her. 'Who is Don's handsome friend?'

Michiko's gaze was fixed on Andy, who was doing a poor job of pretending not to look back at her.

Cherry bit back a laugh. 'That is Andy Williams. He works with Don in Medical. He is a good man.'

'He looks very good.' Michiko smoothed back her hair.

'Andy-san, Simu-san, please meet my friends.' Cherry steered Hana and Michiko towards the Australians.

The sun shone for the entire afternoon, laughter, conversation and cigarette smoke drifting on the air like a gentle cloud. Cherry leaned on Don, and he held her in his arms. An afternoon, a moment of breath to exist together, without caution.

Without fear.

The days fell away, the weather grew cool and Cherry knitted. The jumper was coming together, perhaps a little too big, but that was better than too small. I love you. Be safe. Don't forget me. She finished a sleeve after an afternoon on another island. I love you. Be safe. Don't forget me. She completed the other as Mr Yoshimoto snuck his boat past a Military Police vessel. They weren't stopped. I love you. Be safe. Don't forget me. Progress stalled when she couldn't bring herself to knit in a few rows of grey yarn, the colour reminiscent of the garment she'd made for her mother. Instead, she found an abandoned navy glove and doubled the strands over to match the thickness of the rest of the jumper as much as possible. Don wasn't leaving for another six weeks, but if she gave it to him early, she could adjust anything that needed to be changed and would get a chance to see him wear it. The thought of seeing Don in something she'd made for him felt like pure love.

They were alone in the back garden at Suma's, a rare visit from Don on his day off. He knew the MPs were working in town and felt safe enough to visit. Still, they stayed close to the panel that lead under the house. They were on the grass, Don lying with hands behind his head, Cherry sitting next to him, playing with the fabric of her skirt. He was relaxed, eyes closed against the cool autumnal sun, but Cherry was nervous.

'What is October like in Australia?' she asked.

Don didn't open his eyes. 'It's springtime. The days are pretty warm. Sometimes there's a couple of days of heavy rain but it's mostly perfect spring weather.'

'So maybe January.'

'What's that?'

She made herself ask the question. 'I come to Australia in January?'

A lazy smile stretched over Don's face. 'Now wouldn't that be something.'

He didn't say anything else. Frustration simmered in Cherry's chest. 'So yes? In January I come on boat?'

Don opened one eye. 'You're serious?'

Cherry crossed her arms and Don sat up. The longer it took him to say anything, the more dread crept through Cherry.

'I can't bring you to Australia yet.'

'Yes. Not now. But soon.' Maybe January was too soon. 'Is March okay? That is long time away.'

Don nodded. 'It is a long time.' He caressed the back of her hands. 'Look, Cherry, I want to take you home with me. I'd pack you in my luggage if I could. But the government … they won't let you in.'

'Why?' Cherry frowned, confused. What problem did the Australian government have with her?

Don sighed. 'It's because you're Japanese. They have this immigration policy. It won't let you move to Australia with me.'

Cherry was about to argue, to remind Don that there were many Japanese women with Australian husbands, but her heart sank. Thinking about it, none of the women she knew had left Japan for Australia. Most of the husbands were still serving with BCOF, and those that had returned hadn't been home long at all, certainly not long enough to organise a visa and travel for their wives. Was that why none of the girls had left Kure? The men weren't allowed to bring their wives home?

Cherry tried to make sense of this. 'Do you want me to come to Australia?'

Don went white. 'Yes, of course. All I want is to bring you to Australia. I just have to sort out some things first. Talk to some people. Get you a visa. I'm not sure how long it'll take. Could be three months. Maybe six. So we just have to wait.'

She looked at him closely then. Was he lying to her? She wouldn't be the first woman a soldier had lied to.

Her silence made him fidget. 'Cherry, you have to believe me. I'll send for you as soon as I can. We just need to do the whole thing right. Tell me you believe me.'

His face was so earnest, his hands warm and tight around hers. Was she going to trust this man?

She put her hand on his cheek. 'Okay,' she said. 'But you send for me quick as possible.'

Don kissed her palm. 'As fast as lightning.'

The jumper was nearly finished. Cherry cast off the final few stitches as Suma cooked rice for dinner. The rations were still in place but they were getting more food now. One of the girls was convinced it was because so many Japanese were dead that there were more supplies to be allocated. Running her fingers over her handiwork, Cherry checked it for loose stitches or small holes. It hung together well and she pulled it over her head, the garment far too big for her. The wool brushed against her arms, mimicking Don's embrace and warming Cherry from inside her chest.

'You need to be careful,' Suma said as she rinsed the rice. 'He may forget you. You need to be ready for that.'

'He won't.' Cherry sounded stubborn but she truly believed it. 'Don will book me on the next ship possible.'

'He said that?'

'He said that.'

Suma clicked her tongue, unimpressed. 'You don't want to end up like Yoneko. It's worse for her – she has baby Setsuko now!' The arrival of Yoneko's daughter had done little to draw the new mother out of her darkness. 'It happened to another girl too. She was Amari's friend. She took up with an ex-enemy soldier, he went back to Australia and she hasn't heard from him since they kissed goodbye on the dock.'

'Don-san is different. He won't leave me here. I know he won't.'

'Nobuko-san!' Charlie's panicked voice rang through the house. Cherry rushed to the door. He was red-faced and breathless. 'You must come. Now.'

'What is it?'

'Don-san. He is leaving.'

Cherry froze. That was impossible, they still had weeks together.

Charlie had no time for her shock. 'Now! He is going to the ship now!'

She snatched up the jumper and ran after him, the two of them sprinting down the hill. There was an Army truck waiting for them, Slim and a man Cherry had only met a few times sitting in the front seat. Patrick, a friend of Don's.

'Quick sticks,' Slim said, voice tight, as Cherry and Charlie dived into the truck. They'd barely sat down when Patrick put his foot on the accelerator, lurching them forward as they sped through the streets.

'Why leaving early, Simu-san?' Cherry asked, mind reeling.

'Typhoon warning for Hong Kong. They want to get ahead of the weather so they pulled it forward to avoid delays. I think it's nonsense but I'm not the one making the decisions.'

'Don will wait for us?'

Slim turned in his seat. 'Look, Cherry, Paddy and I will do our best to get you there before they leave. Hopefully that's enough.'

Don's jumper sat on her lap. Cherry pulled it closer to her.

I love you. Be safe. Don't forget me.

The ship was still in port as Patrick sped to the dock, pulling up near the gangplank. Cherry and Charlie clambered out the truck as Don sprinted off the deck, running down the ramp to get to them, pulling Cherry into his arms.

'Cherry, thank God. It was killing me we mightn't say goodbye.'

She couldn't breathe. 'I thought we miss you.'

'You've got me. You've always got me.' Don kissed her hard. There were tears on her cheeks; whether hers or his, she didn't know.

Don drew himself up and looked at Charlie. 'You look after Cherry while I'm gone.'

'Yes Don-san.' Charlie saluted Don, who returned the gesture then pulled Charlie into a quick hug.

'Slim and Andy'll keep an eye on you too. They both got extensions when I couldn't.' Don moved back to the gangplank,

Cherry following, her heart breaking. 'I thought we had more time. I'm so sorry.'

She refused to break down in front of him. He gave her another kiss, lingering and regretful, before he stepped onto the gangplank.

'Don-san, wait.' Cherry pressed the jumper – nearly forgotten in her rush – on him. 'A present. So you don't forget me.'

Don stared at her, his brow furrowed. 'You're my wife,' he said, his voice thick. 'I will never forget you.'

As the troop carrier sailed out of Kure Harbour, Cherry and Charlie stood on the dock, watching, until it was only a speck in the distance.

Cherry let out a long, shaky breath.

I love you. Be safe. Don't forget me.

CHAPTER SIXTEEN

GORDON: Melbourne, December 1948

'You want to what?'

Three equally shocked faces stared at Gordon. His mother and father were speechless. His sister June had been the first to say anything.

'I want to bring Cherry here.' Gordon picked up his teacup, one of the set he'd sent back for Christmas two years before, bluebells skirting the gold-rimmed china. 'Japan's no place for anyone right now, let alone a girl who has no family.'

'Though she has you – is that correct?' Venn tapped her fingernails against her saucer, fixing Gordon with a look he would've once cowered under.

'Yes. She's my wife.'

Gordon didn't miss the concerned glance between his parents. He reined in his impatience, wishing they would understand. He hadn't meant to blurt out his news as soon as he walked in the door at Greenwood House, but Cherry had never left his thoughts. He'd barely noticed the bustle of Port Melbourne when they'd docked, the somehow strange white faces that surrounded him now. There were Christmas decorations in shop windows, carollers on street corners, but Gordon didn't care. Every second he dawdled under the gum trees was wasted time spent away from Cherry. After two years away,

Australia seemed foreign. The city felt claustrophobic, the money was different and sat oddly in his pocket. Even the train ride back to Ringwood, on which he stuck out in his Army uniform, felt somehow unfamiliar and new.

He rushed back home, where the Christmas tree in the corner of the lounge room was laden with homemade decorations. He had barely been home twenty minutes when he told his parents and June his plans to bring Cherry to Australia. If he stayed calm and rational, it may prove he had grown up and matured. That he had made the right decision, even in difficult circumstances. That they could trust his judgement.

June shook her head, trying to understand. 'You actually married her?'

Gordon shifted, frustration growing. 'Of course I married her. That's what you do when you love someone.'

'Why didn't you tell us?' Venn asked.

'Because someone got us into a whole load of trouble when we were still only friends, so imagine what that someone might've done if I'd told them I married her.' Gordon's words were sharp. Venn's jaw tightened but she said nothing.

Harry lifted his pipe from his mouth. 'Surely she has parents. What do they say about this?'

'Her mother died at Hiroshima. Her father is gone.' No-one pushed for more information, all in shock. 'I'm not asking your permission. Although, if any of you wanted to help, perhaps, Mum, you can write a few letters. The last one you wrote to a government establishment was incredibly effective. You nearly got me kicked out of the Army.'

Venn threw up her hands, exasperated. 'I was trying to protect you. I'd been talking with some of the other BCOF mothers and we were concerned about you young men having your heads turned by pretty girls.'

'Did any of the other mothers send letters?' Gordon shot back. Venn sniffed but didn't respond. 'I suspected as much. If you had concerns, you should've written directly to me.'

'Would you have been honest about Cherry if I'd written my concerns in a letter?' Gordon faltered. 'I think not. And I was right. Look where we are now. You with fanciful ideas of bringing some woman here.'

That was enough to spark Gordon's anger. 'She's not some woman. She's my wife. It's only right that I bring my wife here so I can provide for her and we can build a life together.'

His mother sipped her tea. A shout came from outside. The rest of the Parker siblings were playing in the garden. Gordon had returned to find his siblings familiar but somehow unrecognisable. Robin seemed as though he'd been stretched, as tall as Venn now. Donald was trying to grow a moustache. Jennifer chased Jim, who was no longer a baby but a little boy. Jeanette was reading, an echo of June on Gordon's birthday a couple of years earlier, just before he'd shipped out of Australia.

Harry moved next to Gordon, both looking out the window. 'You are not to tell your brothers and sisters.'

Gordon turned to his father. 'I beg your pardon?' Harry didn't speak. 'You're telling me I'm not to tell the rest of my brothers and sisters they have a sister-in-law trapped in another country?'

'It does no harm not to tell them.'

Gordon's head whirled and he looked at June, who shrugged. 'You think you can just bring some Japanese girl here and call her our sister?'

'Have I ever said anything against your boyfriends?' Gordon snapped. 'I'd say your choice in romantic partners is far more controversial than mine.'

June bit back a laugh and Gordon's frustration eased. She, at least, seemed to be on his side.

Jennifer appeared in the doorway. 'Who's trapped in another country?'

Silence among the adults. Gordon tilted his head as Harry and Venn shifted.

June snorted. 'You're fooling yourself if you think anyone can keep a secret in this house.'

Gordon knelt down to talk to Jennifer. 'I met someone in Japan whom I care very deeply about. I married her. And I intend to bring her home.'

She considered Gordon carefully. 'Why didn't you bring her with you?'

'The government wouldn't let her in.'

'Why?'

'Because she's Japanese.'

His younger sister blinked. 'Why would you marry someone who's Japanese?'

'Because I love her.' Gordon refused to look at his parents but he could feel their disapproval radiating from behind him. 'Is that okay with you?'

'May I think about it?'

'Of course. June will go with you. Tell the others.'

'I'm not sure Donald or Robin will like it. They still love to play-fight the Japanese.'

June stepped forward. 'Come on. Let's leave these three to their conversation. We can eavesdrop from outside the window.'

The sisters headed outside, June mouthing, 'Good luck,' to Gordon as she passed him.

No-one spoke. Venn continued sipping her tea, clearly not planning to speak first. Gordon crossed his arms and leaned against the wall, hoping he appeared more casual than he felt.

His father broke the silence. 'What exactly do you intend to do?'

Gordon shrugged. 'I'm going to get her here. Bring her out to Australia. I can worry about the rest of it later.'

'I understand that. Dare I ask if you have a plan?'

'The Army's already set me up to finish my medical studies at university. I reckon people will take Dr Parker more seriously than Mr Parker. But university doesn't start for a few weeks yet, so I want to do some research.'

Every morning, Gordon caught the train to the State Library in the city, spending the day poring over books, newspaper archives, anything he could find to learn more about Australian immigration policies, the White Australia policy in particular. After a week, he had pages of notes, including quotes from journalists and interviewees, thin lines of blue ink on yellow paper.

To make sense of his notes, Gordon commandeered the dining table after dinner each night, constructing timelines of events and underlining anything he didn't fully understand, to investigate further.

'I hope you dedicate half as much attention to your studies.' Venn stood in the doorway watching him.

'I hope my studies are half as interesting.' Gordon rummaged through sheafs of paper. 'I never really knew about this White Australia policy. Seems the government brought it in because they were scared of the Chinese miners coming out during the gold rush, and so restricted anyone who wasn't from Britain. I mean, they say Europe but they bang on about preserving the British colony. And here, Mr Charles Bean, a war historian during the Great War, said that it's a "vehement effort to maintain a high Western standard of economy, society and culture".'

'Astute words from Mr Charles Bean.'

'He also said it is, "however it might be camouflaged, the rigid exclusion of Oriental peoples". So which is it then? Something to preserve the Britishness of Australia or something to exclude anyone from Asia?'

There was a faint smile on his mother's lips. 'Is there a possibility it could be both?'

Gordon scoffed. 'Of course there is. There doesn't seem to be two ways about it. But what do we need it for now? The gold rush is over – it was fifty years ago. Who cares if people from Asia and Europe want to live here?'

Venn sat opposite him. 'Many people. Particularly our current Immigration Minister, Arthur Calwell.'

Gordon grimaced. 'You know what he said about Japanese wives of Australian men?' He didn't need to find the piece of paper he'd made the note on – the words had burnt themselves into his memory. '"An Australian marrying a Japanese can live with her in Japan but it would be the grossest act of public indecency to permit any Japanese of either sex to pollute Australian shores while any relatives remain of Australian soldiers dead in the Pacific battlefields. No Australian is permitted to outrage the feelings of widows and mothers by flaunting Japanese women before their eyes."' Anger threatened to spill out of him, to incinerate the words that hung in the air between them. 'Apparently my wife and I would be committing the grossest act of public indecency.'

Venn flicked through some pages, a wry smile on her face. 'So there is no hope? All is lost? You'll languish and waste away, pining for your Japanese bride?'

Gordon ignored her teasing. 'Not quite.' He clicked his tongue as he looked for a particular bundle of newspaper clippings and notes. It was wrapped in string, an inch-high collection knotted together. He untied it. 'There's Mrs Annie O'Keefe. She's Indonesian, a war refugee because of the work her first husband, Samuel, had been doing for the Dutch in Indonesia. They sought refuge here, in Bonbeach.'

Venn frowned. 'I've heard about them. They have several children?'

'Yes. Eight. Samuel went back to Indonesia to work for the Dutch war effort and was killed in service, but Annie and the children stayed here and have been here for the last seven or so years.' Gordon pulled out a newspaper photograph of Annie and her children, a black-and-white picture of young smiling faces in school uniforms, Annie sandwiched in the middle and a white man standing behind them.

Venn pointed to the man. 'Is that her husband?'

'Her second husband. See, after the war ended, the government started deporting all those who had come over as refugees, and a neighbour who had become very close to the family, John O'Keefe, offered to marry Annie, so the family wasn't sent back to Indonesia.'

Venn nodded, studying the photograph. Gordon couldn't sit still. Nervous energy thrummed as he stood and paced.

'The government still tried to send them back, didn't they?'

'They did. Calwell refused to see the marriage as legitimate and went ahead with trying to force the whole family out of the country. Even though most of the children had lived their whole lives here, had no memories of Indonesia and considered themselves Australian. And,' Gordon fished an article from the bottom of his stack, handing it to his mother, 'Mrs O'Keefe took the case to the High Court and, just a few weeks ago, the court decided that Calwell had no right to deport Annie or the children because of the refugee status that was given to them when they arrived in the country.'

'Yes, of course. Calwell wasn't happy, if I remember correctly.'

'I can't imagine so. And there's another family, in Brunswick.' Gordon fumbled to untie a second stack, smaller than the other but no less significant. 'Mr Lorenzo Gamboa. A Filipino-American man. Met his wife, Joyce, in Melbourne while he was on leave from the US Army. They got married, he stayed in Melbourne, worked at the railways. The government found him, said he couldn't stay even though he had a job and a legitimate marriage, and sent him back to America.' Gordon threw the stack on the table in front of Venn, the pages fanning out in front of her. She was less amused and more interested. 'He rejoined the Army and served in Tokyo at the same time I was in Kure, if you can believe that. Now, he's trying to get back to his wife and kids – he's got two kids who haven't seen him in years – but Immigration won't let him in either.'

'But he's American,' Venn said.

'He's *Filipino*-American.' Gordon plucked out a photo of Lorenzo and Joyce. 'He's got brown skin. It's called the *White* Australia policy. They're keeping him away from his kids even though he's an American citizen, because he's got brown skin.'

Venn exhaled slowly. 'I wonder if you can find a way to contact Minister Calwell. Through the correct channels.'

Gordon nodded. 'I have an address for his office in Canberra. You're quite deft at writing letters, aren't you? Perhaps you can help?'

The question was too pointed. Venn stepped away from the table, mouth tight. 'I was worried for all of you boys. Over there, impressionable and foolish. Turns out I was right. I was trying to look after you.'

'I was fine without your meddling.' Gordon pulled his research back to him, stacking it haphazardly, ready to storm out of the room to make his point.

'Well, I was going to offer to meddle but if, as you say, you're fine without it, please yourself.' Venn disappeared into the kitchen, the regret bitter in Gordon's mouth. His mother's help would have been useful, but it was too late now to backtrack.

Gordon started with letters. He detailed his service with the Army, his time as a medical officer in Japan. He described how Cherry had been employed by BCOF in Kure and had good English, and explained that they were married, weaving in a gentle reminder that, technically, wives of servicemen were considered war brides and thus were exempt from usual immigration policy. He finished by saying that he would appreciate any guidance as to what the process would be to get her to Australia; perhaps a visa could be considered under compassionate grounds, given the post-war state of Japan.

Venn avoided speaking when Gordon was curled over the typewriter, tapping at the keys. Harry wasn't thrilled but said nothing, watching with disapproval as Gordon wound a new leaf of paper into the typewriter. When the first letter didn't get a response after three weeks, he wrote a follow-up. Then another. It was difficult for his frustration not to leak out onto the page, to keep things polite but urgent in the face of deafening silence.

After months of waiting, it became clear that Calwell wasn't intending to reply. There had to be another way to reach him. It probably wouldn't work to go to his office at Parliament in Canberra, demanding to see a senior member of government with a handful of unanswered letters. Instead, Gordon sought out a telephone number, hoping he might get through to speak to someone, to put a voice to his and Cherry's story, to make it more than ink on paper.

He resisted the urge to ask his father to help connect with Calwell, even though he was certain someone in Harry's council circles would be able to find a telephone number for the Immigration Minister's office. Harry had made it clear that he wasn't pleased with what Gordon was trying to do. His lack of support hadn't been easy to deal with, but Gordon had other avenues to explore, old friends and contacts who had gone into public service over the past three years. Surely someone would be able to help.

Gordon's medical studies started, but he was distracted, worried about Cherry alone in Japan. He sent her a letter every three days, signing every one of them 'from your loving husband, Gordon' and adding fifty hugs and kisses in a small cloud around his name, just so she could see how much he missed her. He numbered all his letters and parcels to make sure they were all accounted for. The Japanese postal system was notoriously unreliable, so he sent things for his wife to various soldiers at BCOF, to pass on to her or to sell and give Cherry the money. It was the only way to do it without raising suspicion, although he was concerned with how expensive shipping was to Japan. He had to do what he could to provide for his wife. Every letter reminded him of how hard it was to be away from her. Cherry didn't write back as often, which Gordon understood. It was difficult for her to write in English. He wished he had more from her but he savoured every word she did write. Updates about Charlie and Suma, small stories about life in Kure, all ending with her hope that she would be in Australia soon. It was agony.

One day, as he was about to leave university for home, a young man Gordon didn't know approached him.

'Gordon Parker?'

'Yes, that's me.'

'Been told to deliver this to you.' The man thrust a scrap of paper into Gordon's hand, before disappearing.

It was the number for Calwell's office.

The fifty-minute train ride home felt longer. He had no clue who had come through for him. He'd asked so many people for help. It didn't matter now. In his head, Gordon rehearsed what he would say to the Immigration Minister, jotting down notes as the train shuddered along the tracks, wanting to make sure he made the best possible case. It was still early. He would get home with enough time to call Calwell that afternoon.

Picking up the telephone in the living room at Greenwood House was terrifying. He took a deep breath, ignoring the curious gazes of Robin and Jennifer, who sat in the room with him. He dialled the number.

'Immigration Minister Calwell's office.'

'Hello. Hi. My name is Gordon Parker, I was wondering if I may be able to speak with Minister Calwell.'

'Do you have an appointment, sir?'

'I'm afraid not.'

'I can't pass you to the Minister without an appointment.'

'May I make an appointment?'

'What is it regarding?'

'I'd like to discuss organising a visa for my wife to join me in Australia. I'm an ex-serviceman, you see, and—'

'I'm sorry but the Minister doesn't examine individual cases.'

'Of course, I appreciate that he's a very busy man and I don't wish to encroach on his time. I was hoping to talk about having a visa granted on compassionate grounds—'

'I suggest you put your request in writing and Minister Calwell will get back to you presently.'

Gordon clenched his jaw. 'I have written to the Minister. Several times over the past few months. He hasn't replied to my letters, which is why I thought a telephone conversation may be a better route.'

There was silence. Gordon's heart sped up.

Calwell's secretary leafed through some papers, the rustling echoing down the telephone line. 'What did you say your name was, sir?'

'Gordon Parker. I met my wife while serving in Japan as part of the Occupation Force.'

'And your wife is an American woman? English?'

'No, sir, my wife is Japanese.'

More silence. Heavier now.

'And was your marriage approved by the Army during your time in Japan?'

'We got married under Japanese law – it was all above board. I have the paperwork with me in Melbourne, I'd be happy to send it to you.'

'Did the Army sign off on your marriage?'

Gordon hesitated. 'No. No, they didn't.'

'Unfortunately, Mr Parker, weddings conducted under the Japanese fashion aren't recognised under Australian law. Unless your wedding was signed off by the Army, we cannot authorise any kind of visa for this Japanese woman.'

Gordon's stomach dropped. 'But no weddings with Japanese women were signed off by the Army.'

'Then I'm afraid we cannot help you.'

'Perhaps if I can just speak directly with Minister Calwell, I can explain.'

'Unfortunately Minister Calwell has no available appointments and regrettably he will not be able to speak with you.'

'Wait, please—'

'Good day.'

The telephone connection clicked off. Gordon stood, receiver at his ear, stunned.

'Not sure that went so well,' Robin said, concerned.

Gordon slammed the telephone onto its hook. The sound drew Venn out from the kitchen.

'Calwell has always been very supportive of the White Australia policy,' she said. 'He's a man who believes in the processes of previous governments. It worked for us in the past so it works for us now.'

'Why?' Gordon asked. 'The war's over now. Surely we don't need it.'

'That policy has never been about the war.' Venn headed back into the other room. 'But Imperial Japan certainly gave our government an excellent excuse to uphold its views on immigration.'

Gordon soon memorised the Immigration Minister's direct number, calling every second day to try to get past Calwell's secretary. The pompous man on the other end of the line came to recognise Gordon's voice, hanging up as soon as Gordon greeted him, leaving a tinny echo in his ear as the line disconnected. One solitary letter arrived from Japan, in skinny, wobbling English from Cherry that made his heart ache. Words didn't seem enough to convey how much he felt for her. The little Japanese he knew was already slipping from his mind and, even though he could've written pages and pages to her in English every day, it was difficult to know how much she could understand. His mood didn't improve when he saw an article in the newspaper, a full-page spread, welcoming English war brides to Melbourne: a sea of white, perfectly made-up faces waving to their servicemen husbands on the shore at the Port Melbourne docks. A festival of celebration for these women, who wrapped themselves up in their spouses' arms, smiling for the photographs and the press.

A fog of frustration sat on his shoulders the entire day, Gordon eventually surrendering to desperation and distraction, leaving his class early. Sitting in the pub alone, he nursed a beer, the bubbles racing to the top of his drink. He'd been home for five months and he'd barely achieved a thing. He was no closer to getting Cherry out of Japan, it was expensive and difficult for him to get a civilian visa to return to Japan himself, and it seemed he may have annoyed the Immigration Department so much that any potential visa would be blocked out of spite.

At least the beer in Melbourne was real beer.

Laughter rang out from the Ladies' Lounge next door. Standing on the other side of the pub were some couples, on a double date. Jealousy flared in Gordon's chest. Not once had he been able to take Cherry to a nice restaurant or go on a proper date. All their moments had been cautious and clandestine.

One of the women shifted to the side and when Gordon caught sight of the man with her, his heart leapt.

It was Toby.

Jumping to his feet, he crossed the room and stepped through the door. Almost as if he could sense Gordon's presence, Toby looked up.

'No bloody way.' Toby darted out from his place at the bar and within moments they were wrapped around each other, grinning and laughing. 'Don Parker. Aren't you a sight for sore eyes.'

'What are you doing in this neck of the woods, Westy?' Gordon clapped his friend on the shoulder, unable to believe it. 'I thought you were a Newcastle boy.'

'I am, I am.' Toby walked Gordon towards his group of friends. 'Moved down here a couple of months ago because Hel's family are here. Her mother would murder me if I stole her away. Hel, you won't believe this.' A blonde woman smiled at Gordon, face rouged and made up, a reminder of the English war brides in the newspaper that morning. She linked her arm through Toby's. Intimate. Close.

Dread crept through Gordon as he fought to keep his smile intact.

'Helen, this is Don. Don, this is Helen.'

'It is an absolute pleasure,' she said, holding out her hand for Gordon to shake. He took it, polite. There was a golden wedding band on her left hand. 'Toby has told me so much about you.'

'Only good things, I hope,' Gordon said, the lightness in his tone belying the sudden anger in his chest. He looked to his friend. 'You married an Aussie girl.'

'Can't fight love at first sight.' Toby put his arm around Helen and squeezed her close. 'Mum introduced us when I got back, and I was smitten right from the off.'

Gordon couldn't speak.

Helen smiled. 'Why don't I let you two catch up? We'll sit – you're welcome to join us, Don.' She gestured to the other couple hovering by the bar, keeping a polite distance.

'Oh, I can't hang around,' Gordon said. 'Couldn't pass up the opportunity to have a chat to this bloke though.'

Toby grinned as Helen gave him a kiss on the cheek and walked away.

'She seems nice,' Gordon said, ice in his tone.

'She's all right,' Toby said. 'But you can't be mad.'

'I wrote to you.' Gordon struggled to keep his voice low, to keep his calm. 'Yoneko wrote to you. We were worried.'

'You didn't need to be. I was fine. I'm here, aren't I? And you know what?' Toby took a sip of his beer, almost bolstering his courage. 'It's better, isn't it? Being home again. Japan was a different world. Different rules. No sneaking around here, no threat of being punished if you're caught with a pretty girl. And I've got a real wife now.'

'Yoneko is your real wife.'

Toby sighed. 'Look. She knew I was leaving sometime. Sure, I left earlier than we expected but what was I gonna do? Stay in Japan? Eat rice and fish for the rest of my life?' He ran a hand through his hair. 'Yonnie stopped writing eventually. I never read her letters anyway, so it was probably for the best. I had to keep them hidden from the family so I just stashed them away. Never even opened any of them.'

'So you just abandoned her? Did you even try to do anything to get her here?'

'Do what?' Toby's voice had an edge to it now. 'What was I meant to do? I tried to make it legit. The Army shipped me home. I had no way of getting anything through that bloody Immigration Department and every letter that arrived from her, from you, just reminded me how much of a failure I was. How was I supposed to get her here? It's bigger than me. I'm no-one.'

'You have a daughter.'

That stopped Toby in his tracks. He stared at Gordon, not comprehending. Gordon refused to look away. Toby shook his head and took another sip of his beer.

'Nah, mate. I don't have any kids. Hel and I are hoping one day, but right now we're just enjoying each other.'

'Her name is Setsuko.'

Toby sniffed. 'Dunno anyone by that name.'

'Wonder what Helen would think of that.'

Toby drew himself up to his full height, short but still imposing. Both refused to back down. Gordon squared his shoulders, but it was his friend who spoke first. 'I reckon you should skedaddle, mate. It's been real nice to catch up. Let's not do it again.'

Rage and sadness coursed through Gordon, unsure whether he should throw a punch or get out of there. It seemed a waste to walk away from someone who had been his best friend for three years, but Toby had made his choice. He'd chosen Helen, he'd chosen a future that Gordon couldn't even begin to imagine, a future that forced you to abandon the woman you loved in another country, to somehow forget that your child even existed.

With difficulty, Gordon held his hand out for Toby to shake. He took it and gave a firm squeeze. Toby retreated to Helen and their friends, making a comment as they looked back to Gordon with a wave.

Gordon didn't wave back. Toby put his arm around Helen, the golden wedding ring on her finger a smug talisman of the injustice of how Japanese women were treated by most Australian men.

Unable to let it go, Gordon strode back to the table and looked directly at Helen. 'Did Westy tell you he has a wife? A Japanese girl? Her name's Yoneko.'

Toby stood up. 'I reckon you've had one too many, mate.' He put his hand roughly on Gordon's shoulder, but Gordon shook it off. Helen stared at him, silent.

'And he's got a daughter. Setsuko. Hope she doesn't grow up to be as gutless as him.'

'That's enough.' Toby shoved Gordon towards the exit of the pub.

'He's got letters,' he said, gaze locked on Helen, who was pale with shock. 'Kept them. You should find them. They'll tell you the truth. He promised her they'd live in Newcastle. They're married according to Japanese law—'

Toby's knuckles against Gordon's jaw sent him staggering into a nearby table. He blinked, ears ringing, gingerly opening and closing his mouth to see if anything felt broken. Toby glared at him, fist still curled, ready to swing again.

Gordon let out a tight chuckle and turned to Helen. 'If you don't believe me, ask yourself why your upstanding husband just socked someone who's supposed to be his mate.'

The entire pub was watching now. Gordon was tempted to release all his anger until there was nothing left except bruised knuckles and satisfaction. Instead, he gave Helen a small salute. 'Sorry to cause a fuss. I miss my wife. She's a Japanese girl. And she's not allowed to be here.'

'Maybe you shouldn't have married a Japanese girl then, mate.' It wasn't clear who spoke but the words resonated.

Gordon nodded, guilt coursing through him. 'Maybe I shouldn't have.'

He spilled onto the cool streets of Melbourne. It was too early to go home and there was a whisky bottle somewhere in the city that would help him scrub the image of Helen's horrified face from his mind. He was sure of it.

The lights were on inside his house and the front steps blurred beneath his feet. Were there five stairs or six? The whisky winked at him, refusing to give an answer. Harry and Venn appeared at the door as Gordon navigated the steps with difficulty. The image of his parents, faces serious, looking at him as he concentrated on not falling backwards, made Gordon giggle.

'This feels rather ominous.' He pushed past them into the house, collapsing onto an armchair. The room spun as his body settled, head swimming.

'You had a telephone call.' Harry was silhouetted in the lamplight. 'From a signalman at the Victorian barracks.'

Gordon frowned. 'I don't know anyone at the Vic barracks.'

'There was a message from Japan.' Panic engulfed Gordon. Had something happened to Cherry? He sat up, trying to catch this moment, struggling against the alcoholic fug that clouded his head.

Venn spoke next. 'Cherry's pregnant.'

The world stopped. The lights in the house seemed to dim and a shiver ran down his back.

Cherry was pregnant.

'You're a damned fool,' Harry said.

'No.' Gordon pushed himself out of his chair, standing to meet his father at eye level. His body was steady, the alcoholic cloud whisked away in a second. 'I am her husband. She is my wife. My *wife*. And the mother of my child.' Gordon grappled with the idea that he was going to be someone's father. 'She's your daughter-in-law. And she's having your grandchild.'

Harry stared at Gordon, a whirl of emotions flashing across the older man's face, then walked out of the room. Venn watched him leave before turning to her son. He steadied himself, still trying to comprehend the news. How had Cherry got word to someone at the Victorian barracks? She must've told Slim or Andy, who snuck it through, the message bouncing from receiver to receiver until someone telephoned Greenwood House.

'Do you think it's yours?' Venn asked. The question was a sucker punch, knocking the wind out of Gordon. As he opened his mouth, furious, she threw up her hands. 'All right, yes, fine. You don't need to get twisted up in knots, I wanted to ask because people will.' She sat on the lounge, Gordon instinctively sinking into the space next to her.

'I'm going to be a dad.' The words sounded strange in Gordon's mouth. A dazed smile stretched across his mouth.

'Lord help us all.' His mother laughed. 'Another Parker running around.' She hesitated, frowning. 'Mind you, they'll have to stay in Japan, won't they?'

A throb of pain jolted through Gordon's chest. 'I expect so, yes.'

Her mouth tightened. 'I may never see my first grandchild. Never hear them call me Granny.'

Gordon groaned, grief threatening to spiral.

Venn cleared her throat. 'Enough self-pity,' she said. 'You've got more than yourself to think about now. If you want my advice, we need to figure out what you're going to do next and do it quick. Babies don't wait.'

He tilted his head in surprise. '*We* need to figure it out?'

She shot him a look. 'You're clearly making very little progress on your own. So *we* need to figure out how to bring your wife and child home.'

Warmth spread through him, quickly extinguished by the reality of the situation. 'What am I supposed to do? I already married her. It's not good enough. A Japanese shrine is somehow different from an Australian church? They're both places where people pray to God, right?'

Venn shrugged. 'So get married in an Australian church.'

He rolled his eyes. 'You may have missed this very small fact, but Cherry cannot get into the country.'

'Then get married in a Japanese church.'

'We did.'

'A Christian church. An Australian church but in Japan.' He sat up. 'There has to be a church somewhere in that country. It can't all be temples and shrines.'

His mother's words whirled around him, the whisky keeping them just on the edge of total comprehension. 'Wait. Say that again.'

Venn gripped his chin so that they could see eye to eye. 'Find a Christian church in Japan. Get married there. If you're not a soldier, the Army doesn't have to sign off on it. If you're in a church, it will have to be recognised in Australia. Find a church.'

The words echoed before they finally sank in.

'Mum, I reckon you're a genius.'

Venn let go of him. 'I reckon that's obvious. And I reckon you need a big glass of water, my boy.'

CHAPTER SEVENTEEN

CHERRY: Kure, January 1949

The nightmares started early. The night after she discovered she was pregnant, Cherry's dreams were plagued with visions of horror. Images of birthing a dead child; a child who was half human, half animal; a child who tore her apart from the inside; a child who never even existed. Her worries didn't leave when the sun rose. Every day was filled with constant fear: that her body would fail her and the child, that Don would never meet the baby, that she would do something to kill the life inside her. That Hiroshima, the devastating moment that had taken her mother from her, would somehow find a way to poison her child too. She battled those thoughts and acute morning sickness, struggling to keep any food down or to summon the energy to do anything.

The sickness didn't abate as her pregnancy continued. Most days, Cherry sat in a quiet corner to cry. Her husband was on the other side of the world, she was no longer in control of her own body, and Suma offered only the barest support.

'This is something many women go through.' Suma's refrain had become rote. 'You are blessed to carry a child. You should be grateful.'

Cherry was grateful. So grateful that if she thought about it too much, it would overwhelm her. At first, it had been easier. It had been her secret, a knot in her stomach only she knew about. People pitied her, knowing she was another Japanese girl abandoned by an Australian soldier who had gone home. There were a lot of them, a silent group of women, some who had babies with dark hair and pale eyes, immediate evidence that their father was not a local man. People tried to remind Cherry that Don had left her too, that she wasn't different to any of the false war brides. She fought not to listen, to trust in her husband. He wrote to her often, although the letters sometimes arrived at the same time, so there would be weeks with no word and then Andy would appear with four letters in Don's sloping handwriting, his x's and o's on the bottom of the final page. Cherry struggled to find paper to reply, constantly frustrated by her poor written English. Speaking was easier. Writing in the strange, stark symbols was far more difficult.

Once when Yoneko visited with Setsuko, she suggested Cherry not have the baby. She could get what Cherry needed to abort the child, then she could wait and see if Don would come back. The flash of rage that shot through Cherry was the strongest she'd felt since she'd been pregnant.

'I will keep this child.' She glared at Yoneko, who took a step back.

'What if Don-san doesn't return? Do you want to be like me?'

Cherry shook her head, ignoring the jolt of fear that ran down her back. She had to keep believing in her husband. She had nothing else. 'I know Don-san will come back.'

Yoneko sighed. 'Yes.' She glanced at Setsuko, crawling on the floor. 'Maybe he will bring Toby-san too.'

Reluctant to risk a letter with such important news going missing, Cherry asked Andy to get a message to Don about the baby more directly. Since then, every mail run was filled with letters and packages. Some were for Cherry, the baby and Charlie; others were for Andy and Slim with items to sell at the market so that they could give the money they made to her. Cans of vegetables, tennis balls, cigarettes – she never asked what they sold but gratefully took the profits. She hadn't worked at the barracks since Don had left, feeling unsafe without him to protect her, and many people didn't want to work with a fallen woman. With little choice, Cherry pawned her emerald ring at the market. The last tangible memory of her mother. She refused to cry when she handed the ring to the merchant or when she took the small bag of coins that held far less than the ring was worth. It wasn't until night fell that she gave into her grief, sobbing silent tears in the middle of the night, hands over her stomach, praying and hoping that her ancestors would forgive her.

Packages from Australia always lifted her mood. There were letters and handmade clothes for the baby, a knitted hat from Venn and a letter talking about how excited she was to be a grandmother, something that warmed Cherry's heart. After Cherry mentioned she wanted to improve her reading, Don sent issues of a magazine called *The Australian Women's Weekly*. Poring over every page, translating the English, staring at the glamorous women in the photographs, was a balm. One evening, she was reading about the latest trends in dresses when Riyoko, one of the women staying with them, stopped to look.

'They're so pretty,' Riyoko said, touching the page. 'I would love a dress like that but I could never get one in Japan.'

'You could make one,' Cherry said. 'If you had the material, it would be easy.'

Riyoko laughed. 'I don't think so. I never learnt how to sew. But maybe you could make one for me? I would pay you. Then I could look like a film star.'

The dress didn't look difficult, a few panels and some shaping, some hand-sewing to bring it all together. Cherry's mother had been an incredible seamstress, often tailoring clothes for Noboru or making pieces for her daughter. She had taught Cherry how to use newspapers to measure the fabric, cutting out the shapes and pieces needed to create different looks for dresses and blouses. Like her knitting and yarn work, Cherry had a natural eye for sewing and, after Riyoko had paid her, she set about estimating the best way to recreate the dress from the picture.

It took over a week by the time she found the materials, took Riyoko's measurements, and created the dress. It wasn't exactly like the picture but it was unmistakably Western-style and Riyoko loved it. Cherry was glad that her mother could live through the stitches, even in only one dress.

That one dress was so perfectly made, it drew attention and stares as Riyoko wore it through town. As word spread, young women showed up at Suma's doorstep to order a garment. Cherry set up a workshop in the house, cutting out pictures from the *Women's Weekly* magazines as a folio of samples and moving through orders. Some of these women would cross the street to avoid her in public but were happy to come to her in secret. If the girls were rude during a fitting, it was tempting to leave a few stitches loose in a garment so the piece would fall apart, or place a pin in the hem to jab them at an inopportune moment, but Cherry never succumbed to the temptation. Her mother wouldn't have stood for such vengeful thoughts. The best way to treat people was with respect, regardless of how they treated you. Cherry's reputation was so tenuous that if she could bolster it through stitches in fabric, she would do what she could to protect it and make her mother proud.

Twice a week, she went to the market to pick her materials. The older woman who ran the stall, Sachiko, always made a fuss when she arrived, serving tea and regaling Cherry with tales of her youth. The hour she spent at the fabric stall with Sachiko recalled memories of her mother and aunt, nurturing a longing for maternal figures she could never sate.

Cherry sat with her cup of sencha as Sachiko flitted between the tables, pulling out new fabrics to show her. The older woman threw them on top of one another with a bouncing thud, urging Cherry to touch the fabric, showing her the detail, the sales-speak almost an afterthought as Sachiko gleefully recounted the time she was chased off a boy's property by his mother, caught half-dressed in the fields of daikon.

'The daikon doesn't grow tall enough to hide in and before we realised, she was screaming at us!' A bolt of navy cotton landed on top of some white lace, Cherry unwinding the soft fabric to study the drape, to see how it would sit as a skirt. A rush of bubbles danced through her stomach and she placed a steadying hand on her growing bump, feeling for the baby twisting inside her. Two more months and the baby would be in her arms. Cherry swallowed the knot of anxiety in her throat at the thought.

Sachiko talked as she dug into a pile of material at the back of the stall, but Cherry was only half listening, thinking about how many dresses she could make with the fabric that was already here. Her neck prickled. Someone watching her. She glanced up, glad for the table between her and the market lane, readying herself for insults or abuse for being pregnant to an ex-enemy soldier.

It was Noboru.

Her father stared, any warmth she had remembered long gone. His eyes drifted to her swollen belly, his lip curled in revulsion. Instinctively, she covered her stomach with her hands, trying to protect her child, but her father's disgust seeped into her skin. He was older, colder, and still her feet shifted, her knees threatening to bend, her back wanting to bow, to show him respect.

He drew breath, as though to speak, then his lungs gave way to coughing. He turned from her as his body shook with the expulsion of air, hands shaking as they covered his mouth. Sachiko shot forward, screeching at him to get away from her fabrics, shooing him into the tide of shoppers as they moved down the path of the market.

Noboru half turned, eyes red and watering, watching her through the crowd. Cherry took a step towards him and her father snarled, disappearing into the shadows. The last echo of her lost family.

She sank into her seat, stomach turning. The baby or her own body, she didn't know. She pushed her hands against the seat underneath her, trying to hold on to anything real, to avoid the spiral into despair.

'Where did he go?' Sachiko's anger brought Cherry out of her thoughts. 'He damaged my fabric! Look at this!' She held up the edge of a yellow striped cotton, marked with flecks of blood. 'Coughing everywhere. That man will be dead soon and it's just as well or I'd hunt him down and kill him myself.' Sachiko clicked her tongue and tucked the blood-stained fabric under her arm. 'Now, would you like me to deliver the navy cotton this week?'

The bigger her belly grew, the more scared she was to leave the house, even though Suma insisted Cherry needed to walk to help the baby stay comfortable. After seeing her father at the market, it was harder to keep control of her fear. Her paranoia grew. People stared when she walked through the market and she was certain men were following her home. She stopped eating. She struggled to put on weight. Her energy fell. Her fears rose.

She was terrified she could go into labour early, in public, and be left without medical help because of her Australian husband. The thought of a hospital was equally frightening. There had been stories of ainoko babies, so-called mongrel babies, that had disappeared from hospitals with no explanation from the doctors, much to the anguish of their mothers. Cherry begged Suma not to get a doctor to the house when the time came.

'By the time a doctor comes, the baby will already be here,' Suma said. 'You will have me. You will have your mother watching over you. Your body will know what to do.'

Still, when the time came she was not prepared. It was rolling waves of pain over hours, sticky sweat that trickled down her back, in her eyes, salty tears slipping into the corners of her mouth. Fingers clenched tight around Suma's, around knees, around anything to help channel the pain. Screaming and sobbing, drifting out of her body then slamming back in. She couldn't do this. She couldn't. A soft voice in her ear, real or imagined.

'You are very strong, Nobuko-chan. Your strength is not measured in muscle, you know.'

Tsudo's words echoed as Cherry slumped back onto the floor. The high-pitched shrieks of the baby filled the room.

'Is it okay? Is the baby okay?' Breathless words as Cherry drifted back into her body. She was dizzy, light-headed, in pain, struggling to breathe.

'It's a girl.'

A tiny girl. Pink skin, black hair, dark eyes. No marks or scars of Hiroshima, no wounds or illness. Cherry stared at her daughter, in her arms, tucked into a blanket. An impossible thing, a part of her and Don mixed together, undeniable evidence of their love. Terror seized her. She was responsible for this baby, this tiny thing that couldn't fend for herself and knew nothing of the world. A deep pang of longing for her own mother throbbed in Cherry's chest. She would do whatever she could to protect this little girl. Whatever else happened, she had a chance to build a new family, to replace the one broken by war. Even if it was only the two of them.

'Take her.' Cherry's voice was a croak. 'I'm—' She never finished the sentence. She fainted.

When she woke up, the house was dark. She tried to sit, her head swimming, looking for her baby. Where was she? Had someone taken her? Shaking uncontrollably, she tried to call out but couldn't speak. She pushed herself up, arms wobbling, trying to see.

The movement caught Suma's eye. She bustled in and knelt next to Cherry.

'Lie down. You're not well.'

'Where is the baby?' Cherry whispered. Suma shifted, revealing the newborn strapped to her chest, asleep. Cherry bit back a sob as she slumped onto the futon. Suma held a cup to her lips.

'Drink.' Cherry did as she was told, a sweet liquid pouring into her mouth. 'You've been asleep for ten hours. The baby is well, if a little small. A woman down the road has fed her twice, but she hasn't drunk much. She was screaming for you. Once you drink, you should try to feed her.'

Guilt gripped Cherry. She'd barely been a mother for a day and she'd already failed her daughter. Her heart beat in her throat and tears prickled in her eyes.

Suma didn't seem to notice. 'I did have a doctor come to see you. He didn't touch the baby. He said you are too skinny. Both of you. You must rest and eat so you can look after her.'

Cherry nodded, forcing the last sips of the drink into her mouth. She needed to be strong. She reached out to Suma.

'The baby?'

She tried to stop the shake in her hands, to show that she was all right. Suma nodded and withdrew the baby from her chest. The baby squirmed as the older woman passed her over, murmuring quietly to soothe the child. Cherry held the baby close. Her daughter wriggled in the folds of a warm blanket, then grimaced, letting out a soft cry.

'Try to feed her,' Suma said, shifting closer to help brace her. Cherry lifted her shirt, vaguely noting the tang of sweat and illness on her skin, and resisted the urge to burst into tears.

Suma leaned down and gently pushed the baby's head against Cherry's breast. The crying eased and the baby started to suck. Cherry let out a laugh of relief, of gratitude, ignoring the odd sensation at her chest as she leaned back against the wall.

Suma smiled. 'She's been waiting for you.'

Cherry couldn't stop the tears then. They slid down her cheeks as she watched her daughter suckle, exhaustion creeping in at the edges of her vision. She could hold it at bay for a little longer. Just long enough to feed the baby.

'What will you call her?' Suma asked.

Cherry shrugged.

'You'll need to choose something. We can't call her Baby forever.'

But Cherry didn't choose a name immediately. There were rumours that the Japanese government took mixed-race children with no fathers in Japan and put them into orphanages. She didn't want to register her daughter in case it put her in danger. Being a mother, with no support from a family or income from a husband, was her main focus; learning how to recognise the difference between piercing cries, trying to stay awake during constant feeding, working to keep the lines straight on her garments between naps. Weeks stretched on with no decision on Baby Parker's name. It wasn't an easy choice. A Japanese name with Parker as the surname felt wrong, a clash of cultures and syllables. Cherry had an Australian name, after all. Her daughter should have the same so they would fit in when Don rescued them and took them back to Ringwood

Western names leapt from *The Australian Women's Weekly.* Every page offered a new option, a collection of names begging to be picked. Only one caught Cherry's attention. It appeared in almost every edition she had, attached to a woman who was constantly in focus. Princess Margaret.

It was regal. It was beautiful. It was perfect.

Cherry didn't recover quickly from the birth. She was weak and tired. It seemed that as soon as she fell asleep, Margaret would already be awake and squalling. Letters arrived from Don, promising he would visit soon, promising he was saving money to purchase his passage to Japan and a visa. She could barely read them. Tired, haggard, unable to remember when she'd last bathed, she rocked Margaret to sleep in the middle of the night.

'Soon. Soon you will meet your father. He will come for us soon. Don-san will be here soon.'

She hoped.

CHAPTER EIGHTEEN

GORDON: Melbourne, September 1949

Gordon was worried. He'd only had one letter from Cherry since Margaret had been born in mid-August, arriving three weeks after the birth. Her words were apologetic and thin – sorry for not having given Gordon a son, sorry for not having written sooner or sending him the news of Margaret's birth herself. He didn't care if he had a son or not. All he cared about was that they were healthy. Andy had sent a message announcing Margaret's arrival, a letter following from Suma after that.

It was the second letter from Suma that concerned him most. While the letter revealed the name Cherry had chosen for their daughter, Suma also wrote that Cherry was quite unwell after Margaret's birth. Money was a problem too. One package Don had sent to a new link in his postal chain, to a mate of Slim's called Neil, had gone missing. It turned out that Neil had sold the contents at market but never passed the money on. Suma begged Gordon to send food from Australia, even if only biscuits and sugar.

Gordon was furious. He'd chosen men he trusted that were still serving in BCOF to send parcels to, so they would be sure to arrive and get to Cherry. The mail network needed to be big enough to avoid detection, so he wasn't constantly sending huge packages to Andy and Slim. Slim had suggested Neil as another soldier to post to and, clearly, Slim needed to choose his friends better. Cherry relied on that money to survive, and Don was working two jobs around his medical studies to save the money to buy goods to sell. He picked up work anywhere he could, most frequently babysitting around Ringwood. These were the easy jobs. Once the children were asleep, he could study, although he was finding it more difficult to concentrate on his textbooks. He also took shifts in a pub and put his hand up to help farmers with their fencing. Anything he could do that had a bit of coin in it, he would.

He saved as much as he could for his return to Japan. He had wanted to be there for Margaret's birth, but he was well short of the money he needed for the ship's fare, let alone the civilian visa, and he felt immense guilt he hadn't been there to support Cherry.

Now his wife needed him more than ever. He should have stayed. It didn't matter that he thought he'd had no choice, he should have found a way to make it work. Appealed Kerr's decision not to extend Gordon's service. Transferred to the Air Force from the Army, although the Air Force was a much smaller unit in Kure and they were shipping out of Japan in the next few months, according to the newspapers. There would have been some way to stay in Kure. He should have found it.

Civilian travel to Japan was more difficult to arrange than he expected. He found passage from Melbourne to Japan via Sydney, Brisbane, Manila and Hong Kong. The price of the trip was an eye-watering £96 (at a time when the average weekly male wage in Australia was £7), but there was no other option. The ship, the *Merkur*, was due to leave at the start of December. Gordon had three months to get his visa organised and save as much money as he could. On his way from college to his babysitting one September evening, he sent his visa application to the Australian External Affairs Department. From there, it had to go to the US State Department to the Supreme Commander for the Allied Powers (SCAP), General Douglas MacArthur. Given BCOF were a subcommand under SCAP, Gordon had included a letter that detailed his service in Kure, in case MacArthur did read every visa application himself.

Then he waited.

The hardest part was telling his mother he would be away for Christmas.

'You've barely been home a year.' Venn was furious. 'I need your help with the food drives and delivering parcels for the Red Cross.'

'Get Donald. He'll be better at it than me.'

His mother was about to launch into a tirade, when Gordon cut her off.

'You'd rather I leave my wife and daughter on their own for another Christmas?'

'Of course not. But there are other ways to do this.'

'What other ways? Please enlighten me. I'll try anything at this point.'

Venn hesitated, unsure, when Harry strode into the room. She turned to her husband. 'Have you heard about your son's plan to go back to Japan for Christmas?'

'Nonsense.' Harry didn't look up as he searched the table. 'He won't have enough money. Has anyone seen my pipe?'

'I've saved some,' Gordon said. 'Not quite as much as I'd like but if we're careful, it'll last a few months. And I've still got two months of work. I was thinking about cutting back on my classes for the rest of the year to give myself more time.'

Harry looked to Gordon then. 'Stop going to class?'

Gordon faltered. 'Just for a few months.'

'Surely you have your exams soon.'

'November. Shortly before I leave. The results will come through in January. You'll have to send them on to me.'

Harry looked at Venn, who threw up her hands, exasperated. 'Don't look at me. This is the first I've heard of it.'

'What happened to Dr Parker?' Harry asked, tucking his hands into his pockets. 'I thought that was part of your plan to get the politicians onside.'

'It is.' Frustration rose in Gordon's chest. 'I feel like I'm ready for the exams. And the class is mostly textbook revision, which I can do from home. I don't need to be at school for that.' Gordon didn't mention he was struggling to focus in class, his concern for Cherry invading his thoughts nearly every moment.

Harry and Venn said nothing, which unnerved him more than anything else. His parents always had an opinion. He shrugged. 'I'll get on with things then.' He gave a curt nod, then unearthed Harry's pipe from beneath a few sheets of paper. Harry took it and Gordon left the room before his father could thank him.

Guilt attacked him from two sides now. He had left Cherry on her own with no support and, at the same time, he was letting down his Australian family. He didn't know how to reconcile the two. He started smoking and drinking more, even though he could hardly afford it, and he struggled to sleep without being awoken by anxious thoughts and dreams.

His visa still didn't come.

He rang the External Affairs Department after six weeks and was assured that his application had travelled on to the US State Department as required.

'There's always a bit of a backlog at this time of year.' The clerk on the other end of the line was chirpy and cheerful. 'Although it's because a lot of soldiers are requesting time back home, more so than people like you trying to get to Japan. Why are you heading there, anyway?'

'Just want to see some mates,' Gordon said. It wasn't strictly a lie but was worried SCAP wouldn't look favourably on an Australian ex-soldier trying to see his Japanese wife. The Americans were more lax with their fraternisation rules, but Gordon couldn't be sure who would read his application and decided to err on the side of caution.

'I wouldn't worry,' the clerk said. 'I expect it will come through in the next two weeks.'

It didn't. As they moved into November, Gordon couldn't enjoy the warm sunshine or the late spring days. He worked hard to save what he could, sending Cherry packages and letters, intending to take some products to sell himself. He had told his wife he'd be there for Christmas, but if the visa didn't come, he'd fail her again.

He took to calling External Affairs every few days, always getting the same response: it should arrive in the post imminently. No matter how many times he looked through the mail, it never arrived.

Hope came when the departure of the *Merkur* was delayed by a week so they could load more cargo. It gained Gordon some time, but when the visa still hadn't arrived, he called External Affairs once again, fighting to keep his voice polite.

The clerk gave a different answer this time. 'Ah, okay. I think I know what's happened here.' The air rushed out of Gordon's lungs. 'There's been a breakdown somewhere along the line. This process is so convoluted sometimes.' The clerk laughed but Gordon sagged into his chair, devastated.

'So I don't have a visa to enter Japan?' he asked, voice low.

'Not yet. But you'll be able to pick it up from the Australian Trade Commissioner in Hong Kong.'

Gordon sat up, hope blooming in his chest. 'What's it doing in Hong Kong?'

'Sometimes when they sign off on paperwork late, they leave it along the passenger's line of travel. Manila doesn't have a Trade Commissioner so, as long as you don't disembark in the Philippines, you'll be right to get your piece of paper in Hong Kong.'

He'd done it. Gordon laughed with relief. 'Mate, thank you. This is the best Christmas present anyone's ever given me.'

'My pleasure. Merry Christmas, Mr Parker.'

The next problem was that, with the delays for cargo loading, the *Merkur* pushed its departure once again: to the afternoon of Christmas Day. Not only that, but the delay meant they wouldn't be taking passengers until Sydney. With no time to catch the train north, Gordon reluctantly dipped into his savings to purchase an airfare from Melbourne to Sydney.

He struggled to get excited on Christmas morning, itching to make his way back to Cherry and Margaret. He helped Jim put together his new bike (although it was secondhand itself) and sang carols with June and Robin. Shortly before he was due to leave for the airport, Venn pulled Gordon away from the family and handed him an envelope. Inside were Australian pounds, enough to cover the airfare.

'You don't have to do this, Mum. I have enough money.'

'We both know that's not true.' Venn sighed. 'Don't tell your father.' She cleared her throat. 'I'm sorry that this hasn't been easy. But you go and give my daughter and granddaughter a kiss from me.' She pulled him into a tight hug. Gordon relaxed into it, only then realising how much he needed one. 'You look after those girls of yours and hopefully something changes before you come back.'

'Fingers crossed,' he said, trying to keep the sudden tremble from his voice.

His mother took a shaky breath. 'Promise me you'll come home.'

'I promise.'

Not wanting to miss the bus to the airport, Gordon said a quick goodbye to his siblings, then sought out his father. Harry was in his study.

'I'm off,' Gordon said, hovering in the doorframe.

His father lifted his pipe from his lips. 'You still have time to change your mind, son.'

Gordon's heart sank. 'Merry Christmas to you too, Dad.'

Hollowed out, he left for the bus with a suitcase in each hand, at the start of his journey back to Kure.

Gordon kept to himself on board the *Merkur.* A few passengers tried to speak to him over the first few days of the journey, but when he barely responded, they left him alone. No-one else seemed to be travelling all the way to Japan, most disembarking in Brisbane or Hong Kong.

Gordon stayed aboard, as instructed, in Manila, writing a letter to Cherry. This one he could deliver in person. It was almost a habit now, putting his thoughts down on paper, simplifying his language so she could translate it easily.

Every minute brought him closer to her.

He could barely wait for the gangplank to be lowered before he raced off the ship in Hong Kong, following a hand-drawn map to get to the offices of the Australian Trade Commissioner. Out of breath, Gordon paused by the doorway, checking his reflection in the glass. Once his breathing had settled, he strode into the office.

'May I help you?' The man behind the attendant's window called Gordon forward.

'I'm here to pick up my authorisation to enter Japan. From SCAP. I was told it would be waiting for me.'

The clerk frowned. 'Name?'

'Gordon Holroyd Parker.'

The clerk moved to a set of cabinets behind him. Gordon tapped his foot as the clerk flicked through one drawer, then opened another.

'Parker, you say? With a P for Peter? Not a B for Brian?'

'P for Peter, yes.' Gordon's heart sped up.

The clerk returned to the first drawer, flicking through it more slowly this time. He pushed it shut and returned to the window empty-handed. 'My apologies, Mr Parker, but there is no permit or visa here for you.'

Gordon stared at the man. 'There must be some mistake. I was told my SCAP permit would be waiting for me in Hong Kong because it took so long for them to approve it.'

'The mistake, I'm afraid, was you being told that. That scenario does happen, on the rare occasion, but we are always told when that paperwork is coming in and I have had no such missives. I do apologise.'

Gordon tried to think, heart hammering in his ears. 'How am I supposed to get to Japan now?'

'I'm afraid you can't,' the clerk said. 'You won't be permitted entry without that piece of paper.'

'But that piece of paper was supposed to be here!' Gordon said, the words exploding from his mouth. Immediately, he was contrite. 'I'm sorry, I'm sorry, Mr … ?'

'Briar.'

'Mr Briar, I apologise for my outburst. It's already been a long trip and I promised my wife that I was coming to visit her. She had our first child in August and she's alone in Japan without any family. I need to see her. I need to meet my daughter.' Gordon was babbling but he couldn't control it. 'Would you like to see a photograph? My wife sent me one last month.' He pulled it from his breast pocket and pressed it against the window. Cherry was thin and wan, and it broke his heart every time he looked at her. Margaret was wrapped in a long dress and bonnet that June had knitted for them. His universe in one photograph.

Briar's gaze flickered as he registered the pair in the photo. 'Your wife is Japanese?'

There was no denying it. 'She is. I served in the Occupation Force and we met when she worked on the base.' He waited for Briar to nod and then ask him to leave, perhaps instructing him where to find the next passage back to Australia.

Instead Briar sighed. 'My girlfriend is from Hong Kong. I would love to bring her home to Australia. However, that policy just won't let us do it. I'm fortunate this job is secure and stable so I can stay here as long as I need to.'

That was the opening Gordon needed. 'It's tough. Why do they do this to us? We're just two chaps who fell in love. We shouldn't be punished for that.' Briar shook his head. 'Is there anything at all you can do to help me? I have Christmas presents, supplies, letters from home. It would be a shame not to deliver them in person.'

Briar gave a nod. 'There is one thing. I can issue you a short-term visitor's visa.'

Gordon's heart leapt. 'That's perfect.'

'It's only valid while the *Merkur* is in Japanese ports. Seven days. You'll need to take yourself to Tokyo and get SCAP to issue the correct paperwork for your actual visa once you're there.'

He nodded, excitement exploding inside him. 'Done. And once I've got that, I'm set to stay for a few months?'

'You should be able to, yes.'

Gordon could breathe again. 'Thank you. This is above and beyond.'

Briar beamed. 'Wonderful. Now, I'll just need you to pay for your passage to Japan and back again.'

Gordon faltered. 'I've already paid. My ticket is valid for Australia to Japan, a round trip.'

'Yes, I understand. However, to issue this visa, it needs the accompanying ticket.'

More money. Gordon cleared his throat as he mentally calculated the cost. The Hong Kong to Japan section had been £26. It hurt to think of the weeks he'd taken to save that amount. 'Rightio,' he said. He thumbed through his wallet, laid the notes on the desk, and pushed them over to Briar.

'It's £56.'

Gordon stared at him. 'That's more than twice what I paid in Australia.'

'That's the price in Hong Kong, Mr Parker.'

He fought back his anger, certain now that Briar was extorting him. The smile didn't shift from the man's face. Perhaps that was why they had a window between the public and the clerks.

Trying not to think about how much money he had just lost, he pushed the notes towards the window. Briar snatched them up.

'Your passport?'

Gordon slid that over and looked away. He didn't want to see if the money ended up in Briar's pocket or the drawer. It was a ridiculous amount of money to only have guaranteed seven days in Japan.

Briar copied Gordon's information onto a piece of paper, stamped it and stapled it to the passport before giving it back. The slip of paper simply had a bit of handwriting on it and the Australian coat of arms. It would have been easy enough to fake.

If he was caught with a fake, it wouldn't be worth it.

Gordon forced himself to smile back at Briar. 'Thank you for your help.'

'My pleasure,' Briar said, brightly. 'Enjoy the rest of your journey, Mr Parker. I hope your wife is pleased to see you.'

Happiness shot through Gordon as the familiar ruins of Japan appeared on the horizon. He'd never been to Yokkaichi, the city where they docked, but it had been firebombed by the Americans in the last year of the war. The damage reminded him of Kure. The smell came back to him immediately, a cold winter bite in the air. He was grateful for his jacket and gloves, pleased he had thought to bring warm clothes for Cherry and Margaret.

He was one of the first to disembark the ship, eager to be on Japanese soil, each step bringing him closer to his family. Kure was still half a day's travel away. He made a beeline for the station, requesting a ticket to Osaka. From there, he planned to head to the BCOF newspaper offices and talk his way into a lift to Kure.

The ticket seller didn't speak but simply held out his hand for money. Gordon went to fetch his coins, then hesitated. He had no Japanese yen. When he'd been part of the Army, the trains had been free. Now he was a civilian, that wasn't the case. He could swap his Australian pounds with BCOF soldiers in Osaka, but right now he was effectively penniless.

'Sorry,' Gordon said in Japanese as he stepped out of the queue, looking for a bank or even a hotel. There was nothing around the station, nowhere he could get money. He swore. How could he have been so foolish? He'd planned everything so carefully and had forgotten something as simple as money?

He noticed a Japanese man in uniform watching him. As Gordon looked more closely, the man averted his gaze. He was a customs officer. It was a sought-after job in post-war Japan, bringing a decent, regular income.

His hands were bare, despite the cold air.

Ten minutes later, Gordon had a handful of yen and the customs officer had a new pair of black leather gloves.

It was late afternoon by the time he arrived in Osaka. There wasn't a huge BCOF presence here, but all the soldiers knew where the newspaper office was. Gordon ducked through the ruined city to get there, hungry and tired. He was hyper aware of people staring. A white man in civilian clothes was a rarity here.

There were two soldiers in the offices when Gordon walked in. Both were surprised to see an ex-serviceman back in Japan. When he introduced himself and explained he needed a lift to Kure, the atmosphere cooled.

'Can't help you.' The skinny man walked away before Gordon could say anything else.

The dark-haired man sighed. 'He's a man of many words, but he's right. There's a lot of talk about you on the base. Parker, the bloke with the Japanese missus.'

Gordon frowned. 'Everyone's got a Japanese missus.'

'Yeah,' the man agreed. 'But you've come back, haven't you? So what will our missuses expect from us now? That we come back too!' He snorted. 'She's fun, my lass, but she's not my wife.' He glanced back to his fellow soldier and leaned towards Gordon. 'Look, there's no way you can get a ride to Kure from here for at least another week. I'd jump on a train. The lines are clear now.'

'Got a spare travel card I can use?' Gordon asked.

The man laughed. 'Jeez, you're funny.'

'Change pounds for me then?'

'I've got about fifty yen. Doubt that'll help you much.'

Gordon walked back to Osaka Station and bought the cheapest ticket he could, an uncomfortable third-class seat taking him to Hiroshima. He leaned back, closing his eyes, reminding himself that soon, so soon, he would be in Cherry's arms. Then none of this would matter.

When he arrived at Hiroshima, the last train to Kure had already left.

He stayed still, breathing hard, trying to keep a lid on his temper. He couldn't walk to Kure from Hiroshima with his luggage when night was already falling. Neither did he have anywhere to stay. He had done everything right and everything had gone wrong.

There was a sudden honk and an Army Jeep pulled up next to him. A dark-skinned US soldier leaned across the window. 'You lost?'

Gordon forced a smile. 'I know exactly where I am but it isn't where I want to be.'

'Where do you need to go, Aussie?'

Gordon let out a shaky sigh. 'Kure.'

'Get in.'

Gordon didn't speak as they drove. He didn't have the energy, spent emotionally and physically. There was another soldier in the car, who kept throwing Gordon curious glances but didn't say anything either.

Soon enough, the Jeep pulled up outside Kure Station.

'Where do you need to go? We'll take you.'

Gordon considered it, but the image of Cherry's horrified face at an Army Jeep pulling up outside Suma's quashed the thought.

'I'll walk. Thanks for bringing me this far.'

The two Americans threw an amused look between them as Gordon picked up his luggage.

'All right, Aussie. Good luck in this place.'

They drove off, the tail-lights disappearing into the darkness.

Then he started running.

CHAPTER NINETEEN

CHERRY: Kure, January 1950

Cherry's life had completely changed. She was exhausted, slow to recover from Margaret's birth, and she lived entirely for her daughter. If she didn't focus on the baby's needs, Cherry was worried she would simply float away.

She was waiting for her husband to come. If she could just keep going a little longer, Don would arrive. His letters promised he would, even though his visa was delayed. She tried not to think about Yoneko and Toby, tried to ignore the whispers that drifted into her dreams, strangers calling her 'butterfly' as they did to the women who had taken up with ex-enemy men. They were Madame Butterflies, Japanese women abandoned by soldiers like in the Italian opera.

At least she had Suma. The days when she was too ill or too tired to move, the older woman would take Margaret, keeping her close but showing her off. Some people were scandalised by the young baby being out of the house so soon after the birth, but it was common post-war. Women had to work. Suma waved their concerns away. She had long done what she thought was best.

Suma's biggest complaint was Margaret's name. Even as Margaret grew out of being a sleepy newborn, her face puffing out with rounded cheeks and dark brown eyes, Suma railed against the name Cherry had chosen.

'It is impossible to pronounce.' Suma shook her head, wiggling her fingers over Margaret, the five-month-old baby staring up from where she lay on the tatami in the main room.

'I wanted her to have an Australian name. She's Australian.'

'She's Japanese.'

'I'm Japanese. I have an Australian name.'

Suma rolled her eyes. 'You are still Nobuko-chan to me.'

Cherry smiled, bending over another dress. Orders had picked up again, fuelled by curiosity about the kangaroo baby. Many women were surprised by Margaret's dark features, the Australian in her not obvious at first glance.

Suma pulled faces at Margaret, still grumbling. 'Ma-ga-ra-te. Ma-ga-ra-ta? Ma-ga-ra-to?'

'Margaret.'

A chill ran through Cherry. Had she imagined that voice? That deep, lyrical Australian accent she only heard in her dreams, a low rumble that was followed by a quick smile, an easy laugh. But Don was in Melbourne. He couldn't be here.

She turned.

Standing in the entrance to Suma's house, next to his suitcases, wearing the jumper Cherry had knitted for him over a year earlier, was Don. He was a mirage; something she had thought about so often that she was clearly caught in a daydream.

'Don-san?'

He smiled as she said his name. 'Konnichiwa, Cherry.'

They stared at each other, then Cherry was in his arms, Don wrapped around her, a blur of movement and touch and warmth and intensity, trying to melt into each other, to become one. He kissed her head, Cherry fought her tears, neither aware of anything else until Margaret laughed.

Suma had disappeared, leaving the baby on the floor. Don kicked off his shoes and padded across the tatami, kneeling next to Margaret. Her heart threatened to burst as he touched their daughter's hand.

'Hey little girl,' he said in English. Margaret's fingers closed around Don's thumb, almost possessive. With his other hand, he ran his fingers through Margaret's dark curls, a mirror of Cherry's waves. Cherry's breath caught as his hands shook, a giant next to the baby before him. She moved to put Margaret in Don's arms, but he picked up the baby with ease, bobbing her gently as she squirmed.

'There's Mum,' Don said, pointing at Cherry. 'There's Mum and here's Dad.'

Cherry properly took him in, feeling safe for the first time in months. 'Hello,' she said.

'Konnichiwa,' he replied. 'I'm here to bring you home.'

There was no fear of being caught. Don was no longer a soldier. Cherry could walk through the market with her husband by her side and not worry about the Military Police. She could cook her family dinner, sleep in the same room as the man she loved; she could do anything. After Don travelled to Tokyo with Patrick in a BCOF truck to get his visa stamped, they had months together ahead of them. He went out during the day, sneaking onto the BCOF base to get extra supplies and catch up with old friends, in search of a casual job. Her money from dressmaking wasn't much and he wanted her to save it.

They were still careful out in public, around others, not knowing how people would react to them. Despite this, word still flew through the town that Don had returned, prompting Yoneko to make an unexpected visit to Suma's house, with her young daughter, Setsuko, at her hip.

'Don-san?' Yoneko was awed by him, bowing deeply as he stood in front of her. Cherry hung back, taking Setsuko so the two of them could talk.

'G'day, Yonnie. It's real nice to see you.'

'Is Toby-san here too?' Yoneko looked around, as though he was hiding in another room, ready to surprise her.

Don let out a nervous laugh. 'No, no. It's just me.'

She nodded. 'Melbourne and Newcastle are far apart, yes? Like Hiroshima and Tokyo?'

'Yeah.' Don caught Cherry's eye. 'Something similar to that.'

Cherry passed Setsuko to Yoneko. Don looked at the little girl in shock. With brown eyes and chestnut hair, she was unmistakably Toby and Yoneko's daughter.

'I have written many letters,' Yoneko said. 'Toby has not written back. Maybe I have the wrong address. Do you know?' She offered Setsuko to him to hold, but the little girl protested, refusing to leave her mother's arms. 'Maybe you write to Toby-san? Tell him we are ready to come to Australia.'

'Yes, good.' Cherry beamed at her husband. 'Maybe we all come together.' She was about to suggest she make tea, when fear flickered over her husband's face. It vanished quickly, but she had seen it.

Don put a hand on Yoneko's shoulder. 'Yonnie. Don't wait for Toby to write. You've got a beautiful little girl. You can make a life here in Japan. You don't need Australia for any of that.'

Silence fell. Yoneko stared at him in shock. He didn't look away, an unspoken apology on his face.

She nodded suddenly. 'Thank you, Don-san. I will go now.'

She moved towards the door to collect her shoes. Cherry followed. 'Maybe I make tea?'

'No, no,' Yoneko said, slipping back into Japanese, voice high. 'If Don-san is here, you must be very busy. I have errands to run.' She put on her shoes, then looked at Cherry sadly. 'He came back for you. Congratulations, Nobuko-chan.'

Yoneko adjusted Setsuko on her hip and walked out, leaving Cherry with an odd sense of guilt.

Don had a plan. He wanted them to get married again. If they were married in a Christian church, it might be a way to get the Australian government to recognise them as a legitimate husband and wife. He had asked around and found a small Anglican church in Kure. Spending the afternoon charming the priest, via BCOF translator Cliff, Don convinced the priest to marry them.

'It's the same church we go to for Christmas mass and Good Friday,' Don explained, Cliff translating for Cherry as they sat in the garden at Suma's house. Margaret wriggled around in the grass, laughing at the butterflies that bounced through the spring air. 'The same type of church, I mean. I played it up a bit, made it seem like I was more devout, but he's good for it. We'll need to start going every Sunday. Gotta do the whole thing properly.'

The small white building was nestled among houses in an unfamiliar area of Kure. They went every Sunday morning in their best clothes, sitting in a wooden pew and listening to services in Japanese. Don was usually the only white person there. It was different from the Shinto and Buddhist practices Cherry had grown up with, praying with her mother and father, but there was love at the centre of all of them. Cherry could go to church on Sunday and learn about Jesus, then stop by the Shinto shrine on her way home and make an offering to the gods. All that mattered was that they attend regularly, especially in the lead-up to their wedding.

It was a small ceremony. Andy, Slim, Patrick and Cliff came in uniform and the rest of the guests were Cherry's friends – Suma, Hana and Michiko. Margaret sat with Suma, Charlie sticking with the soldiers on Don's side of the church. It was also a farewell. Hana was moving to Kyoto to marry a Japanese man, something she was both excited and nervous about.

Don was every inch the handsome groom, dressed in a black suit he'd brought from Melbourne. Cherry had spent weeks sewing her wedding dress, inspired by photographs from the *Women's Weekly*. She picked a simple floor-length design, Sachiko giving her a discount on the white silken fabric. Cherry paired it with soft lace over the bodice and neckline, the kimono-style fold over her chest a small nod to her heritage. Suma sewed white flowers into a long piece of tulle for the veil and Charlie had spent the morning picking wildflowers for the bouquet. When he brought them inside Suma's house as Cherry was getting ready, he was also carrying an envelope.

'This was at the door for you.'

Cherry didn't recognise the handwriting, her name written in Japanese characters. She opened it and slid out a letter with a mizuhiki knot tucked into the folded page. Her heart dropped. It was from Yoneko. It was identical to the knot Cherry and Don had been about to purchase as a gift for Toby and Yoneko when Billy had seized Cherry and taken her to the Japanese police.

The note from Yoneko was short.

Good luck, Nobuko-chan.

Cherry tucked the knot into her flowers.

Checking herself in the mirror before they left, Cherry felt like an imposter, a Japanese girl pretending to be Australian. When she appeared in the door of the church and saw Don's eyes widen, she settled. She was no imposter. She was this man's wife. The ceremony was a mix of Japanese and English, translations courtesy of Cliff jumping between both languages, making it easier for everyone to understand. It was a blur, Cherry unable to tear her gaze from Don; the quirk of a smile on the corner of his mouth, the strength in his shoulders. All she could feel was her hands in his, warmth radiating into her palms, holding her in this moment.

Outside the church, they posed for photos. Cherry's friends converged on them, chattering compliments and touching her dress. The small silver band felt strange on her finger, a weightiness to remind her of the life she had chosen, the promise she had made. Don laughed as the Japanese conversation flowed, their shared happiness almost tangible. There was something bittersweet about the absence of Yoneko and Setsuko. Still, every time Cherry looked at Don, she couldn't see how this was a mistake.

Don double- and triple-checked that the paperwork at the church was in order, the priest assuring him via Cliff that it was all legitimate. Satisfied, Don beamed at Cherry.

'In two days, we'll get the train to Tokyo to get everything stamped and signed off.'

'Another wedding?'

'Sort of, yeah. You want to get married again?'

Cherry laughed. 'If we get to Australia, I marry you again and again and again.' Her heart burst at the smile that spread across Don's face.

'You bet we will.' He took her hand. 'Now, let's leave Margaret with the girls for a tick. The boys are throwing us a bit of a party but I want to show you something first.'

It was a small shack out of town. A mish-mash of materials hammered together to make a structure. Wooden walls, a green front door that was too ornate for the rest of the house around it. By the front door was a blooming sakura tree in a pot. The shack was reminiscent of the rebuilt house at Kazuo's but it was cleaner. Stronger.

Don slapped his hand against the door. 'I thought we should move out of Aunty Suma's house now we're married. Again.'

'This is for us?'

'My word. It's not much, but I've spent weeks scrounging things together – you wouldn't believe how hard it was to find a stove or anything to put in the kitchen. And that back door is a bit dodgy. Paddy says he'll come round and fix it soon. But we'll have something better in Australia, I promise—'

Cherry flung her arms around Don, a lump in her throat. This sweet, gentle man had not just come back for her, he'd given her a house. A home. A place for her family. Overwhelmed, she untangled herself from him, bowing apologetically.

He laughed. 'I guess that's a thank you?'

'Thank you. Very much.'

Inside was a simple space, barely enough tatami to cover the dirt. A window, a wonky cupboard door, curtains over shelves in the kitchen. She could make it work. It was a space for them. It was their home.

'Only for a little time?' Cherry asked.

He nodded. 'Yep. Once I send the paperwork back to Australia that says we've got a proper, ridgy-didge Christian wedding signed off, I reckon it'll only be a month before they approve you to come home with me. They can't argue with a church wedding. Why would a church in Kure be any different to a church in Melbourne? And there's a new bloke as Immigration Minister. They say Holt's less of a stickler for the rules than Calwell was.'

Cherry beamed. 'I have surprise for you too,' she said. 'Maybe tomorrow I make recipe for you.'

'You don't have to do that.' Don put his hands on the beam above him and leaned towards her. 'I just want you.'

'Apple crumble. This is Australian recipe, no?'

His face lit up. 'It is, yeah, but how do you know that?'

'*Women's Weekly*.' She looked away from him, his gaze too intense. 'I get apples and make for us.'

Don swept her up in his arms. 'Cherry and apple crumble. Sounds like my most favourite dish in the world.'

He kissed her and Cherry melted into his embrace.

They were finally home together.

After they returned from Tokyo, where they signed the marriage certificate in the British Embassy and sent copies back to Australia, they settled into an easy routine. Unable to find a job, Don spent most of his day on the base, disguising himself as a soldier to swipe food and supplies, helped by men who were happy to see him back and wanted him to get Cherry into Australia so their girls could follow. He and Charlie sold what they could at the market, some days more lucrative than others. Sometimes they would head into the city and forage for a mat or a futon, finding what they could to make the shack more liveable. Cherry swept it out every day, the wind whistling through gaps in the walls as she tidied. She cut wildflowers to bring colour into the bare room and made whatever food she could with their limited rations. Don didn't like fish, which was a problem when that was the main meat she could get with her ration book, but he was adjusting. She hadn't managed to get apples to make an apple crumble, but she'd charmed her way into a bit of sugar.

Charlie was the one who found apples for her. There was a woman, Tanaka, who lived two miles away, making money from an unseasonal harvest on her heaving apple tree. Charlie had moved off the base when Don left, living instead in the city. It was easier for him to find jobs in town, taking whatever work people would give a thirteen-year-old boy. When Cherry had mentioned the apple crumble, Charlie made Tanaka promise to save three of her best apples for her. It was a long walk and a warm day, but she was excited to finally try an authentic Australian recipe.

Her paper fan was a relief in the heat of the day. Margaret's body weight and warmth made Cherry hotter as they walked, the baby tied to her chest. The bus would have been more comfortable, but it was harder to avoid the stares of strangers. People in Kure knew who they were, knew Cherry was waiting for an ex-enemy soldier, and it made them a target for attention. Cherry preferred being invisible, moving through the shadows without anyone realising she was there. If the walk took too much out of her, there was always the bus back.

They walked along the road beside the train line, Margaret babbling to Cherry. She spoke back to her daughter in Japanese, every so often switching to English. Don wanted Cherry to speak both languages, to get Margaret used to the sounds. She tried to speak English as much as possible, but when she was tired, Japanese was far easier.

In the distance, there was a blast of a train horn. Margaret's deep-brown eyes grew wide at the sound, Cherry laughing at her.

'Yes, that's a train. Train. There's a train coming.' Margaret grabbed at her mother's hand, her pudgy fingers wrapping around

Cherry's own. Ahead, someone moved off the road towards the tracks. It was Yoneko, pulling Setsuko with her, the toddler scrambling to keep up.

'Yoneko!'

She didn't hear Cherry. A train appeared around the bend, but she still moved for the rail line.

Cherry's heart dropped. 'Yoneko, be careful!'

There was a fence in the way. With Margaret tied to her front, it was too difficult to step over without falling. She picked up her pace as she tried to find a break in the rope to slip through and get to Yoneko. Yoneko picked up Setsuko as the train grew closer, blasting its horn, a cacophony of sound and vibration. She seemed not to notice the train, her dark hair drifting loose around her head. Margaret burst into tears as the horn sounded again, loud and frightening.

'Yoneko!' Cherry's voice was a scream, lost in the wall of noise. Her friend clutched her daughter to her chest, standing on the side of the train line, waiting for the last possible moment. Cherry turned away as there was a screech of brakes and a sickening thud. It was too late for the train to stop. The wind whipped at her hair and tugged at her skirt, Margaret shrieking in her arms.

She couldn't stay there. Her breath hiccoughed in her throat, gaze blurred from tears as she hurried back the way she'd come, trying to calm Margaret but unable to calm herself. Everyone stared as Cherry pushed past strangers to get home, her red, tear-streaked face echoed in her distraught daughter's. There was sanctuary behind the green door and she scrambled through it, collapsing to her knees, clutching her daughter close, still tied together. The two of them sobbed and screamed until Cherry had no breath left, rocking Margaret in her arms until the baby fell asleep.

They were still like that when Don returned at nightfall.

'Cherry?'

'Yoneko and Setsuko.' Her voice was a whisper. 'They dead.'

He knelt next to her, a flicker of confusion racing over his face.

'A train. She step in front of a train. Because Toby leave her.'

He shook his head. 'I told her to forget about him.'

'Maybe he forgot her but Yoneko never forgot him.'

Don frowned. 'She wouldn't. She had a little girl.' He reached for Margaret, slumped and sleeping, twisting his finger around her curls. 'She wouldn't do something like that.'

Cherry stiffened. 'She did do that. I saw her.'

He stilled. 'What?'

She caught his gaze. 'She had nothing else. She only had Toby-san. And you told her he wasn't coming back.' She didn't soften her voice. 'She needed to believe Toby-san was coming back.'

Don slumped to his knees, devastated. He sat in silence for a moment, then looked to Cherry, anguish clear. 'I was trying to help. I was just … trying to help.'

He sat back on his feet. 'I did see Toby in Australia.'

She inhaled sharply. 'You see Toby-san?'

He nodded. 'He was married. To an Australian girl. I told her about Yoneko, but Toby was always the bloke to talk his way out of anything.' Don rubbed a hand over his chin. 'I was trying to help her by telling her not to wait for him. I didn't want her to hope for something false.' He choked on his words.

Cherry turned away, lifting Margaret from her chest and setting the baby on the floor. 'Sometimes hope for something false is better than no hope at all.'

There was no apple crumble that night.

Don grew sullen and withdrawn. Someone had reported that he was sneaking onto the base and he was barred, heavily curtailing his ability to get products to sell. He had got an extension on his visa to stay another month, but there was no word from the Australian government on whether Cherry and Margaret would be allowed into the country. Cherry suggested Don stay in Japan with them and he lost his temper, pointing out how impractical it was for him to stay with no access to rations or money, especially as he was charged a 'foreigner's fee' most of the time: a hefty mark-up on anything sold to him. It was the first time she had seen him angry and she had taken Margaret into the kitchen as he stormed out to find an izakaya, a bar.

It was the first time she stopped to think if she really knew this man she had married.

Today, while Don had been trying to talk his way into another visa extension so he could stay longer than its two-week expiry, Cherry had found apples closer to home and, even though it reminded her of Yoneko, she set about making apple crumble for that night's dessert. She wanted to cook the Australian meal she had promised, proving she could be a good wife. A good wife deserved a good husband.

She was cutting the apples into small squares when Don threw open the door, angry. She snatched up Margaret from the floor and stepped out of the small kitchen alcove. He grappled with his bootlaces in the entryway to the house.

'What's wrong, Don-san?' Cherry asked.

'They won't extend my visa.' He kicked his foot, the shoe flying across the room and skidding into the shadows at the back of the house. 'Couldn't convince them otherwise. Bloody idiots, the lot of them. And then … oh, and then—' Don let out a harsh laugh as he stormed into the house. 'Then I ran into a bunch of MPs – Billy Richardson is still here, you know? – and they accused me of being a ship's deserter. They reckon I'm still a bloody soldier, even though I'm banned from base, and they refused to let me go and wanted to escort me back to my ship. Wasted my entire afternoon, took hours to convince them I was here as a civilian and not under anyone's command. Told them they could pick me up in two weeks and give me a lift to the port for all I care.'

Don spoke faster when he was angry and Cherry struggled to follow along. One thing stuck out. Don couldn't get a visa extension. She shifted Margaret on her hip. 'Only two more weeks in Japan?' she asked. 'Not much time to organise things. But we don't have many things, so maybe it is okay.'

The sadness on Don's face shattered her heart.

'Cherry, I can't take you with me. Not yet. I thought things would've been easy to get you to Melbourne after we sent the marriage certificate and paperwork, but I'm getting nothing. And if I put you and Margaret on a boat with me, they'll just send you straight back when we land in Australia.' He threw his hands up, exasperated. 'It's easier for them to ignore me when I'm here. I need to go home and sort things from there.'

His unspoken words shimmered in the air between them.

Without Cherry. Without Margaret. He would go home alone.

She resisted the urge to nod, to tell him it was okay. It wasn't okay. None of this was okay. She shook her head, anger bubbling. 'No. You promise. You say you are here to take us to home.'

'I'm trying, Cherry.'

'You are lying!' He took a step back, shocked. 'Tell the truth. When can we come to Australia?'

Don sank to his knees. She resisted the urge to rush to him, to make this easy for him.

'I don't know.' The uncomfortable truth was finally spoken aloud.

Cherry glared at Don before her on the ground.

He took a shuddering breath. 'I promise you this. I'm not stopping until we're together. I'm not giving up on us.'

His earnest words wrapped themselves around her, pleading. The heat in her chest ebbed. She put Margaret down and knelt next to Don, brushing her fingers against his legs. 'I can't say goodbye again.'

In his light blue eyes, rimmed with red, emotions crashed together. Regret, love, upset, longing and resignation.

He shook his head. 'Neither can I.'

Head whirling, Cherry slipped her hand into Don's and placed it on her stomach, spreading her fingers over his. Margaret gurgled and the implication dawned on him.

'Another baby?'

'Maybe. I think yes.'

It was far from a joyous celebration, the news tempered with Don's impending departure.

Too soon, it was the night before Don's ship sailed away. Cherry tried to memorise the shape of his body on the futon next to her, determined not to fall asleep too quickly. He slept, his breath falling into a gentle rhythm as his chest rose and fell. She watched him for as long as she could before she finally surrendered to slumber.

When she woke in the morning, Don was gone.

No agony of a goodbye, simply the quiet hush of loneliness.

CHAPTER TWENTY

GORDON: Australia, August 1950

Time moved differently when Gordon was apart from Cherry. Minutes felt like hours, moments extended into infinity, an aching reminder of their separation. Then whole days would rush by in a blur, weeks flying past, taunting him that he wasn't moving fast enough, letting Cherry and Margaret and his unborn child languish in Japan. It didn't seem enough that a new Prime Minister, Robert Menzies, had been elected. Calwell was gone, replaced by Immigration Minister Harold Holt. Holt had been supportive of the O'Keefe family and Mr Gamboa, but it was impossible to know how much of that was election promises and how much was a genuine indication of a potential change in policy direction.

Gordon disembarked in Sydney to find June on the docks with a young man in a blazer and flat cap. He wrapped Gordon in a bear hug before she introduced them.

'You wanted a journalist. Here he is.'

'Jack Evans.' The man adjusted his round, gold-rimmed glasses then shook Gordon's hand. 'A pleasure. June's told me all about you.'

'Don't believe a word of it.'

'It's all true.' She sniffed. 'If you don't want Jack's help, we'll go to the cinema instead.'

'Wait on,' Gordon said, grinning. 'Don't get carried away. Let me buy you both a drink.'

The pub was steeped in the smell of cigarette smoke and stale beer. The Ladies' Lounge was only marginally more palatable, decorated with dark mahogany wood and touches of luxurious ruby red. A fresh beer sat in front of each of them, the mood light.

'So, June says she has a Japanese sister,' Jack said.

'I do.' June bumped her friend with her shoulder before picking up her glass. 'Cheers to Cherry, hey? And my little niece, Margaret.'

'And the new one on the way.' Gordon sipped his beer, waiting for the bombshell to hit. June stared at him, shocked.

Jack spoke first. 'Congratulations—'

June leapt across the table and pulled Gordon into a hug, laughing almost maniacally. 'You didn't write that in your letters, you sneak! Just a small thing you didn't think to mention?'

'Very small.'

She cackled. 'Righto. Cheers to Cherry, Margaret and the new baby.'

They clinked their glasses and warmth spread through Gordon. He'd take the excitement while he could get it.

'Another baby's great, actually,' Jack said.

'Thank you. That's kind of you to say.' Gordon touched his breast pocket, where a photograph of him with Cherry and Margaret was safely tucked.

Jack nodded. 'Of course, for you. But for the articles, too. If you'll let me write them. See, the White Australia policy's a big topic right now. Especially after Mrs O'Keefe and Mr Gamboa. Mrs Parker could be the next name on that list.'

'I hope so.' Gordon's fingers traced patterns in the condensation on his beer glass. 'I really hope so. I don't want to mention the new baby in the articles yet. It's still early.'

'Understood.' Jack pulled out his notebook. 'Perhaps a short statement from you then. June tells me you've married your wife twice now.'

Gordon couldn't hide his smile. The memory of Cherry walking down the aisle, an angel gliding towards him, was an image he visited frequently. 'My word, I did. It was the best chance we had of getting her out here. It's technically three times, if you count us heading to Tokyo and signing the paperwork at the British Embassy too.'

Jack scribbled in his notebook. 'Perfect, that's perfect. Now, tell me about your wife. What is she doing in Japan? How is she caring for herself and your daughter? Margaret is one, is that right? Tell me everything.'

June winked at Gordon. He ignored the ache in his heart that throbbed every time he thought of his family alone in Kure.

'You want to know everything? We're going to need a few more beers.'

Every night, he dreamed of them. Cherry laughing as they walked along the beach together. Margaret staring with her big brown eyes, frowning. Afternoons hidden away in their shack, washing daikon for dinner, lifting his daughter high so she could touch the sakura flowers when they bloomed. For hours every night he got to spend time with them, to see them, to feel as though he was with them.

The shrill ringing of the telephone woke him. Cherry and Margaret slipped away, buried in his memory. Someone answered the telephone and he rolled over to fall back asleep, when the ringing tore through the house again. It stopped, then the receiver was slammed down. Curious, Gordon got out of bed.

As he padded into the lounge room, the telephone rang again. Venn, wrapped in a dressing gown, picked it up, exasperated.

'Hello?' She listened for a moment before hanging up.

Gordon frowned. 'Is everything okay?'

'You could've warned us.' Venn pointed to the newspaper. It was open to Jack's article. Accompanying the brief text was a grainy reprint of the photograph that was presently sitting on his bedside table: Cherry and Margaret smiling for the camera and Gordon looking at Margaret. He touched Cherry's image as the phone rang again.

His mother threw up her hands. 'I'm not answering it.'

He snatched up the receiver. 'Hello?'

'Is this Gordon Parker?'

'Speaking.'

'You married that Jap girl?'

'I did.'

'We're gonna find you, you traitorous bastard, and we're going to show you exactly what we do to people who spit on the memories of our dead brothers and mates who were killed by those mongrels.'

'You're going to find me, are you?'

'Yeah. We've got your telephone number, we've got your address—'

'Perfect. Tell me your name, fella, and we can sort out the time and place. I'm happy to meet you anywhere you like.'

The call disconnected. Gordon hung up. 'Real brave to do an anonymous phone call, isn't it?'

His mother was not impressed. 'If that goes off all day because of your article—'

'Unplug it.'

'I am expecting calls from people other than those who are angry about your wife.'

'What does it matter to them if I bring my family here? I don't know them from Adam. How are Cherry and Margaret going to affect their lives?'

The telephone rang once more. Venn sighed and picked it up. She barely held it to her ear before she put the receiver down.

Gordon shifted. 'I'm sorry, Mum. I've got to do articles or else the government won't pay attention.'

Venn dusted off her hands, saying nothing, and walked out.

The phone was off the hook when he returned that evening from his work at the Victorian barracks. He was now working as an auditor for the Army, which was a far cry from his previous ambitions of being a doctor, but it was a solid job and the pay was fair. Most nights Gordon came home to chaos as Robin or Jennifer tore through the kitchen, but tonight the house was quiet. Harry sat in the closest seat to the phone, sipping a sherry, the radio quietly broadcasting in the corner.

'How's work?' Harry asked.

Gordon sat on an armchair. 'Fine. Simple. Gets me money, which is the main thing.'

'I would strongly advise you to continue your medical studies.' His father's judgement was clear.

Gordon bristled. 'Can't support my family on textbooks. Plus, I failed the exams. They won't let me back, even with my service history.'

'Perhaps if you hadn't been so distracted, it wouldn't have been a problem.'

'My family is not a distraction.' Gordon put the phone back on the hook, a clang as the metal caught itself. Harry took Gordon in, his eldest son straightening under his father's scrutiny.

The telephone rang.

They both reached for it, but Harry answered first. 'Parker residence.' He gave Gordon a steady look as an indistinguishable voice warbled through the receiver. 'I'm afraid we don't want any more publicity.'

Gordon leaned forward, alarmed. They did want more publicity. Harry stopped him in his tracks with a look.

'I suppose while he was away, it was his business. Now it's mine. Thank you for your call.' Harry hung up before Gordon could stop him.

'Why wouldn't you let me speak to them?' Gordon asked, furious. 'The more journalists that want to take on our story, the better it will be!'

Harry lifted his pipe to his mouth, inhaling deeply. 'Shall I be honest with you?'

'I find it's the best way to be.'

'Your sister was laughed at today at school for having a Japanese sister-in-law. Your brothers were targeted and insulted. The phone has not stopped ringing, your mother is stressed, and this is one insignificant article. Imagine how much worse things would be if there were more.'

Gordon's heart thudded hard. He never wanted to put his brothers and sisters in the firing line for Cherry and Margaret. He was supposed to be the one to cop any attention, something he was happy to wear if they got the right result in the end.

Harry levelled his gaze at his son. 'You need to think about this. This is affecting our family now.'

Anger flared in Gordon's chest. 'Yes,' he said. 'It is. Because there's a pregnant woman and your granddaughter living alone in Japan with no money and half a house, and they're our family too.' Harry started, taken aback. 'I don't care how many phone calls we get or interviews I have to do or articles that get published in the newspapers, I will never be able to live with myself if I abandon my wife and children without having tried absolutely everything I could. I'm sorry that's making things difficult for Jennifer, but Mum can handle a couple of phone calls and Donald and Robin are smart enough to defend each other. Cherry and Margaret are alone. All they've got is me.'

Gordon paced the room, wringing his hands. Harry was still, observing him. His father's silence irritated him more. 'Of course, if you'd rather I forget about them, stop being distracted, as you say, I can do that. With enormous difficulty, but I'll do it. But I didn't think you raised me to be that kind of man. And I refuse to be the one to tell Mum that I'm leaving her grandchildren to fend for themselves in another country that's been completely ravaged by war. I'm trying to be responsible. I'm trying to do what's right. What's right by them. I'm sorry that it affects the rest of the family. I am.' The thought of his family having to defend themselves over his choices weighed heavily. 'But I don't want to give up on Cherry because a boy in Jim's class got mouthy about things he doesn't understand.'

Gordon's words hung in the air. Harry drew on his pipe, tobacco flaring, before he removed his round spectacles, cleaning them on his handkerchief.

'Very well.'

Gordon hesitated. 'Very well?'

His father slid his glasses back on. 'Allow me to apologise. A man's first instinct is to protect his family. I was protecting mine … but so too were you protecting yours.'

Harry moved to the liquor trolley and poured a small sherry. He offered one to Gordon, who nodded. He had never been offered a sherry by his father before.

'You need to be careful.' Harry passed over a glass. It felt tiny in Gordon's hand. 'It makes things more difficult for everyone if you're doing articles every possible moment. The Japanese are not our friends. Many Australians are grieving sons and brothers and husbands lost at the hands of Imperial soldiers.'

This was the most amenable Harry had been so far to Gordon's cause. Keen not to waste it, Gordon nodded. 'I understand. I understand. The last thing I want is to upset anyone. Perhaps there are other ways I can reach out to Holt. I want to be more strategic with him than I was with Calwell. Find a way to get an introduction instead of calling out of nowhere or writing letters that can be easily ignored.'

Harry took a deep drag of his pipe. 'You're that serious about this girl?'

Gordon squared his shoulders. 'I'm that serious about this girl.'

'Let me get in touch with some people. I can't promise they will help but they may listen.'

Gordon sipped his sherry. The taste made his eyes water and he resisted the urge to cough. Harry gave him a small nod and Gordon cleared his throat, choosing to ignore his father's amused smile.

❀

Harry spoke to his colleagues at the council, many of whom knew Gordon and the family well. Despite his standing in the community as the previous mayor of Ringwood, there weren't many who were willing to come on board to help. The only man who agreed to write to Holt was Councillor George Reid, an old friend of the family.

'George is very sympathetic to you and Cherry,' Harry said.

Gordon sat at the dining table, leg jiggling, as his father stood tall and still.

'Sympathy is good.' Gordon exhaled to quell the burst of hope in his chest. Hope was dangerous.

'He remembers you fondly,' Harry said. 'Recalls you both discussing the Melbourne Football Club with great fervour at one of your mother's Christmas luncheons.'

'That certainly would be something I would talk about. I don't quite remember him, but if I made a good impression, that's excellent.'

'George mentioned too that he is an acquaintance of Holt,' Harry said.

'An acquaintance of Holt's is wonderful.'

'He makes no promises, but he has agreed to contact Holt on your behalf. I will also write to the Minister, so perhaps a dual approach from two councillors in Melbourne's east may make him take more notice.'

'Shall I write to him too?' Gordon asked, eager. 'Perhaps three letters are better than two.'

'I suggest we wait until George or myself have heard back first,' Harry said. 'We don't want to play all our cards too early.'

'However, we want to play some.' Venn stepped into the room, dressed neatly in a matching powder-blue skirt and blazer, a black handbag resting on her gloved wrist. 'I have been speaking with the Archbishop.'

The men stared at her. She placed her handbag down. 'I'm not sure why you're so shocked, Gordon. You, after all, were the one who pointed out my excellent letter-writing skills so I thought it best I put them to good use.' She held up a crisp envelope. 'It seems the

Archbishop is very concerned the government are forcing you and Cherry to live separately. As you were married in the church, it's considered a crime against God for the government to keep you apart.'

Gordon let out an amazed chuckle. There were many things that could be said about his mother, but she certainly was not someone to be underestimated.

She shrugged. 'Unless you'd rather I didn't meddle?'

'I'd very much appreciate it if you did.' Gordon couldn't hide his grin. 'Especially as I think a crime against God is possibly the best argument we have yet.'

They sent three letters first. One from Reid, one from the Archbishop and one from Harry. A less aggressive approach, with no media coverage to cause too much attention. With three missives from well-respected men in the community, Gordon was confident they would get a reply from Holt.

It took three months. One evening Harry returned home from the council offices with an envelope stamped with Holt's name on the back. Harry handed it to Gordon. Apart from June, who was riding her motorcycle through country Victoria, the entire family was there, waiting to see what the Immigration Minister said.

Gordon's hands shook as he tore the envelope open. This could be the turning point for all his hoping and wishing. This could be the moment they had been waiting for.

The envelope contained one piece of paper. On it was a neatly typed message from Holt's office.

Gordon read it aloud. 'Dear Mr Parker. I refer to your letter in regard to your son who wishes to obtain permission for his wife, a Japanese national, and their child to enter this Commonwealth. I am at present considering this matter and will communicate with you again as soon as possible.'

He turned the page over to check he hadn't missed anything on the back. There was nothing else.

'They're considering it,' Venn said, breaking the silence. 'That's nothing to turn your nose up at.'

The air left Gordon's lungs and he sat down, his head in his hands. This was supposed to be it, the seal of approval. Holt had positioned himself as supportive of wartime refugees, applauding the efforts of the O'Keefe family in their fight against Calwell's attempts to deport them. The Gamboa case had reappeared in the news too, Holt granting Lorenzo a visa to join his wife and children in Melbourne once Lorenzo's service with the US Army had finished. Why were Cherry and Margaret different?

'At least Holt replied,' Harry said, but he didn't seem satisfied either.

A surge of anger constricted Gordon's chest. 'Replies filled with empty words are useless.' He stood. 'We should write back. Push harder, show a little fight.'

'Let's not rush into anything as a reaction,' Venn said. 'Presumably the Archbishop and Councillor Reid will have received replies too. We should wait to hear from them in case Holt has told them something more.'

Reid spoke to Harry the following week: Holt had given the same response. When a note from the Archbishop arrived three weeks later, it held no other information or hope. Despite Jack wanting to do another article, Gordon told him they couldn't. The agreement had been for Harry to use his contacts and Gordon to not do any further interviews. Gordon would keep his word.

He worked as hard as he could, determined to save his money to return to Japan. Knowing how much more expensive living there was, he wanted to have twice what he thought he needed. His heart ached for his family on the other side of the world: wishing Cherry could see the gum trees, imagining Margaret waddling along the veranda at Greenwood House, dreaming of Christmases spent together. Gordon had sent packages to Japan with gifts to make sure

Cherry's first Christmas as part of the church was celebrated, but the Yuletide of 1950 was bittersweet. It had almost been a year since he'd gone to Japan as a civilian and there seemed to be no genuine progress.

Then letters began to show up.

The first two had the BCOF stamp on them. It seemed Andy and Slim had been talking about Gordon to other soldiers in Japan.

The first letter was from a Lance Corporal Tom Brammich, who was currently serving in Japan. He was writing to support Gordon and Cherry, whom he had heard about through Andy in Medical. Tom told Gordon about his Japanese girl, Emika, who worked in the kitchens in Kure; the only girl that made his heart race when he saw her. The letter ended with Tom thanking Gordon for fighting for Cherry. If Cherry got to come home to Australia, then surely other Japanese girls could follow.

The second letter was from a Corporal Anthony McWard, pledging his support for Gordon and offering his help in any way he could. McWard also had a secret Japanese wife, Mariko, whom he wanted to bring home when his service ended in six months' time. Many of Mariko's friends had been abandoned by Australian soldiers and Anthony was determined not to be a black mark on Mariko's name.

There weren't many letters like this, but every time another appeared in the mailbox, it buoyed Gordon's spirits. Any support, no matter how small, felt like treasure, a reminder that he wasn't doing this alone. It was more surprising when other councillors began to write to Harry to offer what assistance they could, whether that be a missive to Holt on Gordon's behalf or some other way. Councillor Reid had spoken with Richard Casey, the Minister for Works and Housing, who saw Holt most days in the corridors at Parliament House. Casey wanted to visit the Parkers the next time he was in Melbourne, to speak with Gordon.

On the day of Casey's visit to Ringwood, the entire Parker family were dressed in their Sunday best, doing what they could to impress the politician and convince him of how easily Cherry and Margaret would assimilate into Australian society.

Casey smoothed his dark bushy moustache as he listened, his face grave, but he was quick with a joke or a comment to spark a laugh. Gordon nodded along as Harry and Casey spoke of mutual acquaintances. They had known each other socially before Winston Churchill had appointed Casey as Minister-Resident for the Middle East and sent him to Cairo during the war.

Eventually, Casey's attention turned to Gordon. 'So, tell me about this wife of yours in Japan, son.'

'I'm afraid I could talk about her for days, sir, so I'll do my best to keep it short. The moment I met Cherry, I knew she was someone special. Lots of other lads have come back from Japan and left girls behind, but I'm not that kind of man. I've got a wife, a daughter, another child on the way, and I'm going to do everything I can to get them home. But it's not been easy.'

'Quite.' Casey nodded. 'Tell me, this Cherry, how is her English?'

'When I first met her, she barely understood a word of it. She's a quick learner and an intelligent girl, and these days her English has really come along.'

'Wonderful, wonderful. And your daughter? She is well?'

'My word.' Gordon couldn't help his grin. She would be so much bigger now. Guilt shot through him. He was missing so much of these early years with Margaret. It strengthened his resolve. 'She's a strong little thing. In her last letter, Cherry mentioned Margaret was starting to show more personality. Our next child is due any day now. In fact, Cherry may have already had the baby and I'm delayed on the news. The post isn't always reliable, you see.'

'They're little miracles, aren't they?' Casey said, his gaze settling on the Parker children as they spread out in the garden to play a game of tag, calling to one another as they evaded capture.

Gordon nodded. 'They certainly are. And incredibly hard to be away from. A child needs their father.'

Casey turned to Gordon. 'And how do you think Cherry would

go here? Be truthful. She'd be alone in this country, no other Japanese around. Your neighbours might not take kindly to an enemy in their midst. Do you think she'd be happy here?'

Gordon smiled. 'I reckon if Cherry was here, she'd be happy because I'd make her happy. And she wouldn't be alone. She'd have me.'

The day Gordon received a message from Casey was also the day he discovered his second daughter had been born. Kathleen Parker, a healthy young baby, who apparently looked nearly identical to Margaret. Gordon re-read the letter, heart soaring. He was father to two children, even if he was separated by oceans from them. He took a steadying breath as Robin ran in, clutching a letter from Casey.

In the neatly folded pages, Casey reported that Holt had received several representations on behalf of Gordon and Cherry, but Holt wasn't able to see a way to grant Cherry permission to travel to Australia. There was considerable opposition to allowing Japanese entry to the country, especially given the Japanese treatment of Australian prisoners of war. The anti-Japanese sentiment across the country, and within the government, was still strong.

Consoling himself that they had finally received more than empty words from Holt's office, Gordon considered his next steps. They were gathering support, but they needed to be strategic. Given the line from Holt was that nothing could be done now, it didn't make sense to go on the attack. There had to be another way forward.

Around Gordon and Cherry's first wedding anniversary of their Christian marriage, Gordon received two letters. One from Cherry, the other from Slim. Slim wrote to say he was shipping off to Korea to fight but was arranging some other soldiers to look in on Cherry. The idea that BCOF were pulling out of Japan, taking Gordon's postal network with them and leaving Cherry without support from

Gordon's friends, was one massive disappointment, but Cherry's letter sent chills through him.

Their house had been broken into.

He could barely read Cherry's handwriting, it was so jagged and hurriedly written. She wrote of a man who had forced the window open one evening, wanting her Australian riches, refusing to believe she didn't have any. She only just gathered the children and got them out safely, trekking across town to Súma's. Slim had checked on the place the next day. It had been trashed. Cherry now didn't feel safe enough to stay there alone.

Gordon sat on the floor of the front room, at a loss. Venn was quiet, her knitting paused.

'Maybe I should stop,' he said. 'Cherry's being targeted because of me. If she wasn't living in a house that belongs to a "rich Australian" – what a joke – then people would leave her alone. She could live in peace with her two children and people would forget about her. It could be better. For her. For the children. For everyone here.' Gordon rubbed his eyes. 'Besides, Holt's just as bad as Calwell. Worse, even. He replies to letters, but it's been the same response for over a year. An indefinite consideration with no changes. What's the point?'

Venn nodded, thoughtful, and set aside her knitting.

Then smacked Gordon in the arm.

'Ow!' Gordon rubbed his smarting bicep, skin blooming pink, as she stood, her eyes flashing.

'It's taking longer than you want, so you give up?' His mother towered over him, in full flight. 'I didn't raise you this way. That girl over there in Japan, the one you've fought so hard for, she believes in you. You've got two little girls who want their father. That should mean more to you than any government policy or any indefinite consideration. If you're going to let one small thing stop you, you are not the man I thought you were.'

He slumped back against the armchair. 'You reckon the entire Australian government is one small thing?'

Venn shrugged. 'You reckon it isn't?'

Her words awoke something in Gordon. The government wanted him to roll over and allow small-minded thinking and fear-mongering to keep him from having the life he deserved. The life that Cherry and his daughters deserved. Why was he letting that stop him? He was months away from having enough money to return to Japan; Gordon could only think of one scenario that might help.

He was waiting when Harry returned from drinks that evening. Venn hung back in the corner of the room.

'Dad, I need to do more articles with Jack.'

His father's cheeks were ruddy. 'We've discussed this.'

'We have. Months ago. But things have changed. We have more people onside. We are gathering support. This is a wider appeal, a way to bring more people together. Look at the O'Keefes, the Gamboa family. Their cases garnered huge support through the media. We can do the same.'

'I'm afraid not,' Harry said, lurching to take off his coat. 'We must think of the children.'

'I don't mind.' Donald stepped out from the hallway where he had been hiding. He gave Gordon a small wink and Gordon nodded at him, grateful.

'Me either,' Jeanette said, standing next to Donald.

Jennifer and Jim joined their siblings, Robin following behind. 'We want to meet them,' he said. Venn smirked and Gordon threw her a smile before turning back to his father.

'We Parkers have got one another. Cherry's just got me.'

Harry cast his eye over the unexpected ambush from his children and smoothed over his moustache with his fingers. 'Well, that's completely false,' he said.

Gordon frowned, unsure what his father meant.

'Cherry has us too.'

It took a few weeks for Jack to get the sign-off from his editor. The article Gordon had done the previous year when he arrived back from Japan hadn't had a strong response, nor had a rival newspaper's publication of Harry's comments on the phone, requesting the press leave them alone. It wasn't until Jack showed his editor a photograph of Cherry with Margaret and Kathleen that he changed his mind.

'They look great in a photograph,' Jack said, sitting with Gordon on the veranda at Greenwood Avenue. 'And I reckon that's the key. I've been thinking about it. Mrs O'Keefe by herself? War widow, refugee, very sad story, undoubtedly. But she had eight children. All of whom were an intrinsic part of their Bonbeach community, all of whom considered themselves to be Australian when Calwell tried to deport them. Mr Gamboa? A Filipino-American soldier, upstanding member of American society, without question. But add in a distraught Australian wife, a young son and daughter at home, missing their daddy … it tugs on the heartstrings. Sparks people into action. Cherry on her own, regrettable. But keeping two Australian daughters away from their father because they had the misfortune to be born in the wrong country?' Jack exhaled. 'That's just cruel.'

'Do you think people will be sympathetic?' Gordon asked. 'The girls are still Japanese, after all.'

'Your story will make people sympathise.' Jack leaned forward, delighted. 'It's the ultimate star-crossed lovers' romance. We play up that Cherry and the girls are in danger—'

'Cherry and the girls *are* in danger. This isn't some game, Jack. My family's lives are at stake. Cherry doesn't feel safe enough to live in the house I built for her, for Christ's sake.'

'Perfect.' Jack scribbled on his notepad. 'That's exactly what I'm talking about. It's dangerous for your family in Japan. Japan is a dangerous place – people already think that, so we play on that. They'd be far safer in their country Victorian paradise.' Jack looked up from his notes. 'Are you ready to begin?'

Gordon took a nervous breath.

It was the only way forward.

'What do you need to know?'

The first article was a short column in the Melbourne newspaper, *The Argus*. The headline screamed 'My Japanese wife is in danger' and the article described Cherry as a marked woman, something Gordon didn't remember saying. Jack had emphasised that they were a Christian family, something that would be important to many people who read the newspaper on a Monday morning. Different versions of the story also appeared in Sydney and Adelaide, as Venn received a bemused phone call from a friend in Adelaide and June rang from Sydney saying she'd raced around the city telling anyone who would listen that her brother and sister were in the newspaper.

There were a few hostile phone calls, but the family were ready for them. They answered the phone claiming a different residence, explaining to the caller that the number was incorrectly listed in the phone book and they had not reached the Parkers in Ringwood at all. Cautious, Gordon installed a second phone with a different number that Venn could give to people she genuinely wanted to speak to, leaving the main line for any unwanted attention.

Newspapers picked up other angles of the story. *The Argus* published an editorial piece about foreign wives. There were eight soldiers who were currently requesting their Japanese wives join them in Australia, something that was news to Gordon. Eight was a higher number than he had thought. The editorial asked whether allowing eight Japanese women and their children into the country would have any real impact on Australia.

Hate mail began to arrive. Gordon refused to let anyone open anything addressed to him, afraid of the threats that lay within each envelope. To his surprise, there were a few letters giving him support and wishing him luck in among the death threats and promises to find Gordon in a dark alleyway and teach him about Australian pride.

It was the threats to Cherry, Margaret and Kathleen that were the hardest for him to bear.

Reid and Casey stayed in regular contact as the conversation opened up. While Holt replied to most letters with his familiar refrain – that he was considering the matter – extra information sometimes came their way. Holt and his office were concerned that Australia wasn't ready to welcome any Japanese, especially given how difficult it had been to get the population used to the idea of welcoming Germans and Italians after the war. Once a peace treaty with Japan was signed, the circumstances may be different.

The year stretched on. Gordon spoke with Jack and other journalists who were interested in comments from the Parkers. Even on the weeks no articles were published, letters still arrived at the house. Gordon was heartened by strangers who told him they'd written to Holt and criticised him for his lack of empathy and heart by keeping Cherry, Margaret and Kathleen in Japan. At the advice of Reid, Gordon wrote a letter to Holt, outlining the situation, his relationship with Cherry and how his entire family were willing to accommodate and teach Cherry how to find her place in Australia. Holt wrote back several weeks later, promising that he was considering the matter.

Jennifer got married. The celebration, the excitement and blending of the two families made Gordon's heart ache. It was so easy for her. She'd fallen in love with a local man, he'd proposed, and now they could start their life together with no trouble. Gordon raised his glass with everyone else at the ceremony but, in his mind, he was with Cherry and his daughters thousands of miles away. He began detouring through Chinatown in Melbourne on his way home from work, just to find a sliver of Japanese life. The languages and cultures were different, but the starchy smell of cooked rice took him straight back to Kure.

In September 1951, the San Francisco Peace Treaty was signed and Japan joined the United Nations, the war and hostilities officially over. The attitude of the Immigration Department didn't change, though. Media attention swelled as more people heard their story. Gordon was set upon several times on his way home from work, fighting off his attackers with help from kind bystanders who intervened.

By the end of spring, he found sleep elusive. It seemed impossible he hadn't seen his family in almost two years, that they weren't already in Melbourne with him. They seemed to have more support than ever, as well as fierce opposition, but there was certainly more of a balance now. Jack had published two articles in the past month that had evoked a powerful response from the public. The first had the headline 'Afraid to bring Jap wife here', outlining the vitriol and abuse Gordon had been subjected to as he fought for his family. This had created a strong outpouring of support from strangers. The second was 'Ex-Digger's Jap Baby asks "Where's Daddy?"' with a photograph of his daughters together, Margaret now two-and-a-half years old and Kathleen ten months.

Jack had been right. Photographs of the girls evoked the strongest reactions, both good and bad.

Except in Holt. He promised to take the matter to Cabinet but continued to claim that he couldn't see a way forward. According to Casey, the main concern of the Immigration Department was that, now that there was a large contingent of Australian men serving in Korea, any rules changed to allow Cherry to move to Melbourne would have to apply to brides of any Asian nationality. Government officials believed they had halted a Japanese invasion of Australia at the end of 1945, so why would they allow a migration invasion through official channels in 1951?

To make matters worse, Cherry was attacked on the street by a crazed Japanese man while she was walking in Kure with Suma, Margaret and Kathleen, the man shouting at her for her betrayal of Japan by having children with an Australian soldier. Suma chased the man off and no-one was hurt, but Gordon couldn't sit by any longer. He set about organising a visa so he could return to Japan and see his family again. Last time his visa had taken months and disappeared in Hong Kong, so he allowed plenty of time. This time, however, his permission to travel came through within weeks and, when the newspapers published that Gordon was returning to Japan to see his family, kind strangers sent money to cover a plane ticket.

Venn wasn't thrilled about Gordon returning to Japan for another Christmas. She hadn't been well, the doctor saying she had a viral infection, but it seemed the stress of the last few months had got to her. She was on bed rest, Gordon sitting with her and Jack hovering in the corner, recording their conversation for his next article.

'I wouldn't leave if I didn't have to,' Gordon said. 'It's too hard to be away from them. I want to meet my daughter. I want to kiss my wife.'

Venn nodded. 'I understand. Of course.'

'I have to go back.' Gordon took his mother's hand, heart thudding as his next words caught in his throat. 'And this time I'm not coming back without them.'

She squeezed Gordon's hand and looked away. Trying to quell his own rising emotion, the idea of never returning to Australia or seeing his mother again seizing in his chest, Gordon looked to Jack.

Jack was beaming. 'Can I print that?'

'You bet.'

CHAPTER TWENTY-ONE

CHERRY: Kure, December 1951

There were footsteps outside the shack.

Cherry paused over her sewing to listen. It was too late for visitors, too cold to be out in the dark. The wind whispered words she couldn't understand, a soft snore from the toddlers asleep on the futon, but the footsteps stopped.

A hallucination in the dark.

Weary, she lay next to her daughters, curling around them, ready for sleep. The end of another day waiting in Japan.

There was a scrape at the window.

She sat up as a man dressed in rags smashed through the glass, fragments scattering across the floor. She scrambled to shield her children.

'Give me your money!' The man shouted. He grabbed her shirt. 'Your money!'

'There is none!' she stammered, terrified. The man threw her aside and stormed into the other room, opening the cupboards, searching for anything of value.

Cherry grabbed Kathleen and Margaret in her arms, but the man blocked her way out.

'You're an Australian wife,' the man screamed. 'Where are the riches your husband sends you?'

'There are none!' Cherry said.

The man spat at them. The spittle landed on her temple, sliding down her face. He began to laugh when another voice rang out.

'What have you done?' Her heart fell. She knew that voice. It was the ache in her bones on the days she was lost, the voice that guided her. Now, it was filled with venom and hate.

In the doorway stood her mother, Tsudo, snarling.

'Mother?'

Tsudo recoiled. 'Don't.'

'Please.' Cherry swallowed as desperation welled within her. 'Please stay. I need you. I need help.'

'Where is your husband?' Tsudo asked. 'He should be helping you. Where are your children?'

Cherry stopped. Kathleen and Margaret were no longer in her arms. Neither was she in the shack in Kure. She was in Hiroshima and her mother was opposite her, a grey knitted jumper around her shoulders, kneeling by the table in front of a bowl of rice.

Cherry's heart sped up. She knew what came next.

'Let's go. Please.'

She picked up her mother's hand, trying to pull her to the other side of the table so the cupboard would fall on them both, but Tsudo didn't move.

'Nobuko, you're being rude. Please sit down.'

Cherry couldn't stop the words that came next. Her heart was thundering in her ears, tears spilling from her eyes. 'Of course,' Nobuko said. 'I won't be rude. I'll be polite—'

A flash of bright light swept through the house, followed by an ear-splitting explosion.

Cherry awoke with a start.

She curled into her knees, dimly registering the sleeping faces of Margaret and Kathleen on the futon next to her. She tried to calm herself, to come back to the present. They were safe. They were at Suma's. It was a nightmare. Just a nightmare.

Exhausted, she lay down, staring into the night. Perhaps one day it would no longer feel like this.

Each day was the same. Every morning, Cherry cleared away the futons and blankets in Suma's main room, pulled out her fabrics and sewing equipment, and began work on her dressmaking orders, Margaret and Kathleen at her feet. Today a bolt of woollen fabrics was due to come into market, Charlie working as Cherry's courier to bring it over when it arrived. The dress she was finishing today was one of her most popular designs, a buttoned dress with an A-line skirt. She had made it so often that it was almost second nature to bring the pieces of material together. Between stitching the bottle-green fabric and tending to Margaret and Kathleen, Cherry lost track of time. When Charlie appeared, she was startled to realise half the day was already gone.

'I'm here!' Charlie called out from the door.

'Welcome!' She set aside her material. Margaret waddled after her mother as Cherry headed to the door, Kathleen babbling as they left her on the mat. Charlie set down the fabric and whisked Margaret into his arms.

'There is a package from Don-san,' Charlie said. 'The new man is bringing it. He will be here soon.'

Cherry nodded. Slim and Andy had finished their service with BCOF. Slim had gone to Korea and Andy to Australia. Before Andy had left, he'd introduced Cherry and Charlie to James Mason, a soldier who had offered to help Cherry by managing Don's packages for her.

James had visited a few times and only stayed briefly. Slim and Andy had felt more like friends; James was different. He showed little interest in Cherry and the girls, often talking about his Australian family who lived halfway between Kure and Hiroshima at Nijimura, the Rainbow Village. Cherry listened politely but was always glad when he left.

'Hello, Cherry.' James stood in the doorway, a small box tucked under his arm. His face was red with a slight sheen of sweat. The walk up the hill had been taxing for him.

'Hello, James-san. Come in, please.' Cherry stepped aside to let him enter.

'I can't stay, thanks.' James handed over the package. 'For you and the girls.'

She bowed as she took it, itching to tear it open, brushing her fingers against Don's loopy, slanted handwriting.

James hesitated. 'Look, it's Michael's birthday and we're having a party for him at the village this weekend. I thought it might be nice if you wanted to bring the girls along. Have them meet some other Australian children.'

Cherry's stomach clenched but she didn't let her smile fall. 'Thank you. That is very kind.'

After James left, she considered the invitation. He was a friend of Slim's and Andy's, and she didn't want to be rude to the person who was bringing her packages and letters from Australia. Plus, James had called her children Australian.

She didn't want to go alone, so asked Michiko if she would come with her. Michiko agreed. She had become Andy's girl after their regular trips to the outer islands and was keen to spend time with anyone who knew Andy.

The following weekend, Cherry and Michiko got dressed up in their best kimonos. Cherry hand-sewed a new dress for Margaret and put Kathleen into one of Margaret's old ones. It was rare for the girls to be in anything except basic clothes and now they looked as though they belonged in the pages of the *Women's Weekly*.

It was a long trip to get to Nijimura. It took almost an hour and a half for the four of them to arrive at the house in the Australian village, and it took only three seconds to realise coming had been a mistake.

The room was filled with blonde-haired, blue-eyed children who stared at Margaret as she clung to Cherry's leg. The house was an odd blend of a Japanese-style home with Western furniture inside.

Tatami had been replaced with floorboards and rugs, there were florid pink armchairs on the side of the main room and a painting of the King of England was on the wall. One of the Australian children squealed, drawing the attention of the adults. Conversation stilled.

'Did Susan tell the housegirls to bring their children?' one woman asked, perfectly curled hair bouncing as she looked around the room for the hostess. 'I thought they were serving the food.'

'We not housegirls,' Michiko said, shifting Kathleen's weight on her hip. 'We guests. Mr James invite us.'

'I doubt that.' The woman wrapped her manicured fingers around her glass of wine. At Cherry's feet, Margaret took a step forward as a blonde girl in pigtails came towards her.

'Hello,' the girl said. 'My name is Scarlette. What's your name?'

Margaret stared at her.

'Margaret,' Cherry said. 'Her name is Margaret.'

'Hello, Margaret,' Scarlette said. 'It's nice to meet you. Would you like to—'

'Scarlette!' A woman rushed forward and snatched the girl away. 'What are you doing?'

'Saying hello.'

'We don't speak to them. They're servants, not friends.'

'We not servants,' Michiko said, her voice sharp. 'Mr James invite us to Michael-san's party.' Cherry put her hand on Michiko's arm. They shouldn't be impolite. Scarlette's mother's mouth fell open at Michiko's response.

Cherry pulled Margaret close. 'My baby Australian too.' She brushed her daughter's hair out of her face. 'Both of them.' She rubbed Kathleen's cheek, as though that proved their light olive skin and dark features were the same as the blonde and mousy-haired children in front of them.

'I hope not,' Scarlette's mother said, glaring at Cherry.

A clatter of heels on floorboards and a woman entered, pearls around her neck, hair curled and immaculate. She stopped at the sight of Cherry and Michiko.

'Susan, these girls are insisting they've been invited to the party.'

The women looked at their hostess expectantly. The heavy powder on Susan's cheeks couldn't hide her embarrassment.

'Of course they aren't. Why would I have invited any Japanese into my house?'

'Mr James invite us,' Michiko said.

'My husband would do no such thing.' Susan's voice flew up an octave and Cherry's heart sank.

Michiko frowned. 'He did. He friends with Don-san and the soldiers and us.'

Susan laughed, panicked, as the other mothers watched. 'Now now, sweetheart, the soldiers are not allowed to fraternise with you Japanese. It's the rules.'

No-one looked at Margaret or Kathleen.

Michiko pushed Cherry forward. 'Cherry-san, you say. Mr James said we can come.'

An army of hostile, lipstick-mouthed mothers turned to Cherry, coiled to protect their children.

Cherry scooped Margaret into her arms. 'Please say to Mr James we are sorry.' She gave a quick bow and left, Michiko chasing after her.

'Those women were horrible!' Michiko was furious as they walked away, Kathleen on her hip. 'Mr James did invite us!'

'We weren't welcome.'

'We were welcome. We were allowed to be there.'

'Michiko, please. We shouldn't have come. They didn't want us there.'

Her friend stopped walking. 'Why didn't you say something? Ugly white women who think they know better.'

'It wouldn't have changed anything.'

'What if it did?'

Cherry resisted the urge to laugh. 'They were not kind women. Let's go. Please.'

James never came back to Suma's house. Charlie became the delivery boy when he could sneak onto the base and pick up the packages intended for Cherry. It was more difficult for Charlie to sell things at the market as he was often doing odd jobs for others in town, and it was dangerous for Cherry to do it herself. Cutting out Don's small source of income reselling goods meant she could only rely on her dressmaking money, which wasn't enough to completely sustain them. Other women had started similar businesses and if Cherry put up her prices, she would lose her customers.

It was always harder to get food in winter. The cost of food went up, rations still limited, and Cherry didn't have the money to buy enough for three mouths. She wouldn't accept leftovers from other women. She knew they weren't really leftovers, as much as the kind women insisted they were. Often Cherry wouldn't eat, just so Margaret would have something. She could skip two meals without affecting her milk too much. Her energy waned. One night, a man stood outside Suma's house screaming obscenities at Cherry for marrying an ex-enemy soldier for hours, until he exhausted himself and left. Cherry wrote a letter to Don, begging him to come back. It was easier when he was here.

She sustained herself by re-reading his letters and going through his parcels. The packages themselves were treasures, Cherry grateful Charlie could still collect them for her. Sometimes there were newspaper clippings in the boxes, grainy reprints of photographs she had sent to Don months ago. Kathleen was much bigger now, Margaret unable to sit still for more than ten seconds at a time, the girls in the photographs already a distant memory. The newspaper ink smudged easily, making it difficult for her to read the tiny English lettering, but Don assured her many people wanted Cherry and the girls to come to Melbourne. To her, it seemed unlikely. Don wanted them there, of course, but she and her daughters didn't belong anywhere. They didn't belong in Kure. They didn't belong in Melbourne. They didn't have a safe place of their own.

She missed her husband. The sparkle in his eye, the quick smile on his lips, the way his hair fell when he knelt down next to Margaret on the floor. She relived moments with him as she fell asleep and he was her first thought on waking. It seemed indulgent, naive even, to give herself over to daydreams and memories when there was a growing weight in her chest, a doubtful voice that questioned if he was going to keep his word and return for them. It had been over three years since they were first married at the Shinto shrine and there were many other women who had been abandoned by their Australian husbands. Surely there would come a time when Don would decide it was too hard. Her own resolve slipped a little each day, the weeks of silence in the post becoming a wall of uncertainty. Perhaps now, after all this time, her husband had finally given up.

The end of 1951 was coming. The weather chilled as they crept towards the Japanese winter, Cherry exhausted by sewing heavy woollen materials by candlelight. The other women who stayed at Suma's helped her sew or taught Kathleen to talk or chased Margaret around the small garden. Cherry still didn't feel safe, worried for her own wellbeing from angry Japanese men on the streets, or concerned that someone would declare she was an unfit mother and take her children away. She stopped leaving the house. There were days when the world outside the door felt terrifying. Her nightmares increased, reliving Hiroshima every night. Only it wasn't always her mother who died. Sometimes it was Noboru. Sometimes it was Don. Sometimes it was her daughters.

Still, she forced herself to get up every morning and work. Today, Kathleen had been uncharacteristically clingy and it wasn't until she was quietly sleeping near Margaret that Cherry could start. She was sewing a skirt from tartan fabric that had made it to Kure from Scotland, although it was a mystery as to how. The blue-and-red tartan was a strange pattern, but it reminded her of Don's Demons scarf and gloves. She still wore them, with a pang of longing when she pulled them on in the cold Japanese air.

There were footsteps outside. They sounded too close to be on the road. Margaret and Kathleen were asleep, curled around each other at Cherry's feet, and there were no other women staying with

Suma for the next three days. Suma had left for the evening to look after a friend who needed help after she'd broken her arm.

Cherry set her sewing aside and listened. Charlie hadn't mentioned he was coming by, but that wasn't unusual. She knew his footsteps, though. This wasn't Charlie. Maybe Suma had come back early? It didn't sound like Suma either.

Her heart sped up. If it wasn't Charlie or Suma, there weren't many other people it could be. It may be a woman needing a place to stay, but it was late and that seemed unlikely. Occasionally they had men stop by the house to try to find a woman who had sought refuge with Suma, but that hadn't happened in months.

She grasped her fabric scissors, the sharpest thing she had nearby, and moved closer to the door. Another attack? Other Japanese wives of ex-enemy soldiers had been targeted. Perhaps she was a target once again. If she was, she wouldn't hesitate. She would protect her daughters.

The footsteps stepped onto the small wooden threshold. Cherry raised the scissors up, ready for whatever the person on the other side was about to do next.

The door opened.

A man filled the doorframe, taller than any other man she'd seen for a long time.

It was Don.

'G'day, Cherry. Did you miss me?'

Cherry stared at him, then set down the scissors and leaned against the wall for support. Her heart was racing; she needed to steady herself.

Don was in front of her, holding her up. 'It's all right, it's just me.'

She slapped his chest, fear melting into relief. 'Next time tell me when you come!'

He laughed as he caught her hands. 'You don't want me here?'

'Yes, I want you here very much. But surprise is scary. You could be enemy.'

The amusement died in his face. She looked away, fighting to compose herself. She was being ridiculous. It was her husband. She was safe.

Don held her and she stiffened at the unfamiliar touch before relaxing into his embrace. He kissed the top of her head, then her mouth, his lips shaping into a smile. The weight of his mouth on hers reminded her of how sweet it was, this intimacy between them. He made to move away, but she grabbed his face with both hands and held him there for one more kiss, his smile widening.

'Mama?' Margaret's voice interrupted them. Don turned to look, surprised.

'I'm here, Magi-chan.' Cherry walked over to her and Margaret sat up, puffy with sleep, taking in the strange man in front of her.

'Morning there, little one. How's my girl?' Don asked in English. Margaret shrank into Cherry's arms.

'This man is your father,' Cherry said in Japanese.

Margaret shook her head. 'My father in Australia.'

'He has come to see us.'

'No.'

Cherry laughed. 'Yes!'

Margaret laughed too and collapsed against Cherry, stealing looks at Don.

He watched them both, puzzled. 'Does she speak any English?'

Cherry shook her head. 'For here, Japanese is better. You know Japanese.'

'Forgotten most of it,' he said. He seemed at a loss. Eager to shift any tension, she picked up Kathleen.

'Don-san. This Kathleen.' She put Kathleen into his arms. Margaret climbed into Cherry's lap and they watched as he lost himself in his youngest daughter's sleepy face.

Margaret tapped Cherry's arm.

'Mama?'

'Yes?'

'He is Father?'

'Yes. He is your father.'

Margaret timidly stepped over to Don, who beamed at her approach.

'Hello there.'

Margaret crawled under his arm so that she could sit against his chest, between him and her little sister. Cherry shuffled over and curled up next to Don. He lay on the floor, holding all three of them in his arms.

They lay there in silence and, slowly, the children fell asleep.

Cherry listened to his heartbeat, her ear pressed to his chest. The rhythm was soothing, and she matched her breathing to it.

'Cherry.' Don spoke in a whisper. 'I didn't mean to scare you. I wanted to tell you I was coming, but I wasn't sure about the visa again. But, I tell you what, we've definitely caused a stir back home. Last time it took months. This time it took a couple of weeks and people donated money for my airfare. I came here on a plane, Cherry. A ridgy-didge passenger plane – not anything to do with the Army or the Air Force.'

Cherry's English comprehension had faded now Andy and Slim were gone, and she struggled to keep up with Don's words. Letters were easier for her; she had time to translate them, to prise sense out of the strange symbols. Forcing herself back into listening to English, with its sloping 's' sounds and interchangeable d's and t's, wasn't easy.

'How long you stay?' Cherry asked, unable to look at him.

He sighed. 'I'm not sure,' he said. 'I've got leave from work for three months. The visa is about three months too.'

'Then you go back to Australia?'

'Not if I can help it. But maybe. We've just got to have hope.'

Hope. A four-letter word that belied the pain and suffering that was so often attached to it. Cherry had spent her entire life with hope. Hoping for peace. Hoping for calm. Hoping she could trust Don to do the right thing by her. Hoping her daughters wouldn't be ostracised for their mother's decisions. Hoping one day she would have a complete family again. Hoping one day she'd belong.

Cherry tilted her head up to look at Don. He was already looking at her, his whole face shining.

'Okay,' she said. 'We have hope.'

Once again, Cherry was living in an impossible dream. To wake up every morning with Don in arm's reach, to know he would be somewhere in the city, it gave her strength. After he had been in Kure for two days, he went with Charlie to investigate the damage to the shack. No-one had moved in yet, even though it had been empty for months. As they carried the few possessions Cherry had at Suma's back to the shack, Charlie told Cherry that one of her neighbours said the place had been cursed by an angry Australian spirit. When Don had appeared from behind the house, the neighbour had squealed and scampered away.

'I don't think you'll have any problems with break-ins now,' Charlie said, laughing.

Don was having trouble finding his feet in Japan. There weren't many BCOF soldiers left in the city, one hundred men when there had previously been tens of thousands. A few of them knew Don by reputation, but it was difficult to know whether he would get a positive or negative response until it was too late. One night, he came home with a black eye after an Australian soldier had punched him for wanting to bring Cherry home. Another night, he came home with a ceramic jug that had been pressed upon him by a soldier's wife who wanted Don to help them get to Australia.

'Why you keep going to base?' Cherry asked as she washed his knuckles. Don had needed to defend himself when he was set upon by a group of unsympathetic soldiers walking through the market.

'I need to find a job,' Don said, wincing as the water cleansed the grazes on his hand. 'I don't know how long I'm going to be here, but I'm going to provide for my family while I am. And it's expensive for me, so I want to make money somehow.'

'Maybe I put prices up,' she said. 'I take more orders.'

'You've got to look after the girls too.' He brushed his thumb against her fingers as she lifted his hand from the water. 'I'll head back to the base tomorrow. There's a CO there who might be able to sort something out for me.'

'You will have job tomorrow?'

'If everything goes according to plan, yes.'

The next day, Cherry moved through her order quickly. Wanting to prepare a celebratory meal for Don's new job, she finished the collared, yellow dress and cleaned the house from top to bottom, Margaret helping by awkwardly sweeping the floor. They were still on rations, but the portions were less strict, Cherry sometimes able to get fresh pears or fish. Don liked all his fish cooked so she decided to do a steamed fish over rice, with sticky pears for dessert.

She had almost finished preparing the meal, wondering the best way to use the small amount of sugar she had on the pears, when Don stormed inside.

'Don-san?'

He didn't reply, pacing the small tatami room, not seeming to see anything around him. He muttered to himself, brow furrowed. Margaret withdrew to the kitchen, staring at her father, surprised. Kathleen was on the other side of the room, lying on her stomach on the floor.

Cherry softened her voice. 'Don-san?' she asked again.

He put his hand on the ceiling beam above him, taking a breath to calm himself. He picked up Kathleen, turning to face Cherry and Margaret. His anger simmered, but he was fighting to get a handle on it.

'No job?' Cherry asked, already sure of the answer.

He took a breath. 'They reckon I'm too much of a troublemaker. The COs don't want me on base 'cause I'm too friendly with the Japanese. Even though half of them have got a Japanese girl of their own. Hypocrites.' He held Kathleen to his chest. 'What do they reckon I'm going to do? Cause a riot? Jokers, the bloody lot of them.

Told me to re-enlist, even though they'd probably just ship me straight to Korea and I wouldn't see Japan at all.'

Just as Don's frustration rose, Kathleen stuck her hand out. It crashed against his cheek, and then she stuck her fingers in his mouth. He nibbled them, Kathleen giggling. He continued to play, squawking and making noises, tension easing. Margaret stepped out of her hiding place to watch her father and sister.

He noticed the preparation for dinner. 'What's all this?'

'To celebrate,' Cherry said. 'For your future job.'

Don smiled and nodded. 'My future job.'

Don's future job eluded him. There were offerings in Tokyo but none that were worth moving to an entirely new city. Cherry took in more orders, but she was already close to capacity. Now that Don was back, many of the vendors at the market refused to sell to Cherry, or they tried to charge her the gaijin-tax, a high mark-up for foreigners. It hadn't taken long for word to spread that the Australian was home and, in a way, things were even more difficult with Don around. Without him there, people treated her with pity, another fallen woman with an invisible white husband. With Don back, they were ostracised both by people who hated that Cherry had betrayed Japan by marrying a foreigner and by the Japanese women who had been abandoned by their own Australian soldiers.

On Don's last trip to Japan, he'd been able to get extra supplies from the base to supplement the rations. This time, he wasn't allowed on the base. Charlie was even stopped from entering, although he still slipped through occasionally with other Japanese kids who would search for scraps from the soldiers. There was a limit to how much the boy could smuggle out, though, and it wasn't enough for all of them.

One evening, Charlie brought a daikon he'd been given as thanks for helping a family clear the rubble of a destroyed house so they could build their own. Cherry prepared it for dinner as Don and Charlie sat by the table and talked. She barely paid them any attention until her husband's voice cut through the room.

'Osaka?'

Charlie nodded. 'Hai. Osaka. Uncle needs help with his business so I go to help him.'

'You're leaving Kure?'

'Yes. Soon. Just after Christmas time.'

Cherry stopped chopping and looked at Charlie and Don. The fifteen-year-old boy whose round face shone with delight seemed to be a completely different person to the child she'd discovered hiding under Don's bed five years ago. To anyone else, he and Don would be a strange pairing, but now, trying to imagine life in Kure without Charlie seemed impossible. If Don had to go back to Australia and Charlie was in Osaka, Cherry would only have Suma to rely on for help.

Don threw Cherry a worried look and she did her best to hide her concern. He nodded at her, then shot Charlie a wide smile.

'That's great news, Charlie mate. A job in Osaka is great news.'

For Charlie, yes.

For them, less so.

CHAPTER TWENTY-TWO

GORDON: Kure, December 1951

The weeks ticked over as Christmas came and went, Gordon and Cherry's celebrations small and subdued. Gordon was haemorrhaging money, given the extortionate mark-ups at the market and unable to find anyone who would hire an Australian. The official word was that BCOF would pull out of Japan entirely at the beginning of 1952, the end of the Occupation of Japan falling to the American soldiers who were based in Tokyo. He didn't want to think about how much harder it would be without any BCOF presence in Kure. All he wanted to do was provide for his family, and he could barely do that. The small shack trembled in the winter winds, Gordon repairing it every day. Kure itself had changed since he'd last visited. Buildings were going up where there had previously been ruins. Glimpses of the future. Soon enough the war years would be a distant memory. But it felt like Gordon and Cherry were stuck living in that past.

A glimmer of hope came in the form of a letter. The Minister for the Army, the Honourable Josiah Francis, wrote to Gordon, asking to meet his family while Francis oversaw the withdrawal of the Australian forces from Kure. Gordon agreed and organised for the meeting to take place at Suma's house. Their wind-torn, cobbled-together shack wasn't the place to present the perfect family.

Dressed in their best Western clothes, they welcomed Francis into Suma's home. For Gordon, it was a strange echo of Casey's visit to Ringwood. Francis was a well-built man with waves of grey hair, and he was wrapped tightly in a navy woollen coat and scarf. He struggled to take off his heavy, wet boots and eased himself to the floor to drink tea with Gordon. Cherry stayed back, even though Gordon tried to include her in the conversation. They were all nervous, not wanting to offend. It was the closest they had come to meeting with someone from the Immigration Office and he was determined to make a good impression.

Francis stayed for half an hour. One cup of English breakfast tea, the tea leaves smuggled into Charlie's pocket from the BCOF base. The Minister seemed uncomfortable in the small Japanese house, amazed by the two young children who played together in the corner. He and Gordon pushed through polite conversation.

'You do have a … lovely home, Mr Parker.'

'Thank you. This is our friend's house. We live much further out of town, you see. We didn't want to trouble you to travel far – we know you're a busy man.'

'That's kind of you. I appreciate that. Tell me, how does civilian life compare to that of a soldier in Japan? I'd be fascinated to know your take.'

'It's certainly different.' Both men laughed. 'Each have their benefits and their downfalls, of course. But I must say, I prefer the civilian life here.'

'Oh, is that right?' Francis's eyebrows flew up as he sipped from his near empty tea cup. Cherry picked up the teapot to refill his cup, but he raised a hand to stop her. Gordon's heart sank. Francis wasn't planning to stay. Gordon needed to play this right.

'Absolutely, sir. As a soldier, I was never permitted to spend time with my wife and children. As a civilian, I see them every day. It's an easy choice.'

Francis surveyed the girls. Margaret was talking to a peg doll Venn had sent and Kathleen laughed, watching.

'Very easy, yes,' he said. 'I see you live quite a simple life.'

'A necessity, sir.' Gordon forced a tight smile.

'And to think this is the family causing such a stir in Australia.'

'We just want to go home,' Gordon said. 'Nothing more, nothing less.' He held his wife's wrist gently, she slipping her hand over his.

Francis nodded. 'Quite.' He stood. 'I'm afraid I must be off. I have another appointment.'

'Of course. Thank you for your time.' Gordon stood too. Francis nodded at Cherry, who bowed, which made him offer a small bow of his own before the two men walked to the entrance of the house.

Gordon opened the front door as Francis pulled his boots on. 'Tell me honestly, sir. In your opinion, what are our chances of returning to Australia? You'll have a more comprehensive appraisal of the situation than I, and I would genuinely appreciate any guidance you may have.'

Francis stood, ready to leave. 'When does your visa expire, son?'

'February. I'm hoping I'll get an extension through until the end of March, but there's no guarantee that will happen. And, even then, the extension will likely only be a few weeks.'

The Minister glanced to where Cherry knelt on the floor next to Margaret and Kathleen. 'Son, I'd suggest you look into New Hebrides. Perhaps New Guinea. There's an Australian base in Port Moresby. It would be more preferable for you and your family to be with other Australians, I'd wager.'

'We would prefer to be with other Australians, yes.' His frustration was bubbling now. 'We would prefer to be at home, in Australia, with my family.'

Francis shrugged. 'You have my sympathies, son.' He clapped Gordon on the shoulder, the weight of his hand definite, then he walked outside.

Gordon pulled on a pair of outdoor slippers, following Francis, unable to let him go. 'Sir. Please. We've done everything right. We've asked permission from the government, we've been married three times, we've done everything that's been asked of us.'

Francis crossed his arms. 'You may have done everything right, but you picked the wrong girl.'

Gordon shook his head. 'She's the right girl for me.'

Francis studied Gordon with a measured gaze. 'Then you had best hope other people start to believe that too. Good day.'

The older man turned and walked down the small hill, taking all that was left of Gordon's hope with him.

For days, Gordon was quiet. He couldn't explain to Cherry what Francis had said and neither did he want to tell his family in Melbourne that he had failed to bring the girls home. The devastation was absolute, Gordon unable to drag himself out of his deep despair. It was such a simple thing he wanted, to bring his family home, and yet it was the most difficult thing he had ever faced.

Night fell. The sun rose. Night fell once more. Gordon stayed awake, watching Cherry and the girls sleep, heart aching. He hadn't done what he'd promised. Everything he'd tried, it still hadn't been enough.

Fuelled by a burst of righteous indignation, he moved to the low table, pulling out writing paper and a pen. Lighting a candle to illuminate the page, he paused for only a moment, considering what to write, and then the words flowed.

Dear Minister Holt,

I am writing to you now not as a soldier, not as a husband, but as a man. And, man to man, I ask that you please, for one last time, consider our request. If you decide now that you will never permit my wife and children to enter Australia, the country I loved enough to serve during the war, then I vow this will be the last letter I ever write you. I will accept your final decision, even if it means I never return to my home country. This is not a decision I make lightly but it is necessary. As I once swore to protect my country, so too have I sworn to protect my wife and children. We are not 'other'. We are not 'enemy'. We are an Australian family who simply want to come home.

You are the only man who can make it so.

Humbly yours,

Gordon Parker

He sealed the letter in an envelope and blew out the candle.

Sleep finally came.

Too soon, it was Charlie's last night in Kure. To celebrate his departure, Gordon took him to a nearby izakaya for a farewell drink. The boy was determined to only drink sake, the rice wine strong enough to make Gordon's eyes water.

'To Charlie's adventures in Osaka. Kampai!'

Charlie grinned. 'Kampai! Cheers!' They sipped their drinks, Gordon resisting the cough in his throat as the alcohol burnt down to his stomach. 'Uncle wants my English, so thank you, Don-san, for teaching me so well.'

'Thank you for looking after me and the girls,' Gordon said. 'I don't know what we'll do without you once you're gone.'

Charlie set his cup on the table. 'Me either.'

Gordon laughed and took another burning sip of his sake. 'Charlie—'

His words were cut off by a crash at the door. A drunk man burst in, smashing into the table and knocking glasses to the ground. The men sitting there caught the man and threw him backwards. As he stumbled to the bar, Gordon recognised the man in the dirtied BCOF uniform, dishevelled and haggard.

It was Billy.

Billy focussed on the alcohol behind the bar, leaning heavily to prop himself up. 'One bottle of sake—'

'No! No.' The izakaya owner's eyes flashed with anger as he spoke in Japanese. 'I will not serve you! Get out!'

'One bottle of sake. And I'll take the BCOF discount.' The MP officer snatched up a bottle of sake, the izakaya owner grabbing it back.

Gordon caught the Australian by the shoulder. 'Hey, mate. Why don't we get you out of here?'

Billy frowned at Gordon, alcohol potent on his breath. 'Gordon bloody Parker. Should've known you'd hang around like a bad smell.'

'Thought you'd be well shot of this place by now.'

'Nothing in Australia for me anymore.' Billy threw his arms open, knocking a lamp over. 'Mum died last year. Brother killed by these vermin. Off to Korea soon enough. Here I can get some of my own back.'

'Why don't we get you back to base?' Gordon made to steer him out of the bar, but Billy shoved him away.

'I want a drink.'

Gordon shot an apologetic look at the izakaya owner, but the man remained stony-faced. Charlie watched, silent and afraid.

Gordon sighed. 'They won't serve you, mate.'

Billy scoffed. 'They always do.' He turned to the bartender, expectant, but the man crossed his arms, not budging. Billy's face turned dark and he took a step forward, Gordon moving with him to block any punches if needed. 'Fuck you.' Billy turned to the room filled with Japanese men. 'Fuck all of you!'

He deliberately crashed into tables as he stumbled to the door, swiping down what little decoration hung on the walls. As the soldier staggered onto the street, he yanked at the curtain hanging in the doorframe, the red material tearing as he brought it to the ground. His cackling echoed through the izakaya as he moved down the street.

Feeling guilty at the carnage, Gordon knelt to pick up pieces of smashed ceramic and glass.

The izakaya owner rushed over and waved him away. 'Sorry for disturbance.'

Gordon scoffed. 'I should be apologising for him. Helping you clean up is the least I can do.'

As Gordon continued to tidy, the owner spoke a string of Japanese and Charlie appeared by Gordon's shoulder.

'Don-san, please stop. We keep drinking. He clean up.'

There was no point arguing. With difficulty, Gordon returned to the small wooden table with Charlie, a palpable tension in the air. He was aware of several pairs of eyes on him, but if he turned to look at anyone, no-one was looking in his direction.

With no other choice, he picked up his sake.

'Kampai.'

It was well after midnight when Gordon and Charlie left the izakaya. Once the mess had been cleared, Gordon used what little money he had to buy a round of drinks and had instantly become friends with every man in the place. It was an apology and a small way to assuage his guilt as an Australian over Billy's contempt for the Japanese. It hadn't eased his conscience, but it had cemented a free flow of drinks to his and Charlie's table for the rest of the night.

'Train tomorrow,' Charlie said as they wobbled down an empty road. On one side were rebuilt houses, on the other were pockets of rubble that hadn't been cleared. Japan was erasing all signs of battle, but there were still sections of the city that lay as a stark reminder of the war six years earlier.

'Charlie, it's already tomorrow.' Gordon laughed as the two of them crashed into each other.

Charlie grabbed Gordon's arm. 'Don-san. For you, I have something.' He opened his hand. Sitting on his palm was the shiny penny Gordon had given him the first day they met. 'Your lucky coin.'

Gordon grinned. 'You keep it, mate.'

Charlie handed it to him. 'Don't need it. I'm already lucky.'

The moment was punctured by a groan in the dark. Both Gordon and Charlie stopped, alert. Another moan rang out from a ditch at the side of the road. They moved together towards the noise.

The moon drifted out from behind the clouds. Lying on the ground, facing the sky, was Billy. His shoulder had been impaled by a short iron rod, his shirt soaked dark with blood.

'Jesus.' Gordon rushed over, Charlie close behind.

Billy struggled to make his eyes focus, settling on Gordon. He let out a harsh laugh. 'If it isn't the Jap sympathiser and his cunning little sidekick. Such a hero, Parker. You're such a bloody hero.'

Gordon ignored Billy's jibe. He turned to Charlie. 'We have to get him up.'

Charlie nodded and moved to Billy's other side. As he reached out to grab Billy's shoulder, the Australian hissed at him. 'Don't touch me with your dirty Nip hands.'

'Don't be a fool, Billy,' Gordon said. 'I can't get you up myself—'

Billy snarled. 'He killed my brother. And my mother. She died of a broken heart.'

'Charlie didn't have anything to do with your brother. He's a kid.'

The wounded man shook his head, his breathing rapid and hoarse. 'He's a Japanese man. And you can't trust a Japanese man.' His eyes rolled into the back of his head. Desperate, Gordon tried to lift him before he completely passed out but, even as Gordon moved his body an inch, Billy's eyes flew open as he slammed back into consciousness. 'Fuck you, Parker.' His words were venom. 'Fuck you and your wife and your half-breed children.'

Gordon pulled away and Billy began to laugh. Blood leaked from the corner of his mouth, flecks of dark crimson spitting as he spoke.

'You coward.' His voice was raw and rough, the voice of a crazed man.

Charlie sighed. He looked weary and far older than his fifteen years. It wasn't fair that this kid had to go through so much at such a young age. Who was to say that Billy wouldn't drag Charlie in front of the MPs and manufacture some kind of punishment, after they got him to a hospital and saved his life?

Gordon put his hand on Charlie's shoulder. 'Come on, Charlie. Let's go.'

'We will not help?' the boy asked, voice laced with confusion and relief.

'He doesn't want our help. And you can't help someone who doesn't want it.'

They left, Billy's shouts fading into the breeze. Gordon didn't look back, silent as guilt rippled through him, only relaxing when Charlie slipped a hand into his, guiding each other home in the night.

Heeding Francis's advice, Gordon threw his energy into investigating other places where he and his family may be welcome. His visa expiry was looming, January and February slipping by in the blink of an eye, and it wasn't an option to leave Cherry and his daughters on their own. He would not be parted from them again. Of the few choices they had, Port Moresby in New Guinea seemed best. It was an Australian Army base, the closest thing to an Australian colony without being in Australia itself. It wasn't perfect, but it would allow them to be together. The rules there weren't as strict on fraternisation and the rumours were that there were plenty of mixed-race families on the base.

The challenge was arranging a post there before his visa expired and he was deported from Kure. He had begged an extension until mid-April, but it was already almost the end of March. There hadn't been many letters from Australia either, the postal system still unreliable, so it was impossible to know what was happening back home. They had to consider any contingency plans, no matter how remote or difficult they seemed to pull off.

Gordon pored over maps of New Guinea, trying to familiarise himself with the land around Port Moresby, smoking a cigarette and keeping half an eye on Kathleen, who was sleeping nearby. A message had arrived from a CO Michaels, who knew Gordon by reputation and had written to say he would vouch for him in the medical unit. The job was still unconfirmed, but if Gordon could move the family to New Guinea, it would be easier for him to step up should the offer arise.

If they were going to move countries, it needed to be in the next two weeks, which seemed near impossible with everything they would have to arrange. They had to be sure it was the right decision.

Cherry, an apron wrapped around her waist, came into the house with an envelope.

'Telegram,' she said, handing it to him.

Gordon's heart leapt into his throat. A telegram only meant bad news. It was urgent and fast, which never boded well. Heart thudding, Gordon's panic rose when he saw his father's name printed at the top. Something had happened to June. Robin. Or worse, Venn. She had been sick before he left. Maybe she hadn't recovered.

Unable to stop his hands shaking, Gordon read the typed words.

Then read them again.

And again.

Cherry touched his shoulder, terrified. 'Don-san?'

'It's from Dad.' He couldn't hide the tremor in his voice as he read the words typed on the single piece of card.

'Cabinet voted yes. Visas to be approved. Cherry and girls first priority.'

The words hung between them.

'Cabinet?' Cherry repeated.

'The government. They took a vote. They took a vote on us.' Tears spilled from his eyes. 'They voted yes.' Laughter now, an edge of hysteria in it. It was impossible. It was impossible to believe it or trust it. He crossed the room and wrapped Cherry in his arms, kissing the top of her head, delighted laughter still tearing from his throat, sobs and joy mixed as one as the news sank in.

'Cherry. We're finally going home. All of us.'

CHAPTER TWENTY-THREE

CHERRY: Kure, June 1952

The next few weeks were a blur. A combination of passport appointments, photographs, interviews for Australian and Japanese newspapers, farewells and medical tests. Any war brides approved for passage to Australia had to pass a medical examination to make sure they weren't bringing infectious diseases. Cherry was terrified, scared of what the examination by a foreign doctor would require, but the physician who attended her was a kind man from New Zealand who spoke good Japanese. He switched between languages, explaining everything to both Cherry and Don as he looked over Cherry and the girls. They all passed their health checks with flying colours. The final surprise came at the end of the examination, when the doctor called them back in after getting the test results.

'Congratulations,' he said. 'You're expecting.' He threw an amused look at Margaret and Kathleen, who were sitting on the examination bed together. 'Again.'

Distracted by working longer hours to earn more money through her dressmaking, and caught in the whirl of getting their paperwork in order before they left Japan, Cherry hadn't realised she might be pregnant. It made sense. She had been exhausted and tired, appetite thin, nauseous and ill, all things she had attributed to the stress of moving. It was another baby, due in January: seven months away, six months after their arrival in Melbourne. It would be a completely different delivery for their third child. No support from Suma, no community midwives, no risk of a mixed-race baby being stolen from her arms in the hospital.

Don's civilian visa was extended until they could all leave together, their departure date 7 June 1952. Don assured Cherry they would want for nothing in Australia, but that didn't stop her from packing her best kimono. There wasn't much from Japan she wanted to bring, preferring to leave as much of her old world behind her as she could. She found the mizuhiki knot, gifted to her by Yoneko, tucked into the pages of a small Bible Cherry had been given by the church. She carefully put the knot and the Bible into her suitcase.

Don went to the docks to check again that all their papers and tickets were in order, leaving Cherry with Kathleen and Margaret at the house to go through their last few belongings. Most of what they weren't taking with them, they were giving to Suma. There weren't as many women living with Suma these days, but there were always people who needed a room or support.

'Hello?' a voice called from the front door.

'Come in!' Cherry dusted off her hands and stepped past Margaret and Kathleen, who were playing together on the floor. Suma came in, carrying a deep-blue iris.

'For you.' She passed over the single flower, the petals thick with veins.

'It's beautiful.' There was no vase in the house so Cherry laid it with reverence on the table. 'I'm sorry, I'll put it in water soon.'

'That's okay,' Suma said, kneeling on the floor. 'Did your mother ever tell you about this flower?'

Cherry shook her head. 'I will make some tea and perhaps you can tell me.'

Suma settled back as Cherry boiled the water. 'Flowers have many meanings. This one, the iris, was often used on shields by samurai. It protects and makes one stronger.'

'I see it often on kimono.'

'Yes.' Suma nodded. 'Many people like to wear it for the same reasons the samurai did. For protection. For good health.'

Cherry set a pot of tea to brew on the table, aware of the older woman watching her. When Cherry looked up, she was surprised to see tears brimming in Suma's eyes.

'I cannot give you anything for your journey but I can give you that.' She gripped Cherry's hand. The weight was warm, a soft tremble in Suma's fingers. 'You have a new family. Two beautiful daughters and a husband that loves you. But I will always consider you part of my family. A family we forged in war. I am sorry that I couldn't give you more.'

'None of us had more to give,' Cherry said. 'And you gave me more than most. I can never thank you enough for that.'

Suma cleared her throat. 'When I left my husband, I vowed to do anything I could to help women whose worlds were torn apart. When this war started, it became more important than ever. I am honoured to have been even a small part of your story, Nobuko-chan.'

Cherry drew a shaky breath, slipping her hand out from beneath Suma's, tears threatening to overwhelm her.

'Would you like me to get a message to your father?' Suma asked.

Cherry couldn't move, a lump in her throat forcing her to be still. She swallowed hard and, without looking at Suma, shook her head. Suma nodded.

Cherry stood. 'Please wait. I will get the girls.'

Pulling herself together, Cherry bundled Kathleen into her arms and coaxed Margaret to walk out to see Suma. Their adopted Japanese grandmother, a woman they would be swapping for an Australian stranger.

The tea was poured when Cherry and the girls re-entered the room, and Margaret made straight for Suma, fascinated by the blue iris on the table.

No more was said of contacting Noboru.

A few days later, the Parker family were on the Kure docks ready to board the SS *Taiping*. Charlie hadn't been able to come from Osaka to say goodbye and had sent a letter, the ink smudged with tears, the simple kanji wishing them luck for their journey. Don was upset they hadn't been able to see Charlie before they left, but it couldn't be helped.

There were another ten war brides travelling on the same ship, meeting their own husbands on Australian shores. The goodbyes were brief, punctuated with photographs for the media on the dock. Suma and Michiko were there, even Hana had come from Kyoto to say goodbye with her young son. When it came time to say farewell, none of them showed any outward emotion. The women bowed deeply to one another, Cherry unable to find words. Suma gripped Cherry's hands tightly and nodded, before bowing to Don, who bowed back.

The SS *Taiping* was the first ship Cherry had ever been on. She clutched the railing, not trusting herself to stay steady on her feet. This was what she had wanted for so long, but now it was here, she was terrified. She needed to be Brave Nobuko, but Brave Nobuko was difficult to summon.

Japan receded from view, the only home Cherry had ever known disappearing into the distance. The place she had been born, the place her mother had died, the place she had lost everything and discovered the path to a new life, now a small pocket of mountains at the edge of the world. Soon it would be gone, the place of her past merely a hazy memory.

Don joined her at the stern of the ship and put his hand on her shoulder. 'Finally on our way home. I can't wait to show you Australia.'

Cherry nodded but didn't speak.

Words wouldn't come without tears.

The boat trip took a month. The ship stopped in Hong Kong and Singapore, but the Parkers didn't disembark. Don kept the girls occupied while Cherry stayed in bed, dealing with a combination of seasickness and morning sickness. Every pitch and roll of the ship made her stomach lurch. Barely able to move, she lay in her bunk, staring at the azure sky through the small porthole that revealed a glimpse of the outside world. Sometimes Don would return alone, having given the girls to another war bride to watch for the day. There was no shortage of babysitters on the ship, all grateful to help, knowing they wouldn't be there without Don's lobbying of the government. Gifts appeared regularly at their door. The one day Cherry felt better was the day someone left a package of sencha green tea to steady her stomach.

It wasn't until they arrived in Cairns that Don coaxed her off the boat. She was feeling steady enough to look at the tropical coastline of Queensland as they sailed towards it. It looked similar to Japan in parts, until tall leafy palms began to sway on the skyline.

'Let's get off for an hour in Cairns,' he said. 'Be good to get you on land for a little while.'

The dock in Cairns was empty as the Parkers trudged down the gangplank. The fresh air was blissful after so long in their small cabin.

Cherry breathed deeply.

This was her first step in her new country. A symbol of the hope she had placed in the man she fell in love with many years ago, finally coming true.

Her legs didn't steady as she walked off the gangplank, the ground mimicking the movement of the ship. Margaret stayed close to Don, Kathleen in his arms. It didn't need ceremony to be an exciting moment. Don flashed Cherry a smile, and she felt a small jolt of excitement.

They were here. In Australia.

She smiled back as footsteps approached them on the dock.

'Excuse me. Are you Mr and Mrs Parker?' A young man with a dark moustache took off his wide-brimmed hat. Next to him was a young woman with perfectly curled hair, wearing a red button-down dress that Cherry recognised from the *Women's Weekly*.

Don stepped forward to stand in front of Cherry. 'We are.'

'We're the Andersons,' the man said. 'Trevor and Annabelle.'

Annabelle thrust a paper bag at Cherry, face flushed. 'We just wanted to welcome you to Australia.'

Tentatively, Cherry took the bag, whatever was inside hard and spiky under her fingers.

'A small gift,' Annabelle explained.

'It's a pineapple.' Trevor scratched the back of his neck. 'Locally grown here. You need to keep it in the bag for a week or so – it's not ripe. But after that, she'll be right.'

Don looked at the bag, then held out his hand for Trevor to shake. 'That's awfully nice of you.'

'We're just so happy to see you all together,' Annabelle said, waving at Margaret, who wrapped herself around Don's leg. They turned to Cherry, who felt the weight of three pairs of eyes on her at once.

She offered a faltering smile, pushing aside her nausea and summoning her best English. 'That is very kind. Thank you very much.'

From Cairns, the boat stopped at Townsville, but they didn't disembark. Don's theory that Cherry would feel better once she had been on land backfired. She was more ill than she had been before. By the time they arrived in Sydney, any idea of stepping off the ship seemed impossible. The pineapple lay on the bed next to her, still wrapped in the paper bag. Cherry lay her hand on it when the nausea was acute, a reminder of the kindness people had already shown her.

Their arrival in Sydney would be different to Cairns. There were journalists and photographers waiting for them, people wanting interviews as they disembarked. Whether it was seasickness, morning sickness or nerves, Cherry was in no state to face any questions from a group of strangers.

Don disappeared, leaving her with Margaret and Kathleen, who were dressed in their best Western clothes, ready to leave the ship. Cherry sat up and the room spun violently. She gripped the bedframe to steady herself, ignoring the shake in her hands and the fear in her stomach. Her outfit hung on a hook on the wall: a two-piece suit and blazer, gifted to her from a well-wisher in New South Wales, and a string of pearls. There was a jacket for her too, given they were walking off the boat into the Sydney winter air. As nice as the soft woollen material was, Cherry couldn't put it on without losing her balance. Bile leapt into the back of her throat as the boat rocked, the waves lapping against the bow. She exhaled as the door opened and Don came inside, handsome in his wedding suit.

'Cherry. I've got a surprise for you.' He stepped aside to let someone else into the room. Behind him was a woman around his age with the same quick smile. Cherry's heart leapt. She knew that face, even though she had only ever seen it in photographs.

It was June.

Don's sister walked in, dressed in a white shirt with tan high-waisted trousers, her hair perfectly coiffed. Her eyes flicked over them: Cherry braced against the bed, Margaret and Kathleen sitting on the floor.

'Well,' June said, voice breathless. 'Aren't you all just little dolls?' Warmth radiated from her. 'It's a real honour to meet you, Mrs Cherry Parker.'

'June-san?' Cherry's words were tight and, at her new sister's genuine pleasure, she burst into tears.

June crossed the room in a second, her warm hand over Cherry's clammy, cool one. 'My sweet girl, it's okay.'

Cherry tried to compose herself, hiccoughing as June shot a look at Don, who left the room and closed the door. Cherry was barely aware of the other woman moving around, but a cup of water was thrust into her hand and a wet cloth was pressed against the back of her neck. Immediately, Cherry felt better.

'You gotta come out and say hello to everyone. They're going crazy out there wanting to meet you.'

Cherry shook her head, fear rising. She couldn't face everyone, not when she was feeling this sick. 'No,' she said. 'I not brave enough.'

June squeezed Cherry's hand, earnest. 'Come on now, you don't think you're brave? You left your home country to come halfway around the world. You survived the atomic bomb. And you married my brother. I reckon that makes you just about the bravest person I know.'

The earnestness in June's words settled Cherry. She took a breath as her sister smiled.

'Come out and say konnichiwa to all these fellas, then you get to come home to Melbourne once and for all. Gordon'll be by your side the whole time. And you don't just have him. We Parkers are an army. And you're one of us now, whether you like us or not. We're family.'

June's words nearly brought Cherry to tears once again. 'I like you very much,' she said, swallowing hard to find her strength. June thought she was brave. Perhaps she was. Perhaps she was Brave Nobuko.

June grinned. 'That's the spirit. Come on, let's get you dressed.'

Cherry felt like a new woman as she stood on the dock with her husband by her side, Margaret holding her hand, Kathleen in Don's arms. The media shouted questions, camera flashes going off in their faces. Cherry's cheeks hurt from smiling but she felt strong in her body, grounded, as Don fielded questions she wasn't sure she understood.

'How are you finding Australia so far?' one journalist yelled.

'It's great to be home,' Don said. 'We've received many encouraging remarks from total strangers.'

'How does it feel to be finally reunited after four years?'

Don shifted to be closer to Cherry. She took strength from it. 'I wish I had the words to tell you. It's wonderful.'

'Cherry!' A third journalist muscled his way forward. 'How do you think you'll get on in Australia? You won't be able to eat rice and fish every day.'

She hesitated. Had she understood the question? The man seemed to be asking her about rice and fish. What did that have to do with being in Australia?

Don intervened. 'She'll be well fed, I assure you.'

'Cherry, how do you feel about Australia?'

The journalists quietened to hear her response. Don looked to her, waiting for her to answer. She glanced over the crowd and spotted June at the back, who gave her two thumbs-up. Cherry couldn't help but smile.

'I think I will like Australia very much.'

With that, the cameras burst into an explosion of flashes and the smell of burning bulbs drifted over them. It seemed to last for an age. Thankfully, they were on a tight schedule. A shining black car was waiting outside the docks, the chauffeur dressed in a black suit and white gloves to drive them to the airport to fly to Melbourne. They had the plane to themselves, a generous donation from Trans Australia Airlines, who wanted to be the ones to fly Cherry and the girls home. Cherry found the idea of flying, of being suspended in mid-air, disconcerting after weeks stuck on a ship. She wasn't sure how she'd cope. There was something strange about the idea that a bomb had been dropped from a plane, changing her life forever, and now, only a few years later, another plane was changing her life once again.

Everyone wanted to meet them. The pilot greeted them as they boarded, the flight attendants bright and talkative, although Cherry stayed quiet as exhaustion crept over her. She was grateful June was with them so there was someone to keep an eye on the girls. In the end, she slept for almost the entire flight, the pineapple cradled in her arms. It was still in the paper bag, not yet ripe. Her good-luck charm.

Cherry was woken by the flight attendant as the plane began its descent into Essendon Airport. Fear rippled through her. This was the final test. On the tarmac below were Venn and Harry, Don's mum and dad. If they didn't like her, if they didn't want her, that would change everything. There was no easy way for Cherry to get back to Japan and there was nothing for her to go back to. She would be stranded in a foreign country with a family who didn't want her.

'Don-san, what if your family don't like me?' Cherry's voice trembled.

Don spoke from where he sat, pointing out the plane window with Kathleen. 'Well, I love you. So if they don't, stuff them.'

She didn't know the English phrase 'stuff them' but the cheeky grin on her husband's face reassured her. Her anxiety eased, just a little.

'You go first,' Don said as they waited to disembark. 'They want to see you the most.'

Cherry eased past her husband clasping Margaret's hand, the pineapple bag nestled in the crook of her left arm. She straightened the loose bow in Margaret's hair then smoothed down her own, a dark braid wrapped around the top of her head. June had helped Cherry pin it, becoming exasperated quickly, admitting she never fussed this much over her own appearance. Cherry loved having her sister do her hair.

The flight attendant by the door smiled at her warmly. 'Ready, Mrs Parker?'

Cherry barely took her eyes off Margaret as they descended the steel steps from the plane, only vaguely aware of the crowd gathered behind a wooden fence. There was shouting and cheering, but Cherry just wanted to make sure neither she nor Margaret fell. Behind her, Don called out to his family, but she couldn't make out what he said. Margaret leapt down the last few steps, Cherry rushing to join her, the flight attendant at the bottom stopping the girl from going further. She stood with her daughter, looking for faces she recognised from photographs, someone familiar, but there were only strangers and flashes of camera bulbs.

Don joined Cherry on the tarmac, Kathleen in his arms, the four of them standing together in front of the plane.

'Mum,' he said, the word light on his lips as he moved towards the crowd who had been let onto the tarmac. Cherry followed, shy, hanging behind Don as he rushed towards a woman who looked like an older version of June. Venn. The woman who had sent her packages of knitted clothes, yarn, books and letters for years, in handwriting Cherry would recognise forever. Behind Venn was unmistakably Harry, a kind smile beneath his grey moustache, and a group of young faces – Don's brothers and sisters – that seemed both familiar and strange at the same time.

Don was surrounded, a gaggle of excitement, as he embraced Venn. Cherry, on the outer, watched as a tall young man she thought was Robin shook Don's hand. Unsure what to do or who to speak to first, Cherry looked away, only to make eye contact with Harry. Eyes identical to Don's shone at her behind round glasses, and she couldn't help but match his smile with her own. He hesitated, then reached for her hand. She slipped it into his and he beamed. Impulsively, she moved forward and gave him a kiss on the cheek.

'Welcome home, my daughter,' Harry said, his voice rounded and warm. 'Welcome to Australia.'

'Thank you.' Cherry blushed, the man refusing to let go of her hand.

'It's simply wonderful to finally meet you. A valiant effort from everyone to get you here. Quite valiant.'

They were interrupted by Venn enveloping Cherry in a tight hug. 'My lovely girl, here you are!' Venn smelt of lavender and butter, and her pearl earrings and necklace set matched Cherry's. 'Aren't you a tiny little thing. I could snap you in two.' Her maternal energy washed over them as Venn turned to pick up Margaret. Cherry was suddenly breathless. 'Are you all right, my dear?' Venn asked her in a quiet whisper.

'I'm okay,' Cherry said.

Venn saw straight through her attempt at bravery. 'Come now, stay near me. We'll let them take photographs, then we'll whisk you away. I'm sure you'll want to put your feet up as soon as possible.'

The media pressed closer, Cherry not leaving Venn's side. 'You all have five minutes,' the older woman said, her voice strong. 'Then we are leaving.'

Harry pinned a sprig of daphne onto Cherry's lapel and stood beside her. Margaret was in Venn's arms on the other side of Cherry, Don next to his father with Kathleen. They smiled for the cameras, the media shouting questions but getting no responses. Someone said something that made the Australians laugh. Cherry hadn't heard what was said, but she laughed too, grateful for Venn's arm wrapped firmly around her waist.

They piled into a convoy of several cars, Cherry struggling to remember everyone she was introduced to. Some she knew from photographs, Don's brothers and sisters, but there were friends there too, names of strangers immediately forgotten. The cars left Essendon Airport and headed across the city to Ringwood. Leading them was a police car, with a second police vehicle following up the rear.

'Why police?' Cherry whispered to Don.

He hesitated. 'Ah, well. There's some people who aren't happy about you coming home. No-one we know, of course. But the police are here to make sure we all stay safe.'

She drew back from the window as the strange Western streets rolled past. The houses here were far bigger than any in Japan, with leafy green trees that stretched towards one another over the road. Was there someone hidden among the trees waiting for their chance to hurt them?

Don placed a reassuring hand on her knee. 'You don't need to worry. Everyone we know can't wait to meet you.'

The longer they drove, the more the houses thinned out. Soon they were driving through farmlands and orchards, tall silver trees jutting out of the ground and reaching towards the sky. This kind of open space rarely existed in Japan. Even in agricultural spaces, much of the land was farmed or used for other purposes.

Japan now seemed impossibly far away.

Kathleen began to grizzle as they passed a sign that welcomed them to Ringwood. A small town that didn't seem to have much more than a few shops near a railway line and houses on farming properties. The convoy turned into a long driveway with more silver trees and a two-storey farmhouse at the end. It was the biggest house she'd ever seen, a wide veranda sweeping around the outside and a small crowd of people gathered on the steps. Cherry took a deep breath. Another mass of people to meet, to remember. The travel was catching up with her and it would still be hours before there was any chance to rest.

Greenwood House was packed with well-wishers and gifts. Cherry stared at the pile of presents in the luxurious front room. A cot, toys, clothes, books, wool – so much wool – knitting needles and crochet hooks.

'You always have this many things?' Cherry asked Don.

'No. Since your visa was approved, people from all over the country have been sending presents.'

The kindness of strangers threatened to overwhelm her. 'Many people are very kind.'

'That's right. We won't think about the ones who aren't.' Don's face darkened at this. 'Listen, why don't you go freshen up and then I'll introduce you to some of our friends. Don't worry about the girls; I'm sure Mum and June have got their eyes on them.'

Cherry took her time in the strange bathroom. She didn't want to break anything, and it took her a moment to figure out the odd tap handles. The luxury of the bathroom was a stark contrast to what she was used to in Japan. The only time she had ever been in a similar bathroom was at the British Embassy in Tokyo when she and Don had submitted their Christian marriage paperwork.

She wanted more time to collect herself, so she stayed in the shadows of the hallway, watching the merriment from a distance.

Margaret darted through legs but miscalculated her step and tripped hard onto the floor. Cherry's breath caught as her daughter screamed, stepping forward to go to her. Venn got there first. Cherry stayed hidden, watching as the older woman scooped Margaret up, bouncing her to soothe her tears.

'All right, you're all right.' Venn brought Margaret away from the celebrations to calm her, closer to where Cherry was tucked away. 'You silly duffer. Someone put their big feet in your way, did they?'

Margaret wailed, but her tears were settling, eyes fixed on Venn, curious.

Venn patted Margaret's back. 'It's all right. Granny's got you.' Cherry's heart lifted as Venn gave the toddler a gentle kiss on the forehead. 'You're a Parker girl. We Parker girls are tough.'

Margaret stopped crying and Venn wiped the tears from her face. A grandmother tending to her granddaughter for the first time. The affection in the gesture eased the tension in Cherry's stomach, a sense of family growing within her.

Calm now, Margaret grabbed at the pearls around Venn's neck. Concerned her daughter would break the strand, Cherry rushed forward.

'Okay, okay,' Cherry said as she reached for Margaret, laughing apologetically.

Venn swung her hip away. 'You don't need to worry.' She squeezed Margaret close. 'She's no bother.'

Cherry nodded, suddenly scared to speak to her mother-in-law. She didn't want to offend her, to say something unintentionally clumsy.

Venn grasped Cherry's hand, rings squeezing against her fingers. 'I am very glad you're finally here. That we finally got you home.'

Heat crept up Cherry's cheeks. 'Thank you, Mrs Parker.'

Venn scoffed. 'Oh, please. Call me Mum.' Cherry blinked in surprise and the older woman hesitated. 'If you want to, of course. You're part of the family now. All three of you are. Harry and I would love for you to call us Mum and Dad.'

It was strange, looking into the face of a Western stranger who seemed familiar, traces of Don in her smile and the shape of her nose. She knew Venn wasn't asking to replace Cherry's mother, Tsudo. Tsudo had wanted her daughter to know peace. It may not have been what Tsudo imagined when she thought of her daughter's future – a new country, surrounded by foreign faces, far away from Japan – but this was the world Cherry could build a future in, with the help of her new family, the Parkers. Tsudo would always be Cherry's okaasan, but perhaps Venn could be her mum.

Cherry patted Venn's hand. 'Yes. To call you Mum, I would like that.'

'If I could have everyone's attention, please.' Harry's voice cut across the hubbub. Venn led Cherry to stand with Don at the front of the gathering. Her husband flashed Cherry a smile and she concentrated so she could understand what her father-in-law was about to say.

'First of all, I'd like to thank all of you for being here today to celebrate Cherry's arrival home.' The guests burst into applause and Cherry blushed, wishing they would stop looking at her. It was difficult to get used to being the centre of attention. Harry winked at her and she gave a small, reflexive bow of thanks. 'It is marvellous to see all of our family and friends here to welcome the three additions to our family in Cherry, Margaret and Kathleen. Plus the little one on the way.' Harry took a breath.

'Today is a significant day in so many ways. It marks our family being finally reunited. It marks a change in government thinking as to who is permitted to live among all of us as our neighbours. And it marks a fundamental truth in that the power of love is stronger than any of us could have imagined. My son fell in love. Everyone told him it was the wrong type of love. His fellow soldiers. The Army. The government. But Gordon, channelling a level of stubbornness that can only be inherited from both myself and my wife, refused to listen. Why should the government decide whom he could marry? So Gordon fought. And he kept faith. Even in the face of impossible odds, he never gave up. Why?' Harry smiled, and Cherry stepped closer to Don, wanting to draw on his strength.

'Because he loved his wife, his two daughters, his third unborn child. He never stopped believing that he had a right to bring his family home. He never stopped fighting. And here we are. His belief changed a fifty-year-old immigration policy, a policy some would argue is carved in stone, to allow his family to be here today with all of us.' Harry raised his glass to Gordon and Cherry. 'It is my deepest wish that today be only the beginning of a long and happy life for both of you.'

The guests broke into cheers and applause as Harry made his way over to them. He kissed Cherry on the cheek and shook Don's hand. Don's face was flushed too, something that only further endeared him to his wife.

'I didn't think you were going to make a speech,' he said to his father, nodding at well-wishers when they clapped him on the back.

Harry shrugged. 'Just a small way of telling everyone how proud I am of you. And to welcome the girls officially home.'

Don's smile widened, and Cherry bowed deeply to her father-in-law. 'Thank you.' She hesitated. 'Dad.'

Harry stared at her, then a delighted chuckle burst from him. 'Oh, you are simply delightful, my girl. Simply delightful.' He pulled her close for a hug. It was a strange thing, this physical affection. Something to get used to.

'Mama.' Margaret reached out to Cherry from a teary Venn, who passed her over to her mother. She spoke in simple Japanese. 'I'm tired. We go home now?'

'Magi-chan, this is our home now. This is your family.'

The chatter at the party hushed. The unfamiliar sound of Japanese between mother and daughter seemed to rattle the guests. Self-conscious, Cherry switched to English.

'Come. Bedtime.'

Cherry hid in the room that had been set up for Margaret and Kathleen, soothing her eldest daughter to sleep. After a while, Don appeared with Kathleen in his arms, their toddler already dozing. He lay her down in the crib and surveyed Cherry.

'Nice party,' he said.

She nodded. 'Yes. Your friends are very kind.'

'My word.' He paused, considering something. 'You and the girls can't speak Japanese anymore. They've got to speak English here. We need to blend in.'

Her heart sank, but she knew he was right. 'Yes. We Australian girls now.'

Don seemed relieved. 'You are. And we're an Australian family.' He embraced her, pulling her into his chest. She hoped he couldn't feel the thud of her heart, revealing her worry that, no matter how hard she tried, she would never truly be an Australian wife.

It was a thought that haunted her, clawed at her chest, howling madly to be heard. She buried it beneath smiles as she learned how to use the strange, big kitchen, struggling to use unfamiliar English words with Don's family and make sense of their quick, easy sentences. At night, she would pretend to sleep until Don's breaths evened out. It was only then she allowed herself to sob, to miss Kure, to wonder if she had made the right choice.

On her third morning in the big Greenwood Avenue house, so big she was never sure where everyone was, Cherry padded down the stairs to the dining room, Kathleen on her hip. Margaret was already awake, Venn having collected her from bed an hour earlier so Cherry could sleep in. Don sat at the dining-room table, hunched over a pile of mail, a bucket at his feet. He slit open an envelope and tiny pieces of paper fell out. It was a photograph of them from a newspaper, cut into pieces. He swept the pieces into the bin below. There was a lot of torn paper already in the small bucket, evidence of how much they weren't welcome here, ill wishes and threats for them all.

'They hate us,' Cherry said.

Don turned, almost surprised she was there. 'They don't hate us. They don't know us. They're all gutless fools, hiding behind pen and paper. None of them even sign their names. That's not bravery. That's cowardice.'

Don tore open another envelope. The letter was three crude words, torn into the thick paper with black ink: *DIE PARKER FAMILY.* Almost as soon as Cherry translated it in her head, he scrunched it up.

'We should go for a walk,' he said, standing. Cherry took a step back. Since they'd arrived, she and the girls hadn't left the property. The telephone rang often and, although she never would have anyway, Don had forbidden her from answering the phone after a man had rung up and abused Jennifer for being a Japanese sympathiser. Cherry wasn't allowed to open the mail either.

She wasn't ready for a walk outside. They should wait until the media attention had died down and people had forgotten about them.

'Not today. Maybe a walk tomorrow.'

'It's a beautiful day. I want to show you my hometown.'

Cherry fidgeted and he took her hands.

'I promise I won't let anything happen to you.'

It was a beautiful day. The winter Melbourne sun shone above them, sparkling through the gum trees that shuddered in the cool breeze. Don pulled a leaf off a tree and tore it open, letting Cherry inhale the sharp eucalyptus scent. Margaret sniffed too, screwing up her face at the rich smell. Together, the four of them walked towards the Ringwood town centre, Don pushing Kathleen in a pram, Cherry holding Margaret's hand, and Margaret clutching a doll in her other. It was the only gift the girl had been interested in from the pile left for them, a present from Don's journalist friend Jack. He'd been caught in Sydney and not been able to join them for the arrival celebrations, but had promised to visit as soon as he could. Venn had taken the overflow of gifts, to give them to others who needed them more.

A rolling cry of laughter echoed around them. Cherry frowned, unable to find the source of it.

Don grinned. 'That's a kookaburra. An Australian bird. It sounds like someone laughing, doesn't it?'

'Kooka-burra?' she repeated.

'Yeah, they're beautiful birds. There's always heaps nesting around here.'

There was so much to learn about this new world, so different from Hiroshima and Kure. There was nothing familiar, nothing she knew except for her daughters and her husband. Even the sound of the pram on the footpath was foreign.

As they neared the centre of town, people stopped to look at them. A man stared, open mouthed. Ahead of them, a couple crossed to the other side of the road to avoid them. Cherry glanced at her husband, Don's jaw set and the vein in his forehead pulsing. This hadn't been a good idea. They needed to stay hidden for a few more days, perhaps a few more weeks. She turned around, ready to go home, when a young blonde-haired girl just older than Margaret sprinted over to them, making a beeline for the eldest Parker girl.

'Hello!' The girl was flushed with excitement. 'I really like your doll. It's so pretty. I wish I had one like that.'

Margaret and Cherry stared at the young girl, who beamed.

'Jan!' The girl's mother chased after her, exasperated. 'What are you doing talking to them?'

The birthday party at the Australian village in Japan rushed back to Cherry, her breath catching in her throat.

The mother turned to Don, apologetic. 'I'm so sorry, she's got a mind of her own.'

'Not at all,' he said. 'It's lovely to meet someone new.'

The woman nodded, then turned to Cherry. Her smile faded. 'You're the Parkers, aren't you?'

It was almost accusatory. Cherry didn't trust herself to speak.

Don straightened. 'My word we are.'

This was the moment. The woman would scream, shout the words Don had thrown into the bucket this morning, the derision of the Australian women in the Rainbow Village in Kure, and demand they return immediately to Japan. Cherry clutched her daughter's hand tight. Margaret squirmed away from her mother and the slight movement brought with it a single thought.

Was Cherry Parker going to be brave?

Margaret stood next to her, Kathleen watching with toddler-like curiosity. There was another child inside Cherry, another child to raise and nurture and teach. Were her children's lives going to be filled with fear? Even in this new place, filled with silver trees and laughing birds? Was fear going to follow her forever? Or could she let it go?

Cherry steeled herself. 'My name is Cherry Parker. Sakuramoto Nobuko. Very nice to meet you.'

Silence.

Then the woman clapped her hands together. 'Oh, you're enchanting, Mrs Parker. Just wonderful to meet you.' She leaned closer, her necklace sliding against her collarbone. 'I'm sorry, you said something that I didn't quite catch.'

'Sakuramoto Nobuko. My Japanese name.'

'Beautiful. Beautiful. Does it mean anything?'

Cherry glanced at Don. A daydreaming, excited eighteen-year-old boy was buried beneath the twenty-four-year-old man in front of her now, shining with pride. Tension eased from her shoulders and Cherry nodded at the woman. 'Yes. Means at the foot of the cherry tree.'

'Ah, and so you're Cherry Parker!' The woman laughed, excited. 'How clever. My name is Hester Saunders. I don't know what that means in Japanese. But I live around the corner and I am just so pleased to see you. Finally, after so long.'

Don squeezed Cherry's shoulder, electricity running through her at his touch. It was exhilarating being brave. It might not be easy every time, but she could summon it when she needed it, her mother's words reminding her that her strength was measured in more than muscle.

She was Brave Nobuko.

She was Cherry Parker.

She was home.

EPILOGUE

CHERRY: Melbourne, October 1952

It had been three months since she had arrived, and Cherry still wasn't sure how to use the oven. She had cooked over fire and coals for so long that the white box with its door and blue flames along the back seemed unnecessary. Cherry had watched Venn use it nearly every evening but was still not confident in how to start the gas, to light the flames, to get the temperature right.

Even though the Parkers had welcomed her, Cherry still felt like a guest. A guest that other visitors stared at when they dropped in, a guest that stopped whispered conversations when she entered the room.

'Konnichiwa, Cherry.' Robin walked into the kitchen, flashing a smile that reminded her of Don. All the boys were so alike, it made Cherry wonder what her next child would look like. 'You cooking?'

'Maybe not today,' Cherry said. 'This oven is much confusing.'

'My word.' He nodded. 'I wouldn't know where to start with it either.'

'Post!' A voice called from outside. Robin moved quickly to the door, Cherry following. She loved the visits from the postman. Simon always took the time to chat, although she knew he had strict instructions to never leave the post with her. When she was the one to answer the door to Simon, they would wait together until someone else from the family came to collect the mail. He was filled with wild stories about everyone in town and he was the closest thing she had to a friend outside of the Parker family.

'G'day, Robin. Here you are. Miss Cherry around?'

'Hello, Simon.' Cherry stepped forward and Simon tipped his hat, his green eyes shining. 'I have something for you.' Cherry handed him a paper crane she'd made out of newspaper.

'What's this for?' He studied it, tilting it to look it over from all angles.

'I give to my friend.' She bowed to him and Simon bowed back. 'It is called origami.'

'She's beautiful. I'll treasure her. Keep her safe in my bag. You got any letters to send back to Japan?'

She hesitated. 'No.'

He gave her a small salute. 'You have a ripper day, Miss Cherry.'

The truth was, Cherry did have a letter to send home. She'd written half a letter to Suma, detailing the generosity and friendliness of the Australians, the people she'd met and her new life in Melbourne, but she couldn't bring herself to finish it. It felt like a lie. Not that she wasn't grateful to be here; she was with Don every moment they possibly could be and there was always someone to keep her company. But this world was so unfamiliar, so different to what she was used to. She hungered for the simple things. The smell of frying spices in the market, the starchy smell of rice as it cooked over fire, the sakura waving against a Kure sunset. She missed the days she wasn't exhausted trying to keep up with rapid, strange English. Cherry didn't want to lie to Suma to say all was well, so she had stopped writing mid-letter. The truth was harder to express.

'Cherry?' Don called out to her. His voice was tense. Something had happened.

On the armchair in the living room was a Japanese woman, dressed in a grey woollen suit, sobbing into a white handkerchief.

'Are you okay?' Cherry rushed to the woman's side. At the sight of her, and hearing familiar words of Japanese, the woman burst into a fresh wave of tears.

Bewildered, Cherry looked at Don. 'The airport sent her here. No-one's been able to make head nor tail of her since she got off the plane. Don't think her English is very good.'

Cherry focussed on the woman. 'My name is Cherry. It's nice to meet you,' she said in Japanese.

'Ah, Cherry-san! You are Cherry.' The woman bobbed her head. 'I am Kiyoko.'

'Kiyoko, you don't need to cry. What's happened?'

'I was coming to Australia to meet my husband. He said he would wait for me at the airport but he wasn't there. Then they put me in a car and drove me here and I don't know what to do!' Kiyoko let out a cry, shoulders heaving. 'He promised he would be waiting. He promised he would be there. He lied to me!' Kiyoko gripped Cherry's arm. 'What am I going to do, Cherry-san? I can't go back to Japan. I have no money. Mother won't help. She didn't want me to marry an ex-enemy soldier. She didn't even say goodbye.'

Cherry wasn't sure what to say to that. 'What is your husband's name? Where does he live?'

'Lyndon Mansfield. He lives in Swan Hills.'

Cherry looked to Don. 'Her husband didn't come to the airport. Lyndon Mansfield. Do you know?' He shook his head. 'He lives in Swan Hills.'

He exhaled. 'Swan Hill? That's right on the border up north.'

Dread crept through Cherry as she turned back to Kiyoko. 'Do you have a phone number?'

'Only an address.' the other woman took in a sharp breath. 'I don't know anyone in Australia. I don't know anyone here. What am I going to do?'

Cherry patted Kiyoko's hand. 'You know me. You know my husband, Don. My daughters, my family. You just need to be brave.'

Kiyoko nodded. 'I will try.'

'Good. Do you know English?' Kiyoko nodded. 'My Australian mum is lovely. We will look after you.' Cherry stood as Venn emerged with a tray of tea, Margaret and Kathleen in tow. Cherry paused by her, switching languages. 'Kiyoko is scared but she speaks English. A little shocked.'

Venn nodded. 'I bet she is. Coming all this way and no husband. Quite a shock.' Venn delivered the tea, introducing herself and the girls to Kiyoko and picking up the teapot.

Cherry moved to her husband. 'Maybe we can find him. Tell him Kiyoko-san is here.'

Don was skeptical. 'Let me see if I can get a telephone line.' He picked up the phone. 'Hello, I'm looking to be connected to a Lyndon Mansfield in Swan Hill.' He listened. Laughter burst from the other room, and Cherry rubbed a hand against her rounded stomach.

'Ah, I see. We're just trying to get in touch with him.' Don's voice wasn't hopeful. 'Thank you kindly.' He hung up and shook his head. 'No telephone connection for Lyndon Mansfield.' He glanced to Kiyoko and whispered to Cherry. 'What if her husband didn't want to show up?'

'We will find him,' she said, stubbornly.

'Short of driving to Swan Hill, I don't see how we can do anything from here.' Don crossed his arms. 'How else can we find him?'

Cherry crossed her arms too, mimicking his movement. He smirked.

'You find number for place in Swan Hill who knows everyone.'

'What number's that?'

Cherry smiled. 'Post office.'

The call connected quickly, the woman's voice on the other end so loud Cherry could hear her clearly.

'You're looking for Lyndon? He's not in town at the moment.'

'But he does live there?'

'Yes, he does. He left this morning to head to Melbourne.'

A thrill ran through Cherry and Don grabbed her arm, excited. 'Do you know why he was heading south?'

'It's such a sweet story. He's picking up his wife from the airport. They met in Japan. She's a beautiful Japanese lady flying out here to live on the farm with him. He's lucky to have her, I reckon. I'd hate to work on that farm.'

'So he definitely left town?'

The woman laughed. 'He's been telling anyone who'll listen about it for months. There's no way he was going to miss that plane.'

Cherry frowned. Don's face clouded over. 'Thank you for your help. We've actually got his wife here with us.'

'You what?'

'Lyndon never arrived at the airport.'

There was silence, then the woman sighed. 'I told him that hunk of junk would barely survive an hour on the highway, let alone getting to the airport. He's probably broken down somewhere. Fancies himself a mechanic.'

'If he does get back into town, could you give him our number and let him know Kiyoko is waiting for him here?'

'Absolutely. Happy to help.'

Cherry beamed as her husband hung up, but he was still concerned.

'I hope it's nothing worse than a broken-down car.' Don looked at Kiyoko. 'For her sake as much as his.'

Kiyoko didn't leave Cherry's side the whole day, the two conversing in Japanese, putting the children to bed and discussing the strangeness of Australia as night settled.

'This is where we live now.' Kiyoko pressed against the window, staring out into the dark fields. 'It's not what I imagined.'

'Me either,' Cherry said. 'It's very different to Japan.'

'Good.' Kiyoko sat on the armchair. 'I want it to be different. Maybe here my life will be better. A good husband. A family. Peace.'

Cherry smiled. 'I hope all our lives finally have peace.'

The other woman caught her eye and the weary knowledge of what it had been like to live through war, to survive every day not knowing where safety lay, to wake up each day not knowing who would be there at the end of it, passed between them. Survivors recognising survivors.

The phone rang. A call this late usually brought drunken abuse on the end of the phone line, so Don answered it, voice tight. 'Parker residence.'

A burst of noise exploded from the receiver, Don pulling it away from his ear. Then he grinned. 'Yes, Lyndon, we have her here. Safe and sound. Missing you – my word she's missing you.'

Kiyoko squealed and seized the receiver, sobbing, to speak with her husband.

Chuckling, Don gave Cherry a kiss. 'Broken-down car halfway between towns. Thought she was lost to him.' He smiled. 'I reckon she might've been too if you hadn't had your brilliant thought. What made you think to call the post office?'

She shrugged. 'Postman Simon is very nice and knows all people in Ringwood. I think maybe it is same in Swan Hill.'

That night was the first night Cherry didn't cry herself to sleep. Don was snoring beside her, but she was still awake, pleased with her day. Kiyoko was staying in one of the guest rooms until Lyndon could get his car fixed to drive to Melbourne. The house was still.

Cherry eased herself out of the high bed and crept out of the room. She pulled on her boots by the door, leaving the lantern behind. The moonlight made the gum trees shine, glowing in the dark.

She pressed her hand to the trunk of the gum tree, fingers slipping on peeling bark. The leaves reached down to greet her, a muted green compared to her sakura, but they welcomed her.

They welcomed Cherry Parker, the first Japanese war bride, with an Australian husband and Australian children. She was someone who could help people like Kiyoko who needed support. She could build her life here as she wanted it, filled with her brothers and sisters, her children, their children. A life without war, a life of safety and opportunity.

The gum tree rustled, a breeze ruffling Cherry's hair as she breathed deeply, contentment settling in her chest. It wasn't her sakura. It wasn't her Japan.

But it was her new life.

Afterword

Although this is the end of the novel, this is hardly the end of Gordon and Cherry's story. After Cherry became the first Japanese war bride to arrive in Australia, other women and children left Japan to enter Australia to join their soldier husbands. By the end of the 1950s, 650 visas had been granted to Japanese war brides and their children. Some struggled to find their place in Australia and chose to return to Japan. Others settled around the country. In 1957, Cherry became the first Asian person ever to be naturalised as an Australian citizen.

Even with the admission of Japanese war brides, the White Australia policy stayed in place and was only abolished by the Whitlam government in 1975, twenty-three years after Cherry arrived in Melbourne. Immigration laws in Australia still come under scrutiny today, with many asylum seekers and refugees, predominantly from non-European countries, placed in immigration detention across the country for indefinite lengths of time while simply trying to find somewhere safe to call home.

Gordon and Cherry built a small house on the Greenwood Avenue property for their family. Despite Cherry's fears about not being able to have children due to radiation poisoning from Hiroshima, she and Gordon had eight children. Margaret and Kathleen were born in Japan. Harry, their first son, was their first child to be born in Australia. Then came Robert, Jenny, Edward, Ian and Linda. They all grew up in Ringwood, the large family well known and respected in the town due to Gordon's community work and involvement in the local Australian Rules football club. Cherry often volunteered in the canteen and always cut oranges for the players on game day.

As of 2023, Gordon and Cherry's family stretches to seventy-six people – children, grandchildren, great-grandchildren and great-great-grandchildren. Even with eight children, Cherry still found time to work. Among a range of jobs, she worked for a Japanese diamond company and a sukiyaki restaurant. For years after her arrival, Cherry was invited to every Japanese event in Melbourne. Japanese businessmen would travel out to Ringwood to visit the Parkers, Cherry always the perfect hostess. In the late 1950s, Gordon and Cherry were invited to the premiere of a Melbourne production of *Madame Butterfly*. Cherry wore her kimono, the only Japanese woman in the audience. The curious and judgmental stares were a reminder of all she had endured in Japan when she had been the focus of people's disapproval and hate. After that, she packed away her kimono and didn't wear it again for a long time.

The children spoke a little Japanese at home, but as soon as they were of school age, Gordon instructed them that it was rude to speak Japanese at school where people couldn't understand them. Slowly, all of them lost their Japanese language skills. Even now, only two of Cherry's granddaughters can speak it, and only one with decent fluency. The children were targeted for looking different, unable to hide their tanned skin, dark eyes and dark hair. Their connection to Japan was quashed for their own safety in Australia. The death threats didn't stop after Cherry's arrival; they continued to get abusive letters and phone calls long after. The entire extended Parker family remained fiercely protective of Cherry and the children, the rule preventing her from opening the mail or answering the phone staying in place for years. Whenever Don could, he would stop by Chinatown to pick up bags of rice for Cherry to cook at home, the only reminder she had of Japan, until the day she found soy sauce in the supermarket.

It took Cherry twenty-five years to return to Japan and, when she did, it wasn't a world she recognised. Entire cities had been rebuilt in that period, technology and work had moved to the forefront of Japanese culture, and even the language had changed. Cherry's Japanese was so outdated that she struggled to make herself understood.

In 1958, Harry, Cherry's father-in-law, was killed in a car accident by a drunk driver. He was in the car with Venn, his youngest son, Jim, and Cherry and Don's firstborn daughter, Margaret. Venn managed to save her son's life but couldn't save her husband's. Margaret's leg was badly broken in the crash. As a tribute to the work Harry had done in the municipality, H.E. Parker Reserve in Heathmont, near Ringwood, was named after him in 1962. Venn stayed in the big house at Greenwood Avenue until she passed away in 1984.

Charlie stayed in Osaka and married a woman named Yumiko, the two of them creating their own family. Charlie worked at the same printing business for over fifty years, eventually running the company. He stayed in touch with Cherry and Gordon for years after they moved to Australia, visiting when he could and hosting them when they visited Japan. After being diagnosed with dementia, he passed away in 2019.

It wasn't until the 1980s that Cherry told her family that her father had still been alive when she left Japan. In the 1990s she revealed that Noboru had passed away in 1957, due to lung cancer. It's unclear if they ever spoke again after Cherry left Kure. Cherry doesn't talk about it.

In 2023, a bench was installed at Nagahama Park in Kure, to commemorate Gordon and Cherry's story and remember all the war brides who left Japan to join their Australian husbands. The bench was placed underneath a cherry blossom tree.

In 2010, after he and Cherry had been together for sixty-two years, Gordon passed away after a battle with cancer and dementia. In 2019, Cherry turned ninety, surrounded by family and friends. She's survived war, the atomic bomb, forced separation from her husband for four years, disownment by her family, relocating across the globe, eight children, constant racism and micro-aggressions, a husband with terminal illness and a global pandemic.

She truly is, and always has been, Brave Nobuko.

ACKNOWLEDGEMENTS

I would like to acknowledge the Djiru People, the Kombumerri families of the Yugambeh Language Region, the Wurundjeri People of the Kulin Nation, and the Gadigal People of the Eora Nation as parts of this book were daydreamed, written, shaped and edited on their lands. Always was, always will be Aboriginal land.

This novel was once a screenplay and I have to thank Iris Grossman at Echo Lake Entertainment for listening to my rambling pitch and encouraging me to write it. To Anton Russell and Kim Ho, who read early drafts of the script and gave stellar feedback, your notes are in these pages too. Billy Bowring (I promise, the villain was called Billy before we knew each other), thank you for your thoughts and excitement in the middle of a pandemic. Wok and Luke, thank you for your love and support, and for handling our project when I needed to work on this one. To Gi for sharing my excitement when I got an email about the book and never telling PM how distracted I was when I was supposed to be working, you're a superstar. Pad, it was an honour to help your dream come true and thank you for allowing me the space and support to work on mine at the same time (definitely always outside of work hours). To AA, I will forever be grateful for your constant support, your notes on scripts, your offers of introduction and your unwavering belief in me and my work over all these years. Meaghan Wilson-Anastasios, thank you for helping me enter the literary world and for your determination to get this into the hands of the right people. I wouldn't have ended up with my team if it weren't for you.

Without the support of Clare Forster, Benjamin Paz, and the entire Curtis Brown team, I would be writing this book under entirely different circumstances. To Catherine Milne, who I knew I could trust from the first conversation we ever had about this book, please know you are the only person to slide into my Twitter DMs with an unsolicited message I was actually interested in, and I thank you from the bottom of my heart for your guidance, expertise, and belief in this novel. To Jo Butler and Rebecca Sutherland for your astute, on-point edits, for helping me weed out the extra words to find the right ones buried underneath; I am a better writer for working with you. To the HarperCollins Aus editing team, thank you so much for fielding all my questions! Louisa Maggio and the HarperCollins Design team, I cannot thank you enough for my jaw-droppingly beautiful cover. And to everyone else at HarperCollins who worked on this book in any way, shape, or form – your love for these pages reflects my love for all of you.

Angela Slatter, thank you for feeling so moved by my first draft that you felt compelled to shout it out into the Twitter void. To Fiona McIntosh and my fellow Masterclassers of April 2022, thank you for being excellent cheerleaders. To Anne Cavalieros, Kaitlyn Newell and Ceinwen Langley, I am indebted to you for your notes, support and genuine delight on reading early drafts of this book. I look forward to returning the favour! To my Debut Authors 2023 group, thank you for your support, advice, stories and celebration. I am so proud of all of us. To Genevieve Novak, thank you for all your support for a chaotic, anxious newbie author, for creating Very Tired Writers and filling it with beautiful people I adore. My deepest thanks to Dr Keiko Tamura for reading this book and giving notes from both a Japanese and historical perspective. Thank you too to Nikkei Australia, an incredible organisation that documents the history and experiences of Japanese diaspora in Australia, for all your support. To all the men of BCOF who recorded their stories, thank you for sharing them so I can share them again.

To my extended Parker family, my aunts, uncles, cousins; especially Aunty Jen – thank you for trusting me to tell Grandma and Grandpa's story. It's our story too. Thanks for giving me your memories to weave in and discovering pieces of our history so I could put them together. To Uncle Robin and Aunty Wendy, Aunty June and Uncle Hugh – I love you all so dearly, thank you for telling me your stories. I'm just sorry Uncle Hugh is the only one who will get to read this book. I'd also like to mention Mrs Clay, whom I sadly couldn't quite fit in the book but who was a crucial extra member of the Parker family for many years. Clay, you aren't forgotten. To my Hart family, for your unfaltering support for as long as I can remember, I am so grateful to all of you.

To Mum, Nath, Em, Charli, Stace, Ryan, Mila, and Holly, I love you all so much and I couldn't have done this without you. I know you've all been waiting to read this for so long, so I hope it's worth the wait. Dad, I can't even tell you how much fun I've had giving you updates, telling you stories about your own family, and I am so excited that you're finally going to Japan with Anne. I love you. To Bobby, my constant companion, who reminds me to take breaks by demanding pats and attention if I've spent too long at my computer, I promise we can sit in the reading chair for a whole day now this is done.

Finally, to Grandma and Grandpa. This is a fictionalised version of your story, I know, but I kept the real, terrifying, heart-breaking, and hopeful moments. Some of the truth was impossible to discover, some you gave freely. What you both did was bigger than just the two of you, so forgive me for layering in stories from other soldiers and their war brides, to make this book really sing. You challenged thinking in Australia and I hope this novel will do the same. This entire book is a symbol of my everlasting love and gratitude to you both for standing up for what you believed in and fighting for what was right. I quite literally would not be here without you.